Draakensky

A Supernatural Tale of Magick and Romance

Paula Cappa

Crystal Lake Publishing
www.CrystalLakePub.com

Follow us on Amazon:

WELCOME
TO ANOTHER

CRYSTAL LAKE PUBLISHING
CREATION

Join today at www.crystallakepub.com & www.patreon.com/CLP

For my mother, Antoinette, who loved to sketch,
sailing her pencil across paper, creating her own magick.

Table of Contents

BOOK III
BE THE MAGICK

Book I
Magick Lives Here

"There is another world. It is hidden in this one."
—Anonymous

Prologue

Still Falls the Rain on Draakensky

If there could ever be a dark whisper in the wind, I am that darkness. The town here is full of chatter about the murder. A quiet death, no screams heard, no cries for help. The Chief of Police found the woman's body in the Mianus River, her hands stiff in an X over the chest. Killer unknown. Murderers are easy to figure out: envy, greed, power, furious opposition. At times, something else strikes. The locals here think they know death, but not a single one knows how the dead breathe—neither present nor absent, and yet both.

These days I exist on the Draakensky estate near the Mianus River in Bedford, New York. The Mianus River churns inherently over twenty miles of fierce rolling white rapids with treacherous rocky falls bordered by ferns, weeds, and old-growth forests of giant yews and oaks. A tad dangerous, though—gravel pockets line the banks that can slide quickly with the slightest weight. And then slap, down you go into the river's snapping teeth.

I came forth at the conjuring with my jazzy voice in autumn of 2021. I have no taste for gray magick. Fleeing to safer avenues is my preference. I am no legendary figment or Victorian in a black cloak who has trumped death. I don't swipe at chilly shoulders or snap at faces. I remain thin as a toothed elm leaf absent its green color. When the village people see me, they veer away and twist their mouths. Since the calling on that dreary night, I learned to attach to earth and weave myself into daily existence. Only then can I fling my voice, words shivering in the air.

Still falls the rain on Draakensky. At present, a winter rain. Old leaves flattened on the hills smell dank and moldy. Groundsheets flow everywhere in this liquid world with crooked roads and houses mutely swallowed up. Paths along the river lead to Yew Crag, a mountainous terrain twisting into sudden cliffs and ravines.

Yew trees are the oldest, all twists and hollows, burn, poison, and thrum. An owl, the color of ashes, perches on an obliging limb. Fearless, he hoots a song. He becomes his own vanishing. All he wants is to fly the river.

With each sunrise, river and sky are my patient acquaintances. In the past, I used to sit at my desk every morning by my window, sipping good coffee in a Delft porcelain cup, ripe yellow pears in a blue bowl on the table to cheer me—my cherished solitude with pen and ink inside notebooks. Now I have learned the secret of death. Eyes extinguished, I still see. Dead ears, I still hear. Legs without muscles, I still walk. Most important, this disintegrated ribcage still holds my heart.

I love the dark hours of my being. I remain, watching the days turn like pages in a book in this garden of trees, river, sky, and rocky crags. Here I can find, as in old letters, the days of my life already lived. I have one urgent purpose—to make the darkness conscious.

Chapter One

Ghost Watching Draakensky

Jaa Morland warmed her arthritic hands at the fire in the hearth. The winter dampness in Draakensky Windmill wrapped her in a pall. Rain pelted the capped roof and steel-plated sails. She knew with all her senses that rain often came from the past to create the future. Even the drops' *tap-tap-tap* against the four sails promised reflecting echoes. Their airfoil blades delivered vast circles. Ghosts sleighing across Draakensky.

Like an ancient camel getting to its knees, Jaa struggled up from the armchair. Alone, except for the presence of her ghost, she observed the dark eyes and horribly bright cheekbones at the window.

This ghost made no leaping sounds and possessed no flailing skeleton. Still, Jaa trembled at the thought: a ghost watching her. She stepped up to the mullioned windowpane streaming with rain. In the exterior floodlights, the cottage next door shone in a fine pearlescence. The winter garden and its stone walls, paths now frozen, wore a white blindness. The young woman would arrive tomorrow night. Waiting became such a task. Charlotte Knight was her name.

Jaa had a way to remember her name. Knight was easy. King Arthur. But Charlotte. A rhyme, maybe. "Charlotte, Charlotte, rhymes with . . ." She fondled the ring with two red stones on her finger. "Garnet." If she forgot the woman's name, she only had to look at her garnet ring. Her sister's jeweled wedding band. Heida had worn it the day she died.

Jaa sat in her chair, head up, trying to be strong. She raised her vision to the paned glass as shadows slipped side to side. Dark eyes shone like gigantic raindrops. Eyes that didn't blink.

A ringing echoed as if glass shattered above her head.

What did this ghost want? Why was it watching her? Death creates a traumatic wound in those left behind. Maybe ghosts were just faulty repetitions of the loss. Ghosts didn't exist in linear time, but they did in circular time. The whole world was a circle, the moon giving rise to the sun, birds' nests, raindrops, wedding rings, eyes. Clocks, time running around itself. And the everlasting magician's circle of power.

The ghost pressed its face against the window. Draakensky's sails spun circles behind the head. Were the windmill's circles manifesting this ghost? Jaa covered her face with both hands. Maybe having Charlotte Knight here, having her companionship, would calm Jaa's thoughts.

The quiet inside the windmill fell upon her, spreading wall to wall, stealing all the air in the room.

"*What is it?*" the jazzy voice splashed. "*Are you afraid to look the dead in the face?*"

Chapter Two

Ghost-Witch of Hanover Hill

Charlotte Knight didn't think of herself as an especially talented sketch artist. Mediocre mostly, but on occasion she produced worthy, even inspiring illustrations. Sketching ghosts, however, would prove an unnerving challenge.

"Do you believe in ghosts, Charlotte?" the lawyer asked.

She tugged at the black jeans riding up her calf in the uncomfortable chair in Attorney Leland Kent's office. The broad winter sky sent dull light through the bronze-tinted windows on the seventy-first floor in Chicago's famous Willis Tower. Leland sat behind his oversized mahogany desk. His gaunt face, like a shriveled roasted onion, revealed too many sunny vacations and kale salads.

"I'm not experienced with ghosts," she answered softly, although not entirely true. During her childhood, Charlotte had encountered a ghost-witch in the neighborhood vacant lot. The witch's scratchy voice repeated in her head: *Ghosts must live inside you to see them, my little Minerva's girl.*

The legend claimed witches who died in dishonor were cast into the tree shadows as ghosts, left in exile to haunt little boys and girls.

Leland Kent gave a slow, patronizing nod. "I expect a ghostly experience might be an adventure for an artist as yourself." He raised his brows. "Don't we all desire to discover the supernatural? It's exciting to be brave at your age. The thirties are so ripe. You have a lot to win in the game ahead at Draakensky." A plaque on his desk boasted Winning Is Everything.

Winning. Charlotte recalled words from her ex-boyfriend Don on the merits of triumphant lawyers—*Winning is the crown. We're driven to sell the story, feign ignorance, bluff, and twist facts in our client's favor. We're practically gods.*

"Leland," she said, shifting forward in her chair, "I don't see what winning has to do with this. Nor do I see what ghosts have to do with this commission for Jaa Morland. Before I make the drive to Draakensky, I need to settle something. Jaa called me last night. She sounded panicky. She asked me if I appreciated drawing ghosts."

"Well, you are highly skilled in black-and-white illustrations. Ghosts are rather colorless, are they not?" he smirked.

Was that supposed to be clever? True, Charlotte's art portfolio lacked color renderings. Black-and-white art exhibited solid clarity without the added influence or distraction colors often dominated.

"Drawing ghosts?" Her voice cracked. "Why would Jaa ask me that? During our two previous Skype interviews, she didn't mention drawing ghosts as part of this commission." Charlotte crossed her legs. Automatically her foot started swinging. She caught herself and stopped, recalling Mildred's hand slapping her knee to stop fidgeting—back during those awful teen years. As if kicking her foot could kick away her need to rebel. *Sit still. Do as you are told.* Her foster care memories would strike at the oddest times.

Chicago's police sirens wailed from the streets below, holding the lawyer's pause with those pebble-sized eyeballs on her. "Jaa's question likely refers to her sister Heida Mead. You know about the murder?"

"Murder? You told me Heida accidentally drowned in the Mianus River."

"Local authorities have declared it a homicide. Jaa didn't mention it?"

"No." Charlotte stifled a groan. "And where was Heida murdered? Not on Draakensky estate? Or at the cottage I'm staying in?"

"I don't know. The investigation is ongoing."

"Have they a suspect?"

"I don't know."

"How was she killed?"

He shrugged.

"Jaa told me her sister died in October. Surely an autopsy

would have revealed the cause of death by now. February 1st is tomorrow.”

“I have no details. Or any further information.”

Was that sincere ignorance or a lawyer's conscientious stupidity? “Leland, this ghost sketching that Jaa wants is of whom? Her dead sister Heida?”

“People Jaa's age need to reach into the beyond. You believe in the dignity of old age, don't you, Charlotte? Your poet Rainer Maria Rilke certainly claimed to believe in old age.”

Charlotte nearly closed her eyes in exasperation. Instead, as usual, she smiled politely. “Leland, you need not test me. I've read Rilke's poetry and biography in preparation to sketch the poems' renderings. Our contract does not specify sketching ghosts at the whim of a seventy-four-year-old woman.” She cleared her throat. “I didn't agree to that,” she added gently.

“You're very sweet, Charlotte, but Jaa Morland is my client. We have been protecting the Draakensky Windmill estate for decades. Let's be clear: are you saying you are refusing to accommodate Jaa in this small matter? Refusing to sketch what Jaa directs as your collaborator for Sterling Publishing?”

Charlotte sat back in her seat. “Rilke did not write poems about ghosts.”

“Fine. Shall we terminate the contract? I can call Josh in the New York office right now.”

Her leg went into automatic kicks again. Silence huddled between them. Not the soft silence of contemplation, more the hard silence of renunciation. He thought she was weak and intimidated, the way he stared at her short nose, a dead giveaway for weakness—just as Mommy Mildred had drilled into her.

“Shall we terminate?” he pressed again.

She would not be flung down so fast by a bully. She sat up straight in her chair and stopped the kicking. Terminate now? She had resigned from her job, sublet her studio apartment to an accountant for six months, crowed to her friends she was off to a creative adventure in the New York art community, packed and loaded her car, ready to speed away.

“Charlotte, the contract states explicitly that you create the illustrations for Rilke's poetry, as Jaa Morland directs. If she believes you should draw a ghost, you are compelled to do it. You're being paid handsomely for all your trouble.”

True, it was far more money than her pay as demi chef at the Bluebird Restaurant where she was affectionately deemed Bread Meister, baking scores of loaves until she felt floured, crusted, and kneaded into oblivion. But this? Ghosts now? And a murder?

Leland tapped his pen on the desk. "And you wouldn't want to lose Sterling Publishing's deal for your art show at the prestigious Van Cleeves Gallery in Manhattan for when they launch the book. Hyper-realism, is how I think Frederik at Sterling described your art. And Jung May, the art director, absolutely believes in your . . . how did she express it? Oh yes, your 'creative vision.' "

Leland was quoting from a nasty art reviewer who wrote, "Knight's apple tree sketches are delirious creative visions wearing amateurish ghostly subtexts." Doubt came down hard, causing her to question her talents, her years of art classes, and most disturbing, if that ghost-witch had in fact haunted her thorn-apple trees. *Did* the ghost-witch live somewhere inside her?

Charlotte had so regretted trespassing that vacant lot the night of the ghost-witch hunt with her ten-year-old pals. The property had been overgrown for years with thorny wild bushes, trash, and broken beer bottles strewn end to end. No Trespassing signs. Even the air shivered a warning to stay away. It took Charlotte five full minutes to gather the courage to place her foot on the vacant lot, each step building fear as the gang cheered her forward.

At the back lot, the ghost-witch of Hanover Hill had hovered on the dirt beneath the leafless thorn-apple tree. Draped in a monstrous feathered cape, barefoot, her black-and-white streaked hair hung wild, thick as an angora cat. She carried switches in her hand. One look at the ghost-witch, and hearing her fierce voice sing out—"I see you. You see me. Come here, little darlin', you've set me free"—Charlotte bolted.

Her stomach roiling, salty tears flooding her mouth, she had raced to the street where the gang waited, thrilled she was the champ who had actually seen the Hanover Hill witch. That night, with the bedroom windows locked and the closet light on, buried deep under her bedcovers, she trembled that she had truly set the ghost-witch free.

"Charlotte?" Leland annunciated.

With a blink to clear her mind, Charlotte squared her shoulders to match the lawyer's stiff form. Remaining calm, she said, "Leland, I've changed my entire life to take this commission. A strange man is now living in my apartment, and while it's not much, it's my home. I've said goodbye to my dearest friends whom I depend on. I'm exploring a new art form, working for a woman I barely know, and have agreed to live in Heida Mead's cottage—one I've not seen yet." She pressed her knees together, feet hard on the floor, and drew up all her grace and poise. "I fully intend to enforce the contract. But to be clear, you're telling me this contract requires me to sketch ghosts because Jaa Morland requests it? Then I shall do my very best to please her."

"I expect you will dazzle us all, Charlotte Knight."

Chapter Three

Edge of Night

Charlotte drove her refurbished sunflower-yellow Fiat through the stop-and-go traffic to Route 190, anticipating the quiet woods of Bedford and a fresh start. The best part of New York was the *New*. Jaa Morland's job opportunity had come to her through a friend of a friend. The contract offer appeared a month after her breakup with Don Drake. Timing itself was an art.

It's over, Don had said in his most lawyerly voice. *There's someone else.* No apologies, no regrets, no excuses. He strutted out, leaving the apartment door open a crack behind him. She kicked it closed so hard that her boot heel left a gash in the wood.

As she accelerated on the open highway, Charlotte watched Chicago's skyline fade from view. She knew this commission to illustrate Rainer Maria Rilke's poems had the markings of a game-changer for her career, even though she certainly was no Gustave Doré. Admittedly, she was an outsider in the thriving Chicago art scene. Most artsy 30-ish vanguards in her circles had traveled to Europe, Africa, or exotic islands on study grants to sketch. Her applications grew heavy with rejections. She grew weary of watching others' succeed in their artistic adventures, while she meandered on the outside, stuck in her tiny career rut. Well, six months illustrating Rilke's poetry in a sleepy town in New York would have to do. Ghosts or no ghosts. Slapping a Billy Joel CD into the player, she changed lanes and sped eastward.

The drive required fifteen hours, with one overnight stop. Halfway there, the Fiat's heater blew out lukewarm and remained stuck on the low fan. By the time she exited the Merritt Parkway and made her way to the Mianus River Road that led to the Draakensky estate, her shoulder muscles had tightened into stiff knots. Even though she had worn her long red wool coat and hood, she fought off shivers.

The backroads lined with glistening naked trees drew her eye at every curve. Her headlights flashed on a dead blackbird, feathers smashed flat with blood. She swerved to avoid it when the old earworm surfaced.

Be kind to the witches in the trees, trespass them not, or cursed you'll be. Ghost-witches lived in the trees, conversed with blackbirds and ravens, holding to earthly life to curse and perform magick on all who trespassed. Charlotte had trespassed.

All thoughts about the ghost-witch vanished the second she saw the street sign for Willow Pass. Turning off Mianus River Road and onto the private drive, she quickly spied the opened black iron gates. She didn't pause; she didn't even pump the breaks. Her foot automatically gunned the gas.

Light snow pelted the windshield as she maneuvered through the narrow driveway, the rock walls and evergreens bordering both sides creating a tunnel. No turnaround space. No retreat.

Jagged ice shone on the tall hedges—February in the northeast woods. Charlotte didn't mind harsh winters. But bleak wilderness and isolation might prove daunting.

" '*The woods are lovely, dark, and deep,*' " she announced Frost's famous lines. "Guess we'll see about that, Robert."

She inched the Fiat slowly up the steep driveway. Snow-smothered pine trees blocked the view to the surrounding property, which Jaa had boasted spread nearly twenty acres over unspoiled land and the charging Mianus River.

Charlotte stopped the car to examine the pine trees. A picture-perfect black-and-white sketch formed in her mind. Silhouettes riding the air. Long shadows wearing bumpy hooked faces. Three smaller trees shouted with grim empty mouths, their branches fat tongues. *If I were a tree.*

She held her foot on the brake while she flipped on the high beams. The river windmill materialized on a curving hillside, a milky phantom with square-hatched windows emitting white light. Oddly medieval in style, she imagined a castle in the air—Don Quixote charging on his white steed, Rocinante, sword flying in hand.

The gray clapboard tower blinked an unearthly glare at fifty feet high. Four steel blades turned, emitting hoots. Or was that an owl? A sudden urge to flee hit her. *Just a fugitive moment. Ignore it.*

Beyond the windmill, under bright floodlights, a vast square revealed snow mounds rolling far and wide, humpbacked and whale-esque. Clusters of high trees created odd nooks dotting the property in clear blue air.

"There you are, Draakensky. I have arrived."

She opened the window. Sudden winds raced up from the mounds. What a fragrance. She could almost smell the buried tree roots and mossy trunks. At least twelve silver birch trees, coated in frost, lined both sides at the entrance walk. Bright supermodels.

Charlotte pulled into the carport, per the written instructions, across from the cottage hiding behind snow-laden cypresses. Exterior lights flooded a field-stone walled garden. She cut the engine just as a worry-wave hit her. That old fear struck every time she had entered a new foster home—enemy territory. But she wasn't walking that path now.

She stepped out. A sobbing noise swept by. Could have been a child's cry. Of course it wasn't—only the creaking of the windmill blades.

At the entrance to Jaa Morland's windmill, Charlotte pushed open the garden gate. A holly bush's withered ghost greeted her with crippled leaves. The gate latched behind her and clanged a singular chord.

At the windmill door, ajar by an inch, she knocked. "Hello? Jaa?" Spotlighted against a terrible darkness sat Jaa Morland. In an armchair by the fire, as the gray smoke curled strings at the walls, Jaa lifted her head.

"Finally, Charlotte, my little dear, you are here." She wore white silk pajamas and black embroidered slippers. With a dramatic outward throw of her arms, she grinned. "My 1940s Lauren Bacall look. What do you think?"

Charlotte laughed. "All you need is the cigarette and a champagne glass."

"Oh yes, that would be stylish. Let me stand and welcome you properly." She fumbled with her cane to rise.

"Oh no, please, don't get up. I'm terribly late, so sorry." Charlotte glanced at the mantel clock—no hands on the face.

"That wacky clock. Pay no mind to it. Heida hated clocks keeping time in our lives. Come sit down and warm up by the fire. What a lovely red coat you have. Is it vintage?"

Charlotte slipped the hood down. "You might say that." Taking off her coat, she scanned the room—half-dark walls, the lamp's light seeping over flower-patterned stuffed chairs and sofa. A black-lacquered box covered in painted dragonflies rested among books at the center of the coffee table. She sat on the chair opposite Jaa as the woman blatantly examined her from head to toe.

"You're a bony young thing, aren't you?" Jaa said, her voice coming through large, slightly protruding teeth. Even though she had a strong face to carry them, they gave the impression of serious choppers for such an aged woman.

"When we met on that ridiculous Skype interview," Jaa continued, "I thought you appeared sullen with your mousy hair and tiny face. What pretty gray eyes you have. I see now you are surprisingly pleasing. Your nose is cute as a tinker bell."

"This," Charlotte sniffed, "is a child's nose. Thirty-four years old and it never grew up with me."

"Are ponytails still the fashion these days? Yours is so sleek and proud-looking."

"It's my go-to style most days. Jaa, you must be tired, waiting up for me. The instructions said to be sure to knock on your door when I arrived, no matter how late."

"No worries, dear. I'm relieved you've arrived safely. Stay a few minutes with me, please."

"It's quaint here. So unusual, this windmill." Charlotte admired the twisted black iron staircase in the corner. The octagonal walls created a cozy shape, and yet the room possessed a comfortable spaciousness with the high ceilings, white-gray slatted beams and trim, and a lantern chandelier. The folk art yellow-painted chairs and table reminded Charlotte of the *Three Bears* storybook. While Jaa bore no resemblance to the innocent Goldilocks, she held a fairyland quality in her expression, with her face all aglow and the dreamy tilt of her head.

"My father built Draakensky. He was a shipbuilder, you know. This is the first pre-fab windmill, a true Dutch version. Best of all, the sails actually turn. Specially designed with modern ball-bearing rotors, so they never have to stop. Even a nine-mile-per-hour wind will set the sails spinning."

"I saw them spinning when I pulled in. All I could think were castles in the air and Don Quixote's windmills into giants."

"Ah, yes, windmills of the mind. I loved that book. Heida and I read it together. I find it reassuring to live in a house that spins with the wind. Northwest wind turns the sails clockwise. Southeast wind counterclockwise."

"Extraordinary. How many floors do you have here?"

"Three. Second floor is my library. My desk was my mother's hand-carved Marquis drop-lid. I'll show you tomorrow. My shelves are filled with children's books. Stacks and stacks! Did I tell you I was a children's librarian?"

"You did. Must have been rewarding to introduce literature to young minds."

"I miss children terribly. Now I spend my days in my literary parlor." She giggled. "Top floor is the attic where the mill mechanisms are housed in a hatch. We soundproofed the attic to keep the house quiet. The attic was our hiding place when we were children. Did you have a secret cubby as a child, Charlotte?"

Charlotte's whole life was a secret cubby, and vacant—having no memory of her mother, knowing almost nothing of her father, lacking siblings and grandparents. "I used to climb trees and hide behind the leaves," she offered.

"You have an affinity for trees, don't you? So many forests in your portfolio." Jaa's voice trailed off, her vision lifting to the portrait on the wall. She snapped back her attention. "Are you feeling chilled, Charlotte? The cottage next door is warmed up for you. I told Alice to leave you a light supper."

"How thoughtful. Thank you. Who is Alice?"

"Alice Eve. She owns the florist shop in Bedford Village and delivers my flowers every week. A dear friend for years." Jaa pointed to wilted red roses in a yellow bowl on the side table. "I can't bear to live without fresh flowers. They die so beautifully, don't you think?"

Charlotte admired the deep red wine color despite the shriveled petals.

Jaa gazed upward. " *'To breathe what drifts about their blooming spirits.'* "

"I'm sorry?"

"A line from Rilke's poem, 'Number Fourteen' in *Les Roses*."

She lifted an old pink book from a basket near her chair. "This is the French edition. Can't recall all the words now."

"I don't think I read that one."

"Rilke wrote 400 poems. We don't expect you to know all of them. He loved how the blooms die into themselves. *Les Roses* might be a good place for us to begin our work together."

"Drawing roses? I will need some practice time."

"Oh no," she barked, her lips pinching. "We don't want you to draw roses at all. We want you to draw their mystery. Their immanence. We want you to illustrate their loss and transformation. Not the rose's flesh. That would be too ordinary."

"Of course. I will give your approach some thought."

Jaa leaned forward, her expression suddenly all sourpuss. "You know what I mean, don't you? We spoke about it on the phone the other night. Charlotte, we want you to draw its ghost."

"Draw its ghost? Rilke's *Les Roses* ghost?"

"Ghosts make sense of life, do they not?"

Charlotte searched for an appropriate reply. "That is a task. I'll need a good night's sleep." She tried to sound enthusiastic, but her voice sagged.

"Oh heavens, you need not fret. I'll direct you at every step." Jaa kept her harsh face on her.

Charlotte had never seen such hot blue eyes. She had to consciously pull her vision away.

"You will love the cottage," Jaa said. "Heida and I grew up there. It's wonderfully snug. Heida's decorating beats the best of them for old-world elegance." Her vision fell to the floor. She turned the corners of her mouth down.

Few people realized how loud their expressions were; Charlotte wanted to reach out and smooth the creases away with an eraser. "You were close with your sister Heida? I'm so sorry. Losing a sister. I can't imagine the loss."

"You're sweet." She glanced over at the dead roses. "Heida adored lilac roses. She would sleep with the petals in her bed. At times, I'm afraid if I stop thinking about Heida, even for a moment, she'll disappear completely from me. We had our special realm, Heida and me."

Charlotte nodded slowly.

"Did you ever hear the expression, 'two sisters, one is the dancer, the other is the watcher'? Heida became my dancer. She lived life boldly. We talked incessantly, read the same books, and wore each other's clothes. Now she's gone." A tear leaked out the corner of one eye. "We're all wounded, aren't we?" She fondled her white hair, which curled in a neat loop beneath her left ear. "Enough about me and my troubles. You mentioned you don't have sisters. Did I recall that right?"

"No siblings."

"No family at all?"

"I have a third cousin in England I write Christmas cards to, but that's about it. My aunt raised me after my mother died. After my aunt passed, I lived with the nuns at St. Sophia's Convent and a few years in foster homes until I was eighteen."

"Oh. What happens if you go missing? Who would miss you?"

Charlotte realized her jaw had dropped. "Go missing?"

"If you suddenly disappeared. God forbid."

Charlotte thought quickly. She had moments of friendships over the years but no long-lasting friends, being on the outside of so many relationships. "I have many friends in Chicago who would miss me," she exaggerated. "My friend Suzanne and I are close. I know a family in my building. Maddy and her husband are always calling me. And Don, an ex-boyfriend who still keeps in touch. And I chat with Sister James every week."

"Sister James? At St. Sophia's Convent? Is that where you learned to bake bread? With the nuns. I understand you are an award-winning baker."

"The nuns, yes. I loved being in the kitchen. Award-winning? Hardly."

"I've not had homemade bread in years."

"I will bake a loaf for you, Jaa. I make peasant bread, everyone's favorite."

"You would do that for me? How kind you are, my dear. We shall get on splendidly. I am grateful you're here with me, Miss Charlotte Knight."

Charlotte hadn't thought she would connect to Jaa Morland. Their Skype interviews were awkward and formal. The woman had a hard face with sad jowls, a bold nose, and a flat wide chin. Her great blues didn't appear as sharp now. Charlotte saw the kind wrinkles on Jaa's face, the wishful smile, and that naked grief. The woman might have been a Hans Holbein's sketch, akin to the famous Jane Seymour in ink and chalk.

"Charlotte, I wish you could have known Heida. But then this day would not be happening, would it? If she were not dead, Heida would be here arranging Rilke's poems and directing the illustrations for Sterling Publishing. This was her book, as you know. No one had greater devotion to Rilke than Heida. She sponsored poetry salons of his work at colleges and universities all over New England. So, now, you see it's my job to complete the book for her. And here you are to assist me in making it everything Heida wanted. I do so want you to meet Heida."

"I'm sorry?"

"Ghosts reside in everything. A person's very absence is a presence."

Charlotte's heart skidded. "I don't know what you mean. Ghosts reside in everything?"

"I mean those moments when you can engage the dead. Have you ever connected to your mother or your aunt? What did you say her name was? Your aunt?"

"Loretta."

"And your mother's name?"

Charlotte stood up, a flush heating her cheeks. "It's late, Jaa. I'm exhausted from the drive. Time I settled in for the night."

"Of course. We can make a plan for our work schedule tomorrow. Heida preferred to work mornings. What time is best for you, Charlotte?"

"Will eleven o'clock suit you?"

The faceless mantel clock chimed. "Time willing. Peaceful dreams, my dear."

Chapter Four

The Dark Hours

A snow flurry whisked the sky as Charlotte followed the garden flagstone path from the windmill to the salt-box cottage, the pathway cleared and well sanded. Standing at the cottage front door, she paused. If the ground suddenly shifted beneath her feet and swallowed her up, she wouldn't be surprised with all that talk about ghosts, dead roses, and engaging the dead. *You're far too intense,* Don had shouted at her. *Let life happen for once, will you?*

Half tempted to get back in her car and run away, she said it aloud. "Let life happen." Charlotte had run from three foster homes, her instincts proven smart, saving herself from intimidating male aggressors. *Running away can sometimes mean the new direction is the right direction if one needs to survive. Trust yourself to know.* Sister James's wisdom.

On the door hung a lady's brass left-hand knocker. Charlotte couldn't resist the urge to lift the feminine fingers. She let go and the brass hand hit the base. Its *tinnggg* lingered, creating an airy space around her. And in that breathing space, she inhaled the February night air and crossed the threshold.

The living room, fully lit, sported a bright chintz sofa in blue florals and twin vessel lamps on a chatelet chest of drawers, a warmth she hadn't expected. A white trestle dining table and high-back chairs. Wooden shoes by the door. Bowed French windows gave views of the snow garden and sleeping trees. She sniffed the room, an old habit when arriving in a new foster home: clean or dust and mold, good kitchen aromas or old food, sweat or wet dogs. Reassured by wood scents and lemon polish, she stepped across the room.

"Oh, my goodness," she burst out, seeing a print of Visscher's *The Large Cat* hanging on the far wall—her absolute favorite engraving she had struggled to trace when she was only twelve years old. A glorious crouched tabby, sleeping, perky ears, paws neatly aligned, and those amazing stiff whiskers begging to be stroked. The terrified little mouse behind the doorway, so cute, made her brighten up. How funny that Heida Mead would have this print. Maybe a good omen.

Charlotte skimmed the single table setting—a Delft blue china plate brimmed with soft cheeses, blond rolls, a yellow pear so perfectly ripened that its juices dripped from the skin, and rosé wine filled the cut crystal stemmed glass.

The old farmhouse in Long Grove where she grew up had nothing of this charm and style, although the beige hutch filled with chipped pottery struck her as similar to the one in Auntie Loretta's kitchen. She dropped her two suitcases on the floor, hung her coat on the Parisian wall hanger, and sat at the trestle table by the window. Exterior floodlights bathed the garden's red-berried branches, silver wind twirlers, birdhouses on posts, and wooden benches.

Feeling suddenly hungry, Charlotte cut into the cheese. The Gouda tasted buttery and sweet, perfect with the ripe pear and wine, which she finished in three gulps. She noticed a draft circling her legs as if someone had opened a hatch or window.

Opposite her, a bookcase stood floor to ceiling with poetry volumes: Arnold, Blake, Keats, Plath. Rilke's poetry occupied a five-shelf case with puzzle boxes of woodsy scenes, birds, wolves, and deer. The basket of colorful yarns by the wing-backed chair reminded her of Sister James's craft corner.

"Charlotte, welcome to the dark hourssssssss."

Startled, Charlotte turned. Had she heard that right? Was someone in the cottage?

"Hello?"

She walked into the dark passage at the end of the living room. An upswing of light drew her into the kitchen. Galley-style, white appliances and cupboards, the kitchen ran straight ahead to a French glass-paned door—left wide open. Presumably by Alice Eve. Charlotte poked her head out the door. Darkened timbers piled up like a great bull under an open shed at the patio's far end. In the snow, a series of shoe prints caught her eye. Narrow heel- and toe-prints exited the patio into the woods beyond—not on the path to the carport, which curved toward the windmill.

Silence had a creepy way of hanging too long. Of all the beginnings a person could have, and despite her fatigue and anxiety, Charlotte decided Jaa's melodrama had seized her. She shook it off, closed the French glass door, and flipped the bolt lock.

On the kitchen counter, lilac-hued rose blossoms stood fully open in a glass bowl. Sweet perfume. "This is a lovely cottage," she said. Maybe the spoken words would convince her. "Jaa will be a fascinating employer. I'll sketch Rilke's poems, sketch whatever ghostly attributes I must, and in July go back to Chicago all the wiser, with a published book of my illustrations, and a New York City gallery art show."

For once, Charlotte would have a shine of gold. No more failures or detours. As for tomorrow, how delicious to wake up in a new place.

With that, Charlotte climbed the steps to the bedroom. Beneath the eaves, an antique French sleigh bed, scrolled in white distressed waves and curls fit for a fairy tale queen, dominated the room. A country-styled ironing station served as a night table in blue forget-me-nots print. "Tastefully done, Heida Mead, I'll give you that."

Thundering winds blew. One doleful screech drew her to the window. The river pounded in the distance, its splashes and churns shouting through the house's structure.

"I love the dark hoursssss."

Again, that voice. Watery. Swaying. A woman's voice? A man's? She might have drunk in each word and swallowed them whole. Did she imagine it? She propped up the bed pillows behind her head, eyes wide in the semi-darkness. Of course she imagined it. A new foster home had often made her mind swim with frightening moments, some so real she would have sworn it was another child in the house playing tricks.

"My mind deepens into them. Charrrrrlotte?"

Each word flowed loose and liquid so close to her ears that she swatted them away with both hands.

"Here I am, inside the spaccce of your imagination, just where you arrrrre."

She jumped up, feet hitting the floor, legs stiff as wooden pegs. Whatever this was, it needed to shut up. "Stop it. Please, stop it."

As she turned to the window, flapping sounds struck—a bird's wings—beyond the trees. Inside the icy blackened view, the river's rumblings became a drumroll she swore had a hiss of cymbals.

Charlotte resolved she would not spend the night in the dark, listening to the dark. After turning on the bedside tulip lamp, the closet light, and the glass globe ceiling light, she climbed into Heida Mead's sleigh bed. She would sleep exactly like Visscher's tabby cat, poised on her haunches, eyes shut but ears primed, ready to leap, geared to wake and run.

The wind never wearied. Gusts knocked at the roof. Monsters in her mind crawled the shingles. Taps at the window glass might have been long fingernails. From the sky, the trees whacked angry branches at each other. Charlotte slipped in and out of sleep. Eventually her dreams spun along with the windmill's sails, making ghostly circles across Draakensky.

Chapter Five

Silent Murder

Morning opened from a glorious beam in the sky. After oversleeping and downing a quick tea, Charlotte hurried out to meet Jaa. The abundant landscape and bright sun lured her to the snowy paths leading to the river. Stepping on the flattened snow, she followed the footpaths. Bony trees loomed. The towering trunks rose like masts of a dozen ships with their highest branches reaching out of the shadows and into gleams of light. Countless blackbirds ploughed the air as if on a mission.

Downriver, as far as her eye could see, at a plateau, the water wrinkled like Old Baba Yaga's face from the Russian fairy tales. Standing a few feet away from the edge, Charlotte dug her boot into a snow patch.

"That's where they found her," came a deep voice from behind.

She nearly fell in her turnaround.

"Thomas Harrogate." A big guy in knee-high boots. With a mechanical smile creeping across his face, he put out a gloved hand for a shake. "Draakensky property manager. You're the guest at the cottage?" He glared from a short-bearded hatchet face and leaned on his snow shovel.

"I'm Charlotte Knight. You've done a great job clearing the paths. I couldn't resist a walk," she said in her friendliest tone.

Pause before judging. That's what this man was doing. And not hiding his critical stare.

"River is gorgeous," she said. "I've never seen whitewater rapids. And that steep waterfall. Must be a hundred-foot drop."

Her comments hung out there. The way he continued to size her up didn't inspire any comfort. River-man brute type, his black knit cap hugged his head, black hair poking out among stray grays. A furrowed brow, dark brown eyes, he wore a heavyweight red hunting vest, unzipped, exposing a faded tee shirt. He had to be in his early fifties.

Charlotte knew to speak again if only to remove the tension. "May I call you Thomas?"

"Anything but Tom. I wouldn't stand too close to the edge. Not as sturdy as you might think. You come from river-folk, do you?"

"River-folk? No, I'm from Chicago." The gushing river nearly drowned out her words.

"Ah, a city lady. Good for you. The river keep you awake last night, did it? Backwaters can get pretty loud. Keeps me awake. River's got a wicked voice some nights, all those whirlpools. And those damn ice blocks tearing at the banks."

"I guess I'll get used to it."

"Doubtful. River's full of tricks."

"Uh-huh," she answered.

He appeared to be searching for words, moving his lips. "If you have any trouble at the cottage, give me a shout. Furnace sometimes quits and needs a manual reboot. I live downriver, past that cross bridge. Timber cabin. Good day to you, Miss Knight." He walked toward the wooded hills, shooting her a back-handed wave.

Charlotte returned her attention to where she had dug her heel in the patch and dug her heel in again, making the print wider until both boots fit into it. Her place in the snow. Amused at her foolishness, she lifted her head. Thomas hovered over her from the nearby slope.

"You best stay back from the cliff, Missy."

"I'm not Missy. My name is Charlotte." She stepped back to safer ground. "What did you mean, that's where they found her? You mean Heida Mead."

"Nobody else died here."

"Did they find her here on the cliff or down there in the river? God, that's horribly steep. Terrifying."

Thomas twisted his shovel in the snow, looking her over again. "They found her body across the river. On Yew Crag. See that flat upper part above the falls? Right there. Beneath the giant yew tree."

Charlotte focused on the evergreen hanging over the riverbank above the falls. Some limbs had grown down, creating giant claws into the earth. "Yew Crag? So, it wasn't an accident? She was murdered?"

He shrugged his right shoulder as if it were half true.

"What do the police say?"

"Cops don't know what killed her. Pack of fools, those guys."

"Did they do an autopsy?"

Thomas twitched his mouth.

"Did they declare a cause of death?" she persisted.

"You best ask Miss Jaa."

"I'm asking you."

He twitched his mouth again. "No accident. No drowning. No water in the lungs."

Charlotte watched Thomas dig the shovel into the snow and toss it.

"What then? A person has to die of something."

"That's true for most people. But for Miss Heida, she had a different story."

"What story is that?"

"When we romanticize the world. When we know magick. Maybe you know about that already."

"Excuse me?"

"Maybe that's why you're here at Draakensky."

"I'm here to illustrate Rilke's poetry for Jaa at Sterling Publishing."

"If you say so." Thomas fished out a cigarette pack from his jacket pocket, pulled one out and lit it.

"I say so because it's true," she told him in a clear, loud voice.

"Lots of things are true. Sky shuts down every night. Hides the sun like a big dark secret. But that secret never goes away for long. Eventually, the sun bursts open and we all see it."

Nothing was as maddening as a secret. "What secret is that? About Heida Mead? Do you know how she died?"

He drew hard on the cigarette. "Somebody pulled the trigger."

"She was shot?"

"Not with a gun. Not with any weapon that the police can say. The dead still have their realms, you know. Don't you think for a minute they don't. My wife is dead. She's living inside her realm. And I'm trapped here without her!"

His anger held her for a beat. "Nice to have met you, Thomas. Jaa is waiting for me."

"I'm sure she is. I'll be seeing you." He flicked a pout at her.

Charlotte trod the paths back to the windmill, the wind buffeting her all the way. What a strange man. Grim, but more than that, he reeked of loneliness. She knew about being lonely.

In her rush, her boots slid clumsily over ice patches, and she nearly tumbled face down. As she approached Draakensky Windmill, the sails whipped fast rotations, the wind cutting through the square airfoil rows on each blade. Everything flowed clockwise. A northwest wind, Jaa had said. The whirs and hums became a faraway voice. A mother saying *"Hushhhhhhhhh."*

Chapter Six

River Magick

Jaa poured herself a second coffee in her sun-streaked kitchen. She watched Alice Eve set three long-stemmed, shocking white blooms into a vase at the sink.

"Aurelian lilies, Jaa. Will they spark your day?" Alice swept her wavy black bangs off her forehead.

"Gorgeous, Alice. Did you bring the single rose?"

"I did. But she needs a little more bloom time."

Jaa admired Alice's thick braid down her back. The rebellious strands had already escaped, forming wisps around her ears and neck. No one over forty wore braids anymore except Alice.

Alice lifted a vase covered in moss so thick and green Jaa had to touch it.

"The moss is called Goblins Gold," Alice said with a crinkle. "I thought it inspiring for your work with Charlotte Knight. Tell me, is she everything you expected?"

"I sense she has a taste for the *abracadabra* we need," Jaa said playfully.

"Jaa," Alice reprimanded.

"Oh, you know what I mean. The moss is a lovely touch for the rose."

"Never mind that. Tell me about Charlotte."

"I expect she'll be here any minute. We agreed to meet at eleven."

"She's late. It's after eleven now. I'll put these lilies on the coffee table. May I move the dragonfly box to make room for the rose?"

"I guess so." Jaa sat down in her armchair by the hearth. "Alice, it didn't come to the window last night. The eyes. The face I can't identify."

Alice stopped fussing with the rose.

"I'm worried though. What if it tries to come inside?" Jaa tilted her head toward the front door. "Ah. That's Charlotte now. Coming up the walk. Stay so you can meet her. We'll chat later." She smoothed down her trousers and sweater. "Come in, Charlotte. Door is open."

Charlotte stepped into the room, face flushed from the cold. "Good morning, Charlotte. My goodness, you look refreshed. Come meet Alice Eve."

"The pleasure is all mine," Alice said. "Welcome to Draakensky. I hope you'll be happy here, Charlotte."

"Me too. And thank you for the lovely cold supper you left last night."

Alice arched her eyebrows. "Was the wine okay? I didn't know if—"

"I do enjoy a glass. I am wondering though, was it you who left the back kitchen door open or do you think—?"

"Did I?"

"Maybe Frau Holle. When she—?" Jaa cut in, catching Alice's glance.

"Oh, no," Alice broke in. "That old latch doesn't catch properly. Heida used to complain about it all the time. Jaa, you must get Thomas to install a new lock."

"I'll call him first thing."

Alice grabbed her jacket. "I must get back to the shop. Charlotte, I am in the Village Green, Eve's Garden, if you need time with some friendly blossoms. I have a coffee parlor, and we can have a chat."

"Thank you, I'd like that."

The door closed softly.

"Well," Jaa said, using her warmest tone, "let us go for a walk so I can show off Draakensky."

The woods unfolded as they walked the elevated boardwalk. At first they didn't speak. Enjoying nature and the fresh air was enough, Jaa knew. "The boardwalk goes all the way to the river. We have a gazebo up ahead and we can sit there and view the falls. We installed lights too. Going out in nature is really going in, don't you think?"

"Yes. How lovely to have this boardwalk. I didn't see it this morning when I walked the footpath from the cottage."

"You've seen the river?"

"A quick peek. I met your property manager, Thomas. He does a good job clearing the paths."

"He's reliable as the day is long. Keeps Heida's Walk clear all winter. That's what we named it because Heida designed it. You should see it in the summer, blooming shrubs everywhere. Broom and meadowsweet. Lilacs especially. I once fainted from inhaling the fragrance. A lovely way to pass out."

Charlotte released a rippling laugh. Jaa wished she had a melodious one like that instead of her hearty bursts.

"I see a deer." Charlotte ran up farther, shading her sight against the sun's glare.

She's a woman but with a child's wonder, Jaa nearly said the thought aloud. "Come on, we are almost to the gazebo. The river shows off some extraordinary waterfowl. If we are lucky, we'll see the blue heron."

Jaa tapped her cane carefully with each step, moving ahead of Charlotte, who kept looking back to catch another glimpse of the deer.

They reached the gazebo as the wind chimes jangled from the rafters. The tinker bells always set Jaa at ease—except for the night Heida died. That night they clanged as if from the devil's forest.

"Is that a hawk over the river?" Charlotte asked.

"That's a Draakensky owl. A deviant winter flyer. We have dozens of owls. Their wingspan is wider than hawks. They glisten like topaz under the moon. Here we are. Charlotte, take a glance back and you'll see Draakensky Windmill in all its beauty. How the sails are spinning now. We shall have an invigorating wind walk on our way back."

"Wind walk?"

"My family has been wind walkers for decades. Wind walking keeps your body aligned to the magnetic north. I can catch the wind's speed and intensity when I wind walk."

Charlotte didn't appear to be listening. The river absorbed all her attention.

"The waterfall here is magnificent, isn't it, Charlotte? Rapids, wild as ever. This one is only a six-foot drop. A Class One with small waves and a plateau. But it drops at the lower ledges by Yew Crag into Class Four and Five rapids at the big falls, which are quite dangerous. Do you see Yew Crag on the far left, down river? The county banned hiking there. Splintered ravines on the south side and ragged rock shelves. There's a 500-foot cliff to the west."

"Sounds frightening. I've never seen rapids. Only in films or books."

Jaa examined Charlotte's face. Was she seeing the vortices of water? Was she following the tree shadows gliding on the river's surface? Did she feel the soft wind? Frau Holle's caresses would not disappoint. "Watch the current in the waves. It hesitates before the waves jump the rocks. A little bit of navy blue shade there, see it? Can you feel the river's breath, Charlotte? This river has been my companion since I was a little girl."

Jaa opened her mouth, inhaling the air. The force nearly whistled through her teeth. Waves pitched, blowing froth and flakes, and the wind bells ringing along with the currents. "Try this, Charlotte. Take in a deep breath of the river's air. Feel the wind move down your throat and into your lungs."

Charlotte inhaled slowly through her mouth. "Ahhhh, yes. Fresh. A little sweet."

A single high-pitch whistle splintered the air. Charlotte shot her vision up. "So many blackbirds here."

"That one is a grackle. Grackles differ from blackbirds. Their feathers have a high gloss and colorful heads. Watch how that one aligns with the wind. There he goes. Wings up. Zoom! Don't you wish you could ride the wind?"

Charlotte raised her chin to the sky. Her hair blew out as great fingers of wind raked her head.

"Keep your eyes on the river. It's a stage in a theatre, do you think? And we are the players. I see you are already struck. Your face is flushed." A shout burst from the river. "There! Hear that? What a greeting for you, Charlotte."

Charlotte suddenly swayed back and grabbed the rail.

Was she dizzy? Might she faint? Naturally, with all that river energy and Frau Holle whipping northwest today. Jaa guided her to a bench.

Charlotte leaned her head back against the post, licking her lips, cheeks white as linen, hands gripping the bench. Her shallow breaths broke into an alarming pace. Jaa held her wrist to catch her pulse—her beats raced in time with the rapids, as expected.

"Charlotte? Are you having vertigo?"

She blinked several times, breathing through her mouth. "Everything is . . . bending . . . and flipping."

"You're sitting down, safe on the bench. I've got you. Keep breathing at a steady pace. It will pass. I promise." A few seconds later, her breathing transitioned to an even rhythm.

Charlotte released her grip on the bench and rubbed her temples. "What happened?"

Jaa patted Charlotte's knee. "It's all right. The force of the currents, the falls, and all that energy centers us. River magick! Isn't it thrilling?"

Chapter Seven

A Deeper Reality

"Let's have an early lunch, shall we?" Jaa remarked as they strolled back to Draakensky. "And I want you to take the afternoon to settle in, drive into the village, and poke around. I want you to feel at home here, dear."

Jaa kept her eye on Charlotte. The girl appeared to be steady enough now but wasn't speaking much. What was that flinty glaze in her eyes? Her mind probably raced with questions. "I have a wonderful applestroop and currant buns. A little sugar will perk you up."

"Actually, Jaa, I think I need a rest."

"Of course. Such an experience can be exhausting, I know. But I hesitate to leave you alone at the moment. In the library upstairs, I have a comfy chaise and you can stretch out there while I prepare our lunch. How will that be?"

Once inside the windmill, she escorted Charlotte up the spiral staircase and deposited her on the chaise lounge, covering her with a white knitted afghan. Downstairs she brewed strong coffee, heated the applestroop and currant buns, and laid thick ham slabs and cheese in the roaster to warm. Half an hour later, she heard Charlotte descending the stairs.

"I can't seem to settle down," Charlotte said. She took a seat at the white enameled table where Jaa had set two china plates. "What a quaint Dutch door." She pointed. "We had a Dutch door in my aunt's house. Reminds me of de Hooch's painting, in his domestic scene where the mother is holding her child, the half-opened Dutch door with sunlight streaming a square on the floor tiles. Do you know de Hooch?"

"I do. Funny coincidence that you admire de Hooch, too."

"Smells good in here. What's cooking?"

"Nothing fancy." Jaa placed the moss vase with the single rose on the table. "We'll start work on *Les Roses* tomorrow. It seems my little friend here needs one more day for her full bloom. Coffee?"

"Please."

"In Dutch, we say *eet smakelijk* . . . enjoy your meal."

Charlotte dug into her melted ham and cheese mound with fork and knife; she slathered the applestroop over the bun. Jaa watched her every bite, the savory chewing, the swallows. The delight. The girl knew hunger. When she lifted the coffee cup to her lips, her left hand trembled.

Jaa sat back, nibbling at her bun and taking small sips of coffee. She preferred to admire Charlotte, such a soft and fine young woman. She handled the river magick well. A good sign. "I shall have to ask Frau Holle about it," Jaa murmured to herself.

"Who is that? Holly? Didn't I hear you mention that name earlier when Alice was here?"

Caught, Jaa gave a dismissive hand wave. "Don't mind me. I chatter my thoughts aloud since living alone. Frau Holle, spelled H-o-l-l-e. She has gentle old hands. Knows everything."

"Where does she live? Maybe I should meet her?"

The Dutch door flew open with a bang. Squalls burst in. A chaos of yellow and green leaves flew floor to ceiling.

Charlotte hunched down, elbows tight against her sides.

"Don't be frightened," Jaa said. "Frau Holle is riding by. You know how flowers bend in the pounding rain? To live on Draakensky, we must do the same."

"Jaa! I don't think—"

"It's all right. Sway with it. Frau Holle is excited to send you her greetings."

"Close the door, please," Charlotte said.

"We never close the door on Frau Holle. Never."

Charlotte let out a little shriek, her hair spinning up in circles, her face flushed, eyes squeezed tight. Instantly, the girl leaped up, bounded to the front door, and ran through the garden to the cottage.

Jaa lifted her coffee cup, sipped the last of the brew, and placed the china cup back into its saucer, letting the leaves drift around her in an infinite calm.

Chapter Eight

Scattered Faces

Charlotte stumbled into the cottage. She slammed the door and pushed on the bolt lock. Stupid old woman. What a crazy old bat. *What am I doing here?*

Closing her eyes, raking leaves out of her hair, she slid down the door, wrapped her arms tight over herself, knees to chest, chin tucked down—*a snail shrinking into her shell,* Sister James would have said. Charlotte punched the floor and let out a small scream, thinking that would help. It did.

In the calming moment, she caught a patch of sunlight on the chatelet chest where a green glass jar filled with purple flowers sat behind the lamp. She was sure they were not there when she got up. But she had rushed out. Maybe she hadn't seen them. Maybe Jaa placed them there while she was resting in the library; Jaa would have a key to the cottage. Charlotte thought again: had she even locked the door when she rushed out?

Oh hell, what did she care about all this? River magick. Frau Holle. So what, a silly wind forced open the kitchen door. How many times had Aunt Loretta's Dutch door flown open from the weakened latches? Let it go. Move on.

Charlotte came to Draakensky for one purpose: to sketch Rilke's poems, to begin a new path. Both must remain her focus. She grabbed her car keys and headed to the carport.

She drove the winding roads too fast, made a wrong turn, and ended up in the next town, Pound Ridge. She stopped for gas, bought some groceries at the local market, and looped around to scenic Route 22. Horse farms, stone estates, and rolling hills dotted the landscape beneath a big sky.

Gusts blew among the naked trees, sun lighting the woods' edges. In Chicago, the dull sun filtered through diesel fumes and smoky dust. Here, it cast down a vivid canary yellow, clear and magnified.

Near Hook Road, she slowed the car and pulled over to stop, suddenly engrossed in a massive oak drenched in the late day sunlight—the great-branching tree wore a mesmerizing face scattered across the sky. Signpost: The Bedford Oak. An urge to touch the tree seized her. Within seconds she exited the car, sketch pad in hand, and stood before the giant. Rich moss cloaked the leafless branches, arms stretching far and wide, a brave gray father—she could climb up there and dream. With her hands on the trunk, she sniffed the fragrance. Woody. Bittersweet. *What mysteries do you have for me?*

Taking a few moments, she rendered a rough sketch: crooked limbs hugging the sky, the sun glinting through its bare crown. For sure, she would return another day and do it true justice in the spring. Quenched, she drove to Bedford center.

In Bedford Village, she found a parking space near the library— a lovely antique house with black shutters. The crisp afternoon invited her to stroll the sidewalks. She passed a few clothing shops, the Post Office, a deli, real estate office, hardware store, and Eve's Garden with a front window filled with colorful blooms. Tempted to go in and chat with Alice Eve, she turned to read a blackboard sidewalk menu boasting blackened chicken burgers at The Grackle Bar and Grill. Something spicy might be the early dinner she needed to drive away her jitters.

Inside, the barstools sported elegant green leather seats. Above, stuffed birds roosted on a round black chandelier among the rafters. Each had iridescent bluish heads, streaked black and green. Grackles, sleek with striking golden eyes, wings fanned out. In the casual dining room to the left, the walls displayed wild bird photographs and enormous landscape oil paintings. An ambiance of flight, flung everywhere.

A few couples sat at linen-covered tables, bright orange flowers in brass urns, cloth napkins folded like wings. Charlotte loved how the daylight streamed through the casement windows, inviting her to a cozy table and chairs with a view of the street, but she didn't relish sitting alone at a table for two. With several barstools unoccupied, Charlotte selected a seat at the corner end beneath an elegant Tiffany chandelier next to potted palms. The bar's centerpiece, a bowl of green apples with their stemmed leaves, as if just picked, tempted her.

"Good afternoon." The bartender strolled toward her, a hell of a cute guy with blond wavy hair and eyes slashed brilliant blue. "Welcome. How are you? Having a good day?"

"At the moment, yes," she said eagerly.

He smiled—*pow!* Instant seduction. His burgundy cable-knit sweater threw cheerful hues. "My first time here," she gave him a gleam back.

"I see you're not a regular at The Grackle. What can I get you?"

She read the cocktail menu descriptions on the wall. "What's *The Grackle*? Burnt whips and gales and stormy hail? Sounds dangerous."

"You'll love it. Our signature cocktail. Cold coffee, Sexton Irish Whiskey, kick of cayenne, spices, two stabs of bacon."

"Bacon?" she said, resisting the urge to lick her lips. "Sounds perfect."

"You got it." He put his hand out for a shake. "Marc Sexton."

"Charlotte Knight." His grip penetrated warm and calming.

He reached for a stemmed goblet. "You passing through Bedford on your way to—?"

"I'm here for a few months. I saw that Bedford Oak on Old Bedford Road. Some kind of god, that tree. Ravishing."

"That oak is our prize citizen. A resident sage. Over 500 years old."

"Really? Forests are a big attraction for me. I'm hoping to spend time in nature and walk the wild woods here."

He tossed crushed ice into a goblet and free-poured from a black bottle with a skeleton in a top hat on the label. "You want to escape into the forests, hike with some wild man, and muse with Mother Earth?"

She wanted to purr at that. "I don't know. Are there wild men in Bedford?"

"A few of us around," he whispered, then splashed coffee and a shake of spices into the glass. "I'm owner, barkeep, and I live in a barn in Bedford woods, chock-full of owls and wild geese." His voice came in smooth notes from deep in his chest.

With a twist of his hand, Marc waved a blowgun to smoke a cinnamon stick under a glass bell; he topped off the drink with two bacon sticks flaring out into dark wings. Smoke swirled as he placed the drink down.

"The Grackle. For the lovely lady looking for a wild man. Enjoy."

Charlotte lifted the glass. The first sip hit her mouth like an explosion. The next gulp shimmied down. "That is one powerful drink." Crunching on the bacon wings, she pointed to the Sexton Irish Whiskey bottle. "Who is the skeleton in the top hat? An ancestor of yours?"

"The Sexton. That gentleman on the label is Old Father, the sexton who dug graves. Not a relative. But the whiskey is my family's brew from over a hundred years ago."

"Impressive. Do you make it in the basement?"

"Not these days. Now Sexton Whiskey is distilled by a premier distiller in Northern Ireland. Excuse me a sec?" Marc walked to the bar's other end to speak to a waiter.

Charlotte kept her eye on him. He didn't look like a wild man. Tall and long-legged, his heart-shaped face gave him an enterprising, slightly boyish character.

She slid off her red coat and hung it on the coatrack near a wall with photos of celebrity patrons: Actors Michael Douglas, Richard Gere, Martha Stewart, Suffragist Florence Jaffray Harriman—Bedford's rich and famous that she had heard about—above a row of local residents. And, two women wearing old-fashioned brimmed hats, standing before a windmill. The photo was tagged Draakensky, 1982.

Charlotte noticed a peripheral flash of burgundy next to her and turned. "Marc, is that Jaa Morland and her sister Heida Mead?"

"Bedford's Bird Sisters, we call them. I left you a menu if you want to order."

"That blackened chicken special is calling me."

"Coming up. Do you know Jaa Morland?"

"Not really. I'm staying in her guest cottage."

Marc's jaw dropped. "In Heida Mead's cottage? I didn't know Jaa was renting it out. I'll put your order in."

Charlotte took her seat at the bar, checking her phone messages and texts. Her friend Suzanne had texted good luck wishes on her "northern adventure," and a few other friends from Chicago had left encouraging one-liners. The last text surprised her. From Don.

HEY GIRL. I KNOW WE LEFT EVERYTHING ON A NASTY NOTE. I AM SORRY FOR ALL THE ANGER THAT'S GONE ON. HOPE YOU ARE DOING WELL IN NEW YORK. MAYBE WHEN YOU GET BACK, WE CAN HAVE A DRINK FOR OLD TIMES' SAKE. YOU KNOW ME. I HATE TO BURN BRIDGES. TAKE CARE OF YOURSELF. YOUR FAN IN CHICAGO. DD.

Not cute anymore, Don. She deleted the message with a firm tap. Her vision wandered to the host podium with purple flowers in a flamboyant vase. She read the display card. *Compliments of Eve's Garden.* So it was Alice Eve who left the flowers in the cottage.

A staff person slipped behind the bar. "Hello there. I'm Liz. Are you the blackened chicken special?" She held a plate piled high with charred meat in a bun. A classic platinum blond, full red lips, eyelashes that could kill, she wore a black sweater tucked into belted blue jeans.

Jeez Louise. She looks like a movie star. Jean Harlow type. "That's mine. Thank you."

"Anything else you need? Refill?"

"One's my limit. An ice water?"

"My pleasure. Lemon or lime?"

"Oh, thanks. Lemon."

Liz fetched it and headed gracefully toward the kitchen door. When she passed Marc, she gave him a knowing glance. Charlotte noticed he had taken off his burgundy sweater, wearing a dark blue button-down sport shirt open at the neck.

She dove into her sandwich while catching some news on her cellphone. A few minutes later, Marc suddenly stood before her. She lifted her head.

"Sandwich okay? Oh no, you didn't care for the bun?" Marc pointed to the bread chunks she'd left on her plate.

"Chicken tasted delicious. But, sorry to say the bun was too dense for me. Your baker probably didn't knead it long enough. Or didn't build enough mesh into the dough."

"Buns come from a supplier. How do you know about dough kneading?"

"I'm a bread chef."

"I would never have guessed. I imagine bread chefs to be beefy women, double-chinned, with pumped upper arms."

"Nope. All the work is in the palms and chest movement. Fancy rocking is all it takes. And patience." Why did she say that about chest movement? Now his eyes went straight to her breasts.

"Sorry about the bun," Marc said. "Next time you come in, you get a free lunch. Hey Liz? Print me a gift ticket. Fifteen dollars."

"That's generous, Marc. Thank you."

"Stop in again sometime? We're only about fifteen minutes from Draakensky Windmill. Jaa and Heida were regulars here for years. Every Friday, smack at noon, a cheese pizza and two Belgian beers, at the front window table." He leaned over the bar, cocked his head. "Come by on Thursday nights. That's my regular shift and our music night."

"I might do that." Charlotte swiveled off the barstool when a sparkle drew her vision back to Marc's chest. A silver wolf's head dangled below his throat from a wide silver-linked chain. Behind the gentle-faced wolf, an inverted rounded triangle framed the pendant. A wolf mounted on a shield. How curious.

As she walked to the back to get her coat, she struggled to remember where she had seen that wolf pendant. Slipping into her coat, she flipped up her red hood and headed to the front door, but stopped again at the bar.

"I'm admiring your wolf pendant," she told Marc, gesturing to his neck. "Is that Gothic style with the scrolled edges? Maybe a famous wolf I should know?"

"This?" He held it up. "Not Gothic. A Celtic design. What, you think I eat grandmas and little girls in red hoods?"

"Hilarious. Are you some kind of wolf man?" she curled a shoulder, feeling herself blush just a little.

Marc tilted his head thoughtfully. "Yeah, that's me, wild man with a wolf."

Snowflakes kicked up as Charlotte keyed the cottage door lock. In the kitchen, she stocked the cabinets with her groceries and got to work on making bread dough. Bread baking never failed to soothe her, and this night would be no exception. Flour, water, yeast—the silky flour coated her hands. Mixing, resting, kneading. Folding, rolling, turning. She set the dough by the stovetop to rise.

Upstairs, she wasted no time filling the closet and dresser drawers with her garments. At midnight, with the hot bread cooling on the kitchen counter, filling the cottage with warm yeasty aromas, she soaked under the shower. Exhausted, she climbed into the sleigh bed by the window.

Snow squalls had stopped, leaving a few snow orphans to drift in the roof's exterior floodlights. Had she forgotten to turn them off? Leaving the warm bed, she stepped lightly downstairs, flipped the exterior switch off, and quickly returned to bed. Snuggled in, her head sunk into the pillow.

A *bump* hit the window. White light shed across the glass. Except the floodlights were off. She tossed off the covers, switched on the table lamp, and stood at the window.

Her face reflected in the darkness. Going in closer, she saw it wasn't her face at all. A pair of dark eyes looked back at her. Big, black, watery orbs watching her. Whitish cheekbones. A forehead? Shadows spinning on shadows like a blackened pinwheel.

Her breath quickened. Was this a kind of psychic impression happening? Mommy Mildred had plenty of those from people's personal objects. Seeing images, auras, or hearing sounds. Still, the image forced a chill across her shoulders. She yanked the shade down. Ringing echoed from outside—glass breaking or maybe those rusty chimes at the gazebo.

"Do you see my dark hourssss? I am sometimes like a tree rustling over the gravesite."

The words splashed over her head. She hugged herself to quell the trembling.

Like a tree? Heart racing, she moved to the bed, lowered her hip onto the mattress, hands tight on the bedsheets. *Dark hours? Over the gravesite?* What was this shivering voice in the air? She imagined a purplish tinge to the ghostly sound. A gray moisture leaked out around the window frame. Vapors? Might it suddenly leap at her from a dark corner? Scream into her ears?

No, no, no. She would not let it get inside her head—ghost, witch, or imaginative phantom. There she stayed, awake, listening, watching, on the edge between denying and believing. Sleep could not carry her away. Legs straight on the mattress, fingers threaded together on her lap, she sensed the bed breathing slips of air—thin anxious rhythms in and out. Breathing with her.

The thing at the window banged its head against the glass. *Thump . . . Thump . . . Thump.* Any brief dips into sleepy unconsciousness broke like a furious wind slamming a door open, again and again, no matter how many times Charlotte shut the door of her mind.

"Why am I so cold?" The words escaped like teeth falling from her mouth. She would not cry out. Instead she turned to the window, eyes wide, willing it to go away.

"Come to the window, Charlotte. See me. Let me in."

A gliding cold caught inside her throat. Charlotte pushed herself back into the gray pillow, knees to chest, eyes blinked shut, rock-rock-rocking herself to the rhythmic moans and groans of the spinning windmill.

Chapter Nine

Then the Knowing Comes

From the second-floor windows, Jaa enjoyed the morning gray mist gathered in the distance. An owl glided the riverbanks. Faint as a whisper, its hoot drifted down. Minutes later, the bird perched on the windmill's sail beyond the glass window. Wide-shouldered, the bird showed off its ash-colored feathers, streaks of black, brown, and white, with thin red hues on the tail. The eyes pulsed as big as darkened moons, rimmed in yellow.

"Camaroon," she said. "Why are you here today? Are you bringing a message from Heida? Is she nearby?" He hooted a *whoo-hooo,* simulating the wind lifting through the tree branches. With a leap and a flap, he soared away.

Jaa had spent the night on the library chaise lounge, warm beneath the white shawl, resting her head on Heida's pink silk scarf spread across the top. This is exactly where Charlotte recovered after she visited the river. Jaa wanted to sleep in Charlotte's place on the chaise, to absorb the young woman's energies that might still be lingering. Today they would begin with Rilke's poem "Number Fourteen." The single rose Alice had brought stood in its peak bloom now. Jaa read over the poem.

XIV
Summer: to be for a few days
the contemporary of roses;
to breathe what drifts about
their blooming spirits.
To make of each who dies,

a confidant,
and to outlive this sister
among the other, wandering roses.

Still feeling dreamy, Jaa drew up an image: Rainer Maria Rilke wearing his neat sweater and brimmed hat, standing in his rose garden at the Castle Muzot in Switzerland. Jaa had designed her library much the same with paintings of summer flower gardens on the walls between the bookshelves stuffed with her children's literature collection. She ran her hand over her favorite wall hanging, a 1901 image of Rilke and his wife Clara Westhoff sitting in their winter overcoats on a balcony. So romantic.

The ceiling creaked. Those structural beams beneath the roof suffered age and wind pressures. Jaa moved to the far corner and put her ear against the wall to listen again, the sound reminding her of a baby's coos.

On a whim, she pressed the small lever at the bookshelf where the illustrated *Alice's Adventures in Wonderland* sat at the secret opening to the attic. The narrow bookcase swung open on its hinges. Jaa reached into the darkness to pull the light chain. Carefully, she climbed up the battered steps. The bookcase swung back into position behind her.

Memories surfaced. She and Heida as children sitting cross-legged inside the attic hatch, snuggled with pillows, flashlights, Dutch chocolates, and their storybooks. "What a Wonderland we had, Heida." As teens, they stole cigarettes and beer from the kitchen cupboard to stash them in the ratty trunk. At night they smoked and drank and play-acted Chekhov's *Three Sisters*, wearing long skirts and shawls. "How bohemian we were."

Tempted to lie down on the trundle bed in the corner and just be in perfect quiet again, she decided there was no time for such reminiscence. Returning to the attic steps, she pushed the bookcase out into the library, her hand on Lewis Carroll's book, then closed the doorway. "Oh my ears and whiskers, how late it's getting," she imitated the White Rabbit's voice.

At the hatched window, she viewed the garden below. Charlotte was crossing the snowy path. The front door clicked open.

"I'm in the library, Charlotte. Upstairs."

Her footsteps tapped hurriedly. Charlotte reached the top step, her complexion wan under the red hood.

"Good morning, Jaa. You're looking chipper."

"I wish I could say the same for you, my dear. Have we exhausted you already? Have a seat on the lounge chair. Did you not sleep well last night?"

Charlotte tossed off her coat and perched herself on the lounge chair's edge. "I'm fine."

"Appearances to the contrary. Frau Holle didn't upset you, yesterday, did she? We do not fight the wind here on Draakensky, Charlotte."

"I'm sure you're right," she answered politely, her vision cast to the floor. "I baked you a peasant bread." She offered the loaf wrapped in a white cloth tied with ribbons.

Jaa took the bread with both hands. "Oh, it's still warm. You're a sweetheart. You baked it this morning?"

"Last night, but I warmed it up for you. Shall we get started? I read over 'Number Fourteen' this morning, Jaa. Gave it some serious thought. I have a few ideas. I'm thinking—"

"Ideas? No, Charlotte. We don't want your ideas." Heavens, this girl was naïve.

"Excuse me? You don't want my thoughts? For the art?"

Her curt tone irritated Jaa. And that frowning face. Eyes bloodshot. What had her so threatened? Was it Frau Holle's greeting? Surely, the girl was more resilient. "I don't appreciate your impatient tone, Charlotte. You seem defensive. Defenses are costly. It shows weakness. What has you so disturbed? Was it Frau Holle?"

"Of course not. I'm trying to do my job. I'm ready to sketch studies of the poem. You know, Jaa, I cannot worry about what I cannot control. I need to focus my energies on what I can create: the visuals for the poem. It's that simple."

"Nothing is that simple. And this book cannot be rushed. Heida and I were in complete agreement that this creative adventure for Rilke's book demands productive optimism. Precision. Accuracy." Jaa banged her cane on the floor. "Shall we begin?"

Jaa gathered the dried rose petals from the glass bowl on the table. "A little rose scent to inspire us and create a calming atmosphere." She placed them on a brass plate and began lighting each dried petal. "We have a little process to help us find the poem's core. Heida and I did this all the time. We focused on the rhythms. The musical beats open doors between the conscious and subconscious."

She struck a second match and lit more petals. With her fingertips, she caressed the single rose in the vase. "Heida liked to say, 'Flowers have secret eyes. They see us completely.' Let's permit the rose here to see us. Let Heida in. Are you ready, Charlotte, for a secret adventure into the ghost living inside the rose?"

The girl's cheeks suddenly flushed—little red charcoals. One might have thought Jaa had slapped the girl.

Charlotte raised her eyes, narrow, hard, the gray light in them turning dark like two clouds ready to storm burst. "The ghost living inside the rose? What does that mean exactly? What about the ghost that was at my window last night? Eyes looking at me. A voice. Speaking to me."

Jaa's hand flew to her mouth, but immediately she shooed the air, sending such worries away. "A ghost at the window? Impossible."

"Impossible? What is the point in using the word impossible about an event that has clearly happened?"

"Oh my dear, dear Charlotte. River wind crashes across Draakensky night and day. Bang, slam, boom. You'll get used to it. We had a north wind last night. Gusts at thirty-nine miles per hour. Wind horses riding the sky. Wild, they were. Heida hated the north wind because it was full of boulders and daggers banging at the cottage windows and roof. You have no reason to fear. We have Frau Holle here from sun to moon. Let's get to work. Stop kicking your leg and follow my direction. Heida wants us to begin with the rose's urgent lips speaking—"

"You know what?" Charlotte interrupted. "I've changed my mind."

"Sorry, what?"

She rose, her heeled boots banging the floor. "I prefer to work alone on this poem." She pointed to the vase. "May I? I'll take the rose and poem 'Number Fourteen' and work in the cottage. I'll bring you my sketches, and we can go from there. That seems fair, doesn't it?" She snatched up her coat.

"Charlotte, it is *our* task to illustrate this poem as Rilke felt it. His intention. Heida was clear on—"

"Yes, yes. I agree with you. But I normally sketch on my own steam, and it produces good results."

"That is not how this works."

"Jaa, didn't Rilke say an artist needs to choose 'aloneness, that great inner solitude' to find the answers? You agree with Rilke, don't you? I need to follow Rilke's advice. See you later." She headed for the staircase.

"Charlotte!"

With one foot on the step, she turned, coat bunched over her arm, the vase tipping askew. "There is one thing, Jaa, I will not tolerate. Anyone controlling my creative process. Not you. And not your sister. I'll bring the sketches to you later."

She banged down the steps.

Jaa hurried to the window. Charlotte, hood up against the wind, crossed the garden path, darted into the cottage, and slammed the door. Just like Little Red Riding Hood desperate to get home before the wolf devoured her.

Chapter Ten

Winter Sun

Charlotte hustled through the cottage door, her head reeling with ghosts, voices, rose petals, wind horses. Let Heida in?

Focus on the work. *The secret power of hyper-focused work—*Sister James would have advised. *Close down all outside thoughts and run at full throttle.*

As much as she hated to admit it, Jaa was right. Sketching Rilke's poems required understanding Rilke's intentions and his feelings. Productive optimism, indeed. She placed the rose on the windowsill and stood back to get the full impact.

*Just keep on, quietly and earnestly, growing through all that happens to you . . . Nothing alien happens to us, but only what has long been our own—*Rilke's advice on the creative process in his *Letters to a Young Poet* to Franz Xaver Kappus. Charlotte had read the book twice, at Jaa's insistence.

After she got comfy in the wing-backed chair by the garden bow window, she read the poem again. All her ideas fell flat. Maybe drawing the structure would get the momentum going. She began with the rose's dark center, looped around, petal over petal.

She read the words aloud, " '*Summer . . . to breathe what drifts about . . . their blooming spirits.*' " For hours, Charlotte sketched a series of studies in an unstoppable hot energy. Her mind soared. She breathed in the rose as if she might breathe in a lover's kiss. At the finish, after far too many failed renderings tossed aside, she placed the three best images against the wall, stepped back, and studied them.

Was this the mystery in Rilke's poem? Had she captured it? To be fully awake in your bloom, such beauty that belied impending death. She copied the three images into her computer file, and with the sun down already, she knocked at the windmill.

To her surprise, Alice Eve opened the door. "Charlotte. Come in."

"Is Jaa available?" she said, her heart throbbing.

"She's struggling with a dreadful headache, poor thing. Not up to preparing dinner, so I brought her a hot meal." Alice wore a perky face. "How are you settling in?"

"Doing okay, yes. I have sketches for Jaa to review."

"I'm not sure she's up to it at the moment. Maybe you could leave them for her?"

"I'm here," Jaa bellowed from the spiral staircase. She banged down, cane stabbing each step. At the bottom she paused, dressed in a pink silk robe, pink ballet slippers, and her gray hair loose over her shoulders.

"Are you feeling unwell?" Charlotte asked. "I've done a few visuals, if you're up to taking a look."

"Certainly, I'm up to it." Jaa dropped into her chair by the fire. "Hand them over."

In tense moments, Charlotte often found herself going stiff, her left knee taking all the stress and locking. But at this moment, she practically floated over to Jaa, sketches in hand, offering them in a generous sweep. "I had an exciting time drawing them. It went quite well. What do you think?"

Jaa examined them one by one, eyebrows knitted, mouth pursed. She spread them out. Alice blinked at Charlotte in approval.

"So," Jaa finally said. "The future enters us. Is that it?" She cut each word with a razor tongue.

Charlotte lost her enthusiasm. "Well, maybe. I was thinking— of the present moment. Alive to the fullest and taking flight. Breathing in the beauty to outlive the past. Or—or something like that."

"Or something," Jaa imitated her tone. "No. No. No."

"No? What do you mean?"

"*No* is a complete sentence, is it not? *No* does not require an explanation."

Charlotte's legs weakened. She slipped down on the sofa, sinking into the cushions.

"This is dreadful, Charlotte. We don't want your avant-garde vision. You've drawn hundreds of what—lacy loops? Spinning outward in a never-ending circle right off the page. And while it does have a flowery influence, this is nothing near what Heida had in mind for Rilke's 'Number Fourteen.' This is not Heida's work!"

"Of course it's not Heida's work," Alice said gently with a hand on Jaa's shoulder. "Heida didn't draw this. Charlotte did."

In a stifled scream, Jaa covered her face with both hands. Alice patted her shoulder again. She signaled to Charlotte to remain calm.

A few seconds later, an eternity for Charlotte, Jaa held the sketches up. "I see this has been a mistake." She shook the papers. "My mistake. To think you could draw this poem as Heida wanted. I've misjudged you. How stupid of me." She leaned her head back, pain on her face, tears filling her eyes, and with a wail, Jaa flung the sketches into the fire, the images blazing into curly ashes.

Charlotte leaped, crashing her knee into the coffee table, which sent it wobbling, the dragonfly box flipping to the floor.

"There, you see?" Jaa pointed to the overturned box. A shock of tied gray-brown hair lay on the carpet. "Heida does not approve of your interpretation. She is angry. And she's angry with you, Charlotte. Heida would never accept this absurd illustration. You're fired. Get out. Go back to Chicago."

Chapter Eleven

Awakening Desire

Inside the cottage, Charlotte flopped down on the sofa. Seeing her sketches ablaze sent a hot sting straight into her gut. The mantel clock struck a single bell tone on the half hour. *You're fired.* Maybe she should have resolved to illustrate rabbits and kittens like Beatrix Potter instead of such lofty ambitions as poetry.

Were her expectations too high in taking this job? Too emotionally attached? Consider the source: Jaa was a quirky, single-minded, aging recluse, struggling with the loss of her murdered sister. Maybe nothing would please the woman. *Go back to Chicago.* As what, a failed artist? To what? She didn't even have her own home to retreat to now.

Charlotte knew she desperately needed perspective. She dialed Sister James in Chicago, but hung up before the first ring, remembering the St. Charles Retreat for the sisters. She tried Suzanne. No answer. One thing for sure, she would not mope the rest of the night inside Heida's cottage. She jumped in the car and sped down Mianus River Road. Maybe she could escape to a movie. She browsed the main roads through Mt. Kisco and, finding few options, headed back to Bedford. She didn't want to sit alone in a movie house anyway. She wanted to chat it up, mingle, find a new friend, be merry, swear, scream with laughter.

Driving the main street through the Village Green, she passed The Grackle Bar and Grill. Thoughts of ice rattling in glasses, conversation, dim lights, and a glass of wine spurred her to grab an open parking space.

After locking the Fiat, she hurried across the street to the bar's entrance with Marc Sexton, Permittee embossed in gold on the front door. Inside, the lively atmosphere saturated her mood. Men and women stood shoulder to shoulder, singing and swaying with Elvis singing "Burning Love" on the bar television, his classic *Aloha from Hawaii* performance.

Colorful glitz flashed from the screen, everyone applauding, cheers circling. Somewhere in all this, she spotted Marc serving cold brews and cocktails. Several minutes passed before he saw her in the crowd and gave her a thumbs-up welcome.

"Hey there, Charlotte," he shouted over the blare. "Place is jumpin', right? Glad you stopped by. Like our Elvis night?"

"Who wouldn't love this?"

When Elvis began "Something," Marc lowered the volume and people resumed chatting and ordering refills. A stylish silver-haired woman sipping a martini gestured Charlotte to the empty seat near her. Plenty of smart-looking men with beers or whiskey tumblers gave her friendly hellos. While she wasn't the most happening gal in this bustling barroom, the jostle, music, and flirty drinkers gave her an immediate energy boost.

A woman sitting next to her spouted amusing quips about society's obsessions with labels, probably a psychologist. Charlotte chatted with a blue-suited lawyer-type reminiscing about noir films, who imitated Hitchcock's deadpan lugubrious voice. Much of the time she kept a fix on Marc as he filled glasses, jiggered shakers, and dashed from customer to customer, his magnetic face charming everyone. An hour later, Elvis in his white cape closed the concert on the television, and the bar quieted down as people paid their tabs and departed.

Charlotte signaled Marc for a refill.

Marc leaned over the bar top, his wolf pendant clinging to his throat. "I don't think you need another drink, Miss Knight."

"You don't want to sell me another drink?"

"See the marble statue at the bar top?"

Charlotte looked up. "That guy in the toga, eating grapes? Great pecs."

"That's Dionysus. His wisdom declares the first drink is for your health. Second drink for pleasure. Third for sleep. Then the wise stop, and go home."

"I have no intention of being wise tonight or going home. It's not every day a gal gets fired on Day One. Must be a world record."

She blurted out the scene between her and Jaa in the windmill. Marc listened with rapt attention, then reached over and squeezed her hand. His touch sent a lusty surge, one she hadn't felt in a long time and rarely with Don.

"You best not drive back to Draakensky," Marc said.

She didn't stand a chance resisting him or those gorgeous blues. "Oh, I'm a honeybee on a little buzz, is all."

"You're buzzing pretty high." He turned and from a hatch he placed a plated baked potato and a tumbler of ice water before her. "Have something to eat. My barkeep's special. Stay a while."

The Latino guy drinking a beer, sitting on the next stool, gave her a grin. "Sexton taking good care of you, is he?"

She nodded, trying not to splash her glee all over the place.

"Marc's famous for his baked potatoes with the ladies."

She dug into the potato oozing with butter and chives. "I'll bet he's everybody's champion."

"In this town, Marc practically walks on water."

"Oh yeah? A gentleman, huh?"

"One hundred percent. Keeps his shoes shined every day." He put his hand out for a shake. "Jimmy Cruz. You're not a regular here."

"No. You're a regular?"

"Pretty much. I never miss Elvis Night. New in town?"

"Soon to be exiting the beautiful Bedford. I got fired today. Royally screwed up." She downed the ice water. "I'm Charlotte. Nice to meet you, Jimmy."

Marc darted in. "Watch out for this guy. Jimmy's a copper. The Chief."

"Chief of Police, here in Bedford?"

"All the livelong day. Where did you work?"

"For Jaa Morland at Draakensky."

Jimmy exchanged a glance with Marc.

"And exactly how did you screw up?" Jimmy asked.

"I think Jaa was expecting me to fill in for her sister on a book we are working on. Heida Mead. You know about that, right? The murder?"

"Yeah. Tough case."

"The property manager at Draakensky, Thomas, was telling me about it. How was she murdered?"

Jimmy gulped his beer. "Everybody wants to know that one.

The autopsy reported the cause of death as undetermined. Could be hypoxia, lack of oxygen, but that couldn't be medically verified."

"Odd, isn't it? An autopsy to be inconclusive?"

"Everything about this case is odd. They determined her heart stopped but could not identify a verifiable cause. Trauma is the best guess. People can die of shock, but it's rare. Neurogenic shock is the medical term, so that's what we're stuck with."

"But then what evidence do you have that it was a murder?"

Jimmy fidgeted with the cocktail napkin. "Several points. The state of the corpse. State of the crime scene, about which I'm not at liberty to say. But most importantly, fresh bootprints on the riverbank. Local news hacks were all over that leak." He emptied the rest of the beer bottle in two long gulps.

"Bootprints? Thomas wears boots. But you probably investigated him, right?"

"He's clean. Harrogate's a cave dweller. Rhodes Scholar for all that's worth. We're still trying to identify the boot pattern on the tread in manufacturers' databases. No luck yet."

"Do you think the killer is still around here?"

"Probably. This doesn't appear to be a random killing though. We think Heida knew her attacker. Listen, maybe getting fired by Jaa Morland wasn't as bad as you think. Might be an opportunity for you to move on." Jimmy swiveled off the stool abruptly. "Great to meet you, Charlotte. Good luck. And no driving." He pointed his finger at her.

Charlotte watched Jimmy hustle out. "Glad you told me he was a cop. No uniform?" she asked Marc.

"Jimmy doesn't wear his uniform while he's drinking at the bar. Bad image."

"He left in a hurry. Did I hit a touchy subject?"

"The Mead case has gone cold. Jimmy knew Heida a long time. He was the first responder on the scene. You know what? I can drive you home. My pleasure."

Now that would be a perfect ending to a perfectly miserable day. But Charlotte sensed an icy stare from the bartender, Liz, a few feet away. Was Marc Liz's territory? Shoot, a ride home was harmless enough. "Well, I don't dare violate Jimmy's no-driving orders. Right?"

"You better not. Give me fifteen minutes."

Inside Marc's white sports jeep, the bitter February air hit. He blasted the heat, turning out of the Village Green. "We have a clear sky tonight. How are you at counting fire-folk?"

"Counting the stars?"

"I mean Orion. I've got him in my backyard every night."

"The Hunter? I've not seen Orion, except on star maps."

"Orion out dazzles them all. My observation deck is perfect for stargazing. Would you like to see it? I love flirting with the stars. After my dad died, I traveled to Whitehaven Beach in Australia on a stargazing adventure. A spectacular off-the-grid experience. I slept on the farthest lip of the beach, at the end of the ocean, with Centaurus, Scorpius, Lupus, and Libra over my head. The air there is clearer than crystal."

Australia. How thrilling. Traveling to another country had not been in her plans, but it was a desire. "How old were you? Did you go with friends?"

"I was twenty. Went solo. Just the big sky and the mysterious universe watching me." He punched the music player, and Johnny Mathis sang "Chances Are."

"So, are you up for stargazing?"

"I love Johnny Mathis," she said, listening to the lyrics.

"You don't want to go back to Draakensky, do you, Charlotte?"

True, she had no desire to go back to Heida's cottage and spend the night in that sleigh bed, near the window, or hear that weird voice, or debate with herself how to confront Jaa. But go to his house this late at night? "Your Chief of Police told me you're a gentleman. One-hundred percent, Jimmy said. Do you really walk on water?"

He let out a hearty *Ha*. "Yeah, that's the Chief. He's always looking out for me. Jim's a good cop. I bring all my friends to view Orion. You've got to see it. He's like a silver cobweb."

Maybe she should let herself enjoy the little mystery ahead. "I'd love to see Orion. But. To be clear, Marc. I don't sleep around. Agreed?"

"Uh-huh," he nodded thoughtfully. "The good girl?"

She cringed. Good girls were meek. Good girls go to heaven. Bad girls get to go everywhere and taste the wild side.

"I like good girls," he made a wide turn onto a backroad with no street lights.

"Really. Why is that?"

"Good girls are the ivory tower. Genuine. High-quality listeners, and deeply affectionate."

"And bad girls?" She said, coaxing him.

"Hellfire. Aloof. Demanding. And they break the rules way too many times. In my youth I wanted the bad girls to win. We all grow up. And, I don't sleep around either, Charlotte."

The jeep bounced over narrow roads and hills. Johnny Mathis sang "Autumn Leaves" as Marc turned onto another backroad. Neither one spoke for a while. How comfortable Marc was not forcing chit-chat. Quite different from her life with Don when everything ran on formalities, discussions ordered, and reordered into priorities as if silence were a foreign intruder.

Only a few houses dotted the way until he turned sharply onto a gravel road. When Marc pulled up a long driveway, a gigantic green barn stood in the distance, fully lit, two stories high, covered in leaded glass windows.

"You live here alone? This big house?"

"Oh, I've got a few fairies who reside with me."

"Only you and the fairies?"

He shot her a cute grin. "And a wizard in the attic."

"Of course, every home needs a wizard in the attic." Marc killed Mathis's song just before the crescendo where Mathis hits a long mellow note that Charlotte loved to linger on.

With a slam of the shift, the car jerked into park, and he turned to face her. "Let's warm up with chai lattes and I'll show you The Hunter. Promise to drive you back later."

The gravel crunched under Charlotte's shoes as she walked the driveway path bordered by snow-covered shrubs and a low rock wall. Heavy pine aromas hit her; she took the air in delicious gulps. Somewhere an owl hooted.

Inside, she admired the arched doorways in pine paneling the color of toasted biscuits. High ceilings. Exposed rafters. A vaulted living room so high one might think there was no ceiling at all. Tall curved windows floor to ceiling, quirky cubbies, and alcoves made her feel she had entered a hideout in the vast woods. Centering the room, a rough-hewn stone fireplace, an inglenook she could have walked into drew her eye—gray and white stone, sparkling in the lamplights.

She scanned his bookshelves: *King Arthur and the Knights of the Roundtable,* Tennyson's *Idylls of the King, The Daughters of Avalon, Life of Merlin, In the Forest of Broceliande,* Malory's *Le Morte D'Arthur,* and other titles she didn't recognize. A battered

The Boy's King Arthur brought up memories. "I read this book in high school."

"My grandmother read it to me every summer."

On a middle shelf, an old red volume, Doré, wrapped in clear plastic, caught her attention next to *Histories of the Kings of Britain*. "You have a volume of Gustave Doré Illustrations? I adore his work. I used to trace Doré illustrations to study his form. What a rare book this is."

"That edition has Doré's *Story of Vivienne of Avalon*. The pages are shredding. You want to open it and—"

"Oh no. It's far too delicate."

"How about this one?" He pulled out *In the Forest of Broceliande* and paged through.

Charlotte liked his hands. Generous, well-scrubbed. No wristwatch.

"This illustration is Vivienne and Merlin under the oak tree. Vivienne is portrayed as the evil temptress in Tennyson's version. She bewitches Merlin. Pretty tricks and fooleries," he said diabolically.

No rings on his fingers, either—only the enchanting wolf face on the silver shield, resting perfectly below the hollow of his throat. Instinctively, she wanted to touch it but would never be so bold.

"Do you know the legends about Vivienne and Merlin?" he asked.

Charlotte sat down with the *Broceliande* volume to study the images. "Not much." She paged through. "Vivienne is gorgeous here, twined like a snake around Merlin. She wears strength and darkness beautifully."

"Vivienne is the Lady of the Lake. She had other names. Nimue or Nineveh."

"I remember the story of Vivienne rising from the lake with her elegant hand on the Excalibur sword, giving it to Arthur. You know that legend?"

"That's the Celtic version. Vivienne is best known as the Water Goddess of Avalon. Of all the legends about her as Lady of the Lake, enchantress, sorcerer, the Water Goddess is her true identity."

"Is that in the story where Vivienne asks Merlin to give her his magick? In the Celtic version?" She certainly hadn't read all the legends of Merlin and King Arthur Pendragon but recalled the films from Saturday movie nights with Sister James at the convent.

"That would be in Tennyson's *Idylls of the King*. Vivienne is on a quest for her highest feminine powers. And she desires Merlin's magick."

"Good for her. I didn't read *Idylls of the King*."

"Not so good for Merlin, though. Vivienne seduces him relentlessly. He succumbs and reveals his most secret magick to her. Big mistake. When Merlin sleeps beneath the oak tree, during a lightning storm, she uses her new magick to make the oak tree rise around him as an invisible tower."

"How beguiling. I can think of a few men I would like to cast into an invisible tower."

That got a chuckle from him.

"What happens to Merlin in the tower?"

"Merlin becomes her prisoner. She makes him her sexual plaything." His cocky little grin made her giggle. "Because what else would a woman do with a man in a tower?"

"Very juicy. Does Merlin get out?" She expected some thrilling escape with magickal intrigue and mystical creatures.

Marc's face dropped. "Without his magick," he said gently, "Merlin dies."

"Oh no."

"Merlin '*lay dead, lost to life, use, name and fame.*' First time I read *Idylls*, I felt such grief for Merlin. But, brave and adventurous Vivienne is the winner. Her magick exceeded Merlin's powers. And she became the mighty Water Goddess of Avalon."

"Isn't she clever. I love it. Even a wizard as gifted as Merlin can fall."

"Tennyson has Vivienne shouting to the woods of Broceliande, '*I have made his glory mine.*' For all Merlin's magick and prophecy, he lacked skills in sex magick." He raised his eyebrows playfully.

"Sex magick? What is that?"

"By all accounts, a powerful weapon."

His winsome expression held her. A little bit of a secret there. Charlotte returned the book to the shelf next to a title she didn't know but pulled the volume because the title intrigued her. "Who are the *Sisters of Avalon*?"

"Celtic women. They possessed the highest magickal powers. After King Arthur's final battle at Camlann, where he is injured, they sailed the river on a barge and rescued the king." Marc leaned in and whispered, "In a land far and away, the sisters sailed him to the Vale of Avalon, to their island hidden in the mists between the known and the unknown. And there they laid the king on a bed of gold and healed his battle wounds."

"I'll bet they did. Do you think Arthur truly existed? Historically, I mean."

"The Oxford's Bodleian Library has a medieval manuscript identifying King Arthur's burial site in Avalon. Truth is patient. She waits to be discovered."

"I like that," Charlotte turned, scanning the room. "You must have hired some fancy decorator to renovate this barn. Where are the fairies?"

"Kitchen. They prefer the herb garden. You know fairies are impossible to catch."

"I knew that," she said. "And the wizard in the attic? Will he be joining us?"

"Ahhh, my fair lady, he prefers the hidden realms. Give me five minutes and I'll have two lattes for us."

The kitchen was lined with white planks, black iron and stainless steel accents. A brick hearth and two industrial-sized ovens banked an entire wall. A small black wood table and two chairs, with X-designed backs, sat before a picture window, floodlights showing off a vast tree grove at the far end. Charlotte imagined Marc sitting there, morning sun rising over the landscape, mug of coffee in hand, alone at a table for two.

On the window shelf, indeed, fairies sat inside pots of thyme, parsley, and rosemary—shiny ceramic figures in green and white curly gowns. Charlotte lifted one. "Are they antique?"

"From my grandmother, Mamó. She was a maven of Celtic folklore. Official Lore Keeper for the family. Almost all my books are from her. Shall we go meet Orion?"

Chapter Twelve

Orion

With steaming mugs, Charlotte followed Marc upstairs, past his bedroom with a huge oak bed beneath a timber vaulted ceiling, and up a third-floor stairwell to a circular deck outside. The wooden door in an alcove at the top had a padlock. "Is that your attic? Where the wizard lives?" she craned her neck to see more before stepping outside.

"It's mostly a dust closet now. Storage for my father's valuables from his cabin. Watch your step." He held the deck door open.

They sat on cushioned chairs with the brilliant swashbuckling Orion hunting overhead. "Spectacular," Charlotte said, gazing through his high-powered binoculars. "Blue starlight? I've never actually seen blue stars."

"Hottest stars are blue. The three brightest stars in a row are Orion's belt. You can see two stars above for his shoulders."

"Oh! A star is red."

"That's the red giant, Betelgeuse. His right shoulder. Orion is looking down at you and he's thinking, I am alone and it's winter. Come sit by me, pretty lady."

She enjoyed the flattery, stirring her chai latte, her head still a little woozy. "I did very little stargazing when I grew up. Spent most of my time reading books and watching old movies."

"Rural life speaks its own language out here. Deep in the woods is the only way to live. I've got birds, owls, deer. I saw a snow hare on Christmas Day. He ran through snow smooth as water rushing in a brook. So, how is Bedford treating you so far?"

"The woods here are dazzling. Charming village and friendly

people. And Draakensky, well, I'm still figuring it out. I don't know, something is unsettling on Draakensky."

"Yeah, the estate is hollowed out. Valley of unrest. What are you going to do about Jaa and your job now?"

"Jaa is difficult. You probably know her better than I do. Any suggestions?"

"She's cute as a lamb, but she does take handling. And she can be hyperbolic."

"I got that part."

"Are you going to ask for your job back?"

"I'm not sure that's even possible. She's so furious with me. I can't afford to lose this opportunity, not for my art, certainly not financially. My illustrations in a book, now that is a dream come true. This is still new to me, interpreting poetry into visuals, but you know what? The poems clicked for me. I loved working with Rilke's *Les Roses*. Discovering the visual of 'Number Fourteen' broke open for me. Those three sketches Jaa threw in the fire might have been my best work."

"The wow factor?" Marc asked.

"Yeah. My illustrations will be exhibited at Van Cleeves Gallery in Manhattan. A solo show. Why should I give that up? Just because Jaa was in a bad mood with a headache? She told me to go back to Chicago. That means giving up. Starting over. Find a job. Find a place to live until I can get my sublet back."

She paused, tempted to reveal her history of failed administrative jobs and freelance illustration disappointments. If the illustration job offer at McKee, Borden & Beck Advertising in Chicago had come through as planned, she wouldn't even be sitting on this man's deck in Bedford. Fate threw curves, good or bad, literally throwing her back to the drawing board; trusting fate wore her down.

For the moment, she said, "I hate starting over. I've done it enough times." Orion drew Charlotte's eyes. "Maybe I'll get myself a tiny boat with wings and fly away to Orion. Live in the stars." She regretted the words the second they fell out. "I'm being silly. Too much Irish whiskey."

Marc breathed a smooth easy laugh. "Orion would love that. He's especially fond of brunettes, you know. And one who can bake bread." He raised his head. "Did you hear that, Orion? The lady bakes bread."

"Ha! Very funny." She wondered if he spoke to Orion like that regularly. Kind of interesting to speak to the stars. "Why do you like Orion so much?"

"Orion is alive. He's a living, breathing soul and he's on my radar. He's all about strength over one's opponents. What you need to do, Charlotte, is get Jaa to give you another chance. Admit to her you got it wrong coming out of the gate, and you want another go at it. Then hand her the moon and see what she does with it."

"Admit I got it wrong? That kills me because it was Jaa's opinion that the illustration wasn't Heida's work or Heida's choice that made it wrong. My illustration theme felt truer than I've ever done. I wonder," she said, tapping her mug, "to get Jaa to give me another chance, I'm pretty sure . . ." Here she paused, hesitant if she should tell Marc what was honestly pressing her.

Marc leaned in. "Pretty sure? Of? You can tell me. Orion's listening too, but he's a great secret keeper. All the stars are listening. All the way from the southern hemisphere in Australia," he said, caressing her hand.

Face to face, feeling his warmth, the strength in his touch—she missed being with a man. "Marc, I'm sure . . . Jaa would require me to engage in what you called the valley of unrest at Draakensky." She watched closely for his reaction.

He shifted in his seat, tilting his head forward. "Like the air is brooding?"

"More than that. I think Jaa requires me to engage with—" Why was she so hesitant to tell him? This was a man who admired fairies, Merlin, and the Lady of the Lake, Vivienne. He conversed with the stars, for heaven's sake. "To engage with Heida's ghost. Or at least Jaa's version of it."

Marc didn't even flinch. "Heida's ghost." The moment idled. "I do believe, Miss Knight, you are on the right track there."

She almost didn't want to ask. "So you know about Heida's ghost?"

He cocked his head in a yes.

"Did Jaa tell you about it?"

"She did not."

"Then how do you know?"

He stood up. "It's too cold to stay out here now. Come inside. I'll build a fire."

Marc lit logs in the fireplace, his back to her. From his peripheral vision, he got a view of Charlotte settled into the tan-leather sofa, her shoes kicked off, legs curled up beneath his green afghan. He felt her attention on him while he poked the logs.

"This room is massive," she murmured, "black and tan. You didn't style it after the black and tan beer, did you?"

"Absolutely not. We call it half and half in Ireland."

"What are those branches in the milk cans over by the fireplace? Are those silver bells on them?"

"Apple tree branches. I had to cut down two apple trees when I rebuilt the barn. I felt like a murderer. Fruit of the gods and all that. The bells belonged to my father." The curiosity on her face drew him. "His name was Matthew. He hung the bells on the bar front door. Old Celtic tradition."

When the flames caught in the logs, he sat in his black leather armchair across from her. He would have preferred to snuggle in with her on the sofa, but he knew better.

"How do you know about Heida's ghost?" she asked.

He placed his mug on the coffee table. "I've seen it."

"Where? At Draakensky?"

"In the bar."

She sat up straight.

"You've seen it too." He purposely didn't phrase it as a question, wanting her to feel welcome to share.

"Not directly. I mean, Jaa talks about Heida and her *presence*. I heard a voice inside the cottage."

"A voice? Female?"

"Not sure. The voice called my name. I saw a face. It banged at the window. Scared me half to death. I felt like it was right inside the bedroom with me. Of course, I could rationalize it. Claim some psychic hypersensitivity going on causing impressions. You know what I mean by impressions?"

"Maybe."

"High emotions, or trauma, can leave accumulated psychic impressions. From objects or people. Jaa seems emotionally charged about her sister. Maybe Jaa is an empath? My foster mom was an intuitive empath. Mildred had psychic impressions all the time. She observed auras, sometimes faces when she touched objects. She knew inanimate objects to carry energy. Psychometry is the scientific name."

Marc saw the fire needed attention and he poked a log higher into the flame. With his back to her, he asked, "Are you looking at me?"

"Caught me. I'm admiring your jaw and sweep of your nose. I'd love to sketch your profile. And those broad shoulders. You must have been a football star in school."

"I played high school football but not college. I was god-awful. I know nothing about empaths," he said, fanning the flames.

"Mildred knew things no one else did. Too much dopamine in her brain is how Mildred described it to me. An overload can heighten visual and auditory reception. Jaa might have similar traits."

Marc sat down, choosing the end of the sofa. He stretched his legs, feet up on the coffee table, half facing her. Flames cracked and stuttered, warming the air in a glow. She was so dreamy. What stunning clear gray eyes.

"When did you see Heida's ghost? Tell me." Charlotte said.

Marc loved how she said, 'Tell me,' almost child-like, waiting for a story. "Only one other person knows what I saw. I've kept this buried mostly, and I'm trusting you to keep it buried, too." Tempted to kiss her, to bond with her innocence, to inhale her sweetness, he controlled himself.

"This happened a few weeks after Heida passed away. The week before Thanksgiving. Heida Mead was a Katherine Hepburn look-alike. The marvelous high cheekbones and jaw. Same sexy square forehead. Even down to that provocative little tremor in her voice. Heida's quivering had a quality that would mesmerize you. We all wanted to go closer to her and listen. Only sixty-nine years old, she was way too young and far too ravishing to die."

"Were you in love with her?"

"Not in love, no. Enamored, yes. Who wasn't enamored with Heida Mead? Anyway, on this particular Friday afternoon before Thanksgiving, Jaa comes into the bar at noon, takes a seat at her usual table in the bar front window, and orders a small cheese pizza and two Belgian beers, as was their customary lunch for the past ten years. I was surprised to see her because I didn't think she'd be out so soon after Heida's death. Anyway, I'm thinking, this must be awfully hard for her to be lunching alone without her sister. My heart goes out to her. I sit down opposite her, and we chat for a while. When Jackson serves her the pizza, I go back to the bar, watching from near the register. Jaa pours herself a glass. And then, she pours a glass for the empty seat."

"Ohhhhh," Charlotte sighed.

"A heartbreaker, right? And in a blink, the chair isn't empty. There is Heida, wearing her famous pink scarf with the owl feather pattern on it. Anybody who knows Heida knows her feathered scarf. Her brownish-gray hair is pinned up at the neck. She's dressed in her khakis and macho collared shirt. Stunning, as usual."

"Was it a psychic impression, do you think?"

"Call it what you want. This was Heida Mead sitting in that chair. No rational explanation, but it was an absolute reality. I could smell her jasmine perfume. At one point, Heida turns and looks straight at me."

"That must have been chilling. And you weren't projecting your own grief? A wish fulfillment dreaminess?"

He admired her intelligence. "You mean Freud's theories? No. When you see a ghost, you know that ghost absolutely exists. You've never encountered a ghost?"

Her slight head shake made him doubt her sincerity. The firelight shadowed half her face. "Charlotte, do you honestly think we know everything about the afterlife or other realms that exist?"

"Well no, but—"

"Our world here is not so far from the world beyond. There are occupants within the invisible realms of eternity. The visible and the invisible move in and out of each other. What do you think?"

She faced him, her neck curving as she thought it over. He imagined pearls lying across her creamy skin. No, that lovely sweep merited a diamond butterfly pendant at her neck.

"Sooo," she said, "you think Heida's ghost manifested—from eternity?"

"I know it did. Eternity is not elsewhere. It's a presence right here." He was unsure of her level of perception about such things until she gave him a look that said *keep talking.* "We Celts know the mortal world and the Otherworld can overlap and even merge.

Eternity is veiled by our worldly time. Do you know the Otherworld?"

"I'm Catholic. You mean Heaven?"

"Not exactly. For the Celts, the Otherworld is an actual realm, an extension of our world where the dead spirits reside and can communicate with the living. And can act. The veil is thin with loopholes."

Charlotte curled up tighter under the afghan. "Loopholes. Let me ask, besides seeing Heida, did you hear her speak?"

"I heard her voice, not the words. The entire event only lasted a few moments. In a second, Heida faded away. Jaa finished her pizza and left. Days later, when I mentioned what I saw to Jaa, she denied Heida sat in the chair. She was lying. I saw the panic in her face."

Charlotte let out an exasperated breath. "I suppose the Otherworld isn't that different from Heaven. Christians communicate in prayer with the spirits of saints, Christ, the Madonna." She rubbed her chin. "For God's sake, what am I to do with all this now?"

"What if you go along with Jaa's directions for the illustrations? Which are probably Heida's instructions because Heida and Jaa were so close. Wouldn't that do?"

An unhappy line etched between her brows. "Marc, if I do that, I'm not being true to my art. I would be drawing Heida's sketches. My illustrations are going to be in a show in New York City. *My* work. What a liar I'd be if my interpretations for the Rilke's poems were actually a dead woman's interpretations, dictated by her sister."

"Hmm, a valid point. I don't know much about artists or how they draw."

"Sterling Publishing hired me to visually interpret and recreate each poem into an image. The art director Jung May loved my test samples. I did the samples on my own, without Jaa's direction. I know I can do this."

He took a minute to think. "You've got quite a dilemma. One thing, if I may make an observation. Charlotte, you don't want Heida Mead as your opponent. Not in this world, and certainly not from the realm beyond."

"Wait. Heida is not my opponent. Jaa is my opponent. Even though Jaa claims her sister is angry with me for doing such a poor job on *Les Roses*."

"Know this. The sisters were inseparable. I think they still are, even in death. What Heida wants, Jaa wants."

Her face froze. "You make it sound like something here is threatening me."

"Look at this from the other direction. Inside the Otherworld realm, Heida is threatened by you."

Charlotte sat up straight, her lovely face gone white. She muttered a stream of fragments under her breath: ". . . ghosts . . . Hanover Hill . . . ghosts living inside."

"What was that?"

She tossed off the green afghan. "Jaa fired me because I failed to produce what she wanted for her sister's book. I don't think she is going to compromise that standard. The smart thing for me to do is to drive back to Chicago tomorrow. Time for me to go back home. Take me back to my car in the village?"

In an uncomfortable silence, Marc followed Charlotte outside to the driveway. He wanted to kick himself for alarming her. When she dashed around the car to the passenger side, his vision darted to a white blur near the driveway rock walls. Between two arching birch trees, the white wolf stood within ten feet—muzzle lifted, teeth bared.

"Stop. Don't move," he told Charlotte calmly.

"What? Why?"

She turned, following where his hand pointed to the rock wall.

"Don't make any sudden movements. Don't run, or she might launch."

The wolf flexed her legs, growling, ready to leap.

"Stay calm, Charlotte. Keep your head down. Don't show her your fear."

With slow steps, Marc made his way to the wolf. He positioned himself between Charlotte and the wolf, and with his back, he shielded Charlotte.

"Hey there, Sky Wolf. How you doing, girl?" He opened his palms up to the animal. "Stay—girl—stay." The amber eyes fixed on them, although he knew the wolf had her sights targeted on Charlotte.

"We're good, Sky Wolf. You and me." He raised his hand out to his side. "Charlotte, take my hand. I want her to see you're safe."

Sky Wolf growled low and long, her snout wrinkling.

"Easy now. This is Charlotte. Stay calm. You're the queen in the kingdom, aren't you, Sky Wolf? Stay—girl—stay."

"Open the door," Charlotte begged.

"Wait. She's taking it all in. Give her a second to get the message."

The wolf held them in her stare for a long moment before sitting back on her hind legs. She stretched up, raised her nose, and howled. Charlotte jumped. Swiftly Marc opened the door a sliver, and she slid in. He made his way around the car and got inside.

"Sky Wolf? You keep a wolf?" Charlotte said, her voice breaking.

"I don't keep a wolf. She runs the woods and comes by here. So I named her. Magnificent, isn't she?"

"Are there wolves in Westchester County? I had no idea."

"No wolves in these parts anymore. Up north, yes, Canada and Maine. Most run in packs and they do travel south." He told her the simplest explanation.

"How is it she came so close to your house? Are you feeding her?"

"No. She's been leaving her tracks in the snow all winter. This is the first time she's been so close to the house. Probably a lone wolf. I don't know for sure."

The white wolf remained flanked between the two birch trees.

"Those eyes are frightening," Charlotte said.

"What a beauty though, right? Sky Wolf can take you right out of this world. No one can convince me there's not a soul behind such light."

He started the jeep, keeping his peripheral vision on Charlotte, and hit the music player. Johnny Mathis's buttery-smooth voice dove into the final lyrics of "Autumn Leaves." As the music floated over them, the trepidation on Charlotte's face relaxed. The dashboard lights, mixed with the house floodlights, sent shadows streaming, and inside those shadows, her face tilted to his. He got her scent, light and floral, warm and green. Mathis's mellow voice swelled on the last trembling note.

Marc lifted her chin, kissing her softly, then once more as she clung to him in the lush music.

Chapter Thirteen

Grave Hours

A strangeness settled over Jaa. Must she grow old, weak, and indolent? The sleepless night had left her heart fluttering and her cheeks burning. Sitting in her chair, her back achy, her arthritic knees stinging, Jaa picked up the telephone to dial the cottage. Oh no, too early. Wait until nine to call her. She opened the back door. Snow flurries sifted down. She lifted her head and put both hands over her heart.

"Upon the wind, below the wind, within the wind, come, Frau Holle, come near." Snow squalls burst through the doorway. The first breath would tell her. She inhaled, shivering, head listing, ears tuned. *Fight harmlessly. Press onward.* Nourished now, she closed the door, put the kettle on for coffee and waited for nine o'clock.

At the stroke of nine, Jaa slipped into Heida's blue-fox coat. Furry hood up, she stepped outside to the walled garden. A white blanket had already covered the ground, and ice too. Each step she made left clean bootprints. *Leaving my wrinkles behind.* Why did she think that now, of all moments? She might have laughed had she not been so jittery.

At the cottage door, she lifted the brass hand and hit it three times, same as she did for Heida. This time, Jaa would not call out her sister's name and enter. This day, she would pause and wait to be asked in. She might have heard Heida's tremulous voice, *Come in,* but she didn't.

When Charlotte finally answered the door, the girl's face was as gray as the dead. Jaa wanted to weep right there on the spot. With much dread, she stepped into the cottage. "Good morning,

Charlotte. I had planned on calling first, but, I decided to pop in, as they say."

"Hello, Jaa."

A suitcase was opened on the sofa and an empty box on the floor. "You're packing already?"

"I'm driving back to Chicago today," Charlotte said with a glance out the windows. "I hope to be on my way by noon."

"Oh no, my dear. This is a storm. It's bringing ice. Mianus River Road will be treacherous. I'm afraid it's a panther wind. I can smell the wind's hands, a pungent zing. You mustn't drive in this."

Charlotte went to the bow window. "Weather report said it will pass, clearing by noon."

"It's not going to pass by noon. My heavens, it's cold in here. Isn't your heat working?" Jaa put her hands on the heating vents. "I don't hear the blowers. We need to call Thomas right away." Jaa reached for the phone on the side table and dialed Thomas's cell phone. Thomas didn't pick up, so she left a message.

When she turned back to Charlotte, she spied Heida's balled yarns by the armchair. The familiarity struck. She found her way to the sofa. "Sorry, Charlotte, I need a minute."

"What's wrong? Are you okay?"

"Feeling weak is all."

"Can I get you water or tea?"

"No. Thank you." She patted her chest to stay calm. "I want to . . . I came to apologize for destroying your illustrations. Stupid of me. I'm a wretched old fool. The sketches were quite good, even if Heida didn't . . . would not have approved."

"I loved drawing them, Jaa. But since you are unhappy, I have to recognize this isn't going to work out."

"Oh, what do I know about sketching art? I've been a children's librarian my whole life at Bedford Village Library. I'm a gnawed-up old bone. Sometimes I get stripped down to the marrow in winter and become quite rude. Aging is such a task. We get cranky. Charlotte, I cannot let you leave."

"I'm a master at starting over. I know the drill. My friend Suzanne is letting me stay at her apartment. I'll land on my feet, don't worry."

"No, you will not," Jaa said. "I insist you stay here."

Charlotte took a step back.

Patience, patience, Jaa reminded herself. *The girl needs to be cradled at the moment, not yelled at.* "Charlotte," she said gently, "maybe we should think about this again. We might be well paired, after all. I'm a trunk dweller myself. But you, dear Charlotte, I see you prefer to swing out and explore the options. You're a branch dweller, aren't you?"

Charlotte folded her arms across her chest. "I am not a branch dweller, whatever that means."

"You most certainly are a thickly leafed branch dweller, my dear. Otherwise, you would not be standing here in this cottage. And more power to you because my trunk is sinking fast into the soil."

Charlotte laughed now. "What is a trunk dweller?"

"A person whose roots grow so deep in life, they get stuck. Happily for the most part, but in the end, we sink into old age."

Charlotte sat down next to Jaa on the sofa. "Here's the thing. I came here to sketch Rilke's poems. To sketch my visual impressions, not draw Heida's interpretations or what you might think are Heida's preferences. I don't see any room for agreement in this. Our contract gives you cause to fire me if you are dissatisfied."

"Heida insisted on that clause. Let me say, Charlotte, my sister was highly esteemed here in Bedford. A college professor at State University in Purchase. English Literature. No one had a better understanding of Rilke's poetry than Heida. She appreciated his verbal beauty. I must honor her in my direction for the illustrations."

"Of course you must. I was hired to make the viewer *see* Rilke's poems concretely as a visual. And even though I'm prepared to do that, it's not what you want."

Jaa knew the girl was right. "There must be a way to work this out?"

"We're at the crossroads," Charlotte said with a confidence that surprised Jaa. "The verbal poem versus the visual poem. You'll have to choose. Designs by your sister, esteemed in the verbal, or an artist's visual renderings. I hear the melody in Rilke's writing. Sometimes I see it take shape."

"Rilke's poetry is intensely visual. I know that. And you do too." Jaa sensed tears rising but fought them back. Would Heida ever forgive her? How could she betray her sister in this way and let Charlotte control the illustrations?

"Should we discuss this with Jung May?" Charlotte prompted.

"Jung May would undoubtedly agree with you. She loved your samples. I had my reservations, I'll admit." Jaa stood up, smoothed her sweater, and cleared her throat. "I prefer you to stay, Charlotte. Please, will you continue to sketch the visuals?"

"Jaa, that will require you to be flexible with my creative interpretations. Are you capable of doing that?"

"I know in my heart Rilke would agree an artist's renderings would be most appropriate. He admired artists greatly. I will make every effort to be cooperative and let you be creative and expressive. Say yes, you'll give us another try?" *Forgive me, Heida. This is for the good of Rilke. And for his poetry.*

The front door knocker banged, startling them both.

"That must be Thomas. Thank our lucky stars he's come to fix the furnace." Jaa threw open the door, Charlotte standing behind her.

Snow blew in a wild blur. Jaa's bootprints on the garden path had vanished already. At the entrance, pinecones and dried leaves dashed inside the cottage doorway.

A pink silk scarf printed with owl feathers swirled in circles over the snow.

It couldn't be. Heida's owl-feathered scarf? Her scarf was on the chaise lounge in the upstairs library. Jaa had vowed to never remove it.

The wind turned like a hook into gusts, practically barking through the open door, driving the scarf inside the cottage. Jaa tried to snatch it with both hands. The scarf expanded and then broke apart as if invisible hands were taking scissors to it.

The printed feathers transformed into a chaos of sharp quills. Gigantic black shafts shot through the air like a storm of hornets. Gray scolding spears plunged past Jaa's head. A fierce cry came from behind. She jerked around.

Charlotte fell, arms batting quills by the hundreds. They ripped her cheeks, drew blood, stabbed her mouth, pierced her neck, and snarled her hair into twisted coils. With her arms, she covered her face, shrieking, legs kicking, rolling across the floor.

"Frau Holle! Make it stop. Stop!"

All halted. Feathers carpeted the floor, crooked and broken, some pinging the wood as they hit. Charlotte crawled to a corner—curled up, head pressing the wall, hands fisted at her mouth, her face streaked with blood. Quills poked her hair in a fool's crown.

Jaa slammed the cottage door. Heida's scarf lay unscathed on the floor. She plucked it up and tied it around her neck in a double knot. Ash mixed with jasmine fragrance caught in her throat, making her cough so badly she had to hold her stomach to get through it.

Jaa sat on the floor with Charlotte. "You're safe, Charlotte." She patted her hand, then wrapped her arm around her, resting her head against hers. "Winds are beating crests. Downdrafts happen. This was a low pouch that burst over Draakensky. We call it a mammatus. Like a whale's mouth storm cloud. No need to fear."

She held the girl, a little bird inside her hands. *Oh dear. What have I done?*

Chapter Fourteen

Ghost Owl

Two *days later*, Charlotte huddled in the wooden chair in Eve's Garden Shop. Every muscle ached; even her breaths dipped in gulps after the chaos in the cottage. She consciously focused on a row of tinned sunflowers, buds still closed. One bloom poked up half opened. She could at least open up too, just a little, to let her body settle and regain stability.

Alice Eve sat opposite her in the coffee parlor, talking nonstop. Asking Alice to meet with her was not a straightforward choice. The last thing Charlotte needed was to tread on Jaa's territory by secretly discussing the situation with the woman's closest friend. With each question she asked about Jaa, Heida, and the Morland family, she felt a twinge of guilt.

The Viennese coffee that Alice served—a delicious smoky cocoa flavor—had a comforting effect. Charlotte wrapped both hands around the white mug to warm them. The shop held a soft humidity like a greenhouse from the mist spouts above the lacy ferns. Towering green palms, birdcages filled with moss, and colorful flowers displayed in rain boots glowed with steamy sunlight from the massive front windows. The air, so moist and warm, created a calming atmosphere. Charlotte drew it in.

Alice adjusted her black eyeglasses and brushed wisps of her curly hair off her eyebrows. "I'll tell you whatever I can to help. Bedford's Bird Sisters. The Morland family was beyond quirky, yet endearing as far as you can imagine. Except the father, Joseph. He was a gruff, opinionated eccentric. Irascible. The sisters never grew out of their sibling rivalry. Heida learned how to strike a nerve by emulating her dad. Still, we all loved her dearly."

"Yes, I've heard that Heida's charms left people enamored."

"The woman was remarkably vibrant. Swank. A thrill-seeker with sparking green eyes that grabbed your heart."

Green eyes, Charlotte thought. On her color palette, she imagined black eyes requiring depth with passion and blues needing light for honesty. But green eyes had to be jungle green, splashing jealous flares.

"Heida's wit could knock you over," Alice went on. "Always the life of the party. She initiated cancer charity events all over the state, served on town committees, doted on babies and children like Mrs. Santa Claus. Every summer she gave an extravagant picnic at Draakensky for children at risk in Westchester. We all loved her benevolence."

"The sisters didn't have any children?"

"None. Heida married a real estate executive right after her fortieth birthday, an elderly man. He died suddenly, heart attack." Alice rolled her eyes. "Heida admitted it was a mistake for her to marry Warren but a financial advantage. She inherited considerable money and real estate investments. Warren's assets saved the sisters from losing Draakensky."

"And Jaa?"

"Jaa never married, although she boasted about a few ardent love affairs," Alice added with a titter. "Jaa is a darling. She has her moments and can bark, but she's harmless."

"She's been very sweet to me since the . . . event. She claimed the attack was a whale's mouth cloud bursting on Draakensky. Mammatus? What a silly word."

"Never heard of it," Alice said firmly. "I see the scratches on your face healed up nicely. And so quickly."

"The cuts vanished within an hour. What do you make of that?"

Alice's cheeks pinked. "No idea. I suppose there's no end to the things we don't understand. Most of the time, I try to just accept them."

"I suppose. Jaa insisted I take three days off to settle down."

"And are you settled down?" She raised her brows in hopeful anticipation.

"Hardly." Charlotte hadn't slept for two nights. Sleeping on the living room sofa had its hardships—no way was she going to sleep in Heida's sleigh bed after that attack, after the voice, after the eyes at the window. "The cottage is freezing. Thomas rebooted the furnace, but no matter how high I raised the thermostat, I couldn't get it warm enough. Maybe it's just me."

"Feeling excessive cold is a symptom of shock. You know that, right?"

"Probably. I've spent the last two days baking bread to warm myself. Oh, here." She scooped up a bag from her tote. "My peasant bread for you. Two loaves. An old Roman recipe. I dropped off a few loaves at The Grackle too. Left them on the bar with Jackson. He's Marc's manager, right?"

"Right. Homemade bread? You're a doll. Thank you. Back to baking?"

"When life becomes stressful, bake." At that moment, Alice's friendly voice was performing a miracle on her nerves. Even the shop's humidity had a soothing effect, gauzy and silky, warming her cheeks.

"I hate to see you leave Bedford over this incident," Alice said, pouring more coffee into her cup. "You don't honestly want to go back to Chicago, do you?"

Charlotte remained unsure but didn't want to say so. Bedford gave her a sense of liberation, the rolling countryside, glorious trees, big sky. She glanced out the window to the tree-lined street, the bricked village shops, and the fashionable window dressings. Local folk strolled by, giving nods and greetings. So different from Chicago's racing hubbub with towering steel and glass, noisy busses, crowds on the sidewalks, and bullish shoulders pushing to cross the street before the traffic darted out. And then there was Marc, and their undeniable attraction.

"Alice," she said, hearing the yearning in her voice, "I need to know what I'm dealing with here. Tell me about the real Heida beneath all the charm and magnanimous reputation."

Alice shrugged. "She knew how to use her power and get her way, despite her bombastic behavior. Which we all tolerated. When men get angry with each other they slug it out. For Heida, if you did her wrong, she got dirty. Don't ask for specifics. I can't say."

"Sounds like she was a sister of sorts for you?"

"We're all sisters at the core," Alice curled her shoulders up. "Don't we love our sisters no matter what? Heida would walk into my shop, wearing a shawl or cape and it would billow out, imitating wings. She'd spin around like a magnificent bird. Entertaining as all get-out. She'd buy flowers by the buckets and give them away to people with my card. She became an investor some years back when I had to renovate.”

“A magnificent bird? You mean owls? Her signature scarf?”

“Heida believed owls were ‘pieces of the sky come to her window.’ How’s that for ego?”

“Sounds more like something Jaa might say.”

“The sisters had the same sentiments. But Jaa possesses a much more genuine love of nature. Jaa was a student of psithurism, you know.”

“Student of what?”

“Interpreting the sound of the wind. She trained with meteorologists to understand wind patterns, planetary winds, the magnetic north. She even studied under a shaman in New Mexico about mythological wind beings.”

“Wind beings? You mean Frau Holle?”

“Jaa keeps these skills to herself. Heida called it wind magick, but Jaa was terrified people in town would target her as a wind witch. That would slay her to the heart. Although I did hear Jaa call it wind magick one time.”

“Psithurism? So, you think the bird feather event was Jaa’s doing? A psychic wind projection that attacked me?”

“Jaa would never cause you harm,” Alice whispered, scanning the room.

Why so secretive? Only two people were browsing the shop and not within listening distance. Had Jaa caused harm to someone? Was she known among the locals as a wind witch? Charlotte guessed small towns probably required closed conversations. Who gossiped about people’s virtues, anyway? The tinned budding sunflowers along the wall snagged her vision again. They were not in the sunlight. How would they bloom hiding in the shadows?

Alice added milk to her coffee. “I will say it’s more in line with Heida to be so . . . aggressive.” She played with the spoon in her cup. “For all her talents, she failed at being a poet herself. Heida wrote a verse named *Ghost Owl*. A small journal published it. Got scathing reviews and nasty comments. She carried on for months about the incompetent reviewers, even wrote them nasty letters.” Alice stood up. “Wait, I have an idea. Hold on.”

Alice crossed the parlor to the far bookshelf. The shop might have been a library with old books displayed on racks, between pottery, marble bookends, and alongside rows of antique coffeepots. After running her finger over the spines, she pulled a book out and rushed back to the table. "Don't think me crazy, but I feel there is some message from what happened at the cottage. Everything is a sign, isn't it?"

"What is that?"

"*The Book of Emblems and Totems*. A modern interpretation of symbols, but it'll do for our needs."

"Our needs?"

"Don't you want to know what caused the attack? Shouldn't we put this to rest so you can get on with your life? The answer may lie in knowing the meaning of owls in the context of that event. Don't you think so?" Alice adjusted her glasses, her black eyes practically popping.

Charlotte didn't resist cracking a smile. First time in days. A sister couldn't have been more helpful. She might not have had a real sister—Sister James being the dearest female in her adult life, besides Suzanne in Chicago who was more like a cosmopolitan chum—but if Charlotte could choose a sister, Alice would be top of the list.

Alice raked her black frizzy hair, paged the Index, then scanned the text. "Owls . . . 'efficient killers' . . . The Celts called owls 'crones from the underworld.' How funny is that? 'Nymphs of darkness . . . historian Pliny named them night monsters.' "

"Does it say anything about owl feathers?"

Alice kept reading. "Hmmm, no. Sorry, I thought maybe we'd get some insights to reassure you."

"May I borrow it?" Charlotte lifted the book. "I'll bring it back in a day or so." She stuffed it inside her tote bag. "You've been wonderful, Alice. Thank you for seeing me."

"Anytime. Call me anytime." Her face grew bright.

Charlotte stopped and absorbed it for a moment before slipping into her coat. From her pocket, she retrieved an owl feather. "Alice, would you hang on to this for me? It was the only feather left after the attack."

She took the feather into her hand. "What happened to the rest? Jaa told me hundreds flew at you. Where are they?"

"Every single one vanished. Within minutes. I found this one in my hair."

She turned the single feather over in her hand; she gave it a sniff. "Jasmine. That's Heida's fragrance. Oh God, I feel like she just walked in here."

"Don't even say it. I don't want to keep the feather in the cottage."

"Of course. But how did the others vanish? Are you sure?"

"The how is not clear. Someone, or something, erased them. Erased the cuts on my cheeks too. Do you think it was Frau Holle?"

That night on the sofa, sleep took Charlotte quickly from sheer exhaustion. No bad dreams. No sudden bumps or jumps in the night. She woke at eleven, remembering sunflower buds standing in their tins in the dark. At least the cottage was warmer. She dressed in a hurry to exit the cottage before Jaa stopped by. Charlotte still had until tomorrow at three o'clock to decide if she would stay or return to Chicago. What was more pitiable than a wavering mind? Would there be another attack? Would the eyes appear again in the upstairs window? And that voice. Were all these signs telling her to jump ship?

A text came in from Suzanne in Chicago. Her luxury apartment overlooking Lake Michigan had more appeal by the minute. Charlotte could manage living with Suzanne for a few months. And Don had texted her at two o'clock in the morning. *Do you still love me,* he asked. In a text. Jeez, Louise.

In Bedford Village, she parked the car near The Grackle. Marc might be at the restaurant by now. Dying to hear his reassuring voice, she admitted she could use a little grounding.

Inside the bar, she found Liz. "Hi. Is Marc around?"

"Good morning. No, sorry, he's out," Liz raised her attention from the stemware she was stacking. "Did you want to leave a message?"

"I'll try him later." Disappointed, Charlotte left and walked along the village sidewalk. She crossed the street to the Orphan Book Shop. A sign hung on the front door handle: CLOSED: Be Back in 20 Minutes. While she waited, she shopped the front window's display of Charles Dickens's novels celebrating his birthdate in February. A tic-tac-toe game board with clever silver and black wolf pups as playing pieces centered the showcase. Wolf pups.

"Look at that," she said to no one. The game was a duplicate of the one she had played with Aunt Loretta on Friday pizza nights. That's why Marc's silver wolf head pendant looked so familiar.

She grew up on tic-tac-toe, learning predictability and blocking. The game set had gone into the donation box, as did all Charlotte's possessions when the state took the house, and she moved into St. Sophia's convent. Including her favorite stuffed white rabbit. The more she examined the game board, the more she yearned to have those beautiful little wolf pups.

Sitting down on the sidewalk bench to wait for the shop to reopen, she absorbed the weak sun speckling through tree branches. Beyond the Village Green, white headstones spotted the hill—The Old Burying Ground, Established 1681, scrolled over the gate.

She crossed the street and walked the shoveled cemetery paths, not sure why. She didn't appreciate cemeteries—tombs holding bones six feet under, decaying flesh, and all that. The hill leveled off at the top where a gate led to a modern expanded cemetery field. Charlotte instinctively walked toward the wooden gate. Trees bordered a frozen pond round as a silver coin. Hedges drooped, swallowed up in snow mounds from the plowed paths. The sun retreated behind giant storm clouds. A turbulent downdraft swiped her cheeks.

Charlotte flipped her hood up. Peace may hover over the graves, but this graveyard held gloomy air. Rows of gray mausoleums stood at the far end. One tomb wore bold letters: MORLAND. The family crypt, no doubt, Heida was likely interred there.

She imagined Heida lying in her coffin inside the stone vault, hair long, yellowed pearls at her neck, the hands holding rotted lilac roses. Guilt hit as if she were spying on the dead. Without thinking, she turned off the center path onto a narrow loop leading directly to the Morland tomb.

Noon church bells rang from the village steeple, sending blackbirds to soar above the cemetery. Not far from her position on the path, a man sat on a bench. Glad not to be alone in the cemetery, she kept her vision on him. He wore a dark wool overcoat, brimmed hat, no gloves or scarf. Tattered, light-brown cap-toe boots.

One leg crossing the other, his head down, face masked in shadows, he read from a thin green book. Both hands cupped the tattered volume as if he were holding a baby's head.

Her boots crunched on the snowy trail as she proceeded toward him. When she passed, ready to offer a friendly hello, he didn't lift his head. Maybe she should sit next to him and start a conversation. He looked lonely. She might ask him what book he was reading.

Abruptly, a low-bulbous cloud broke with sleety rain. Giant droplets fell quickly. She'd be drenched in seconds. Rushing toward the cemetery gate, she stopped to look back at the man.

Rain mixed with icy pellets in a batty wind. The man didn't move. Didn't lift a finger from the book. He didn't even uncross his legs. He let the icy drops bounce off him as if he were made of stone. He must have felt her thoughts on him because he rose suddenly from the bench. With slow steps, he strolled deeper into the cemetery, as soundless as a fish in water.

At the Orphan Book Shop, Charlotte burst through the door, grateful for the dry warmth. The shelves revealed mostly used volumes, although the front corner held current titles.

"No umbrella today?" the clerk said. "Come in and dry off."

A half-eaten sandwich on a plate sat on a stack of volumes. The sign over the register displayed their logo: Vintage and Antiquarian Books. Take an orphan home. The clerk straightened his cashmere vest. An elderly man, groomed in a striped brown tie, he had a narrow chin that ran away from his mouth. "I'm Scully. Can I help?"

"That tic-tac-toe game in the window. The wolf pups. Is it new?"

"Not much is new in this shop. Not me either." He flicked his silver hair. "The board is authentic Egyptian roof tiles and the pups are pewter." He strolled to the front window and brought it to the counter.

"It's adorable. How much?"

"One-hundred fifty dollars. A fun improvement over the old noughts-and-crosses."

"Must be an antique?"

"I'm pretty sure it is."

"May I?" Charlotte gestured to a pup. She chose the silver wolf. Shiny smooth—same weight, fitting perfectly into her palm, the memories flooding back. But one hundred and fifty dollars? An impractical purchase at a time when she didn't know what the next months would bring if she ended up unemployed. "I guess I'll think about it."

"Want to play a quick game?" Scully asked.

His friendliness tempted her. "Oh no, you're having your lunch break."

"Cheese sandwich can wait. You first." He scattered the wolf pups off the board.

Outside, icy rain continued to strike the front window. She placed her silver wolf pup into the right corner square—a strategic first move in the game. When she raised her vision to see Scully's reaction, his vision riveted on the front window. He grimaced.

She turned around. A blurry face shone through like it was old and cracked. Cheekbones wore a chalky dullness. Black eyes inside dark circles. Killer eyes? The man from the cemetery stood beneath drowsy gray mists, quivering like a cat.

He had followed her to the bookshop. She turned back to Scully. "Who is that?"

"Who?"

"That man. Standing at the window. I saw him in the cemetery."

"By the mausoleums? He hangs around the village. I've seen him sitting on the benches there. Odd fellow. Doesn't seem to mind the cold."

Charlotte wanted to turn and see if he was still there, but a shudder held her still. "Do you know his name?"

"No. He probably lives nearby."

"Is he still lurking in the window?"

Scully placed his black wolf on the center square, then tilted his head to view the window. "Gone. Your move."

Chapter Fifteen
On the Edge of Mystery

In the cottage, Charlotte could not shake the gloom hanging over her that night. Reading Alice Eve's emblems book, she paged to the owl section. *Feathers are symbols of the power of air. They are the bird's self. Omens of death.*

Whose death would that be? What if Heida's ghost took form in the chair like she did sitting in Marc's bar? Ghosts haunt because people didn't let go. Jaa certainly had not let go of Heida. Isn't that how these psychic events worked? Maybe ghosts didn't haunt places. Maybe ghosts haunted people.

Ghosts must live inside you to see them.

In bed by midnight, she tossed, legs curling up, heart pulsing in her temples. An old jump rope song beat time in her head. Double-Dutch speed. *Long ago when I was small, one day I ran away. After that, for most days, at home I had to stay. Stay, stay, you runaway. Stay or fly awayyyyy.* Charlotte would fly away, jumping out of the spinning double ropes to land on both feet to the applause of her friends.

She sat up, hair in her eyes, feet cold, throat dry. One place she hadn't flown away from was the convent. Having to leave the sisters when the nunnery closed had left Charlotte devastated in the unsafe foster care system. Homes with dirty bathrooms, no locks, snooping eyes, and rations of food had spawned her fugitive soul.

Finally, she drifted off to sleep on the beats of *fly awayyyyy, fly awayyyyy.*

At noon, she woke with a headache. The daylight grew into a purple sky as the clock neared three PM. She decided a walk would help clear her mind. Her cell phone buzzed.

Suzanne Porter. "Hey Char, when are you coming back?" Suzanne asked without even a hello. Chicago street traffic blared in the background.

"Not sure," was all Charlotte could manage.

"Head's up, Char girl. Marty McKee at McKee, Borden & Beck called me."

Just hearing the name made her heart jump. "What?"

"That illustrator's position you missed by a hair last year? Well, the job is open again and Marty asked me about you. I told him you were presently out of town but planning on returning soon."

"You did what? Suzanne!"

"Marty is hot to hire you. He's calling you tonight with an offer. It's a good one," she sang. "Be ready, kiddo. Come on back, Charlotte. We're dying here without you. Call me tomorrow." *Click.*

Charlotte hung up, locked the cottage door behind her, and walked to the river. Every tree seemed to lean over her like a mom listening. After only a few minutes on the river path, her phone buzzed with a text message from Marty McKee: Need to speak to you tonight. Important. Green light ahead. Will call at nine o'clock.

She replied Rock and roll, Marty, and added a thumbs up. Charlotte used to think, *how lucky do I have to be to get a job with Marty McKee?* And now, luck was around the corner.

The icy path ahead gleamed hard as silver. Birds shot through the air. Their songs ripped the sky, like someone tearing tissue paper. She followed their music to the river.

Maybe luck had nothing to do with it. Nothing happens by chance, anyway. On the riverbank, she placed her feet on the same spot where she had made her shoe prints on her first day at Draakensky. The footprints had worn away, but she sensed the toe-and-heel outline and slipped into position. If this was going to be her last day at Draakensky, what better moment than to take her place *at the last stand?* The drama stimulated her. So did the idea of working under Chicago's advertising rock star Marty McKee. How easy would it be to walk into Jaa's windmill and say *I've got a promising job offer in Chicago and I'm seizing the opportunity?* Say goodbye to Draakensky, goodbye to Heida and Jaa, goodbye to river, trees, and wind. Say goodbye to Marc?

At the river, white rapids crashed with abandon. Sticks and weeds poked straight up like the hair of the dead. Maybe she should cross the river bridge—sit on the crag among the crazy quilt of trees, rocks, and sky stitched together.

Waves streamed the river rocks, disarrayed and cluttered. White foam peaking. Vapory mists clotting. Above, the dark haze held a confusion of flat faces. Watching. The yew tree stretched its witchy branches up. Bark, gray as ashes. Hollows with dark threads, the massive green fur hung in twisted cords.

This was no ordinary tree. Draw it on smooth Bristol paper in muted dark green. Sharp black. Gray strokes. Red lashes on the trunks. Scarlet or dragon-blood red. Charcoal smudges for those fierce orbs staring out of the hollows. Drawing that darkness, what would it take? Bluish streaks will make the whitewater rapids dazzling.

What lay beneath those frenzied rapids? What furious hues hid beneath the surface? The shiny boulders pulled her sideways. Her view submerged into the fractured watery light, waves rushing over her in skewed transparencies like sharp mirrors shooting up, making her eyes pulse.

Imagine falling in, becoming the river, turning as the river turns, dying into the river to the sounds of the water gushing all around you.

"River teeth are sharp."

Alarmed, Charlotte veered back, hands to her chest. Thomas Harrogate, in his opened red hunting vest, leaned against a giant elm, shovel in hand, boots covered in mud, and a stupid smirk on his face.

"Oh! You startled me, Thomas. What are you doing sneaking up on me?"

"I got a soft foot most days. Those waves will give you one hell of a bite." His boots left a dozen impressions around the elm. "What are *you* doing here again? River tempting you? Now with Miss Heida gone, river magick has built a higher force. Lots of howls and hoots inside those waves."

She wasn't in the mood for his river heebie-jeebies.

"How are you sleeping these days, Miss Charlotte?"

"I sleep quite well," she lied. "Probably the ice clogs breaking apart. I'm sure it's normal." The truth was, she had more than a few restless nights in Heida's sleigh bed.

"Nobody sleeps well on Draakensky since Miss Heida died. I certainly don't."

Rain flew between them.

"We got river-rain today. You know, Miss Heida believed if you boil a lizard in oil and anoint it on a person's chest, that person dies. Stops the heart within a few hours. *Poohm.* I'll bet you didn't know that, did you, Miss Charlotte?"

Boil a lizard? "What is this now? Are you trying to scare me? Am I intruding on your territory?"

He sniffed. "You're intruding on Miss Heida's territory. The dead don't go far. 'Nature is a petrified magic city,' Novalis says. 'Perceptibility is attentiveness.'"

She groaned. "Cut it out, Thomas." Who was Novalis, anyway? She didn't ask, wishing she had the courage to shove him. Send him sprawling to the ground. That would shut him up.

He snickered, thoroughly amused with himself. "Oh hell, I'm messing with you, Miss Charlotte," he placed his hand over his chest. Black hair sprouted from the V-neck tee shirt. "My apologies. I get carried away. Living alone too long with my nose stuck in books." His face softened. The mouth relaxed, and he yanked off his hat. He wasn't bad-looking. His river-brute had an appeal. "You know what?" he lifted his voice. "There's a pretty little twist downriver beyond the bridge and the falls." He pointed. "We got a swan family living in the lake. They're marvelously calm. To watch the mama swan lower herself into the slow waves and glide away," he waved his arm out. "She's quite the pomp. I can take you there. I think you'd love it."

"No thanks. You'll be happy to know I won't be intruding on your territory anymore." She let out a frustrated tsk.

"You think you're leaving Draakensky?"

She folded her arms across her chest.

"You're not leaving Draakensky. Once you're touched by river magick, you are forever changed. Magick leaves its path."

"I'm late for my meeting with Jaa. Goodbye, Thomas."

Hurrying down the footpath, she ran each turn, huddling beneath the shivering trees raining voices, which she blocked out of her ears.

When she reached Draakensky, Jaa threw open the door before she had a chance to knock.

"Oh heavens, Charlotte, you're drenched."

"I took a walk to think things through. Ran into Thomas. You know, Jaa, I really dislike him."

"You know what they say, those who are the hardest to love need it the most. He has a big heart if you can get past his gloom and doom."

"Has Thomas been with you a long time?" Charlotte hung her coat on the rack.

"Over ten years renting the cabin. An esteemed philosophy professor at Columbia. Since the car accident, he's had to stop teaching. Lost his wife. A tragedy. Anxiety. Depression. Too much drinking. Heida took him in. Come sit down."

Charlotte sat on the sofa, dried herself off with Jaa's tea towel and clasped her hands on her lap.

"I made a fresh pot of coffee. May I offer you a cup?"

"I'd love it. Thank you. I can help myself, Jaa."

"I'm perfectly capable." She placed her cane against the chair and entered the kitchen. "That walking cane is more for outdoors," she shouted back. "A gift from Marc to me after his grandmother died. The cane was hers, you know. Birchwood. A treasure. Marc's such a good man. He called me every day after Heida died to check on me."

She walked back on sturdy legs, holding the mug with both hands.

Charlotte took the cup and an immediate sip. "Vanilla?"

"You deserve a treat." Jaa sat down in her chair.

The windmill glowed with light from the fireplace, its roaring logs throwing pine and oak scents. She watched the orange flames. The rumbling, the simmer, the *hushhhh*. "Jaa, I think I've—"

"Oh, let's not talk business. Shall we just enjoy each other? I have a lovely pastry to go with—"

A knock at the door jolted Charlotte. She really had to calm down.

"Come in, Marc," Jaa called, clearly relieved.

Marc Sexton strode into the windmill, a knight in a shining gray slicker, bearing flowers wrapped in tissue paper. "Good afternoon, ladies."

Jaa's face lit up. "Ohh! White peonies and lilac roses. How you spoil me. Thank you." She took the flowers and held them like a babe in arms.

"This is unexpected," Charlotte said, trying to hide how glad she was to see him. He looked especially dashing in his buttoned navy vest and tie. "Or maybe not so unexpected?" she added.

"I invited him," Jaa said with a cloak-and-dagger expression. "Marc has news for us."

He tossed his slicker on the rack and sat down next to Charlotte on the sofa. "You're looking well, Charlotte."

She wasn't looking well at all—no makeup, her hair flat from the rain. That kiss in his jeep took over her thoughts. His secret kiss. Was he thinking of their kiss right at that moment, too? His artful little turn of the mouth gave it away.

Jaa straightened herself. "We have a proposal for you, Charlotte."

Marc handed Charlotte a large envelope. "This is for you. Don't open it yet. Let me explain. I've had a request to sponsor a charity event at the restaurant for the children's Homestead in Somers. I often donate food to the Homestead, but they need a fundraiser for renovations. Roof, bathrooms, new furnace, a playground, landscaping for a vegetable garden. I came up with the idea to host an Irish Tea Time on Sunday afternoons, donating all the proceeds to the Homestead. We're thinking weekly for a month or so."

"What does this have to do with me?"

"Everything. Irish Teas are famous for tea sandwiches. I want your peasant bread for our sandwiches."

Jaa clapped her hands, brimming with delight.

"The loaves you dropped off at the bar were the absolute best. My staff loved them. Thank you for thinking of us. Charlie, my chef, thinks your bread is first-rate. Charlotte, would you be willing to bake the loaves every Sunday morning for the Afternoon Teas over the next couple of months?"

"It's a worthy cause, Charlotte," Jaa cut in. "The Homestead has about eight children. They're mostly kids abandoned by their parents or from abusive homes. Children at risk. What do you think?"

Kids abandoned. Charlotte knew all about that. She was one of the lucky ones who didn't have to go into an orphanage. She had been more terrified to be sent away to a "home" than to live with foster parents.

"You'd only have to bake once a week on Sunday mornings, so it wouldn't interfere with our work on the book," Jaa went on. The excitement on her face was practically glee.

"Our work on the book?"

"Surely we can find a way to be agreeable. I promise to be more generous with my guidance. For the sake of the children at the Homestead. For Rilke's book, and for your art, will you give us another try?"

Her art? Jaa was concerned about her art? "What about Heida?"

Jaa blinked thoughtfully. "Leave that to me."

Charlotte didn't appreciate the sound of that. She turned to Marc. "You don't need my bread to make your Afternoon Teas a success for the Homestead."

"I do. We want to advertise freshly baked homemade bread for the tea sandwiches. People love that. I've already discussed it with Alice Eve. She writes our advertising copy."

"We've been conspiring, I have to confess," Jaa said, feigning embarrassment. "We want you to stay, Charlotte. The Homestead needs all of us. I'm donating the initial expenses to get the program off the ground. Heida and I have been Homestead benefactors for years. Marc has local thrift shops donating vintage teapots and cups. And the local bakeries are donating dessert trays. It's becoming a huge community effort."

"I very much want you on board, Charlotte," Marc added.

She didn't doubt his enthusiasm. "Everyone is being so generous," Charlotte said eagerly.

"We're keeping it all in the family." Jaa shimmied in her chair. "We need you, Charlotte. Wouldn't you love to be a member of our family here for the Homestead?"

Member of a family. There was a time when Charlotte thought the only way she'd ever have a family was to marry and have children. That prospect appeared slimmer every passing year.

"Let's talk to Chef Charlie," Marc said, his eyes all over her. "He's got some sandwich ideas on the drawing board already. He's dying to get your thoughts. You can read over the contract in the car. Look at that, the sun broke out. Good sign. Let's go."

"I've not said yes."

"I know we're still at the game plan." He playfully tugged a lock of her hair. "Come with me, anyway."

"I mean, I might have—something's come up—in Chicago for me."

Marc shot a glance at Jaa.

"Charlotte," Jaa said, "Marc and I, and Alice too, we want . . . Please don't go back to Chicago."

Marc rubbed his hands on his knees as if to soothe himself. "How about you read the contract in the car and we'll talk it through. Please don't say no, not yet."

In his jeep, they rode in silence while Charlotte read the contract terms. Thankfully, the legalese read easy enough. She pulled out photos showing the Victorian homestead. As she flipped through, she stopped to study the children sitting on the front lawn, arms wrapped around each other, happy faces. Three rested on their bellies, legs kicked up with feet touching each other.

One little girl with mismatched socks, stringy brown hair, eyes as big as dollar coins, clutched a stuffed white rabbit in a checked waistcoat, the pocket watch dangling. Alice's white rabbit in Wonderland. "This little girl in the front. How old is she?"

Marc had his attention on the road but snapped a peek. "That's Marguerite. A sweetie pie. Five years old. She hides in picture books. I gave her that toy rabbit. Patricia and Daniel have really brought her out. We could take a drive to Somers if you want to meet the children."

"Oh, no. No." She shoved the photos back inside the envelope and turned the clasp to seal it. "I don't need to do that."

Marc slowed the car. "What? I'm sorry. Did seeing the kids trigger—?"

"No. I'm fine. This is so unexpected. I'm feeling a bit ambushed, is all."

"My fault. I'm overexcited to get to the kickoff."

"This is no coincidence, is it? Offering me this job."

He pressed the brakes on a sharp curve that he took way too fast. "I want you on my team. And I want your bread. Are you not okay with the contract offer?"

"The offer is excellent. The money is a surprise. How come you're not requiring me to donate my baking time like everybody else?"

"You're not like everyone else, Charlotte."

"Of course I am," she said with far too much defense.

"That's not what I mean," he said, shifting the gear to pass a slow-moving horse trailer. "My donors run local businesses and are friends of the Homestead. This is business between you and me. Besides, you're new here. And you have enough challenges going on right now,"

"Do I? Exactly what does that mean?"

"Uhhhh, well." He coasted the jeep down a steep hairpin hill, conveniently waiting until they were on the straight and narrow. "Jaa told me about the attack in the cottage."

"Of course she did."

"She was near tears when she explained what happened. Must have been terrifying. I'm so sorry you had to go through that. Do you want to talk about it? Can I help?"

"Marc, there's no making sense of it."

He focused on the bottle-necked traffic at the intersection traffic light, checking the rearview mirror and oncoming cars before he turned. "The threshold between the visible and the invisible usually doesn't make sense. What happened at the cottage remains a phenomenon, mysteriously caused."

"What phenomenon would that be? Jaa's wind magick? Or are we talking about Heida's ghost? It was Heida's feathered scarf that flew into the cottage. Like a storm cloud? And then Frau Holle stopped the attack, at Jaa's command."

"Jaa is pretty good at understanding air currents and atmospherics. She senses what's inside that kind of energy. It carries an imprint. Remnants, if you will, of the past and the present." He skirted a sudden swerve, jammed the car into gear, and gunned the engine on the open road.

Cars, houses, trees raced by; she tracked the scenery, wordless in the dumb quiet, all the way into Bedford Village where he slowed down—much to her relief—and stopped to let pedestrians cross the street. In that split second, he reached over and placed his hand on hers. "Time may work in your favor here. For the moment, can you let the mystery be the mystery?"

"I don't know."

He squeezed her hand before releasing it.

"Good of you to bring Jaa flowers. You're wonderful to her."

"I never walk through her door without an armful." He turned the car into The Grackle's parking lot.

In Marc's cluttered office, she met Chef Charlie, a brawny, young Asian guy with black, curly hair. Marc leaned back in his chair behind a desk constructed of two whiskey barrels topped with a thick glass slab. "Don't let Charlie's Chinese-Italian heritage fool you. He makes the best Irish-American dishes in Westchester."

"Everything Irish, I learned from Marc," Charlie said, his admiration obvious. "And from his audacious mom, Kelsey, who makes a wicked beef and Guinness stew that no one can beat. A secret ingredient that I can't figure out."

"She won't even tell me her secret," Marc said. "But Chef Charlie here is going to challenge her famous beef and Guinness stew with his interpretation, aren't you, my man?"

Charlie cringed playfully. "Working on it."

"She's coming here this summer for her sixty-seventh birthday in August. I can't wait for you to compete with her version. Battle of the Beef Specials."

"I'm scared already. Meanwhile, you want to see the tea sandwiches menu?" He handed her a sheet. "Including my favorite, cukes and cream cheese shamrocks."

"Sounds marvelous," Charlotte said, reading over the varieties. Her desire to belong to this project leaped.

She gave it serious thought as she settled back into her chair. The office decor had a reassuring and comfy ambiance. Bronze and topaz-striped wallpaper made the room yawn. Marc's copper shell desk lamp and glass clock revealing its mechanical movements *tick-ticking* created a hypnotic mood that calmed her. Even the copper sun face hanging on the wall behind his chair, Sun Father, added a paternal blessing.

"We'll need test sandwiches," Chef Charlie said. "Charlotte, can you do pumpernickel bread? It will pair well with the salmon." He peeked at his watch. "Time's up. Gotta check the ovens." He dashed out.

Charlotte held the contract envelope in her hands. Marc sat there, hands on the chair's arms, swiveling restlessly. His eyes were clear as a drink of fresh water. She might have melted right there.

"Don't tell me the pumpernickel is scaring you away?" he said, shooting a rubber band at her.

"I can bake any bread you want. I think the work you're doing for the Homestead is exceptional. I feel guilty taking money, though."

"If you want to donate it to the Homestead, that's your choice. Here's the gold. We can make a difference in these kids' lives. Patricia wants to plant a fruit arbor. Can't you see little Marguerite climbing an apple tree in the backyard? Do you want to be a part of that gift?"

That thought made her bubble up. "I would love it."

"Good. Sign the contract."

Charlotte squeezed the envelope. Clangs and chinks echoed from the kitchen.

"This is not only about the bread," he said with a tenderness she couldn't miss. Her throat swelled with not one lump, but two.

He blinked hard. "So, out with it. What's going on in Chicago?"

She couldn't pull herself from his lock on her. By now, she recognized how deep the blue in his eyes went when he became serious.

"Is there an ex-guy who has made an appearance?"

A glass water pitcher sat on his desk. She poured herself a cup. "No."

"Uh-huh."

She took long gulps. "Anyway, I'd never go back to Chicago for Don Drake."

"Uh-huh."

One more slug of water. "Last year, I was second choice for a staff position at a premier advertising firm. Solid commercial work, top money, senior-level benefits and bonus. I'd be producing illustrations for eco and environmental clients. Collaborating with naturalists, scientists, and academics. It was a crushing disappointment I didn't get it. Today, I got a call. The position is open again, and creative director Marty McKee, known as King McKee, plans to make me an offer. Tonight. If I were in Chicago, I would be leaping at this."

His swiveling slowed down. "Is that what you want, Charlotte? A commercial illustration career in Chicago?"

She gave his comment a few beats before answering. "It's an undeniably worthy career move for me, Marc. King McKee skyrockets his artists. Marty is a master at bringing fine art into mainstream media. I would be exploring high-quality creativity under his direction. He inspires alternative reality art and imaginative realism. The man has got a stairway to the stars and he's inviting me up."

"Uh-huh."

"I'm thinking, maybe, I'd be more secure, more successful at McKee's agency than living in a haunted cottage and sketching Rilke's poetry with Jaa Morland. At the end of which might leave me back in Chicago unemployed, again."

"So, you want security or opportunity? Usually we only get to choose one."

His eyes were piercing hers. The striped walls, the glaring window glass, the copper clock's *tick-tick-tick* were all suddenly piercing her. She turned her view out the window. Clear cerulean blue sky and wide open. She wanted to fly, slap-bang, right into it. "I went for a walk today to the Mianus River," she blurted out.

He stopped swiveling.

"I walked downriver, to the cross bridge where the big falls are. Near Yew Crag. Do you know it?"

"Yeah." He leaned forward. "Jaa is famous for showing off Draakensky. The view from her boardwalk is one of the most stunning scenes of the Mianus I've ever seen."

"The big falls there are wild. Waves angry at waves. Water swallowing water. The rhythms beat like war drums. Today, in the daylight, the waves reflected into a hundred fractured mirrors. I wanted to touch them. Place my feet in the falls. All those whorls and ripples and flashings. Knots and twists. What is that destination roaring beneath those waves?"

She moved to the desk to be close to him and leaned on the edge. "That yew tree is a paradox. It's ancient; it's shrewd. I need to sit there, feel the roots, the trunk, smell the green on its limbs, and dig into the shadowy hollows. All those dark threads moving there. What are they?"

Marc's chest rose and fell rapidly. "For God's sake, Charlotte, where are you going with this?"

"I need to draw the falls. Draw the yew. Explore the shadows."

"Why?"

"Because they speak. When I draw nature, I listen. I see."

"That waterfall is where Heida died."

"Yes?"

"She suffered a muddy death in that river, do you understand that?"

"Meaning what?"

"Jimmy Cruz found Heida, her mouth stuffed with mud, buried under yew tree branches on the river rock. Roots strangled around her entire body inside a cage. The Fire Department had to use a buzzsaw to release her."

A rush of cold sent a shiver through her body.

"We don't know what killed Heida. Do you get that? Charlotte, don't you dare cross that bridge to Yew Crag. Please!"

Book II
Everything Is Magick

Old Yew, which graspest at the stones
That name the under-lying dead,
Thy fibres net the dreamless head,
Thy roots are wrapt about the bones.

"In Memoriam A. H. H."
—Tennyson

Chapter Sixteen

Grinding at the Sky's Edge

On Saturday afternoon, Marc Sexton finished wiping down the bar top. Distracted by a raging headache all morning, he slugged water and two aspirins, grateful the bar action ran slow. Odd for a Saturday, though, not to have a busy lunch crowd. The unusual fifty-degree temps and clear skies no doubt drew everyone outside; he would have preferred to be out running himself. The light pouring in the bar windows drew him to the front corner table with his daily planner. Jaa and Heida's front corner table. He sat down, eyes on his notes. Sudden fatigue taking over, he closed the planner and hurried to his office to catch a power nap on the sofa. An hour later, he woke up in a sweat, headache still throbbing, recalling weird dreams of Yew Crag.

Muted voices told him the bar buzzed with customers. He sat up smelling smoke. The kitchen! He dashed through the swinging doors, expecting a smoking oven or the grill shooting flames. Instead, all appeared normal at the cooking and prep stations, the staff jostling, and Chef Charlie checking the ovens.

"What's burning, Charlie?"

"Nothing. Got a batch of turkeys in the oven for tonight's special. We're good."

Relieved, Marc headed to the bar. Liz had her hands full, serving seven people while a threesome meandered in.

"You okay?" Liz asked him as she filled beer glasses.

"Fine. Busy, huh?"

"I'm up to speed. You look horrible, Marc. Go home. Oh wait, you've got a smudge on your face." She dabbed his left temple with a napkin.

"Stop." In the glazed wall mirror behind the bar, he saw a grayish streak from his cheekbone to his eyebrow. "I must have touched something on the bar when I wiped it down. Rubbed my eye, I guess." His fingertips were clean, but he distinctly smelled ash when he wiped the smudge off. "Is this cigarette ash?" He turned to Liz. "Did you let a customer smoke at the bar?"

"Of course not."

"This is cigarette ash."

"Can't be. No one was smoking. Calm down, babe." She touched his arm.

"Don't call me that." He pulled away.

Two women overheard him, their faces wide with curiosity.

"Matteo?" He called. "Cover the bar."

Matteo came rushing over. Marc thumbed a direction toward Liz to go to his office.

In the office, Liz flopped down on the sofa.

"A smoking violation is a $2000 fine. Shall I deduct it from your paycheck if we get a citation?" He tried to use a polite tone, but his words came out angry. That damn headache.

"I didn't see anyone smoking."

"I've got it on my cuff." He turned his wrist to show her. "Of course it came from the bar top. Where else?"

"No one smokes on my watch, Marc. I've told guys to take their smokes outside. You know I have."

He looked again at the ash on his cuff. Maybe it wasn't cigarette ash. The color seemed too dark and the flakes too big. "If not cigarette ash, what then?"

"I don't know. Maybe you picked it up from the brick oven."

"I wasn't in the kitchen." He let out a breath he hadn't realized he was holding. Ash on his face. Ash on his cuff. If not from the bar, who touched him? He had locked the office door when he crashed on the sofa for his nap. And he hadn't used the men's room. He used to think uncertainty was intriguing. Not this time. "My apologies, Liz. Maybe it's not from a bar smoker. I don't know where it came from."

On the drive home, he kept all the windows open to clear his head. The nap helped, but what were those crazy dreams? Birds flying, a voice calling him, dark swirling air, a feeling of suffocation too. Had he dreamt of smoke? He had. Black smoke rolled across the river and ashes flew in circles.

He needed a run, needed to pound his feet into the earth. He accelerated the car down his driveway, gravel grinding, going too fast as he approached the house. At the curve, he slammed the brakes. From the birch trees, Sky Wolf leaped out. She perched herself on the rock wall like a pet expecting her master. Marc killed the engine and got out.

She sat alone. Peaceful. Wind flowing as if cloaking her presence. Inside her eyes, something. If she could speak, she'd be saying *I am wolf.* In an instant she darted from the rocks and trotted off.

He walked through the front door. The air hung dull and empty while the window light spread out hard on the carpets; the glare stabbed his eyes. He missed Charlotte. Missed her contagious laughter, her charming banter and curiosities, and her irresistible gray eyes on him. He loved the way she looked at him, so eager to connect. Was there ever a woman more kissable? He wanted to call her and let her luscious voice wash over him.

He downed a long drink of water at the kitchen sink. The smell of ash came over him again, this time stronger than before. And something else. In the bathroom, he examined himself in the mirror. On his neck, he found his silver wolf head dusted with black ash.

On Draakensky, Saturday afternoon, Jaa closed the windmill door behind her. Snow had melted in the warmer temps; a breeze hit whistle clean. Instead of taking her daily westerly stroll on Heida's boardwalk to the river, she paused at the walled garden. Softly, she sneaked to the cottage bow window and peeked inside. Charlotte sat in Heida's chair, sketch pad in hand. She was diligently at work sketching Rilke's "Evening in Skane." She had been working for days now, on her own, without so much as a peep.

Charlotte's enthusiasm to sketch the poems reassured Jaa right down to her bones. A thought to knock on the door and offer assistance seized her. Heida had had several preconceived ideas for interpreting "Evening in Skane"—a breaking sky at dawn to suggest the waking into the mind's landscape. Jaa bit her tongue— best to let Charlotte alone and not rock any boats.

North wind today. Greetings to you, Frau Holle! Jaa put her face full into the wind as she exited the garden, walking in Heida's footsteps, heading down the river path—sisters arm in arm, so many times together.

Beneath the blue sky, she strolled the foot trail, cane in hand; at the river's edge, she paused. Four months exactly since she had last stood her ground opposite Yew Crag near the cross bridge. That horrible day when they found Heida dead in the falls.

At the entrance to the cross bridge, she stopped to observe the yew tree with the green limbs hanging in a hundred nooses. No one could tolerate its oily vapors on hot summer days. And the dreadful bloody red sap that leaked every autumn. The ancient yew had remained mute most of the time. Except whenever Frau Holle blew keenly through the crag, the monstrous evergreen would moan across the cliffs.

She raised a foot to the first step on the bridge. Grateful to the sky, she asked Frau Holle to send a few wind nymphs today. Jaa hadn't seen wind nymphs for years. How lovely to have the companions. At the third step, she stood on the bridge as the river burst with muscular high waves over the steep falls. Was the river happy to see her?

With each step forward, Jaa held both hands tight on the guardrails—a difficulty because in her right hand, she squeezed three rose stems. Making a memorial with lilac roses where Heida died had been a nagging desire over the winter months. *Where shall I leave your lilac roses, Heida? On the river rock?*

Wind made her eyes tear. She would make it across safely—of course she would. She had crossed this bridge hundreds of times during her youth. Yew Crag remained familiar territory; she could never forget the safe places to walk to avoid the cliffs.

Shadows piled high between sun and clouds, which threw her own shadow down on the wet planks. Why did her silhouette look so small? In that instant, her right foot slid into a puddle. Jaa swayed back, her hand slipping off the handrail. The roses fell. River wind snapped them into the waves below, gone from sight in seconds downriver. She nearly cried out. Disappointed, she soldiered on.

At least I can be here with you today, Heida.

When she reached the end of the bridge, mists flowed around her. From her position, the massive yew stretched out with five separate trunks holding dark gaps. Gloomy boughs. Leathery green limbs. One might shudder to touch them.

Beyond the yew, dozens of offspring yews had spread abundantly into a grove; a person could barely walk between them, every branch and needle poisonous, already growing pods of their toxic red seed berries.

So this was Heida's last journey. Heida's footsteps crossing the bridge, following the worn-out footpath, climbing the bank to the yews, to her final moments at the falls on that river rock. She had died with no one to cradle her hand.

"I'm here, Heida," Jaa called, hoping the words would draw her forth. "May I see you once more? Come hither?"

She gripped the rails, ready to step down. Ashes gathered across her knuckles. Jaa knew her sister's ash held powerful energy. Ash draws forth and propels energy. *Yes, Heida is telling me she is present here.*

Saying Heida's name aloud, along with the river's tumbling voices, Jaa breathed in, drawing nature's magick net to her. And inside it, she would see her sister again, the same as she did at Marc's bar.

A heartache welled up as the minutes passed. "Heida, Come hither."

Nothing materialized. Another few minutes. She might have wept in the waiting. She stuffed back the tears. Another few minutes.

The river magick failed her. The giant yew shook. What went wrong? Deciding to go to the river rock, she stepped down the bridge steps, feet planted firmly on the ground.

A figure huddled low in the distance. Sunlight shed through the empty woods on a stealth wolf. White as the moon. Ears pricked forward, the wolf jerked his neck back, nose to the air and howled—the song waving across the crag.

The vibrations sent Jaa stumbling back. She reached for the bridge post but failed and spun down to the ground. Collapsed on all fours, hands scraping the loose stones, she struggled to rise. "Frau Holle!"

The wolf charged her. A mass of white, fur straight up, the giant paws stampeded. Jaa grabbed the bridge post and hung on, panting, tears breaking. The wolf ran in time with the descending wind. Fierce galloping broke all around her. A thunder-wolf? A wind-wolf?

The wolf zoomed past her, across the crag, into the forest

beyond. Holding the post with fingernails dug into the wet wood, dizzy, and weakened, she waited to be sure the wolf was gone. Minutes passed before her nerves calmed. With her cane, she managed to stand.

Frau Holle sent a breeze to cool her fiery face. A refreshing mint scent sharpened Jaa's senses. She hurried back across the bridge, tears streaming down her face, but grateful she could walk at all. Once down the bridge steps on Draakensky's side, on safe soil, she took a moment to rest. During that pause, she turned back to Yew Crag.

Vaults of oak, birch, and yews spanned beneath Frau Holle's softened winds. The sun retreated. From beneath the giant yew, trapped inside a dark hollow, a blurry white face stared out through bars of woody branches.

Oh, my dear Heida. What kind of ghost have you become?

Chapter Seventeen

Verge of Darkness

Saturday, at four thirty, Charlotte pinned her study sketches on the wall to examine them. After a productive few days, and pleased with her interpretations for "Evening in Skane," she reached for the phone to call Jaa. A text message from Suzanne lit the screen.

KING MCKEE IS BLASTED. ME TOO. I WOULD HAVE PUT MY MONEY ON YOUR CUTTING AND RUNNING FROM WACKY DRAAKENSKY AND THAT ECCENTRIC CRONE YOU WORK FOR, BUT LOOKS LIKE STAYING THE COURSE IS YOUR NEW BLACK. WISH YOU WERE HERE. ANYTIME YOU NEED, I AM. S.

Staying the course. The smart course would be to choose reliable King McKee and the shiny offer dangling in her face. Their phone conversation hadn't gone well; Marty's disappointment was visceral. By the time she hung up, her mouth tasted of salt and vinegar. Somewhere beneath the mess of doubts, lack of sleep, and all the vacillation, she knew taking McKee's offer meant abandoning Rilke's book of poems, losing her gallery show in New York City, leaving everything Bedford had to offer, and failing the Homestead opportunity. She didn't want to miss meeting Marguerite with her white rabbit. And then there was Marc. Her attraction to him frightened her. He was that new gleaming train pulling into the station, the express ride speeding to an exhilarating new destination. All aboard.

The door knocker banged. Alice Eve poked her head at the window.

Charlotte opened the door. "Alice, what a surprise. Come in."

"Thank you, but I can't stay. Jaa isn't feeling well. I stopped by to bring her the weekly flowers. She's in a terrible state. Can you check on her later and see if she needs anything? She usually retires by ten but if you can knock on her door, around eight thirty, I would—"

"Of course. I was going to call her to see the sketches for—"

"Not tonight." Alice stepped into the room, wringing her hands. "She's had an awful fright. She should see a doctor, but she refused. I left her resting on the sofa. Gave her some tea and toast and she seemed better."

"What happened?"

Alice shook her head. "On her walk today, she encountered a wolf."

Charlotte's hand flew to her chest. "Here on Draakensky?"

"On Yew Crag."

"The crag. Doesn't she normally walk the boardwalk every day?"

"She does. Today, though, I think she wanted to be with Heida. This is the four-month anniversary of Heida's death, the 26th. Poor thing, she was terrified. The wolf charged her at the cross bridge. She fell and bruised her arm. The wolf ran off. Thank God and all that's holy it ran off."

"Alice, sit down."

"I can't stay. My son is waiting for me to pick him up from his game. I'm late already. Please check on her for me?"

"Do you think I should stay with her tonight?" Charlotte offered. "I'm free, except to turn in early. Chef Charlie is expecting me at seven AM to bake the bread for the test sandwiches at The Grackle."

"She'll refuse your offer as she did mine. All her fierce independence. Call me later, will you? Can you imagine being all alone in the woods and finding a wolf on your path? And a white one at that. I've got to run. Talk to you later. Thank you."

Charlotte closed the door. A white wolf. On Yew Crag. Marc's Sky Wolf? Maybe not. Wolves run in packs. Should she tell Marc about it? As she thought it over, her cell phone rang.

"Hey there, Miss Knight," Marc said. The cheer in his voice lifted her right up. "I've been thinking about you. Chef Charlie has a roasted turkey special tonight. How about I grab a bottle of wine and bring you dinner? Have you ever had colcannon?"

She nearly chuckled at the way he barked the word *colcannon* as if it were a military firearm. "What is it?"

"Irish mashed potatoes. Insanely buttery, bacon, chives, scallions, dressed with thin ribbons of charred cabbage. *Shebang!*"

"An irresistible offer."

"Is that a yes?"

"It's not a no."

"I'll be there at seven thirty." *Click.*

If she hurried, she could wash her hair, tidy up the place, and set the table. Maybe wear the royal blue sweater that draped off the shoulders with the white swing trousers. With a glance out the bow window, she observed the windmill's windows across the garden. Jaa appeared and disappeared. Charlotte watched for several minutes as Jaa moved from kitchen to sofa to chair and table, then sat down by the fireplace. Reassured Jaa was steady on her feet and acting normally, Charlotte dashed upstairs to the bath.

At seven thirty, Marc tapped the door knocker. Arms full of bags and a bundle of flowers, he made a hammy bow to her. "Dinner has arrived, m'lady."

"Mmmm, are those lilies? How charming. Where's your white horse, Sir Lancelot?"

"I've stashed my magical mare in your fine stables. Shall we go for a ride later? Through the enchanted Forest of Broceliande?"

She swung open the door with equal drama. "I require fairies to attend."

He dropped his bags, swept her into his arms, and kissed her madly. When he released her, she could hardly stand. With the fireplace roaring and half a dozen candles burning on the table, their conversation went splendidly over glistening turkey slices and cranberry-almond stuffing. "Absolutely succulent," she said, wanting another helping, but holding off. Marc had brought a layered Chocolate Delight, mocha-chocolate pudding, topped with whipped cream and pecans.

Charlotte let her cashmere sweater shift around her shoulders, keeping her eyes strong on Marc. She'd forgotten the pleasures of flirting. With a last bite of the creamy colcannon and crunchy bacon—and a little swoon—she tipped another swallow of white wine. "Your Chef Charlie, what a passion he has for food."

"A virtuoso. We're planning a taste test for his Irish stew variations. I'd love you to be a tester. Next Thursday night in our private dining room. We named it The Kelsey Room after my mom. Seven o'clock. Small group. My local merrymakers."

"I know nothing about Irish food."

"No Irish in your heritage? Not even a dash from somewhere?"

"I'm Italian and English. I'm told we had a Russian Duke way back."

He winced playfully. "Man oh man, if I brought you home to Dublin, my mom would hit the roof. She expects me to keep to the clan. I'm obliged to hook up with an Irish pure-bred. Turns out, I'm not at all attracted to those Gaelic missies."

Charlotte let out a belly laugh. "Why is that?"

"Who knows? Love is mysterious." He stood up and stretched. "Are those your sketches on the wall?"

"Today's work. What do you think?"

He walked over for a closer look.

"I'm afraid the image won't mean much unless you know Rilke's poem, 'Evening in Skane.'"

"I know almost nothing about poetry." He took a moment to examine the drawings. "Beautiful double swirls and lifts. I'm getting a rocking delight. Quite distinctive." He touched the figure gently with his fingertip. "What's the artist's journey like?"

"I'm still figuring it out."

"Hm. What motivates an artist to draw?"

He sounded honestly interested, not just making conversation. "I guess most artists draw because they're inspired about life. Ugh, what a soppy textbook answer."

"Why do *you* draw?"

"If I knew that, I'd be brilliant instead of stumbling around."

"You've got a genuine talent for this, Charlotte. Do you think you're hitting your stride?"

"That remains to be seen." She stepped across the room. "Rainer Maria Rilke's poems are difficult to understand. He wrote in German and French so translations can be tricky. And the biographers think he spoke the barest of Russian and English."

"Odd name, Rainer Maria."

"His original name was René, but his lover Salomé convinced him to change it to Rainer. I prefer René. His biographers claim he became obsessed with death. Only fifty-one when he passed away. Did you know he died with his eyes open? I keep wondering, maybe he didn't want to leave this world."

Marc faced her. "I love that blue sweater on you. You have this glow from the lamp lights." He ran his fingers over her sleek ponytail, cupped both his hands around her face, and drew her to him.

She expected a deep kiss. Instead, she breathed in his small clinging kisses, tasting the toasty flavors, wine mixed with warm flesh.

The mantel clock chimed on the half hour. Eight thirty. She pulled away reluctantly. "I nearly forgot. I have to check on Jaa. Do you mind? Only a few minutes. I promised Alice."

"What? Leave now? You're ruining my romantic timing here." He said with a teasing grin.

She placed a deep kiss on him. "Let's continue this later? Jaa had a bad day."

"Jaa had a bad day. Why is that?"

"She went to Yew Crag on her afternoon walk. A wolf charged at her on the bridge. A white wolf. Do you think it was Sky Wolf?"

Marc's chin dropped.

"Alice found her in a terrible state when she delivered the weekly flowers."

"The wolf charged her? Is she okay?"

"Charged her and then ran off. She was shaken up but okay."

"What time was this?" His expression grew panicky.

"This afternoon. That's all I know, but it must have been Sky Wolf, right? Or, could the pack have come down from the north?"

He let go of her and paced to the window. "I don't know. Sky Wolf was on my property when I got home today at four."

"Marc? I promised Alice I'd check Jaa. I have to—"

"Yeah, yeah. I'll come with you."

They left the cottage and knocked at the windmill door. Jaa didn't answer, although the first and second floors' lights burned bright. Charlotte used her key.

"I'll check down here. You go upstairs." He headed for Jaa's bedroom, calling her name.

Charlotte shot up the spiral staircase, announcing herself loudly. At the stair landing, she halted. Jaa's white knitted shawl draped across the chaise, fringe hanging on the floor, the feathered scarf neatly folded at the top like a pillow.

The ajar closet door drew her attention. She rushed into the room, thinking Jaa might have fallen into the walk-in and lay there unconscious. Stacked boxes, bags, coats, and dresses filled every space.

On Jaa's desk, a photo album lay open under the porcelain lamp. The sisters in pink pinafore dresses and black Mary Jane shoes, holding hands in a garden. More photos of them on the lawn, riding bikes, at birthday parties.

"Anything?" Marc poked his head up from the staircase.

"No. Maybe she went out?"

"Her car is in the carport. I'll check the yard."

In the kitchen, Charlotte found the basement door. She pulled on a chain lightbulb and descended the rickety steps. Musty odors mingled with the sourness of a dead thing. She covered her nose, imagining skittering mouse claws inside the walls. Packed floor to ceiling: cedar planks and bricks, rakes and tools strewn akimbo, cracked mirrors, broken rattan chairs, a utility sink, shelves overflowing with clay flower pots covered in cobwebs, the furnace, the water tank, and a humped shadow with two heads she dared not speculate on. Not expecting an answer, she called out Jaa's name anyway.

Charlotte climbed upstairs where she latched the basement door, a damp chill forcing goosebumps. She dialed Alice Eve. "Alice? I'm at Jaa's and she's not here. By chance, is she with you? Marc is here with me. Please call back right away."

A second later, Marc came through the Dutch door. "Can't see much out there."

Charlotte plopped down on a kitchen chair. "I don't know what to think. Maybe Alice came back and picked her up? I called Alice and left a message."

Marc glanced out the kitchen window. "Alice would tell you if she did that. Are there lights on the boardwalk?"

"I think so. Not sure where the switch is though. Jaa wouldn't have gone out walking after dark. Would she?"

"She's got a fearless streak. Maybe. What's that mess?" Marc pointed to a glass vase on the kitchen counter with loose petals, leaves, and scissors.

Charlotte picked up the paper invoice itemizing red and purple tulips, two bunches, dated February 26, from Eve's Garden Shop. "Must be for the flowers Alice delivered. Gee, where are they?" She leaned around the doorframe into the living room for another look. "No tulips."

"I didn't see any flowers in her bedroom."

"Nor upstairs," Charlotte added.

Marc sat in a kitchen chair. "Why would Jaa remove them from the vase? Alice is an award-winning floral designer."

"And this vase is so pretty with the etchings."

"Does Jaa have a cellphone?"

"All I have is her landline number."

"Jaa goes on her walks without a cell phone? She's smarter than that. I think we need to call Jimmy."

"Jimmy Cruz? You want to call the Chief of Police? Marc, she's only missing a couple of hours. Maybe Alice knows—"

"Charlotte, Jaa was on Yew Crag today." Darkness crossed his face. Tight-lipped, he shifted his weight uncomfortably.

"What are you thinking?"

"You said Jaa was upset. Now she's nowhere in sight. Something's happened."

"Marc, it makes sense that she's probably with Alice."

"And if she's not?"

"Are you worried because Sky Wolf was on Yew Crag?"

His expression told her nothing.

"Or is it the river? Jaa's river magick? She introduced me to it at the gazebo on my first day here. Impressive. And overwhelming. Even Thomas spouts on and on about river magick, petrified magic, and its higher force."

"Harrogate," he hissed. "That Socrates with a shovel. Don't listen to him."

"Guess you're not fond of him?"

"Harrogate's a troublemaker." He stood up. "Jaa must have gone back to Yew Crag. Maybe she fell somewhere. The cliffs there are over thirty feet."

"She wouldn't go out alone in the dark after such a day," Charlotte said.

"Jaa grew up on Yew Crag. I wouldn't put it past her to persevere, boots on, flashlight in hand, and head out. The horn on the north side is treacherous, full of tree corpses, clefts, and caverns all over that terrain. I'm calling Jimmy."

Chapter Eighteen

Watching an Owl Watching Me

In the cottage, Charlotte made coffee with Marc watching over her shoulder. The draft from the back French door added to the dampness creeping in. Even the white tiles were icy cold; she regretted kicking off her shoes.

Chief Jimmy Cruz had arrived with two police cars at Draakensky within a half hour. With their high-powered flashlights and patrol car beams, a crew began searching the grounds, boardwalk, and river paths.

Marc leaned on the galley kitchen doorframe. "Why hasn't Alice called back?"

"Maybe she didn't get the message yet," Charlotte said, spilling the coffee grounds across the counter.

"Here, let me help you."

She turned on him. "Don't do that."

"What?"

"Patronize me. I can make coffee."

"Sorry. We're both feeling edgy."

"Why don't you try Alice again?" She wiped up the coffee grounds.

He pulled out his phone and walked into the living room. At least the fire kept the room warm, shedding a glow over the chintz sofa and dining table still cluttered with dishes. Even the bow window reflected a goldish cast. How lovely it would have been to snuggle in together.

Where could Jaa be all this time? What if she wasn't with Alice? How would tonight end? She listened to Marc leaving a message on Alice's phone.

"Jaa, where are you?" she said under her breath, but she really wanted to scream it. Charlotte grabbed two cups from the cupboard—Delft porcelain, hand-painted scrolled tulips. She scooped out the pudding dessert; the coffee brewed quickly and she brought a tray into the living room.

"Smells good. I need this," Marc said. "Thank you."

"These coffee cups are Heida's."

"Yeah. So?"

"Tulips. It bothers me why Alice's purple and red tulips are missing. Maybe Jaa took them somewhere. To Heida's grave? To the Morland mausoleum in the village? Maybe Alice gave her a ride there."

"Heida isn't buried in the family mausoleum. They cremated her."

"Oh. Are her ashes there?"

"Her ashes live in a box in Jaa's bedroom. At least that's what Alice told me."

A half-hour passed. They barely talked, had more coffee, and nibbled on the creamy dessert. Marc wandered the room, to the windows, to the kitchen, opened the back door a few times to overhear the officers' conversations. At one point, he couldn't sit any longer and went outside.

Charlotte slipped her coat on and joined him. They huddled on the garden bench, watching the emergency vehicles' strobe lights drench the woods and riverbank.

A loud crack made them both jump. Then, loud zig-zagging whirs.

"What is that?" Charlotte gripped the bench. "Is it coming from the river?"

"Is that a buzzsaw? God, no." Marc ran toward the river path. One officer obstructed him at the carport.

"What's going on?" Marc said.

The officer placed a hand on Marc's shoulder. "Stay back. We have the area closed off."

"What's happened?" Charlotte burst, right behind him.

"We found a body."

Charlotte could hardly breathe. *No, please, no.*

"What's the buzzsaw for?" Marc asked.

The officer shook his head. "Go back and wait at the house."

"Is it on Yew Crag? Are your men on Yew Crag?"

"Wait at the house. I don't know where they found it."

"Where's the Chief? Tell Jimmy to call me. Tell him to call."

They sat on the garden bench again.

"Marc, is there another access to Yew Crag besides the cross bridge on Draakensky? Could a vehicle get through from the other side?"

"No way. That easterly region is rocky as hell. The only way to penetrate is to fly in with wings. Or on four legs, if you're a deer."

"Then, you know Yew Crag. You've been there?"

"I've never crossed the bridge."

Charlotte rubbed her arms. Listening to the saw's whirs could have been shredding her own nerves. Exhausted already, she stretched her aching neck. The windmill lights shined masterfully—a guardian tower—sails stirring the air into streaming circles. "It's a beautiful windmill, isn't it? Reminds me of a giant star that fell to Earth. I understand why Jaa preferred not to move into the cottage. She's a princess living in a fairy tale in that windmill. You know those sails never stop spinning? In the weeks I've been here, I've never seen them stationary, not once. The wind never stops blowing on Draakensky."

Marc looked up. "Why are the window lights on the third floor a different color? Almost bluish."

"That is odd."

"Marc?" Jimmy Cruz came walking into the garden.

Charlotte noticed the buzzing had stopped.

Marc darted off the bench. "Jimmy! What's happening?"

Jimmy glanced at Charlotte. "It's not what we thought."

"What do you mean? Your officer said you found a body," Marc said.

"We did. On the river rock in the falls."

Charlotte felt herself swaying back toward Marc.

"We had to cut it free," Jimmy said, his voice cracking.

She gulped. "Tell me it's not Jaa."

Jimmy let out a huff. "It's Tom Harrogate."

The Chief took his cap off, blew out a hard breath, and sat on the bench without another word.

"Harrogate?" Marc said. "On Yew Crag. Did he fall?"

"No, he didn't fall."

"What then?"

"Unclear. Whatever happened, he was covered in tree limbs."

"Yew limbs? Like Heida?" Marc's voice shot out.

"You know what, Marc? Shut the hell up." The Chief's phone rang, and he strode to the garden gate to speak privately. "Medical Examiner is on his way," he said. "And no sign of Jaa, yet." He scanned the windmill structure. "Could she have called a cab and gone out, Charlotte?"

"Probably not."

Jimmy held his vision on the windmill's roof. "What is that, a hawk owl up there?" He pulled his night vision binoculars off his belt and focused on the roof. "Oh Christ, that's the same one we saw on the crag tonight. Same size. Long tail. Big son-of-a-bitch."

"Is that important?" Marc asked.

"If that's the same hawk owl that perched on Harrogate's body, it is." He kept his binoculars aimed. "Damn thing, he's watching us. We tried to catch him, but he flew off."

Charlotte raised her vision to see the owl. She caught a shadowed figure in the hatched pane on the third floor. Familiar head and shoulders.

"Who is that in the third-floor window?" Jimmy yelled.

"Oh my word. I think it's Jaa."

The Chief sprinted to the windmill. Charlotte followed, with Marc behind her. They pounded up the spiral to the second-floor library.

"How do you get to the attic?" Marc said.

"Must be a scuttle hole or hatchway." Jimmy searched the ceiling.

Charlotte didn't see any ceiling hatch. "Inside the closet?"

Jimmy opened the door and began tossing boxes.

"Jim!" Marc said. "Stop."

Charlotte turned around.

A bookcase had swung open. Jaa hobbled down the steps, her gray hair tangled, pink silk robe dragging.

"What's happened?" Jaa murmured. "All those lights on Draakensky. What's going on?"

The bookcase door swung closed behind her with a soft tap.

Downstairs in the living room, Charlotte sat next to Jaa. She could hardly believe Jaa had been in the attic the whole time. How ridiculous. Marc's expression showed more astonishment than anything else.

Jaa rested in her chair by the fireplace, holding her whiskey tumbler with both hands. "I've done nothing wrong," she said, clearly annoyed with everyone frowning at her. "This is my house and I can go into the attic if I choose."

"Of course you can," Charlotte said. "We've been sick with worry trying to locate you." Charlotte regretted the harshness in her voice.

"I'm sorry to have been so much trouble," Jaa shot back. "I had no idea you were going to come check on me and search the house." She downed the last of the whiskey. "I'll have a little more, Marc, if you don't mind."

He tipped the bottle into her glass. "Careful, it's got a knockdown that'll sneak up on you."

"Yes, we've met before—Heida and I, on many a Saturday night. Best whiskey in Belgium."

"What were you doing up in the attic for so many hours?" Charlotte asked. "Didn't you hear us calling you?"

"I fell asleep on the trundle bed. The attic is soundproof, you know, so we don't have to hear the mechanisms turning the sails."

The Chief dipped his head. "Why did you go to Yew Crag today? The account I have is sketchy."

"To bring flowers to where Heida died. Today is her anniversary date."

"And you went there alone?"

"For heaven's sake, yes, I went alone. I've known Yew Crag and the river since I was a child. I crossed the bridge well enough, except when I dropped the roses. They floated away."

"What time did this happen?" Jimmy made notes.

"Afternoon. Then I ran into a wolf! All these years Heida and I walked these woods, and we never once saw a wolf. Although Heida would have loved to have seen a white wolf on Draakensky. But for me, I was terrified. I became so upset that I had lost Heida's lilac roses. When Alice arrived and brought me the tulips—beautiful red and purple—I decided I would bring Heida the tulips."

"You went back to the crag after dark?" Jimmy said, almost aghast.

"I called Thomas and asked him to do it for me. I wrapped the tulips in ribbons and he took them to the river rock. Thomas is such a dear man. I know he's a misfit in this community, but the man does have a streak of tenderness. At least for me."

"What time did Thomas go to Yew Crag?"

"I don't know."

"What time did you give him the tulips?"

She closed her eyes. "I don't recall. Why don't you ask Thomas?"

Marc moved to the ottoman near her. "Jaa, we can't ask Thomas." He placed his hand on hers. "I don't know any easy way to say this. Thomas is dead."

Jaa let out a cry.

"I'm so sorry," the Chief said. "This is a shock. For everybody."

"What happened? Not on Yew Crag?" Jaa burst. "You better tell me how this happened, Chief," she shouted.

"We're still figuring it out," Jimmy said. "What time did you call Thomas?"

"After Alice left."

"Alice left around four thirty," Charlotte added.

"All I wanted was to be with Heida today. I went to the attic hatch to be in the quiet place we used to go as kids. Oh dear. Thomas, dead! What have I done?"

A bell rang. Charlotte jumped up, pulling her phone to her ear. "Alice?" She listened and turned to Marc. "Her cellphone is missing, maybe stolen. She just got home." Charlotte moved into the kitchen and leaned against the Dutch door. "Alice, we have troubles here."

Alice had more questions than Charlotte could answer and after a lengthy and arduous conversation, Charlotte hung up. Alice had insisted Jaa spend the night at her house in the guest room. Thankfully, Jaa agreed with no argument. Alice arrived promptly, helped Jaa pack a bag, and escorted her to the car.

What a relief that Jaa would be in Alice's care because Charlotte needed to escape this horrible mess—the little fugitive inside surging to run away.

Before Jaa climbed into Alice's car in the driveway, Jaa whispered into Marc's ear. Charlotte caught her last words. "Please don't leave Charlotte alone tonight."

Everyone said their goodnights. Marc followed Charlotte into the cottage. He closed the door, then withdrew Jaa's whiskey bottle from his jacket pocket.

"Will you join me?"

"No thanks. You don't have to stay. I heard what Jaa said. I'm perfectly fine staying here tonight."

"Charlotte, please be smart here, I think—"

"I'm good, Marc. I'll be at the restaurant early, as promised, at seven to bake the bread."

He shot his vision out the bow window to the windmill. "That hawk owl is—"

"I know what you're thinking. And I see the hawk owl on the roof. What, you think that owl is going to come after me?"

He stiffened. "Jaa certainly does."

"And why would she think that? You know so much about Jaa. And Heida. And Yew Crag. Enlighten me, Marc!"

He whistled at her anger. "Jaa's perceptions are keen. Her understanding of nature deserves—"

"Ah, yes, Jaa the psithurist. Her wind magic. And let's not forget her river magic. And windmill magick. And flower magick. And there must be some air magick going on in all this too, right?"

"I don't know air magick."

"Of course you don't, Marc. I just made it up!"

"Could you knock it off, please?" he asked ever so politely.

"What is all this magick?" she screamed.

"Look, magick is mysterious and can be frightening as all hell, but at the core, it's a higher self-awareness that fuels power." He lifted his chin, cueing her to pay attention. "Jaa is gifted with that higher power. Her skills trump anything you or I can know. Her warning about the hawk owl is serious."

"What's your problem with owls? You think owls are wicked crones from the Otherworld? Harbingers of death and all that?" She felt her face flush hot. " *Birds of omen dark and foul. Night-crow, raven, bat, and owl.'* Gee, I remember that one as a jump rope song."

"Jump rope. Cute," Marc said flatly.

"The song is actually from a Sir Walter Scott poem. And anyway, why didn't you mention to Jimmy about Sky Wolf on Yew Crag? Don't you think he needed to know that?"

"I don't know that it was Sky Wolf. And what difference would it make? What can I do about it? The wolf didn't attack Jaa."

"Didn't you tell me Sky Wolf had strayed from her pack? A lone wolf?"

"My best guess. There could be a mate out there or other wolves from her pack that followed her south. Sky Wolf is not the issue here. All I know is that Harrogate is dead in what is manifestly the same condition as Heida's death."

She sighed.

"This is significant," he continued. "An owl sitting on Harrogate's body? While I'll admit I didn't like Harrogate and banned him from The Grackle, I am sorry that he's dead."

"You banned Thomas? Why?"

"Because he's a hotheaded bully. Abusive. Contentious. He wrecked my bar in a fistfight with two guys. He pulled the first punch. Harrogate attacked Heida. I can't even tell you how bad it got. Nobody trashes my bar and is permitted back in."

"Heida was there?"

"Heida and Harrogate were pretty tight. Literature buddies at Columbia."

"I didn't know Heida hung out at your bar."

"A regular, every Thursday night."

"What about Jaa? Was she there too?"

"Jaa? The magnificent spinster? She wouldn't be caught dead sitting on a barstool. She only came for lunch at the front table. Heida was the barfly. Big-time talker. You've never seen such emotive power, especially after a few drinks. I'd cut her off more nights than I care to say. Dionysus notwithstanding. I put her in a cab home regularly. A few times I had to drive her home and deposit her on the sofa. Protecting Heida against her indulgences became routine."

"You do live by Dionysus's wisdom, don't you?"

"Of course I do. My permittee license requires me and my staff to deny service to intoxicated patrons. And for myself. My family's Sexton Irish Whiskey practically runs in my veins. I don't have the luxury of indulging." He grabbed two glasses from the bar shelf on the bookcase. "Stay at my place tonight." He filled the tumblers a quarter with the bright golden liquid. "One ice cube makes this perfect."

After a dash to the kitchen and back, he offered her the glass.

She took the glass to please him but placed it on the table. Don used to control her drinks, manipulate events and dinners and friends to his preference. Too often she confused that control with security. "Marc, I'm staying here. You're going home."

He halted, his glass halfway to his mouth, then he gulped the whiskey. "Atta girl, Charlotte. But you need to know, the game here has changed. What happened to Thomas on Yew Crag tonight is no small thing. Danger ahead. Jaa knows it. Do not take that lightly."

"Jaa is hypersensitive and overreacting," she said, her pulse slamming into her throat. "And I'm not taking this lightly."

"Stay at my place tonight. I have a guest room that's all yours. No expectations."

"I'm staying here. How many times do I have to say it?"

Marc didn't move. His silent stare-down might have turned her to stone. Was he thinking she behaved stubbornly? Was he waiting for her to change her mind? Whatever he was thinking, she swung open the door. "This is not negotiable. I don't need a knight to save me. I need my own sword. Go. Goodnight."

He placed his empty whiskey glass on the end table. A second later, the door closed behind him.

In the following minutes, she listened for his car motor to fade down Draakensky's drive. When it did, she downed the whiskey in three gulps. Then poured another.

A glimpse at the windmill confirmed the hawk owl indeed held its position on the roof. Its yellowish eyes glowed under the windmill floodlights. If she had a gun, she'd go out there and shoot its head off.

She dragged Heida's armchair over to the bow window, flopped down, feet up on the ottoman, sipped the whiskey, and focused her sight on the oval bird on the roof.

Watching an owl watching me.

Chapter Nineteen
Owl Vision

Charlotte woke cold and shivering; she curled up with a moan, her thoughts reeling. Thomas dead. Hawk owl. Jaa. Angry Marc. She didn't recall drifting off to sleep in the chair, didn't recall any dreams, didn't even feel she had slept. She shimmied up. A roaring headache sent her falling back. The whiskey bottle stood on the end table. Belgian Eagle, Single Malt Whiskey. "What the hell is in this stuff?"

She forced herself to check the windmill roof. All clear. Revived by a hot shower and yesterday's leftover coffee, she sped to Bedford Village. As she walked into The Grackle kitchen, Chef Charlie talked on his cell phone.

"We're good, Marc." Charlie gave her a wave. "Charlotte just walked in now. See you later."

"Is he checking up on me?"

"Marc rarely does that sort of thing. I guess he's cranky today."

"Where's the staff?"

"We don't open till three. Most arrive around one o'clock. I've got the ovens preheated. The entire kitchen is ours."

"Perfect."

"Marc said there was some bad business last night at Draakensky?"

"Dreadful. Let's get to work."

She crafted ten loaves while Charlie prepped for the day's menu dishes, their breezy conversation sliding in and out as they worked. Ye gods! The soft dough in her hands, squeezing between her fingers, cheered her. *I'm the boss now and you do as I say.* Bread magick!

At about 1:30 Marc strutted in. "Good afternoon. Ahhh, the aroma of homemade bread."

He looked incredibly handsome for a Sunday afternoon. Freshly shaved, classic blonde waves, dressed in a crisp white shirt and sea-green tie sporting muted suns and moons. So different from Don's Ivy League hard side-part and his sword-striped ties.

Marc strode to the menu whiteboard on the wall and erased a line. "Charlie, the Garden Club party canceled. Kill the Wicklow Beef Salad for tonight." Marc turned. "Charlotte," he looked askance at her, "May I see you in my office, please?"

What is this now? They sat down—Marc behind his desk, Charlotte in the opposite chair by the window. Outside, a truck pulled up in the parking lot. "My bar delivery. Finally." He switched back to her, his mouth tense. "Your breads look beautiful." He paused. "Are you cooled off after last night?"

"Are you?"

"How about we agree we both acted . . . impetuously?"

"Is that what we were?"

"We had a stressful night. When somebody dies suddenly, it's a big bang. My dad died suddenly. Felt like a stroke of lightning hit all of us. My mom is still burning." His phone buzzed. "I have to take this. It's my brother." He gestured for her to stay. "Hey, William . . . Yeah, I need to follow up later. Can I call you back? I have Charlotte with me. I'll call you at four. My time." He tossed his phone on the desk.

"Your brother knows who I am?"

"He does. We chat every Sunday. William is the family academic. Psychology professor at Pepperdine. Lives in L.A." A bell sounded at the outside door. "Damn," he huffed. "Charlotte, I have to supervise this delivery. Sorry, bad timing. Can you sit tight for ten minutes? Help yourself to coffee."

Tempted to huff herself, she agreed to have coffee. Acted impetuously? At least he had the good sense not to blame her entirely. She poured the hot brew into a paper cup. Through the window, she observed a man in a baseball cap unload the truck while Marc checked off items on a clipboard. Liz emerged in black jeans and a silver V-neck satin blouse as she leaned in to count the cases. Quite the butt curve.

Their voices carried, but Charlotte couldn't distinguish the words exchanged—only that the three appeared agitated. At one point, Liz touched Marc's chest affectionately. She flipped back her blonde locks and spoke through pouty lips. Was that an eyebrow flash she shot at him? Their faces were close enough that she might have kissed him. Marc didn't appear to be evading it and patted her shoulder. Liz gleamed up at him.

Charlotte sipped her second steaming coffee when Marc returned.

"My apologies. The bar order got messed up. I'm short vodka now." He closed the door. "Give me one more second. I need to call Jackson." He dialed, instructed Jackson to make a vodka run to Mahopac, sat down, loosened his tie, and opened his shirt collar button. "Hot as hell in here today."

"Charlie's had all five ovens going since seven. No wonder."

"I'm not a kitchen guy. I hate the confinement. All that heat. That's the reason I left the Culinary Institute. I need to be out in front at the bar where all the cool people are."

She nodded.

He cleared his throat.

She crossed her legs; she uncrossed them.

He tapped his thumb on the desk; he swept his vision to the coffee pot and then settled on her. "Charlotte, I want to apologize for last night," he blundered out. "I'm sorry. I was pushy."

"You were controlling."

That made him blink. "Okay. I'll concede to controlling. My fault."

"And, I'm sorry I tossed you out."

"Well, I confess you're not the first woman to tell me to get out."

They both got a kick out of that, exchanging nods. Charlotte nudged herself to the seat's edge. She debated whether she should ask but reminded herself of the importance of knowing the absolute truth in relationships. Being naïve—or worse, stupid—had added to the combative relationship with Don.

"You have a thing going with Liz?"

He appeared surprised at the question. "If you mean, are we sleeping together, I'll be honest. That's an old story."

"Not for her, it isn't."

"She knows it's over. My relationship with Liz was a big mistake. A fleeting indulgence, which blew up. And was my fault." He paused. "I'm not in love with her. Liz is a valuable employee.

She messes up on administration sometimes, but that's not why we hired her."

"Why did you hire her?"

"She's a high-quality bartender. Been with us for seven years. My mother hired her and trained her into the professional she is."

"Liz is more than just bar service," Charlotte said, knowing she was pushing it.

He swallowed hard. "Yes, that's true. I'm embarrassed to say this, and I apologize. Liz is also a very attractive woman, a bright asset behind the bar. Look, drinking is sexy. She has that Marilyn Monroe style going for her, and men enjoy admiring her and engaging in her conversations. Communication is a key talent for a barkeep. She knows all the right dialogues to encourage repeat customers. This is business."

Charlotte didn't know whether to scream or throw something at him. "Do you think, maybe, just maybe, that is a tad sexist?"

"I think it's incredibly sexist. I hate that part. Liz is not slinging drinks for big tips. She is a smart mixologist, good at reading the guests and anticipating their needs. A beauty, certainly, without being trashy—because that I would not tolerate. The bar is a line, and each guest seated on my line is important to me. I've worked incredibly hard to make The Grackle upscale. Thanks to Chef Charlie. Thanks to Jackson. And Petrovna who runs an A-plus kitchen."

"And so you have. But, Marc, this needs to be clear. If you're still attracted to Liz, and she's present in your life, I shouldn't—"

"I'm attracted to you, Charlotte. You are my enchantress. Like lovely Vivienne. Under the oak tree." He yanked off his necktie and tossed it to her. "Make me your prisoner."

They burst out laughing. And then Charlotte laughed again.

"Stay for the sandwich tasting? We're going to circulate bites at the bar and trays to the dinner crowd."

"I can't," Charlotte said, checking her phone. "I have a text from Alice. She needs me to pick up Jaa at the flower shop and drive her home. I've got to go."

"Okay. I'll walk you out."

In the parking lot, Marc put his hand on the small of her back, guiding her into the car seat. His touch, so sensuous. Enthralling—she wanted to linger there. He leaned his hip against the open door. "I have a rule: no kissing on the job. I owe you. I'll call you tomorrow. Wait, let me rephrase that. May I call you tomorrow?"

She ached to kiss him. She could let him kiss her all day. That sexy rise in her belly, all that dreamy breathing together, his invigorating aroma, she wanted all of him.

Thump!

Charlotte's head snapped back. Instinctively, she snatched the steering wheel. A dark figure had hit her car windshield. Marc jumped back with a shout.

A striped owl, gray, black, and white, sprawled across the glass, hooked wings spread out, dark eyes, yellow-rimmed, fixed in a dead bolt on her. They blinked, paused, blinked again.

Marc slammed the car door. He waved his arms at the bird. "Go on. Go."

Feeling safely enclosed inside the car, she struggled to make out its distorted face. Between the eyes, the ash-colored feathers puckered in a frown. Swivel-eyed, he held his head oddly poised. The beak appeared too high. His head, propped up and misshaped, wobbled.

"Go! Go on," Marc yelled again, banging the car hood.

The bird's eyes shook, creating an odd buzzing sound. Charlotte grabbed her cell phone, zoomed in, and captured a photo.

"Start the engine. Back out," Marc said, running to the back door where he grabbed an abandoned snow shovel.

The engine's rumbling didn't scare the bird off. That odd face held her tight. She reversed the car slowly and pumped the brakes to jolt him. In a flash, he rotated his head, flipping his face in a half circle. Eyes, beak, and face were now in normal position.

Marc aligned the snow shovel with the owl. Carefully, he nudged him an inch. "Take off, fella, go."

Charlotte placed her face closer to the window for a moment. Transfixed, she reached a hand up to the windshield and touched the glass space over its head.

"Don't engage it," Marc said. "Blow the horn."

She pressed and held it for a long beep. The owl launched, ripped through the air, and disappeared into the trees.

Charlotte climbed out of the car to show Marc the photo. "Have you ever seen this? An owl's head flipped upside down? And then he rotated it, right side up."

"God damn," Marc touched the photo to enlarge it. "Did you see him do that?"

"What a stunt."

"You need to speak to Jaa about this. She knows bird behavior." He put an arm around her. "I have owls on my property. I've never seen one behave like that. Come back inside. Let's make sure he doesn't come back." He shot his vision to the trees.

"Jaa's waiting for me at Eve's. I'll be fine. Really. He's gone."

"Charlotte," he said her name so tenderly, it could have been a prayer. "You know, I'm finding it increasingly more difficult to say goodbye to you."

At the parking lot exit, Charlotte pressed the brakes to wait for traffic. People sat on sidewalk benches in the sunshine. Moms walked strollers and baby carriages across the Village Green. A dad played catch with his two boys on the grass. She loved the drowsy calm, swaying trees, and easygoing community. That lovely Bedford Oak came to mind. Maybe Bedford held the possibility of becoming home. Might she belong here? Why return to Chicago in the summer, anyway? Chicago's art community wasn't much better than New York City's. And it might be exciting to take a stab at the opportunities thriving in the Tribeca art scene in lower Manhattan. She turned onto the main street and found a free parking space at the Orphan Book Shop.

She strutted into the shop. "Hi Scully."

"Ahhh." He grinned. "The Tic-Tac-Toe lady."

She handed him her credit card. "Wrap up those wolf pups for me?"

Strolling the aisles, Charlotte dipped herself around until she arrived at the front window display with a colorful chalkboard sign: Philosophy in the Garden. Fresh blue and yellow flowers in vases surrounded books showing landscape scenes. "Pushing spring, are you?" she said to Scully at the counter.

"I am. We're connecting garden and philosophy books for March's theme. Nietzsche and his thought tree. Sartre and chestnuts. Novalis and his blue flowers."

"Novalis?"

"Are you a Novalis fan?"

"No. What's he famous for?"

"Nature philosopher, the other-worldly type. Mostly known for his 'What we see, sees us' theory. Connectivity, and all that jazz."

"Most philosophy literature is beyond me."

"Novalis is not all that dense. Everything in nature looks back at us. A butterfly. A tree. When you see the moon and admire it, the moon sees you back. All life is connected. Cool, right?" Scully handed her the bagged tic-tac-toe game. "Win brilliantly."

Before getting into the car, she instinctively dashed her vision across the street to the cemetery. The man in an overcoat sat on a far bench, book in hand, head down.

Time running late, she tossed the bag in the car and dashed across the street between oncoming cars to the cemetery. She scanned the benches, headstones, and stone walls. In the distance, at the windy slope, she thought she saw a figure. But a closer look revealed only dust in the air.

Chapter Twenty

Crooked Shadows

March arrived with warmer temps on Thursday. The windmill spun its sails in an unusual rhythm, Jaa noticed—like it was trying to kick the wind. She reclined by the fireplace, her nerves jumbled over the past few days. Thomas's death became headline news. A second death on Yew Crag. Reporters kept calling for interviews. Detectives from Westchester County scoured Draakensky for evidence of foul play.

Snug inside her armchair, Jaa's mind scudded between sleep and consciousness. The river sent liquid whispers. She tried to let that soothe her—the rolling waterfall, the light swimming on curly waves. She had missed her wind walks to the river.

She peeked at the window's garden view. An image formed: Heida, tall as a rake in her red trousers and pin-dot blouse, grayish strands falling around her face, bending over to snip the glory roses in the summer flowerbeds. Jaa could still hear the pruning shears *click-click-click* down the path. Heida, a statuesque beauty, walking among the hollyhocks, butterflies, and bees.

The door knocker banged.

"It's open, come in."

Chief Jimmy Cruz poked his head around the door. Removing his cap, he patched a smile on his lips. For a cop, he had a gentle face with bright black eyes. His neat beard and broad shoulders gave him an impeccable presence down to every button, collar, and the sharp cuffs. The chief's greeting and polite banter about spring weather soothed her as he took a seat. How good to act normal when things were anything but normal.

"Jaa, the autopsy report on Thomas came through today," he said with his charming Spanish accent. "I wanted to tell you myself. Before it hits the media."

"How kind of you, Chief."

"I admit this week has got my head spinning. I can hardly believe we're investigating again on the crag."

"I trust you'll do your best. I expect Charlotte any minute. I do so want to get back to my work and take my walks again. I've not been out since all this happened. Don't be afraid to tell me the facts. I'm stronger than I look."

That made him grin. He pulled out the report. "Thomas's death was caused by—the simplest way to say it is heart failure."

"A heart attack?"

The door opened. Charlotte stepped into the room. "Jimmy? Hello. Am I interrupting? I can come back later."

"No, my dear. Please stay," Jaa said. "The Chief has the autopsy report on Thomas."

Charlotte sat down on the bench near Jaa. She wore a pretty dark green knit dress, trimmed in white piping at the neck and cuffs. "Are you on your way out, Charlotte?"

"Later today. Go ahead, Jim."

The Chief turned to Jaa. "Not a heart attack. Technically, it's called *vagal sudden death*. Direct vagal nerve compression. The medical examiner found a series of bruises on the abdomen—the solar plexus, right below the ribcage—which they believe caused a massive fatal shock to the body."

Jaa felt suddenly thirsty and reached for her water goblet. "Bruises? I don't understand. How could bruises cause death?"

"It's a rare occurrence. The autopsy revealed," he read from the report, "acute cardiac failure due to vagal nerve inhibition."

The words *series of bruises* repeated. "Heida didn't have abdomen bruises, did she?"

"No bruises reported in Heida's autopsy report."

"I see. And what about footprints? Were there footprints on the riverbank, similar to the ones you found around Heida?"

"We did find a set of footprints. Forensics will determine if they match the prints found near Heida's body. Takes time."

Jaa rubbed her hands around and around. "They suffered the same death? Shock?"

"Not exactly. We have physical evidence Thomas was attacked

by something, and it directly caused the bruises, which caused the vagal neurogenic shock.”

“Not the same as Heida then?”

“We found no physical evidence of a direct attack on Heida.”

Jaa let the words sink in. “Is that all?”

The Chief gave a slow nod.

“Are you sure? You know what I am asking, don’t you, Chief?”

He paused avoiding eye contact. “You’ll see it in tomorrow’s paper. We did find an owl on Thomas’s body.”

Jaa returned to rubbing her hands.

“What happens next?” Charlotte said.

“We continue to investigate. But I have to say, two and two are not adding up to four.”

“I remember you said the same about Heida’s case. Two and two are adding up to zero.”

“We haven’t given up on Heida’s case.” His words came out choked.

“Chief, I have to ask. It’s been on my mind,” Jaa said. “Did you find the tulips? The ones I gave to Thomas? Red and purple on the river rock.”

“I don’t think they did. We’ve spent the last few days searching the crag, the cabin, his car, the shed. Are you certain you gave them to Thomas?”

“Of course I’m sure. He knew how important the tulips were to me. And he was happy to bring them. He told me so.” Putting her head down, she gathered her strength. “I can only hope that wherever Thomas is in the afterlife, he is with his wife and happy in their realm together. He was so miserable here without her. Thank you, Chief, for stopping by.”

The Chief said his goodbyes and left.

“Bruises on the abdomen?” Jaa said. “This is so disturbing.” Charlotte held the sketches in her hands. “Charlotte, I’m not up to reviewing the sketches. Shall we do it tomorrow?”

“Of course. Jaa, I’m out tonight. I promised Marc I’d participate in Chef Charlie’s Irish stew tasting at The Grackle. That all right?”

She nodded. “I need some air.” Jaa walked to the door and opened it. “Ahhhh, that feels good. I’m dying to walk the boardwalk. Would you come with me? Twenty minutes?”

“I could use a walk, too.”

Bundled up against the wind stuttering high over Draakensky, they walked Heida's Boardwalk. Jaa didn't have the energy to speak. Neither did Charlotte. They reached the gazebo and sat down.

"I love to watch the waves go by," Jaa said. "You can follow a silvery ripple and follow another and another and float your mind down the river." Charlotte watched with her. Maybe they were watching the same ripples. "Can you hear Draakensky's sails turning?"

"I do. A soft clatter."

"Can you hear the wind's undernotes?"

Charlotte lifted her head. With her fingertips, she touched her left ear. "Oh yes. A rustling? No, something breathy."

"There's an eave in the wind. At the underside of the top layer. Its direction is vertical, coming down to you." Jaa noticed the birds quieted now. Even the river shut its loud mouth. "Can you smell her earthy perfume?"

Charlotte parted her lips, taking in the air. "I hear the hem of a lady's skirt sweeping the grass in a vast meadow. It's a *hushhhh*. She's here, thin and willowy. She's calling me. Is that your Frau Holle?"

"Oh no, my dear. That is your Lady of the Wind."

Chapter Twenty-One

Dark Interval

Charlotte steered the car into a space at The Grackle parking lot. *Lady of the Wind*. Would she meet her again? Would she hear the *hushhhh*? The image remained a blur, but she recalled the Lady to be fine as a thread. Hair flashing. Slender eyes. A graceful figure. So swiftly she moved. Just thinking of her made Charlotte suddenly alert.

"Life certainly is happening to you now," she told her reflection in the rearview mirror, raking her hair loose on her shoulders. "Why is this happening? Because of my art? Because of Rilke's poems? Because of Marc? Because . . . because I said yes."

The dashboard clock lit up 7:25. "And because I'm late."

Inside, she found her way to the back dining room, The Kelsey Room, filled with about twenty-five strangers holding pints of dark beer, a few patrons tilting wine goblets. Women shared their hellos with her as she weaved through the chatty gathering. A couple of guys made drop-dead eye contact as if they knew her. People weren't reluctant to engage strangers in this town. These were Marc's local merrymakers. Now she was one of them.

Tables draped in black-and-white checked linen formed a square, centering the room. Chef Charlie became another centerpiece in his double-breasted chef whites and navy beanie as he schmoozed his taste testers. He gave her a wink and a mocking cringe. *Thumbs up, Charlie!*

Lined against the wall, two modern emerald green loveseats acted as bookends, accenting black-leather barrel chairs in a cozy semicircle. Above hung family photographs of Kelsey Sexton, an elegant strawberry blond matriarch with eyes green as grass.

Scenes of Ireland's verdant landscapes, castles on hills, cottages, barns, and a wishing well with two children labeled William and Sheila, Marc's siblings. Charlotte could not find a single photo of Marc among them.

The waiter Matteo offered her wine. "Can I interest you in a California Chardonnay with notes of pear and vanilla?" he announced elegantly. "Mr. Sexton's specialty of the house tonight."

"Yes, please." She lifted the goblet, feeling flushed even before the first sip.

She meandered to the side wall sporting another photo montage: men wearing vests and Kerry caps in bar scenes, couples drinking at sidewalk tables beneath a bold brass sign, Sexton Whiskey Pub, Est. 1888. The entire back wall showed off 20th-century images: The Sexton Ancestors. A rather fierce and unsmiling bunch of elders posed before rimy caverns and forests. Mustached men held rifles on hilly terrain. Gray-aproned women stood in doorways, babes in arms. Others sat beneath trees—bushy-haired hags. Horses, sheep, and dogs were in every photo. What a family, she thought, trying not to be too obvious in her inspection.

"Charlotte." Alice Eve tipped her head around. "I'm so glad you came tonight. Love your dress. The dark green becomes you."

"Thanks. I'm happy to see a familiar face. So, this is Marc's dad?" She pointed to the full portrait of Matthew Sexton occupying the wall between the double glass terrace doors.

"You might want to step back," Alice batted her lashes. "He's something, huh?"

She did have to take a step back. The patriarch sat in a high-backed chair, burly in stature but heart-crushing beautiful with a serene James Cagney-type face. His aloof radiance was jaw-dropping. Dressed in a wine-colored suit and tie, he had a head full of wavy blond hair—the same as Marc's. The spectacular oil painting was struck in angular proportions, the light and composition exquisite from a glossy blackened background. When she looked closer, she spotted baggy gray storm clouds behind his head. Odd for an interior portrait scene.

The banter grew louder as Alice got pulled away by a red-haired woman. Charlotte sipped the wine, moving her vision deeper into the portrait. The storm clouds swirled thick at the top.

Monstrous paint strokes. Inside the murky depths, she found shapes. Ragged head. Ears. Snout. Tail. A wolf figure.

Alice looped her arm into Charlotte's—"We're just about to sit down,"—and led her to a table. "I want you to meet the gang."

The gang—or, more precisely, Marc's gang—consisted of the local librarian, Martha, two volunteer firemen, the town historian, and the town clerk, Maeve, who had a smart Irish brogue and acted as the official tasting judge.

Chef Charlie reigned, a superstar, serving beef and Guinness stew in Irish crockery mugs, as well as mushroom or lamb variations. They rated the aroma, texture, taste, and presentation. Charlotte ate all three mugs with gusto.

As the guests began leaving, Alice finished off her wine. "How are things at Draakensky? Jaa managing better? She mentioned to me you were going to review the sketches today."

"She wasn't up to it after the Chief's visit."

"I hope this investigation blows over fast. For Jaa's sake. I think the only person in town who cared much about Thomas Harrogate was Jaa. Heida did, but that's history."

"Marc mentioned Heida and Thomas were pretty tight."

Alice cupped her words. "Long time affair."

"I didn't know."

"Marc didn't tell you? Well, he wouldn't. He despises gossip. Heida was fifteen years Thomas's senior. She had an attraction for younger men. Ex-lovers a-plenty. Don't you hate small-town gossip? Always appalling. I'm guilty too, indulging juicy scandals."

Matteo poured them a second Chardonnay.

"And Thomas wasn't a suspect in Heida's death? I mean, he's somewhat freaky." Charlotte kept her voice low as people exited.

"Not a suspect, but a person of interest, as they say. Apparently, Heida and Thomas had had an argument, and he took off to visit his sister in Maine the week Heida died. The Chief said Thomas had a solid alibi." Alice glanced around to see if anyone could overhear. Matteo began clearing the tables. "I think Thomas had an old girlfriend in Maine and Heida found out they were back in touch. At least that's what Jaa suspected. Oh look who's here, did I just speak of the devil?"

Chief Jimmy Cruz strolled into the dining room. "Guess I missed the tasting dinner. Everyone's gone but you two. May I join you?"

"I'm afraid you did miss it, Chief. The mushroom variation was the winner for me," Alice said. "I'm trying to go vegan."

He waved to the waiter. "Hey there, Matteo. Can I have a beer, please? Charlotte, how is Jaa after I left today?"

"Better now. Thomas's cause of death had her upset." Jimmy's dark blue uniform created an intimidating refinement. The badges. The stars on his shoulders. Dark hero-type, brimming with confidence. "Did Jaa know about the owl you found on Thomas's body? Sounded as if she did."

"She suspected as much. Jaa's a sharpie."

Alice slipped on her shoulder bag. "I've got to run. I'll tell Marc on my way out he missed a triumph. Five stars from Maeve! See ya, Jimmy."

Matteo appeared with a mug and beer for the Chief. "Marc didn't want you to miss the stew." He turned to Charlotte. "Marc says he's busy at the bar tonight but please stop by before you leave."

That got a teasing grin from Jimmy.

Oh sure, Charlotte thought. Marc didn't call Monday, Tuesday, or yesterday. Not that she was waiting or wondering. Not much. "Thank you, Matteo."

Jimmy dug into the stew. "You okay, Charlotte? After that owl came barreling into your car on Sunday?"

"Marc told you?"

"Of course he did. We notified Wildlife Control. Marc said you got a photo? May I see?"

She pulled out her cell phone to show him.

"Christ almighty. I didn't believe Marc when he told me the bird flipped its head. That's a 270-degree turn. Will you email it to me?"

"Sure. Isn't it odd for owls to be out during the day?"

"Most owls are nocturnal. But Northern Hawk owls hunt daytime."

Surprised, Charlotte sat forward in her chair. "You think that owl was hunting when he flew at my car window?"

He took another bite of stew, chewing slowly. "They hunt all the time. What else do owls do? Besides sitting on dead bodies."

"Bodies? You mean sitting on Thomas's body?"

"I mean on Harrogate's and Heida Mead's body. We found that same owl perched on Heida's corpse. That's why Jaa asked me."

"You're kidding."

"I'm thinking this owl is a damn corpse-bird."

"What is that?"

He checked his watch. "I need to get home. Rosie's waiting. Ask Marc. He can tell you all about corpse-birds. And it's quite a story." Jimmy stood up. "If you see that same owl again, call Wildlife Control. He handed her a card from his pocket.

Charlotte made her way to the bar and found a vacant stool. Marc hustled cocktail trays and chatted with two men at the far end; he didn't notice her immediately. Behind her, four cocktail tables were unoccupied except for one person sitting alone beneath the single bell-shaped hanging lamp near the front door. A man in an overcoat, head down, reading a menu.

The same man in the cemetery. Trying not to stare from her awkward position facing the bar, she swiveled to keep her peripheral vision on him. No, he wasn't reading the menu. He read the same green book. Long fingers. Thick dark hair. Rounded shoulders. No drink. No cocktail napkin. The waiters buzzed between the dining room tables and bar side. The man didn't seem to mind that the wait staff ignored him.

He sat there, patches of darkness creeping around him. Solitary. Coffined inside a cloud—that's how she would sketch this man. Feeling brave, she considered going to his table to offer a friendly hello. Indecision holding her back, the man suddenly slipped away from the noisy crowd to the front entrance. The door swung shut.

Quickly she withdrew her sketch pad and roughed out a figure from memory. When she lifted her head, the bar had emptied to a handful. A gray-haired man took the stool two spaces down from her. Charlotte admired his sculpted face, especially the forehead and jaw. Without being too obvious, she penciled his face on her pad. The rendering gave her a decent image, but it was poorly executed in the dim lights.

Marc strode past her, threw her a wink, then beamed at the gray-haired man. "Hey there, Sir Duncan. You drinking Irish tonight?"

"I'll have the usual, Marc."

"Sexton and soda, coming up." He swerved over to her and whispered, "I love it when you sit at my bar. What can I get you?" With a touch of his hand on hers, he sent gentle tremors through her. "How about a hot, bossy cocktail?"

She cracked up. "What a tease. I could use a coffee if that's no trouble."

"You can have anything you want."

She admired Marc's black tee shirt and red sports blazer—stylish and racy. She wanted to reach out and touch his jaw, run her fingertip over those lips. She had fallen for this man already in way too short a time. Although if the Chief of Police could brag that Marc 'practically walks on water,' she had no trouble with that vote of confidence.

A few minutes later, Marc returned with Sir Duncan's drink and placed a coffee mug down before her.

"Whipped cream? Thank you." She cupped her hand over her mouth. "By the way, who is *Sir* Duncan?"

"Obscure English earl. From where I can't remember. Cornwall, maybe. We pay him a lot of attention. A bit elderly for you?" he said in a mock warning.

"Stop. Sir Duncan, huh? He might do. I play a fantasy game where I pick out a man and imagine him to be my dad. Everything you can imagine is real. Picasso said that."

"Did he? Good one. What was your dad's name?"

"Charles Knight. Aunt Loretta said he was a good man, an elderly British gentleman, but he left us, so maybe he wasn't so good. Want to know which stew I picked for the winner?"

"The lamb?"

"I did. Oh no, I'm becoming predictable."

"Listen, my apologies for not calling this week. After my meeting at the Homestead, I had to follow up with my attorney on Tuesday in Manhattan. Wednesday, I walked in here and the soda gun had exploded, flooding the bar floor. I hate not keeping my word. Let me make it up to you?"

"No need. I wasn't sitting by the phone waiting."

"I didn't think you would be," he said in the cutest way, then focused on his customers with an OK gesture to a man. "I have to refill a round of mojitos. Takes time to muddle the fresh mint. Don't leave, okay?"

Two coffees later, and after striking up a chat with Sir Duncan, Charlotte convinced the earl to let her do a quick sketch for her private notebook. The gentleman sat still for nearly twenty minutes. She gave him her card. By ten o'clock, the bar folk had thinned out. Sir Duncan left, and Charlotte slid off the stool. She gave a gesture to her wristwatch to Marc standing at the cash register.

He rushed over to her. "Don't leave." He locked his big blues on her. "I thought we could have a brandy together."

"I don't know," she said, thinking it over.

"Charlotte, I've been dreaming about you. I'm not kidding. I have news. It's so noisy here. Come back to the house with me?"

At Marc's house, Charlotte reclined on the sofa, apple brandy snifter in hand. She tucked her feet up and neatly pressed the hem of her green sweater dress around her knees.

Etta James's "At Last" swayed from the speakers in the rafters. Marc kicked off his shoes and collapsed into the cushions with her. "How did your week go?"

"I illustrated three poems," she said. "Sketched seven studies each. Day of Reckoning is tomorrow when Jaa reviews them. I'm half terrified, half excited."

"Are you pleased with them?"

"I am. I've spent time reading more about Rilke. His published letters mostly. It's helpful to know his perspectives on life. I am becoming fond of René."

"You haven't seen that owl hanging around Draakensky, have you?"

"No. Speaking of owls. Jimmy mentioned corpse-birds to me."
"Did he?"

"What does it mean?"

"Jimmy is easily spooked these days."

"He told me about the owl on Thomas and Heida's corpses. That would spook me, too. How is it you know about corpse-birds?"

"My grandmother. Jim knows the story from when we were kids." Marc paused, listening to Etta James's voice croon out tender and soulful. "I love Etta's earthy voice. Kind of serpentine. Each word she sings slides right inside me. Like she's casting her musical spell on us."

"Mm, hypnotic. You and Jimmy go way back?"

"Buddies since third grade. I was a groomsman at his wedding. He met Rosie at The Grackle. They have three boys now, under five.

Jim and Rosie are so fertile—she gets pregnant if Jim just looks at her. I drove him to get his vasectomy last year. Oh no, I shouldn't have told you that."

"I'll wipe it from my memory. What's a corpse-bird?"

He wrapped his arm around her. " 'Stormy Weather' is next. I love how Etta sings that song."

She rested her head against his chest. "Tell me about the corpse-birds. *Once upon a time . . .* "

"This is no fairy tale." He put his snifter down. "My grandparents lived in County Cork. Every summer since I turned five years old, I spent July in Ireland with them. One summer—I was ten—we heard an owl screech in a tree. I sat beneath the evergreen for hours, listening to his hoots. Next morning, my grandfather dropped dead."

"Oh, no. How horrible."

"Corpse-birds hoot warnings of death. My grandmother lived *by the signs,* so she knew."

"Did she know it was your grandfather's death?"

"Mamó never said. I remember her laying out his body with flowers. She opened every window. Screens off. Stopped all the clocks in the house. My parents came with my brother William, and Sheila was a baby. My uncles arrived and smoked pipes outside, making white puffed circles all over the yard. The family brought enough food and booze to choke an army. That's when I had my first Sexton Irish Whiskey. I'll never forget that moment, everyone with their glasses raised to me, smack in the middle. My initiation as a young man in the family."

Etta began "Stormy Weather." He tilted his head up to the speakers. "At the end of the day, Etta is perfection." When the song finished, he grabbed the remote and hit pause.

"We all sat with the body. At sundown, a small white owl flew through the window and sat on my grandfather's chest. Mamó explained the corpse-bird had come to take his spirit into eternity."

"Did that frighten you? About being taken into eternity?"

"Not at all. Mamó wasn't threatened. Everything held meaning for her. Celts are a folklore culture. We're highly spiritual and recognize the sisterhood of nature. Mamó saw the landscape alive with spirit, every tree, rock, bird, water, the sky. Mamó understood the owl as a sign that the man she loved had entered eternity, escorted by a sacred white bird."

"That's beautiful, Marc."

"Some people don't see it that way. When I came home, I told Jimmy about the corpse-bird. He freaked out. He couldn't stop asking me about it. One time, he accused Mamó of being a witch. I took a swing at him. That stopped his teasing. Jimmy Cruz was the goofiest kid in school, always razzing everybody."

"The goofiest kid becomes Chief of Police? How funny is that?"

"Yeah, well, the police academy straightened that out. Now, with what's happened on Yew Crag, he's rattled."

"You think the owl on Yew Crag was a corpse-bird?"

"Corpse-birds are known to be small, white, and female. Corpse-birds don't fly at car windows. And they certainly don't sit on rooftops. They keep to the trees where they can be protected by the tree spirits." He kissed her head. "I hoped we could view Orion tonight, but the rain clouds have him covered." He scooted up. "I want you to see this." At the bookcase, he pulled out a picture frame and sat down. "This is Mamó's house in Cork."

Charlotte admired the white stone cottage, weathered gray, with a curved dirt path and windows trimmed in red, surrounded by meadows and distant hills. "Picturesque. Gosh, how old is the house?"

"Built in the 1800s. Mamó willed it to me. Last year, I replaced the plumbing system and electrical wiring. Next is the roof. See that red door in the center?"

"I love red doors."

"I dreamt of that house last night. And Mamó standing in the doorway."

"A happy dream?"

"Very. You were walking up the path, right there."

"Me?"

"Mamó opened the red door and invited you inside."

"Are you serious? You're giving me chills. Did I go inside the house?"

He groaned. "I woke up."

For Charlotte, being swept into his life, his Mamó, even if it were only a dream, enthralled her. A grandmother—such pleasures she knew nothing about. "In the private dining room tonight, I saw all the family photos. I didn't see you up there. How come?"

"Nope. You won't find me on that wall."

Mamó's house drew her attention again. "Are you planning on living in Ireland someday?"

"I have everything I want right here. That means you, Charlotte."

Would her heart be safe with this man? So many things about him told her yes. Charlotte lifted herself up, threw her leg over him, and sat on his lap, her knees hooking around his hips, thighs open to him. Holding his face, she smothered him with kisses. She drank him in, the same way she had savored the spiced brandy, tasting every note.

Upstairs in his bed, her head butted the headboard from his hungry kisses. She recognized that all her past kisses with men were child's play. Marc's kisses were more than sexual. Each one made her feel deeply connected, their lips bonding with every breath.

His hushed words lulled her, his hands bringing her pleasures she'd not experienced with any man. Charlotte clamped her legs around him, allowing herself to be carried, swayed, and pulsed, rocking the room. This man had the power to shake walls. She wanted the hard ache inside her to throb into him so he could pound it out.

With her fingertips, she dug into his shoulder muscles as he plunged with groans, swelling and breaking. The towering merge overwhelmed her. Never had she cried out like that. His belly grew so hot it practically scorched her skin. Was there more of him to have? How deep could he go?

If Marc had split her in two, she wouldn't have minded. He gave her all he had and didn't stop until they spilled across the sheets, exhausted.

Chapter Twenty-Two

It Will Reveal Itself

Marc awoke with a jump. Something clattered outside. Did he wake Charlotte? One look told him she hadn't flicked a muscle, asleep with the sheet up to her neck. He rose quietly, grabbed jeans off the door hook, boxer shorts, clean white tee shirt, and used the downstairs shower so as not to disturb her.

In the kitchen, he brewed a pot of coffee. After pouring a cup for himself, he placed his guest mug with blue stars on the counter for Charlotte. Man oh man, she was exhilarating in bed. Just shy of wicked. When he wore the blindfold, she performed the mystery game on him like a champion—well done for a woman who hadn't played it before. She was so pretty. So pretty amazing. She released a warm kindness in everything she did to him. He loved how at the end of their lovemaking, lying on her back, she casually raised her knees, her thighs parted by a few inches, secretly calling him back to her for a luscious second round.

"Good morning."

Startled, he turned. Charlotte stood in his oversized black tee shirt hanging an inch below her backside, her brown sugar hair tossed over her shoulders. She leaned on the door frame, one bare foot resting on the other.

"Well, there she is. You feeling okay?"

She lifted her shoulders. "We may have gone overboard. I'm a little bit sore."

"Me too. More than a little bit."

"Oh, no. Was I beastly?"

"No, you weren't beastly. I didn't anticipate your . . . enduring vigor."

"Me either. I don't know what came over me last night." She twisted the tee shirt around her finger. "I normally have the usual boundaries, just as other women, you know? Maybe the apple brandy got me. Been a while since I've been with a man. And Don, well, not the most adventurous guy. Safe and straight. I once asked him to join me for a Tantric Sex session and he declined. Vehemently at the top of his lungs. He wasn't interested in a deeper connection with me. We had a very isolated relationship. That's life, right? Oh well. He was an obsessive, perfectionist workaholic. Gee, I hope you don't mind my wearing your tee shirt. I couldn't resist throwing it on. Smells of your aftershave. The way you took it off last night, pulling it over your head with one hand. I keep playing that image over in my mind. Isn't it funny how the next day after having sex, you focus on one trivial, thrilling gesture? Last night was, what's the word, a stunner. Oh, you have coffee ready? Is that mug for me?"

What a soliloquy. Did she even draw a breath? How cute. After everything they did to each other in bed, she was embarrassed now? He brought her to him, bracketing his hands on her waist. With his lips, he skimmed her cheek down to her chin. "You were thrilling last night. Like Lady Vivienne, brave and adventurous, who I've been in love with since I was sixteen years old."

"I'm not as wicked as Tennyson's Lady Vivienne."

"God help me if you were."

"You were quite generous last night. You have no problems with intimacy, do you, Marc?"

"Not with you." He leaned in for a kiss, when the front door shuddered with a loud bang, jarring them apart.

"Who's here at seven thirty? I didn't hear a car on the drive." At the window in the foyer, he got a half view of the front door entry. He scanned the parking area and turnaround circle. "No car."

Bang! The wooden door shook.

"Marc, that's not a knock."

He stretched his neck to see the outside entry steps and flagstone walk. "Nobody's there." From the living room windows, he searched the driveway. "No cars there either."

Bang!

"What is that? Marc?"

"There's no one standing on the step. Something's wrong." At the desk, he grabbed the key ring, unlocked the middle drawer, and withdrew his six-shooter revolver.

"A gun?" Charlotte yelled. "Marc, are you kidding?"

"Go in the bathroom and shut the door."

Bang! The front door's hinges rattled.

He couldn't decide if he should open the door and fire or wait to see if the banging stopped. What was he even shooting at?

Bang!

The top metal hinge split with a loud ping.

Think! The kitchen window alcove jutted out and would give him a wider angle to the front entrance. He ran to the alcove.

A huge black-and-white owl zoomed through the air, hit the door—*bang!* It surged out and flew toward the evergreen beyond the stone wall. There it flipped itself, a swift recoil into headfirst position, and zoomed back to the door.

Bang!

Stunned, he watched the owl fly door-to-tree, flip, fly tree-to-door, wings to the sky, speeding through the air, a pendulum in a hypnotic, continuous rhythm.

"Marc!" Charlotte cried out. "Marc, where are you?"

The cold metal revolver in his hand refocused him. If he exited out the kitchen door, he could sneak around the side and shoot as it zoomed into the door.

"Marc!"

"Stay there. It's a bird. I've got this." Checking the revolver, he cocked the hammer.

Bang! The foyer side window pane cracked into splinters.

The bird is aiming at the window now? "Don't you dare, you son-of-a-bitch."

He figured he only had seconds before the bird might come crashing through the window. Could he scare it off or would he have to kill it? Marc stepped back several feet, aligned himself with the side window, and with both arms extended, hands steady, he aimed the revolver. Counting the seconds, keeping his aim fixed, he flexed his legs for strength. The bird rocketed straight at him.

With a high screech that jolted Marc's nerves, the owl burst through the window.

Glass shards exploded. He fired once. Twice. Three times. The bird spun out into a blur.

Feathers shook the air.

Marc surveyed the floor and walls. The silence in the house made him whip around. The living room, kitchen, all perfectly still. Where was that damn bird? Gun in hand and cocked to fire again, he kicked over a magazine basket in the foyer. Empty. In the living room, he smacked a rolled newspaper across the sofa, pillows, bookcases, and tables.

"Where are you?" He moved through the foyer, glass crunching under his shoes, to check the kitchen. Nothing appeared disturbed, but he whacked the tables and counters and cabinets.

He pulled out his cell phone and tapped a contact. "Jimmy? It's Marc. I've got an emergency. I need you at my house. It's that crazy owl! It's been flying into the front door. He burst through the window. Hurry."

Back in the foyer, he examined the floor. The bird should be dead on the tiles. But there wasn't a speck of blood anywhere in sight.

Charlotte opened the bathroom door and peeked around the edge. "Did you say an owl? Did you kill it? Marc?"

"I missed."

She came out of the bathroom, avoiding the broken glass.

"Stay there. I'll get your shoes upstairs."

A walk through the upstairs three bedrooms, checking under the beds, reassured him. "He's probably outside," Marc said, pounding down the steps with her the green sweater dress and shoes. "Maybe I grazed him and he flew back out the window."

"I was terrified for you. How can an owl keep thrusting at the door and not get injured or killed?"

"I fired three times. Can't figure how I missed at such close range. He's in the pine tree, that son-of-a-bitch."

"You're not going out there, are you?"

"I'll wait for Jim to arrive. You okay?"

"Me, the coward? Hiding in the bathroom? Why wouldn't I be?"

Charlotte quickly dressed as Marc moved to the broken window, eyes searching for the owl in the sky. Within minutes, a car came screeching to a halt on the gravel drive. Jimmy and another officer jumped out and walked the driveway, inspecting the scene. "It crashed through your window?" he yelled through the broken glass. "Cracked the hell out of your wooden door. Better not open it with the broken hinges. You kill it?"

"Missed."

"Where is it?"

"In the evergreen by the drive. Wait, I'll come out. We'll use the kitchen door."

Jim and the officer walked to the pine trees, weapons drawn.

Marc darted out with Charlotte behind him. "See the branches shaking? That's him." Charlotte stood close, breathing down his neck. "It's okay. Jim knows how to handle this. Better than I did."

They searched the tree from all sides and positioned themselves below the pine boughs. The two officers circled the tree again, guns ready. "Can't get a target point, Marc. The tree height alone creates an obstacle. If the owl is up there, he's camouflaged himself. We could fire and he'll probably take off."

"Marc," Charlotte tugged his arm. "By the shed. Look."

Sky Wolf stood about thirty yards away. White as a lamb.

"Whoa." Jimmy stepped forward and recalculated his aim on the wolf.

"Don't shoot," Marc said. "She runs through here. She's not a threat."

"That wolf charges, Marc, we fire."

Sky Wolf raised her nose and howled a long note to the sky. High and rolling. A gusty commotion broke from the pine tree. The owl zoomed up. Jimmy fired three shots. The officer fired two.

Marc watched the bird jet across the blue expanse, haughty wings tipping in the sunlight. When he looked back to the shed, Sky Wolf galloped into the woods.

"Does she run with a pack?" Jimmy asked.

"Not sure."

Jimmy stepped up to the front entrance and skimmed his hand over the cracks. "Powerful force, this bird. Dive bombing, for sure. Owls are known to fly over forty miles per hour. How many times did he hit the door?"

"I lost count. Nine, maybe ten times before he came through the window. What did it want here?"

The other officer stepped up. "Maybe blazing a track?"

"Track into the house?" Jim asked. "What's this?" Loose petals and stems littered the doorway. He bent down and retrieved dead flowers.

Charlotte gathered up a few stems. "Tulips. Purple and red petals." The color drained from her cheeks. "Jaa's tulips?"

"Not the tulips Jaa gave to Harrogate?" Jimmy said. "Marc, are these yours?"

"No. They weren't here when we came in last night. We would have seen them."

"We?" Jimmy looked at them. "Oh. Sorry. Didn't mean to pry."

"Jim, what do you think happened here?"

"The obvious. This owl has got Charlotte's scent. He's tracking you, Charlotte. Spotted you on Draakensky, pursued you at The Grackle, and now the bird has hunted you down at Marc's house. Three's a winner."

She flinched. "It's not hunting me." Backing away, she shook her head. "Don't say that. What a stupid bird. Why would it be hunting me?" She tossed the tulip stems back on the doorstep.

Jimmy's phone buzzed. "I've got a situation at the station house. There's nothing more we can do here. Board up the window. I'll speak to you later, Marc." In a second the police car sped down the drive.

"Charlotte, do you want to come inside and—?"

"Thank you. No. I need to get back to Draakensky. I have that meeting with Jaa." She scanned the evergreen. "I need to leave."

Marc watched her fumble her keys, slipping into the car seat hurriedly, struggling to latch the seatbelt. With clenched fists on the steering wheel, she gave him an anxious glance and pulled out.

He remained on the driveway, automatically lifting his sight up. Sun brightened the treetops. Winged beauties floated their distant birdsong across the lawn. The woodsy landscape of oaks and pine, meadow and pond, reflected his summers living in the enchanted woods in Ireland with Mamó. When he turned back to enter the house, Sky Wolf sat on the front doorstep, paws neatly aligned, hot amber eyes straight on him. Out of habit, his hand went to the pendant at his throat.

Chapter Twenty-Three

What Lies Ahead

Jaa read the newspaper's front page column while her breakfast remained half-eaten on the kitchen table. She couldn't take another bite. Charlotte had rushed in, all flustered, and now stood at the counter, propping up the sketches against the cookbooks, chattering nonstop about the editor's March 15 deadline for the first fifteen sketches, and being woefully behind schedule, and they must move on to the next poem immediately, and how they would never catch up to the sixty images by June.

"For these studies on 'The Panther,' " Charlotte said, her voice raspy, "I focused on the behind-the-bars theme in the text. The cat's pacing, his grief, the loss of power. Maybe the image should be larger? I've been wrestling with size for this sketch. I almost want the image to leap off the page. What do you think, Jaa?"

Jaa tore her attention from the news. "Behind-the-bars theme?" she repeated, her headache surfacing. She didn't want to disappoint Charlotte again with criticism about her work. The girl did have a genius for form—probably easiest to trust it for now. "I really can't think about it, Charlotte. You know, Heida had some notes on 'The Panther.' And on 'Evening in Skane' too. She kept her notes in a box. I had forgotten all about them. My mind's a sieve."

Charlotte frowned.

"I'm not suggesting you follow Heida's plans. But it might give you insights. On the bookcase in the living room is Heida's box. Painted with blue irises on the top."

Charlotte retrieved the box and placed it on the table.

"Heida wrote her notes on picture postcards and stashed them wherever handy. Terribly unorganized, she was. She might have a note about size for 'The Panther.' You make a valid point. I can't even remember what's in that silly box."

"I'll take a look."

"And Charlotte, maybe it's best you leave these sketches here for today?"

"Leave them? Why?"

Jaa tapped the newspaper. "I'll see them later. I'm so sidetracked today. Front page report on Thomas's case. Have you seen this headline? 'Harrogate's Death Caused by Blunt Force.' They say repeated violent hits to the abdomen with a hard object, possibly a bat or fist killed Thomas."

Charlotte sat down at the table and read the article. "Blunt force."

"The Chief didn't tell us that yesterday, did he? Did I misunderstand?"

"Jimmy only told us about the autopsy results. Not the cause of the shock to the body."

Jaa fought back tears. "This makes me sick. The way Thomas's life ended, all caged up on that river rock. I know he was an angry, scrappy man, but beneath I saw a damaged soul struggling through every day."

A dark cloud beat down outside the kitchen sink window—rain on the way. She wanted a thunderstorm to strike right at that moment. "You know, Charlotte, I keep recalling that week in October when Heida died. Poor Thomas. He had had a terrible fight with Heida. What a fury went on between them. I could hear them shouting at each other in the cottage. Heida often had rages, but this time she was her worst ever, screaming she had never loved him, calling him every name in the book. Heida fired him that day, you know."

"She did?"

"That's why he went to his sister in Portland. Heida threw him out. She confiscated his keys to the cabin. All these years, Thomas served us well. I told Heida the man needed understanding, not hostility. She shouldn't have fired him." The kitchen window darkened. She closed her eyes picturing herself stepping inside a storm, becoming the thunder, lightning, and pounding rain.

Jaa opened her eyes, Charlotte before her like a painting. She noticed the girl's pale cheeks, smudged eye makeup, and untidy hair. Was she wearing the same green dress as yesterday?

"This is not my business, Charlotte. You're a grown woman. But I have to say, you seem frazzled. And you're wearing the same green dress as yesterday."

Charlotte flushed.

"What's happened?"

"I am frazzled." Charlotte withdrew her phone. "Jaa, what do you know about this?"

A whitish, brown-and-black owl, head inverted, glared at her. "Ohh! Dear God. Where did you get this?"

"That owl hit my car windshield on Sunday. That bird tracked me to The Grackle parking lot. At least that's what Jimmy Cruz thinks. And this morning, it came barreling into Marc's front door, battering the door over and over, nearly off the hinges. And when it couldn't break the door down, it came crashing through the window."

Jaa felt heat rising to her cheeks. She hoped Charlotte wouldn't notice. "How awful. Were you there?"

"Yes," she said meekly. "Marc tried to shoot it."

Jaa gasped. "Did the bird get away?"

"It did. Jimmy thinks the owl tracked me to Marc's house. He says it has my scent. Can owls do that, pick up human scent?"

"I suspect it's more a natural radar than a sense of smell."

"What does a stupid owl want with me?"

Jaa licked her lips, needing water. "Owls are largely air, you know."

"Is that true?" she squinted. "But why was its head flipped?"

"Owls are messengers and exhibit warnings. They invite us to use our feminine wisdom. Purple wind is the color for wisdom. Red wind for power. Most people don't see wind as color. But I do." Jaa pointed to the red and purple blurry streaks around the owl's head in the photo. "See?"

"They're so faint. Almost invisible."

"Charlotte, it's so hot in here. Would you open the door?"

Charlotte flapped the Dutch door's upper half open and took the chair opposite Jaa. Arms crossed over her chest, jaw clenched, looking again at the photo, she clucked her tongue. "Red and purple wind? Same colors as the tulips."

A cry gathered in Jaa's throat. She sipped the cold coffee.

"Sisterhood is powerful. Even in battle, sisters protect each other. One is the sword. The other, the shield."

"And which one were you, Jaa?"

The shield, but Jaa said nothing, thinking only of what magnificent sisters they had been together, exchanging muses in their work and sharing loyalties. Jaa was with Heida long before her lovers, long before her husband, long before her career. No one understood Heida's thread of madness. Only a sister could know. If anyone trespassed on her, Jaa felt the pain too. But now, to be left with this horrible burden . . .

"Jaa?" Charlotte snapped.

"Charlotte, we both had the same possibilities, Heida and me." She fought off tears. "How many times men would tell me, 'Oh Jaa, you have the most beautiful and intelligent sister.' But I was the clever one with the vision. We were the same; we were opposites, both passing through identical rooms in our house. The paths we chose, though, were not the same. Rilke said it perfectly in his poem 'Sisters.' In the end, it's her blood that dwells in my blood."

A clean breeze shot through the Dutch door. Charlotte walked to the sink and drank a glass of water. "Jaa, if owls are largely air, then what happened at Marc's house today was what? Was that your wind magick?"

"Not for a minute. Do you honestly think I would hurt you or Marc? He's been like a son to me in a hundred ways. Listen to me, Charlotte. You need to go back to the cottage. We *are* woefully behind schedule for the book. Jung May said they have laid out all the text and all they have to do is drop in the illustrations when ready. Yes, 'The Panther' image should leap off the page. The viewer needs to feel the massive world outside the panther's barred confinement."

She gathered the sketches into a stack and thrust them into Charlotte's hands. "And don't you come back here searching for me. I am going to the attic. I hear the trees beating the wind. A storm is brewing."

Chapter Twenty-Four

Bewitchments

Blood dwells in blood. What dark splendors of sisterhood. Jaa and Heida. *Little Women*, the March sisters, they were not. Move on, Charlotte told herself. Running away to work would serve. The rest of the day, she labored under the illustrations for the March 15 deadline. Charlotte whipped off sketch after sketch. She enlarged "The Panther" image, refined "Evening in Skane," and completed two more poems, three studies each. The quiet in the cottage proved a productive advantage. "Child in Red" and "Let This Darkness Be a Bell Tower" were next on the list and then, "The Dark Hours of My Being."

If she completed two more illustrations by midnight, all would be well. She already had a concept for "Child in Red." Unable to eat a crumb all day, she managed on stale coffee. A storm brewed up with soaking rain, daylight vanishing at 5:45. On the carpet, a last patch of daylight streamed on Heida's blue iris box.

Ignoring it, she checked her phone and realized the battery had run out. She plugged it in and rummaged through the fridge for bread and cheese, deciding a glass of wine would hit the spot. With half a glass, she set the bottle on the dining table and eased into the wingback chair.

Her vision floated to the bright blue irises, hijacking her attention. A pretty loopy key hung on a silver ribbon. Giving in, she sat crossed-legged on the floor and jimmied the stubborn key in the box until it clicked open. The hinges squeaked as she lifted the lid.

She flipped through old birthday and Christmas cards and an *Alice in Wonderland* card deck. French coins and bills, a photo envelope—dogs, cats, a wolf behind a fence, and several scenes of Heida posing with award plaques. A tiny ragdoll with button eyes. Ribbons tied in knots she wanted to unravel.

Crushed on the side, she found a glittery decoration. An owl mask, bejeweled with blue and green rhinestones trimmed in beautiful iridescent feathers. The owl ears pointed up in devilish branches with a horn-like beak for a nose. No, she would not slip it over her face, as tempting as that was.

Loose postcards had been jammed into the back: Swiss Alps, Italian gardens, English landscapes. On the backsides, Heida had scribbled notes in her flowery handwriting. Mostly Rilke's most famous quotations. *I am too alone in this world*, was one Charlotte had not seen. *I want to be with those who know secret things.*

No notes on "The Panther" or any other useful comments. One Paris postcard got her attention: *Child in Red. Limerick, iambic trimeter, maybe use color for this one poem?*

Color? The art editor at Sterling had insisted all illustrations be black and white. Yet, maybe Heida had a point. A splash of red might heighten the visual drama for contrast. She placed the postcard on the end table.

As she put the items back, her thumb snagged against a sharp point. A nail had popped from the warped wood, exposing a gap. Inside the gap, a white stick protruded. A false bottom? Of course, vintage boxes often had secret compartments. With her fingernail, she shimmied the damaged wood aside and found the bottom layer.

Netted dried violets, an envelope filled with ashes, Tarot cards, lace gloves, a pinecone, colored candles, and crystals. And a letter on floral stationery in Heida's handwriting.

My Darling, RMR.

She scanned the text to the end where Heida had signed in big scrolling letters, *Evermore yours, Heida.* A black waxed seal was embossed in the right-hand corner.

Her cell phone rang: ALICE EVE.

"Hi Alice."

"Charlotte, I spoke to Jaa. What happened at Marc's house? Are you okay?"

"She tells you everything, doesn't she? I'm fine. You're sweet to ask. I can't explain that crazy owl and frankly don't want to at this point. I've been working on the Rilke sketches all day. Finally, I have a stride going."

"Work is such a healer, isn't it?"

"At the moment, you'll never guess, I'm going through Heida's wooden box. The one with the painted irises? Do you know it?"

"I've seen it on Jaa's bookshelf."

"You wouldn't believe what I found. A love letter to Rilke. She writes about their rendezvous under the stars. Listen to this: 'When I look at the world through your words, it is a better place. To live everything. To live the questions. Our love can be two solitudes that meet. Will you let the beauty and the terror happen to us? Will you come to me? Tell me your secrets. I will meet you in the darkness, inside the hollows beneath the starry trees. Awaken at my summons.'"

Alice hooted. "Heida *would* fall in love with a dead poet. Is there a date on it?"

Charlotte skimmed front and back. "No date."

"Sounds juicy. Oh, I've got another call. Must be Jaa calling me back. Stop by the shop. And bring the letter. I'm dying for more."

Feeling relaxed, she sipped more wine while sorting through the bottom layer. A white velvet pouch looked intriguing. Inside, a black-and-white photograph, deteriorated with age marks, showed a well-dressed gentleman walking on a grassy path. The man had dark hair, in a single-button suit, tie and vest, with hands shy behind his back. Even the feet were close together in narrow light-colored shoes. On the back, she read the copyright stamp attached:

RAINER MARIA RILKE, GERMAN POET ENJOYING A COUNTRY WALK. DATE: 1875 – 1926 PROPERTY OF THE MARTHA JEAN PRIVATE COLLECTION, ALBANY, NEW YORK. COPYRIGHT 1999. SALES STRICTLY PROHIBITED UNDER PENALTY OF LAW. ABSOLUTELY NO DISTRIBUTION TO RESELLERS.

An original Rilke photo must be worth considerable money if authentic. Why hide such a valuable piece of art in this rickety old box? Charlotte slipped it back into the velvet pouch.

Before she returned it to the secret compartment, she noticed another photograph at the bottom, a nine-by-ten size. A blond guy leaning on a bar top with a Sexton Irish Whiskey bottle in the foreground. "Marc?" Not until she put the picture under the light did she see a lipstick kiss smudged on the corner above Marc's head. Pink as cotton-candy lips. On instinct, she dove back into the box and discovered folded stationery stuck in the corner. When she unfolded the letter, ashes spilled out.

My Darling Marc, I've made some wrong choices in my life, but I'm thrilled I've chosen you. And that you have chosen me. My rescuer! When you looked at me in your office, I felt so beautiful. Our kiss is still warm on my lips. Your arms around me like a king's embrace. Let me be your Aurora, your Sleeping Beauty. Let me laugh with you and cry with you. That touch of gray at your temples makes me want to press my lips there and feel your pulse. Come to my sleigh bed. Awaken me. Our destiny is sealed by the power of the crescent moon. Ever yours, Heida.

A wax seal shaped in a black crescent moon embellished her signature. Had Marc had an affair with Heida? Had he slept with her in the sleigh bed upstairs? Charlotte leaned back and sipped her wine.

Marc's former relationships were none of her business, especially a dead one. Did it matter now if he did have an affair with her? Maybe best not to know—choose neutral gray, Payne's Gray, on the palette. Or, maybe just ask him? Pitch Black, and know for certain.

She felt confident her relationship with Marc had a solid foundation. His gentle power and charming honesty. Skilled in bed, for sure, he possessed amazing knowledge about a woman's anatomy. How his fingertips curled across her thighs, finding the secret crevices, made her feel worshipped. She genuinely knew the thrill of being sexually alive with this man. The walls were falling.

She scooped up the contents, dumped them into the box, and set the bejeweled mask on top, then tucked the two letters and Marc's photo into a folder on the end table.

Torrential rain battered Draakensky. Thunder rolled. With Bach's *Italian Concerto* playing on her phone, and another wine, only half filled, she went back to work. Her imagination blew with the thunderbolts, reading the poems, forming thoughts and images, and drafting the wildest illustrations. Would Jaa appreciate such creative brio? Would Sterling Publishing approve?

The door knocker banged furiously. She bolted up. Thoughts of the zooming owl flashed. For an instant, she didn't move a muscle.

"Charlotte!" Marc's voice broke through. "Charlotte, are you there?"

She opened the door.

Standing beneath the roof's overhang, Marc huddled in a black raincoat, panic on his face. "I've been calling you all day."

"You have?"

He shook off and stepped inside. "Why didn't you answer my texts?"

"I've been working. My phone went dead."

Chest heaving, breath in spurts, he made a frown.

"Why are you here, Marc?"

"Why am I here?" His tone incredulous. "After what happened this morning? I need to know you're all right. When you didn't reply to my calls or my texts, I gave up and drove here." He waited for her to respond. "Aren't you going to ask me in?"

"Oh. Sorry. Come in. Nasty night to be out."

"Sure as hell is." He scanned the room littered with her charcoal pots and pencils, chalk dust and dirty cloths strewn across the floor. The sketches pinned on the wall grabbed his attention. "Look at that. Those are exciting images. I like the movement in that one." He pointed. "First-rate, Charlotte."

"I did have a productive day. And I've got another three or four hours' work ahead," she added as he slipped off the raincoat.

He hung it on the coat stand. "How about I make us a pot of coffee and then I'll take off? Yes?"

"I don't know. I'm working on 'Child in Red' and I don't want to lose the momentum. I've got a mountain of work."

"I come out here during a wicked storm to make sure you're safe and—"

"Sorry, sorry. I'm preoccupied. Coffee break will do nicely."

He popped a smile, and an image of Heida's hot pink lips on his lips kicked her in the belly.

In the kitchen, he made clinking sounds while she watched rain flood the garden.

"I've got the dates for the Sunday afternoon teas," he called out. "We start the first Sunday in April. Chef Charlie will call you for the supply list. You excited?"

"I am. Sounds good," she answered.

He had no trouble finding his way around the kitchen. He pulled cups from the first cabinet, found the coffee grounds on the pantry top shelf. He knew the silverware drawer on first try.

They sat on the sofa together, cups in hand. Marc savored the coffee, the same way he had savored her in bed. If he had slept with Heida upstairs in her sleigh bed, did he play the blindfold mystery with her too? Did he give Heida the power over him as he had given the power to Charlotte? Did he drive his rocking into Heida until she moaned with pleasure? *In the same sleigh bed I'm going to sleep in tonight? How can I lay my head on the same pillows he kissed Heida on?*

Full of doubt biting like a mosquito, she set her cup on the end table.

"You've got charcoal on your chin," he said, wiping it with his thumb. "Oops. I smudged it." He pulled his handkerchief from his pants pocket and wiped her cheek, playfully dabbed her nose, and went in for a kiss.

On reflex, she gave him her cheek.

"What, no kiss? Are you mad at me? Did I do something?"

The question sat in her hands, a burning piece of wood. She had to know. From the folder, she pulled out the photo. "This is you, right?"

One quick look was all he needed.

"That pink lipstick kiss is Heida's," she said.

"Where did you get this?"

"Found it here in the house."

"What, you just stumbled across it?"

"Not exactly. Heida hid it in a secret compartment inside a box."

"I'll bet she did. You know why? Because this photograph hung on the wall in my bar. She must have swiped it. How lame am I? I didn't even notice it gone."

"Were you having an affair with Heida?" she said in a soft tone.

He burst a sarcastic half laugh, then stopped short.

"Did you sleep with her in her sleigh bed upstairs?"

"Are you kidding me? This is a dopey lipstick kiss. An affair? She's my mother's age. I'm thirty-nine. What kind of man do you take me for?"

She didn't answer.

"You think because Heida kissed my picture that I slept with her? That's quite a leap you're taking, Charlotte."

"Is it?" With a flip of the folder, she presented Heida's love letter.

He snatched it. Read it slowly, taking forever to lift his head.

She struggled to decide if his expression signaled guilt or fear—for sure, it wasn't a surprise. The letter fell from his fingers.

"She certainly did make wrong choices in her life," he said in a surrendering tone. "I don't know what this letter is."

"I'm sorry I asked you. Not my business, I know. It's just that I'm so," Charlotte struggled to find a polite word, "uncomfortable, disturbed even, knowing you and Heida were—"

"I didn't." He jumped to his feet. "I did not sleep with Heida Mead."

"Marc." She wanted to phrase this as respectfully as she could. "This letter makes it appear that you were involved with Heida. You're telling me you know nothing about Heida's sleigh bed?"

"Never. Never saw it. Never was in it. I never went up those stairs. I've never even seen this letter. Clearly, if you found it here, she didn't send it."

"But you knew the content. I saw the recognition on your face."

He let out a growl and paced to the opposite side of the room. "Damn Heida," he said. "Flaming bitch."

She scooped up the letter. " 'Thrilled that you have chosen me . . . Sleeping Beauty, Aurora—' "

"Please don't read it aloud. Heida is in fantasy land in that letter. She's playing Aurora. She's delusional."

"Okay, maybe she is over the edge. But is 'Our kiss is still warm on my lips' one of her delusions?"

His pacing halted.

Thunder might have struck on the word kiss. But it didn't. She'd have to create her own thunder. "Did you kiss her in your office? Did you break your rule, Marc, no kissing on the job?"

He didn't jump into a denial. "You did kiss her?" A thunderclap broke the sky. "Was her kiss brave? Adventurous?"

"Stop it."

"So you did kiss her in your office. And it led to what, nothing?"

He withdrew to the bow window, his hand jiggling coins in his pocket. He pulled a chair out at the dining table. "Will you come sit with me?"

Did she honestly want to hear this? Reluctantly, she sat opposite him.

"On a Thursday night in October, Heida sat at my bar. She had brought Halloween gifts. Black crescent-shaped moon candles on tall brass stands. Very dramatic on the bar top. I didn't recognize the candle scent. Strong as hell, though. Heida insisted I turn off the Bills-Ravens football game and show Kubrick's *The Shining*. Everybody agreed, so I streamed it in. Typical, she had a way of manipulating people to her opinion."

"Delightful woman," Charlotte couldn't resist saying.

"She nursed two glasses of wine the whole night. Unusual for her. I noticed she acted off—low-keyed, staring into her drink, whispering to herself. Not at all the gregarious and reliable boozer, Heida Mead, mingling with everyone.

"Anyway, Jackson closed up, locked the front and back doors and left. I had a register that didn't balance out. Missing two hundred dollars, so I stayed to recount the cash and receipts. The office door stood open. Suddenly, Heida appears, poised in the doorframe like some cliché film star, haughty as all hell, dressed in black silk with enough cleavage to kill a battalion. I knew instantly, she was trouble."

"How did she get in if the doors were locked?"

"I suspect she hid in the restroom. Jackson sometimes forgets to check the stalls.

"Who made the first move?"

"She did." His tone was indignant. "This was her playbook. She threw herself at me. I stumbled and fell into the file cabinet. What a humiliation."

"What were you thinking?"

"Shocked. Panicked even." He lifted the wine bottle. "This your glass? Drinking alone?"

"Why, would your Dionysus disapprove?"

"I doubt he cares. You drink while you're working?"

"On occasion. Red wine can turn the imagination more vivid. When did the kiss happen?"

He poured himself half a glass. "After I pleaded with her to get out. After I gave her all the reasons why she needed to stop." He gulped the wine. "She cooed and grinned and mentioned all those things that were in the letter, the sleigh bed, Aurora, and more that I don't have the courage to repeat. Before I knew it, she had maneuvered me against the wall. I pushed her away, but she wouldn't give up."

She had to ask. Pitch Black be damned. "Did you kiss her back?"

He bit the inside of his cheek. She could see the pucker near his jaw. "Heida was unstoppable. The only way to get her off me was by force, and I didn't want to hurt her. Yes . . . regrettably, I kissed her back. This was not one of my better moments. I broke it off quickly. I hated it."

"You hated kissing a beautiful, salacious woman? Why don't you admit you enjoyed kissing Heida and wanted to sleep with her?"

"Charlotte," he said, slumping back into the chair, "you're killing me here." He glanced at the carpet, the window, back to her. "Because I don't want to desire a sixty-nine-year-old woman. It's inappropriate. Undignified. That is not who I am."

"You weren't falling for her?"

"Heida was a friend, an intelligent conversationalist, a loyal customer, a perceptive woman I admired. But never were we lovers." He leaned forward. "Don't think less of me, please. In that moment, there was no abandoning the power of her kiss. To this day, I'm still kicking myself for it. I wish I had found another way to stop the whole thing."

"Did you stop it?"

"Yes. When I broke away, she flared like some banshee. I had to haul her to the parking lot and strong-arm her into her car. She threatened to tell everyone at the bar that I had roughed her up. That pissed me off. I told her she wasn't welcome at The Grackle. That sent her into a tailspin. She threatened to kill me. Her drama would win awards."

"You didn't rough her up."

"Of course not. I held her by her coat sleeves the whole time."

"If she was so angry with you for refusing her, why did she write this love letter to you? And why didn't she mail it?"

"No idea. The next day when I tossed out the candles, I read the label on the bottom. Aphrodisiacs East. Black Horse scent, whatever that is. I was so stupid. I should have known."

"Aphrodisiac candles? Directed at you?"

"Well, who else was standing at the bar all night long, inhaling those fumes?"

"Did you find the missing two hundred dollars?"

"I did. No miscount. Heida threw the cash at me, out her car window before she pulled away."

"Are you serious?"

"How she managed to snatch two hundred in cash from my register completely baffles me."

"Did she show up at the bar again?"

His face dropped. "That night was the last time I saw Heida. Five days later, Jimmy found her dead on Yew Crag, trapped in timbers and mud."

Charlotte couldn't think of a single word to say. Several minutes passed. He twirled the wineglass, watching the rain, then splashed more wine into his glass. This time she joined him.

"I'm sorry, Charlotte, that you had to find out this way. Heida slept with a lot of men. I am proud to say my name didn't make her V list. Woe to the man who did fall for Heida Mead."

"V list?"

"She had a Victory list of all her lovers. Jaa called the list *Mephistophelian*."

Charlotte burst out, "Mephistopheles?" She could barely pronounce the name through her laughter. "After the devil in *Faust*?"

"First time I ever heard Jaa utter a negative word about her sister. But Jaa had had a few that night." He paused and gave her one of his unfathomable stares. "I guess I should leave, so you can get back to your work." He slipped into his raincoat. "Are we leaving this in a weird place between you and me?"

She looked deep into his eyes; blue, bluer, bluest. Maybe it *was* only one coerced kiss and nothing more. She would sense it if he were lying.

"May I at least kiss you goodnight?" He put his palm up for her to take.

She let him embrace her, his powerful arms sheltering her completely. With slow kisses in circles on her cheeks, he made tiny smacking sounds before he captured her lips. She swelled with a rush only Marc could invoke. She belonged to him no matter what. She even belonged to his mystery. He was the mystery.

"You're a magnet," he said. "How am I going to spend the next twenty-four hours away from you?" He clung to her. Then he opened the door and exited, without a look back.

Waiting for his car motor to ignite, which seemed to take a long time, she had the oddest thought he hadn't rushed through the rain to the carport. Was he standing out there like some lost soul? She pressed her ear to the door, and after several minutes, his engine started and hummed down the drive.

Back to the easel, feeling completely energized, Charlotte

worked on "Child in Red." She consulted *Werner's Nomenclature of Colours* to sharpen her eye for the most exciting red tone—scarlet, vermillion, lake red? She chose Venetian Red and sketched over four hours without stopping. Satisfied the illustration benefited from the color red, adding a secret presence into the meaning, she stood up and yawned.

A bright ringing echoed over her head. Like glass shattering outside on the flagstone path. Chimes? Maybe the light rain tapping the metal roof gutters? She glanced out.

At the bow window, a man stood watching.

Square shoulders. Face obscured in black recesses. Overcoat. Brimmed hat. The man from the cemetery.

A sizzling sound waved. *SSSSorrow?* Or, *sssongs?* With her heart booming, she dashed to the window. He stumbled down the drive toward the river path, vanishing into the night.

She threw open the door, searching as far as the floodlights permitted. The lights bathed the garden in a glow. The glass-breaking echoes faded away.

Near the shrubs, beneath the bow window, she found muddy shoe prints.

Chapter Twenty-Five
The Man Watching

Sunday morning, Chief Jimmy Cruz sat down at the table in the cottage. Jaa sat next to him, a frightened expression on her face.

"Charlotte," Jimmy said, "why didn't you call me last night about this? I needed to see these shoe prints fresh in the soil. These might match the prints we found on Yew Crag at the crime scene, but there's no way to be certain from this photo you took. Too blurry, and now after the rain, the prints are destroyed. I'll see what Forensics thinks."

"It didn't seem urgent last night, Charlotte answered. "I got up this morning and thought you should at least know. The man took off quickly."

"You had a prowler at your window after midnight, and you didn't think it was urgent? We've had two murders right here on Yew Crag. What if this guy came back and broke in," he said, using an admonishing tone.

"I understand your concern. I didn't feel threatened by him, Jim."

"You didn't?"

"He's a strange fellow. Sad. Lonely. But harmless, I think. "

"You can't be serious, Charlotte."

"I am serious. I want to ask him to sit for me so I can do a portrait."

"Do not do that."

"Here." She pulled out her sketch pad. "I drew this rough sketch from memory. Not very detailed, though."

Jimmy took the sketch pad and showed it to Jaa. "Have you seen this man skulking around Draakensky?"

Jaa took a quick look. "No. This is so frightening. Someone on Draakensky at midnight? Our doors are always locked, Chief."

"You drew this today?" he asked, taking a photo on his phone.

"No. When I saw him at The Grackle on Thursday night."

"What, you know this guy?"

"I've seen him around. In the village cemetery. I think he followed me to the bookshop. Scully has seen him on the benches there."

"He was at The Grackle? Did you speak to him?"

"No."

"Was he with anyone?"

"He sat alone at a bar table."

"Did he eat anything?"

"He was reading a book."

"Who goes to a bar and reads a book? He's trying to show you he's harmless. Build your trust. Don't believe it. What time was this?"

"After we left the taste testing dinner, maybe nine o'clock."

"You've got yourself a stalker, Charlotte." He scribbled in his notebook, then punched into his phone. "I'll check with Marc and Scully, and have an officer search Draakensky. Maybe we'll get lucky and find more prints. I'll have a patrol car cruise up the driveway tonight." He slapped his notebook into his pocket. "Listen, this stalker is playing with you, building your attention and familiarity. That's what stalkers do. Just like a cat plays with a mouse before it jumps and kills it."

"I doubt he wants to kill me, Jimmy."

"That's exactly what he wants you to think. Do not play his game. Keep your doors locked, lights on. Jaa, we've talked about this before. You need surveillance cameras on Draakensky."

"I'll think about it, Chief. How's the investigation on Thomas coming along? Any developments?"

"No evidence yet. The detective on the case came across Thomas's memoir draft during the cabin search. The memoir contents may lead to information. That's all for today. Thank you, Charlotte."

After taking another sweep of the shrub garden and grounds, the Chief drove out.

Jaa watched his car disappear, wrapping her arms around herself. "Thomas wrote a memoir?"

"Does that worry you, Jaa?"

She hunched her shoulders. "Heida confided too much in Thomas." She shook her head with a tsk. "Charlotte, a stalker here on Draakensky?"

"The man is not a stalker. Probably just a drifter. Jimmy's being a good cop. We'll be fine. Shall we get to work? I've pinned up the illustrations with the poems." Charlotte sat on the sofa. "I'm hoping I can send these off to Jung May at Sterling today."

"Jung is a sweet young thing but not very experienced. Heida thought her tastes were too contemporary. She lacks historical perspective."

"Twelve years at Sterling Publishing. Worthy, I think."

"Have you been in touch with Jung lately?" Jaa asked, standing before the wall, propped on her cane, examining the illustrations.

"Several times."

Jaa paced back and forth, lifting her eyebrows with an occasional nod. "You did better than I expected. 'Evening in Skane' is a distinctive interpretation. I'm not fond of 'Let This Darkness Be a Bell Tower' image. You might want to rethink it. 'The Panther,' yes, much better."

She paused at "Child in Red" and did another walk to view the other sketches before she settled in front of "Child in Red" again for a ridiculously long time.

"A red rope swing? Hanging from a red tree with no leaves? A red crescent moon? What are those faint sweeps at the top?"

"The wind."

Slowly, she curved her head to Charlotte. "Where is Rilke's child in the poem? *She walks through the village in her little red dress . . . she runs . . . she dances . . . life moves on too fast.*'"

Charlotte rubbed the ache in her neck. "Instead of the red dress, I illustrated red shoes. I set them on the ground because this is where she lands. Successfully inside her red shoes—fulfilling Rilke's theme that life is full of risks."

"The child lands?"

"The child has jumped off the swing at the highest point. She catches the swirling wind. She flies into the air and lands on her feet in the soft white grass."

Jaa said nothing. Was she stunned? She turned to Charlotte. "White grass? Where did you get such an interpretation? The swing?"

"The poem's rhythm. The swinging cadence. '*Runs . . . dances*' *. . . 'frolics and ferments.'* I was thinking that Rilke—"

"You were *not* thinking from Rilke's perspective." Jaa's face shone hard as a rock. "Why are the red shoes so far away from the tree? Look at the distance where she lands."

"Because, for a few seconds, at the jump off the swing, she is catapulted into the air. She sails out, taking the risk. Free. Powerful. She lands in a new location. The distance suggests her growth."

"Here's the problem, Charlotte. Rilke does not mention a swing, not even remotely implying or symbolizing a swing. Why did you manufacture such a ridiculous image?"

Charlotte had no idea why Jaa acted so angry. Accidentally, she must have hit a nerve.

"This child," Jaa announced, "who pumps the swing to the highest point and leaps. She flies inside the wind. I see her body outlined in the wind strokes at the top."

"Yes. It's rather abstract, her body flying across the sky. At first glance, the viewer might not see it, but it emerges in a subtle, almost secretive fashion. We all fly when we take risks. But does the child in red land safely? Find her power? She does."

"How does she do that, Charlotte?"

"Excuse me?"

"What kind of *magick* does this little girl use to fly?"

That word came down on her, a slap in the face that made her cringe. Magick? Charlotte struggled to find a reasonable answer. "Jaa, I didn't intend the viewer to think of magick. But now that you bring it up, and I didn't realize until this moment, maybe I have drawn, in a loose sense, wind magick?"

"No, my dear. You did not draw wind magic. You drew a little girl in red shoes, who flies!"

Charlotte couldn't deny it.

"Again! What kind of magick does a child use to fly across the sky?"

"I don't know," she answered flatly.

Jaa walked to the door, hand on the knob, and with a glare at Charlotte, she said, "We're done here. You can send these first illustrations to Jung May. Hold off on 'Let This Darkness Be a Bell Tower' because your interpretation is too muddled. And do not send 'Child in Red.' Trash it. I want a simple illustration. No embellishments. No moon, no tree, no swing. A child in a red dress will do.”

The thought of submitting to Jung May such an amateurish and hollow image for this poem offended her to the core. “Jaa! Rilke’s meaning in the poem points to a little girl soaring toward womanhood. The doubts, the risks, the frolics and fears, the freedom and exaltations. She is *every child*.”

“Absolutely not. Let’s keep this clean. You are instructed to sketch the child in a red dress and leave it at that.”

Charlotte sucked in her stomach. “I’ve already emailed the electronic versions to Jung May. This morning. Including ‘Child in Red.’ ”

Jaa’s face flushed. “Without my approval? How dare you?”

“Jung loved them, especially ‘Child in Red.’ She thinks it will be an inspiring centerpiece. She’s considering using it for the book cover. I would love my ‘Child in Red’ illustration to be on the cover.”

“But I would not. I will have plenty to say to Jung May about that. Have you forgotten this is Heida’s book? Heida’s portrait is going to be on the cover. I’ve already written the dedication to my sister’s memory. Jung has Heida’s published essays on Rilke and her four lectures already in layout.”

“I’m aware.”

“Are you also aware that Heida would despise your flying illustration, especially as a book cover?” She paused, rubbed her chest, and screamed, “Heida would never tolerate such an abortion of Rilke’s poem.”

A razor blade couldn’t have ripped Charlotte open any deeper. She might have bled out right there on the sofa. “I’ve not forgotten whose book this is. In fact, Heida’s note on a postcard said ‘Child in Red’ might be sketched in color.”

“It’s not the color red I oppose. It’s the little girl flying.”

“Why?”

“Because,” Jaa said, her cheeks flaming, “only witches fly.”

Bang went the door as she left.

Charlotte sunk deeper into the sofa, feeling a wall of dread slam down on her.

Chapter Twenty-Six

Death by Fright

Forces of reality, that's what happened here, Jaa told herself, taking each attic step carefully. How could Charlotte have possibly known? The crescent moon. The grass turned silver and white. The tree with the rope swing. The flying!

After opening the attic hatch window, Jaa sat in the rocking chair with hands in her lap, head against the wood. Might she nap? Might she have a peaceful dream? Instead, she remembered that summer day like pages in a storybook.

Draakensky had burst with wildflowers. Sunlight had threaded the trees; birdsong drifted. "I see you," Jaa had shouted into the bushes. "I win." She had expected Heida to jump out, all giggles because that's what nine-year-old girls did when they played hide-and-seek. Heida adored being found. That fearless face, eyes deep as emeralds, drew everybody's admiration.

Only this time, on this hot day on Yew Crag, she didn't jump out. She emerged in an awkward grace, her brown hair streaming her waist like a wood fairy. This time she held a fluffy white baby owl, no bigger than a cup of sugar.

"He must have fallen from the nest," Jaa told her and petted his feathers. "Poor little thing. Put him back. The mama will come find him."

"Oh no, we can't," Heida said. "Look, he has a crescent moon shape on his head. See those black feathers?" Her voice practically singing. "He's a magickal owl. From the moon."

"Even if he is, we need to put him back, Heida. The mother is going to come for him. She's in the yew tree right now, watching."

"I found him. He's mine. Anyway, owls aren't out in the daytime. She's asleep somewhere. Shall we name him? Let's call him Crescent because he's got a magickal quarter moon on his head."

"Heida, put him back."

"Oh, go eat dirt! I'm going to take him for a ride on the swing." She tucked him into her red smock pocket, shimmied onto the wood swing, and began pumping.

"Don't, Heida. He'll die of fright."

"He's a bird. He'll love to swing with me. Besides, nobody dies of fright."

Heida pumped up fast, her hair turning golden in the daylight, the curls flying in butterfly shapes. Oftentimes, Jaa would squeeze onto the swing with Heida and they'd pump in unison, holding on tight, throwing their heads back with wild screams. But not this day.

"Watch me go the highest ever," Heida yelled.

Jaa ran up the rocky hill where she could see the swing climb the sky. Higher and higher, Heida pumped. Jaa watched, scared down to her toes. The swing might twist too high. It might toss her off. She might go flying over the precipice down into the rocky chasm below.

"I hear Mom ringing the bell," Jaa lied. "She has cake and tea ready."

"Tea is stupid!"

"Heida, we have to go home."

"I'm going to touch the moon. There it is."

A quarter moon hung in the sky. "Heida, stop. Please! You're going too high. The swing is going to break."

"It is not. Watch this."

Heida sang out in a high voice, *whoo-who-whoo-who*. A flashing light burst. She let go of the rope with both hands and leaped off the swing, her legs and arms flailing, her body zig-zagging the air.

Jaa screamed, covering her face, peeking out between her fingers.

The hills bleached out to silver. Treetops darkened. Heida sailed up and rode the sky. Hair standing up in points, arms out from her sides, dipping, swaying, circling clouds. Minutes sped by, the whole time Heida zipping the sky as if she owned it, singing *whoo-who-whoo-who*.

A giant wind scooped her, a magick carpet, gliding her to the ground where her red shoes slid across the white grass, landing her on her bottom.

Jaa dashed to her sister, expecting the worst.

"Did you see me? Did you see?" Heida jumped up, her face flushed with sweat and windburn. "I didn't touch the moon, but I was flying!"

Jaa threw her arms around Heida, both trembling. "How did you do that? How were you able to fly?"

"Owl magick," Heida said, grinning ear to ear. "I conjured his magickal moon powers. It came out of his head all dusty with smoke and snowflakes."

"You didn't. How?"

"The *Come Hither* spell. I say it three times. *As I do will, so mote it be*. And more secret words I can't tell."

Jaa bit her fingers. "Where did you learn such a spell?"

Ignoring her, Heida lifted the baby owl from her pocket. It lay in her hand, feathers stripped to the barbs, eyes fixed open, pale ash, the tiny claws curled tight in its terror.

"He's dead. You killed it, Heida." Jaa burst into tears.

"I did not."

"It died of fright."

"Maybe it did. But now I have owl magick!"

"That's stealing. The mama owl will know you stole her baby's magick."

"Will not."

"The mother knows. And she'll know you killed her baby."

"Will not. Swear you won't tell a soul, Jaa. Swear on your heart to keep my magick secret. Just as Frau Holle is your secret with Dad. He says you're gifted to know Frau Holle. Well, I'm gifted too," she said with a pinched face, her eyelashes wet and lids welling. "Dad can love me, too. I can be Daddy's little girl now that I have magick. Swear you won't tell I stole it."

Jaa shook her head. "You killed the baby owl!"

"We're sisters. You have to lock this secret inside our realm."

Jaa could never deny her sister their realm.

"You have to keep our secret," Heida pressed. "I'll die if you don't. Without you, I'll die."

Jaa couldn't stop the tears. She calmed her trembling chin. "I'll keep your secret. I swear never to tell." She made an X over her heart. Heida made an X over her heart.

"Give me the owl. I'll bury it." Jaa said.

Except Jaa couldn't bury the helpless little baby. Wracked with sobs, she sat on the grass. Watching the sky, breathing in the blue vault, skeins of green and blue air skipped the expanse. She knew what to do. In the garden shed, she found a flower pot and lined it with moss. Gently, she placed the bird on the moss, tucked in the owlet wings, and covered it with fresh leaves.

Standing beneath the yew tree, she sang out, "I call upon the wind, upon you Frau Holle, to spin, spin, spin." Frau Holle warped the air purple around the tree. Jaa knew owls were mostly wind anyway and that Frau Holle would look after the owlet. She placed the flower pot inside the yew tree hollow, deep into the darkness among roots and rocks. There it would dwell by the falls to remain forever after.

In the attic, Jaa rocked herself to sleep.

Chapter Twenty-Seven

Live the Questions

Late Sunday morning, Marc dialed Charlotte's cell number. "Hey there, Miss Knight in Shining. What are you doing? I've got a paella in the oven. Can you break away and come over? I want to show off my culinary wizardry."

"Who is this?" Charlotte said.

He rolled out a smooth laugh. "This is your hero, slaving in the kitchen."

"Oh, that guy! I would love a hot meal. Especially after working half the night. I'm famished."

"Another spectacular day at the drawing board?"

"I sent off three sketches to Sterling Publishing. I finished two more sketches this morning and have only four more to go for this first deadline. What's paella?"

"You are a darling but fledgling epicurean."

"I'm kidding. I love paella. Did you make it with sausage?"

"A-plenty. Get over here as soon as you can."

Marc set his grandmother's china and wineglasses on the dining table; he centered a fan vase filled with red Belize sage and yellow marigolds from Eve's Garden when the doorbell chimed.

Jimmy Cruz stood on the front step. Odd. He never popped in.

"Good morning," Jim said, holding up a small white box.

"Hey there," Marc took the box, noting his serious expression. "What's this?"

"Birthday cake."

"Not my birthday."

"It's mine, you dumbass. I brought you a piece."

Marc snorted. "When's your birthday?"

"Turned forty yesterday." He strolled in, gave the place a cop's sweep. "You alone? Or have you got some babe upstairs?"

"I don't have some babe upstairs," he said, half amused. "I hate that word. What am I, seventeen?"

Jimmy walked into the kitchen cluttered with greasy frying pans, vegetable scraps piled on a chopping block, shrimp and clams in the sink and spilled rice on the floor. "What a mess. What is this, Sexton? You don't cook."

"No, I don't cook. But I can."

Jim peeked into the dining alcove. "You're cooking dinner for a lady? Who is it, Little Miss Good-Knight?"

The approval in Jimmy's gleam flattered Marc. He tossed the cake box on the counter. "Nothing gets by you, does it, Chief?"

"This is serious?"

"For the first time, I think. Why, does it show?"

Jimmy's face lit up. "All over you. You feel charged all day? Can't stop thinking about her? Can't stop touching her? Got cravings?"

Marc did have cravings. He desired Charlotte's mind and her mouth, her thoughts and her voice, her sparkle, the pure aroma of her skin, and all that gorgeous hair. Most of all, he craved her heart. He didn't know exactly how he would win her over, but he knew for sure he wasn't going to lose her.

Jimmy chuckled. "Can't sleep, right? Do you pace the house at night wanting to hunt her down? Look at you, all star-struck. You're in love. Jeezus!"

"Okay, okay, you win. She's got me snapped. Are you happy now? Why are you here?"

"To share my birthday cake with you."

"What a crock. You're snooping."

Jimmy sat on the kitchen stool. "Half-true."

"You want a beer? Let's sit in the—"

"I prefer the kitchen. For what I have to say today." He drummed his knuckles on his knees. "I shouldn't be telling you this. I'm breaking a dozen investigative protocols by coming here."

Marc felt the heat of Jimmy's thoughts on him. Sharp, inquiring—a cop's focus interrogating the suspect.

"Marc, expect a call from Detective Anne Horne. She has questions about your relationship with Thomas Harrogate."

"I didn't have a relationship with Harrogate."

"Horne has reason to think you did. And, about an alleged affair with Heida Mead."

"What? There was no affair with Heida. You of all people know that, Jimmy."

"Horne isn't convinced." He cleared his throat. "Here's the bullet. Did you threaten Thomas Harrogate in September?" he said with an expression that could drive nails.

Marc had a hard time pulling back from the sharpness.

"Holy shit, Marc, you've got guilt written all over you."

Charlotte would be on her way soon. He had to clean up the kitchen, shower and change. *Holy shit.*

"Did you threaten Thomas Harrogate?" Jim belted each word out.

"Why are you asking me this?"

"Because we have information that you did. Did it happen, and where?"

Marc sat down on the stool opposite Jim. "At the bar. You want a beer?"

"Do I need one to hear this?"

"I need one to tell it."

Marc opened two beers; they moved to the kitchen table by the window overlooking the tree grove, always a calming sight. He slugged a mouthful. "It happened on a Wednesday night. Around ten o'clock. The dining room had cleared out. Wait staff had swept up and closed the kitchen."

"What date in September?"

"That last week."

"Give it to me straight. Leave nothing out." Jimmy said, not touching his beer.

"I had only four customers at the bar. Heida and Harrogate sat near the TV in the corner. She had insisted I stream *Casablanca* with Bogart and Bergman. Next to Heida, a bratty red-haired kid who just turned twenty-one and cocky as hell to be legally drinking—on his fourth fireball shooter. Two stools down, a bald guy, brawny son-of-a-bitch, fifties, wearing a Minnesota Vikings sweatshirt, drinking Gunshot Black Lager—head down the whole time, texting on his cell. I hadn't seen a Vikings fan at my bar for years." Marc slugged again. "Here's how it went down."

~

Marc had poured Heida another whiskey. "Last call," he said, giving her an eyebrow. She had had enough. They all had had enough, especially the red-haired kid.

Heida perked up, listening to the whiskey burble into her glass, watching Marc stream water in. She lifted the glass, swirled it, inhaled a good whiff, then took a greedy mouthful. She rolled and chewed. Swallowed with a deep breath to get the brightest finish. Marc had taught her that practice—the same drinking skill employed by whiskey ambassadors—much to his regret.

Harrogate sat there, brooding and sullen as usual, fingering his pack of cigarettes and pulled one out.

"Harrogate, you light up, you're out the door."

"Ohhhh, Marc," Heida crooned. "Let Thomas have his smoke. You close in twenty minutes, anyway." She gave the red-haired brat a wink. "We won't tell, will we, Big Red? You're a tall fella, aren't you? I love 'em lean and mean."

Big Red pulled out his own pack with swagger. "You said it. Here's looking at you, kid." With a boozy expression, he stroked Heida's chin, leaned in awkwardly, and planted a kiss on her neck.

She batted her eyes.

Harrogate bolted up. He seized the kid by his jacket, jerked him to his feet, and slammed him against the wall. "You're no *Bogart*. She's with me." He rammed a punch into Big Red's gut. The kid doubled over with a groan and went down.

"Hey! None of that." Marc shouted, the bar confining him.

"Thomas, you gorilla." Heida shoved Thomas away. "He's a kid."

Harrogate came back at Heida with a slap across her face.

"Stop it!" Marc sprang up, grabbed at Harrogate, but the bar top obstructed his reach.

Heida landed her own punches, beating his head, blocking his swings at her, and scratching at his eyes. The Vikings guy pushed off his stool. "Never hit a woman." He elbowed Heida away to get at Harrogate and with one heave, sent him flying into the potted palm. Barstools crashed. Glasses shattered.

Marc hurtled himself over the bar top. His feet hit the floor. Glass cracked beneath his shoes. He plucked Heida out of the line of attack just as Big Red bounced up. The kid's face burned scarlet with humiliation. He swayed and landed a slapdash punch on Harrogate's mouth.

The Viking snickered. "Nice try, girly. Go home to your mommy." He swatted Big Red away.

The kid spun around with a left hook at the Viking—who dodged it perfectly. Big Red swung back, which the Viking ducked again, sending cocktail tables smashing to the floor.

"Everybody out. Right now," Marc yelled. More barstools flipped as the Viking advanced on Big Red, who now backed away. The Viking's two-hundred-and-fifty-pound hulk was about to collide with this lanky, stupid kid. Marc yanked Big Red out of striking range and hauled him to the front door. "Go home, kid. You've caused enough trouble. Out!"

The Viking pumped a fist, downed his beer, threw cash onto the bar, and went into the night, slamming the door behind him.

Marc went back behind the bar. He surveyed the damage. Glass shards, broken lamps, smashed furniture. Harrogate leaned on the bar, blood streaming down his chin. Heida tossed a wad of cocktail napkins at him. "Wipe your dumb face, Thomas."

Mark scooped up ice into a towel for Harrogate's fat lip, already bulging.

"The boy was only flirting, pecked a little kiss. So what?" Heida's voice slapped sharp and cold. "What, you think I want that fireball kid? Maybe I do. You ever hit me again, I'll slash you up in your sleep. You men, you're all the same, thinking you have power over women. I am going to show every man out there, they don't. And don't think for a second you're getting any tonight because I'm not nearly drunk enough to have sex with you. Grow a pair, would you?"

Marc nearly fell back at her tirade. "Here." He handed Harrogate the ice towel.

Harrogate slammed the ice out of Marc's hands, sending cubes flying into the liquor bottles. A dark hate consumed Harrogate's face. He dove at Heida, both hands around her throat, squeezing, her arms flailing. "I could choke the fucking hell out of you and love every minute—"

Marc reached across the bar and jammed the barrel of his Colt Army Revolver hard into Harrogate's temple. "Hands off!"

Harrogate's fingers loosened.

Marc drew the hammer to a full cock. *Click.* "Get your fucking hands off her." He dug the barrel harder. "Nothing would please me more than to blow your brains out, Harrogate."

~

At the kitchen table, Jimmy cringed. He gulped the beer. "Were there any witnesses to this death threat?"

"Staff had left."

"Did you pursue Harrogate outside into the street?"

"Only to warn him never to come back to The Grackle. Heida stayed in the bar. How is it you know about this, Jim?"

"And nobody reported the assaults?"

"Harrogate wouldn't. He threw the first punch. The kid took off. The Viking didn't give a shit. And I had no cause. Do you know what a front-page report in *The Bedford News* would do to my dinner crowd? *Bar Brawl at The Grackle.* I run a family dining room." Marc thought of all the young moms and dads with their toddlers in booster chairs for Kids' Free Mac 'n Cheese night. He'd lose more than half his Wednesday night customers.

Jimmy shook his head. "Let me move on. Do you have any witnesses for your whereabouts between five and seven on February 26th, the night Harrogate died?"

Marc might have fallen off his chair. "Witnesses? Christ, Jim. I left the bar around four o'clock. Drove home, did a quick run, showered, grabbed a power nap, and picked up dinner from Charlie around seven-ish. Drove to Draakensky to have dinner with Charlotte. At eight thirty, we discovered Jaa was missing. You know the rest."

"The M.E. fixed Harrogate's time of death between 5:30 and 6:30 PM. And you were where? Home alone, taking a power nap."

"You can verify on my cellphone location history."

"They did. Which only confirms your cellphone's location at home."

"For Christ's sake, Jimmy. What is this?"

"Listen, Marc." Jimmy placed his hand over his own chest. "I think you're clean. But Anne Horne has a taste for the jugular. At the moment, she has you on her radar as a person of interest in Harrogate's murder. I'm worried that will accelerate to suspect."

"Based on what?"

Jimmy squirmed. "Horne found a manuscript. Seems Harrogate wrote a memoir. Working title is *Artful Truths*. Notes, dates, intimate entries. Heida is everywhere in it. And your name is in two chapters."

"You can make up any shit in a memoir. Harrogate wasn't exactly stable. He had anger issues, depression, and wasn't he suicidal? Jaa said he was."

"Harrogate's mental instability holds a valid point. One other thing in your favor: Horne has no physical evidence that puts you at the murder scene. But, in that absence, she's built a theory from Harrogate's memoir that you and Harrogate were opponents over Heida in a romantic triangle."

He practically had to unclench his teeth to speak in the lingering silence between them. "No romantic triangle. None whatsoever. Zero!"

Jimmy turned to the window in a thoughtful pause, then back on Marc. "I hope not, because Horne's narrative is that you threatened Harrogate with your gun, establishing your aggression. That's malice aforethought. Conscious intent to cause death or bodily harm."

Marc felt the blood drain from his head. "This is absurd, Jim."

"Not so absurd. Horne's got you blaming Harrogate for Heida's murder."

"What? And how is she dreaming up that?"

"Chapter Fifteen in Harrogate's memoir describes your threat to blow his brains out, and his account that you were fucking Heida in her sleigh bed."

"You can't be serious."

Jimmy gripped the beer bottle with both hands. "Marc, this detective has you taking revenge on Harrogate. And in the same fashion that Heida died on Yew Crag, on the anniversary of her death."

"Revenge?"

Jim took a slug of beer. "Horne believes that you barreled into Harrogate repeatedly with a blunt object—possibly a tree stump or bat— arranged his body on the river rock, and covered him with yew branches. Same state we found Heida. Classic lover's revenge scenario."

Jaw dropping, Marc tightened his body to stay calm. He tossed his empty beer bottle into the recycle bin. If he bit his cheek any deeper, he would draw blood.

"Did you have a pet name for Heida? Aurora? Sleeping Beauty? Because that's in the memoir. And if that can be verified in any way, it lends credibility to Harrogate's account."

"Never. I never called her Aurora. But in her fantasy world, she was Sleeping Beauty. Heida likely told Harrogate that to make him jealous. She loved men fighting over her. I've seen her instigate conflicts with guys at the bar."

"Did you ever kiss Heida? Because that's Chapter Sixteen in the memoir. A rather ambitious description."

Marc stood up, his stomach turning to acid. "Jim, Horne's theory is ludicrous. There was no affair between Heida and me. No cause for revenge. And anyway, Harrogate had a solid alibi. He was in Portland at the time of Heida's death. Everybody in town knew that fact."

"Not so solid anymore. Horne thinks his sister lied to cover for Harrogate. The sister's husband now recants his statement about what time Harrogate arrived in Portland that week. It's *possible* Harrogate was still in Bedford the day she died."

Marc's neck stiffened. He wanted to kick something.

"Marc, these suspicions ring circumstantial. But, it doesn't mean Horne cannot drive this investigation right to your front door."

"Meaning what?"

"Horne is determined to locate the owner of the bootprints at Harrogate's crime scene. She thinks they're your bootprints. Forensics claim a man's shoe size eleven to twelve."

Marc refused to bite.

With dread on his face, Jim asked, "What shoe size do you wear?"

"Doesn't matter. I've never set my feet on Yew Crag. Never crossed that bridge."

Jimmy stood up, gave him an eye-to-eye. "Listen to me. Horne might show up here with a search warrant to locate these damn boots. Although, I can't imagine Judge Prentice signing off on such a weak totality of circumstances for probable cause."

"Well, holy hell. If I had killed Harrogate, wouldn't I have destroyed that evidence by now? What does Horne think, these boots are lying around in my garage?"

"Be smart. Consult a lawyer."

"I'll be smart. You can count on that." Suspicious circumstances? If Charlotte got wind of this, how would he ever maintain their relationship? First Liz, then Heida's stupid love letter. Now a murder suspicion? The love letter. Aurora. The kiss. Sleigh bed. *This can't be happening.*

Jimmy walked to the sink and placed the beer bottle down. "I've got to go." He headed to the front door. "One more thing." He turned. "I'm following up on a prowler on Draakensky Friday night. A voyeur at the cottage window. After midnight when Charlotte spotted him. He fled."

"A prowler! Is this guy stalking her? Is she okay?"

"Of course he's stalking her. He probably followed her to Draakensky. She saw him at the cemetery, the bookshop, and The Grackle on Thursday night."

"You going to nab this guy or what?"

"We're chasing it down, but there's not much to go on. Charlotte didn't mention this to you?"

"I've not seen her since Friday night at the cottage."

"Wait. You were at the cottage Friday night? What time?"

"After eight. I only stayed an hour."

"Marc, you didn't for some weird reason stand in the garden at the bow window, did you?"

"Why would I do that?"

"No reason. Do you recall a man in the bar, dark hair, wearing an overcoat, on Thursday night? Sitting at a cocktail table?"

"I don't know. Lots of guys have dark hair. Overcoat? It's winter."

"If the prowler's footprints match the prints on Yew Crag crime scenes for Heida and Harrogate, this stalker could be a suspect in the murders. Forensics haven't identified the treads yet. Until that happens, the only possible suspect is you."

"Jimmy, what are you thinking?"

"I'm thinking we have an overzealous detective on a mission to solve Harrogate's murder. She's named love and revenge as motive. And she's naming you as the devious killer who is cleverly misdirecting the clues."

"Jim, Horne's theory against me hinges solely on one premise. That Harrogate murdered Heida on October 26. Exactly how did Harrogate accomplish that? No weapon? No viable cause of death? No evidence? If Heida did die from shock, what did Harrogate use to stop her heart? How could that stupid bastard have pulled it off without a trace?"

Jimmy growled through his teeth. "I'll tell you one thing that haunts me is that damn corpse-bird."

The pause between them endured horribly. Marc finally broke it. "I don't know what to say."

"Here's what to say. Nothing. We didn't have this conversation. And you know nothing about Harrogate's memoir. Enjoy my birthday cake."

After leaving a phone message with his lawyer and hitting the kitchen with a slap-dash cleanup, Marc soaked under a hot shower. Thoughts on how to clear himself with Detective Anne Horne battered his head as hard as the pulsating water. How would he prove this suspicion as unjustified and a mischaracterization of the circumstances? What would he tell Charlotte? Even if she believed his innocence, she'd have her doubts. Nothing sabotaged a relationship faster than broken trust. He couldn't lose her. He couldn't bear not having her in his life. Hell, he'd marry her tomorrow.

Maybe he should tell her about the suspicions, in case this investigation went down on him. Take the offensive; penetrate the line and run with the ball; hit the red zone. Where would he find the right words? When would be the right time? Tell her tonight? Should he wait? *Damn, that fucking Heida.*

He descended the stairs at the precise moment Charlotte pulled into the driveway. Desperate to clear his mind of the worries that Jimmy had slammed on him and refusing to let the situation jeopardize his time with Charlotte, he paused on the last step. If he gazed too long at this sleeping dragon, the dragon would wake and gaze back. Gathering up his strength and all his will, he sealed the dragon's cave.

"Sleep, *draig*, sleep."

Chapter Twenty-Eight

Sex Magick

Charlotte arrived in a clingy, white knit dress with a sheer yellow scarf loosely circling her chest, her hair an ocean of brandy-brown waves on her shoulders, and a single pearl at her throat. Marc thought she could easily be a brilliant kingdom, fortressed with towers, high-arching gateways and bridges glittering on the horizon, protected by mountains and moat. And he the goodly knight—armored, shield and sword—on brawny horse, smiting the dragons, galloping the wild woods to her castle, far and away from the madding world.

Marc chose vibrant Spanish jazz for its chatty beats and a silky Pinot Noir aged in French oak. At the dining table, they sat opposite each other, ate off Mamó's emerald green china plates and talked about Ireland. When he asked her about the prowler on Draakensky, she dismissed the whole thing as overstated—"a man adrift but not dangerous"—and turned the subject back to his travels.

"Tell me about Australia. What did you do there?"

"Camped out on the beach, did some kayaking. Stargazed every night and collected a bag of seashells like a kid. The paella's not too spicy for you, is it?" Marc asked. "I used some unusual flavorings."

"Not at all. We could be in Valencia, Spain, having this meal on a veranda beneath orange trees," Charlotte said, spearing a sausage slice. "Did you ever read Longfellow's poem? 'Castles in Spain'—'*In the happy vale below, the orange and pomegranate grow.*' That's how I feel tonight."

"Ah-ha, you got the orange zest? I used Sanguinelli blood oranges."

"Very cheffy dish, Marc."

"A high compliment for a Culinary Institute dropout. You're looking ravishing tonight, by the way."

"What a lovely thing to say." She scooped her saffron rice. "It's absolutely beautiful here, this house, the natural colors, high views of the trees. So much swagger out there." After a wistful pause, she said, "You live well. I admire that."

"I'm comfortable. Wasn't always that way. The bar struggled for years when I grew up. Debt all over town. After my dad died, my mom had to run the family business."

"How old were you when he died?"

"Twenty. I had just gone off to college. But my mom turned her grief into work. She called it 'running with the lions'—gutted the bar and dining room, expanded the back end, hired a new chef to create bold cultural dishes and a proficient staff. She invented the grackle theme for a distinctive image. Boom. We had customers waiting in line."

Charlotte finished her wine. "A champion lady, your mom?"

"Kelsey Sexton still is," he said proudly. "She taught me everything I know about running a business, respecting the customer, integrity of our staff. She's a champion. As you are."

"Am I? Well, at the moment, I think I *may* have arrived at Sterling Publishing," she added shyly. He loved her shyness. Women who burst their words out drove him mad. He'd take the quiet and mysterious unfolding of a woman any day. That innocent gleam on her face especially seized him.

"The art director Jung May is impressed with my work. She wants 'Child in Red' to be the book cover." She said it so softly, he barely heard her.

"That red sketch? The swing you had on the wall? Masterful. Makes me want to read Rilke's poem."

"Aww, nice. There is a snag though with Jaa. She's not keen on 'Child in Red.' Wants me to trash it. But you know what? I woke up this morning and thought, Jaa is not the publisher. Jung sent me an email earlier that Frederik said I have exceeded their expectations. Marc, can you imagine my illustration on the book cover?" she said in a subdued scream.

He wanted to leap across the table and sweep her up in his arms. "Remember the question I asked you, why do you draw?"

"Yeah?"

"Well?"

"I guess I love to create scenes. Scenes that a viewer can enter. A small world, alive on the page." She waved her hand, tossing the thought away. "Sounds too dreamy." She fanned her face. "Whew, what did you put in that paella?"

"You *have* arrived, Miss Knight. Your energies are soaring so high right now, it's coming at me like a sunbeam."

She leaned forward, elbows on the table, holding up her empty wineglass.

He refilled the goblet, watching her anticipation as he poured the liquid. "What is that on your face? Are you blushing?" Was it the wine or because she had a sexy little thought going on and didn't want to say it? He had his own sexy thoughts.

She held her focus on him a long time. A bit of a pout there. He used to think smart women were the sexiest. All their savvy confidence and insightful perspectives. But Charlotte held far more. An inner knowing. A dash of whimsy. A subtle awareness. Her foxy demeanor irresistible, for sure. "Do you have something you want to say, Charlotte?"

"I'll save it for later."

"What's going to happen later?" he asked, knowing full well what they both had in mind. Did she want the chase?

"I'm thinking, since we finished your exquisite paella, next should be . . . the bedroom." She shushed the word like a secret.

So much for the chase. "I'm getting a thrill already."

"And then," she added with a slow sweep of her eyes, "we can finish off the night with a vintage movie. *Out of the Past*. Love, money, murder. Noir wiseguys Robert Mitchum and Kirk Douglas in bawdy fist-fights. And a dame with a rod and forty Gs, Jane Greer. I've got the DVD in my bag. The men talk big, smoke excessively, and drink booze in cut crystal tumblers. Nobody beats Mitchum and slinky Greer for hot and steamy. Starstruck kissing. Ever see it?"

She lifted herself in slow motion and licked a drop of wine off her upper lip. He watched her strut across the room, the swing of her skirt hiding those thighs. Curvaceous. She kicked the red-strapped pumps off her feet while she balanced the wine goblet in her hand, pulled a book off the shelf, tossed herself on the sofa, and opened the cover. "I'm going to have to read this one, the *Sisters of Avalon*."

With her legs splayed over the edge, those shiny brown waves flung out, she glanced in his direction at the table. "Would you like to kiss the back of my neck?"

He delighted in her lure.

After relaxing on the sofa together, soon enough they were upstairs in his king-sized bed. She tangled her legs with his. He rolled her around, teasing and tempting, rollicking rough and tumble. She worked her charms, her touches, provoking his body.

A thunderstorm broke in hoarse laughter through the javelining oaks at the window. "Here we are," she said, "under the oak tree, like Merlin and Vivienne in your book." She pulled him on top of her. "You have secrets, don't you, Marc?"

"I admit to nothing."

Her lips were warm and begging. He caught a little gasp in her kiss, urging him on. He pushed himself into her thighs, but her legs didn't part for him. She resisted his separating her knees. "What's this? Am I not allowed in?"

"The gate to the tower is locked."

"Is it?" That alluring little flick on her face sparked him.

"You need the key."

"Of course, I know the key." He began kissing toward her belly.

"Wrong key."

Stunned, he lifted his head. "Really? You love it when I kiss the inside of your thighs."

"Wrong key, Marc."

Sitting up, he rested on his haunches. The gray light in her eyes shined back at him. An odd summons there held him. "Uhhh, this key . . . is it . . . a back-door key?"

A shy nod.

"Oh. So, you've done this before?"

"Never. But I sense that you've done this before," she stated.

"I have."

"More than once or twice?"

"Several times. But with only highly selected women who are worthy of the invitation."

"Then I'm in good hands."

Still uncertain, he gave her a second to explain. She didn't. "Why do you want this?"

"The body is not just a plaything, is it? You know all about that, right?"

"You mean the path? Do you know what this kind of sex is really about?"

She blinked. "I think I do."

Why hadn't he seen this coming? How is it he didn't sense she welcomed *the quest*? Usually he had known when a woman desired such a sexual journey. But with Charlotte, he had somehow missed the signs.

"Do you like doing it?" she asked, and he saw a bit of fear in her face.

"It's very sexy. The male becomes the dark steed. I carry you through to a full body orgasm."

"Is the path painful?"

"Can be very painful."

"You're scaring me," she said, a deep blush flooding her face. "How painful?"

"When the passion rises, excitement takes over, and the pain awareness is subdued. There's a sharp point I know to avoid. I keep inside the limits."

She bit her lip.

"You're sure, Charlotte, you desire this experience?"

She blinked again. "For a long time, yes."

Marc remembered now, her telling him about Don, the recurring conflicts, the isolation, the man's refusal to create a deeper relationship.

He remained quiet with her, their eyes touching beyond vision—he couldn't resist falling for her silent face and heart-aching curiosity. Was that a coil of courage he felt unwinding from her chest? Was she worthy?

Rain walloped the house. A watery wild. No nightingales tonight. No stars or flowering fields. No crystal air. Lightning cracked, splitting the sky. Shadows beat down. From the farthest shore, the Lady's voice sailed in.

She is born of both worlds. You may thread the bridge.

Plunging hoofs sounded on the earth straight into his head. He took both her hands into his. Heart racing, throat swelling, he whispered, "I can give you this. There are conditions."

"Yes?"

A westerly wind stirred her hair into river curves, valleys and peaks. A gentle hand moved around them. Churn and splash, river magick calling her name.

"Charlotte Knight, you never speak of this to anyone. This event cannot be revealed to another, not by me, not by you. Neither confirm nor deny. Say it, neither confirm nor deny."

"Neither confirm nor deny."

"We vow to say nothing. You break the vow, everything breaks. This act remains sealed as a private pleasure between you and me. Do you vow to keep this mystery hidden between us?"

The vein in her forehead visibly pulsed. "I will."

He stretched out on her, his body hugging hers, hands gently around her head, eye to eye.

"I work the front at the same time I penetrate the back. You do exactly as I command. If I say 'don't move,' you don't. If I say 'lift up' or 'push down,' you tighten your muscles and do it. I will tell you when to hold your breath, when to inhale, when to exhale. You do not fail my commands, because it will hurt like the screaming devil. There's no crying, no kicking. All lights are off. You are in darkness."

She blinked, swallowed hard, her brow ghostly white.

"My commands are to minimize the pain, not as a master, but as your lover."

Sweat beads formed on her forehead. Her body grew suddenly warm beneath him, her pleasure circuits priming already as they spoke.

"Charlotte, do you understand where we are going?"

"Not entirely."

He had yet to find a woman who did fully understand the empowerment he had to give. "I can promise this. You will leave my bed a different person. This kind of massive orgasm awakens the goddess fire. The pleasure is excruciating, releasing a delicious hot burn."

Charlotte's chest rose and fell. She would start panting any second.

At the windows, silent lightning flashed in the dark glass. Her face illuminated with shadows of the dripping oak branches. He read her thoughts moving across her face. Her eyes, cat's eyes on the hunt, hungry for the burn—she certainly was. Her lips apart, breathing slips of air in high anticipation. Her lower belly swelled against him in a slight buzz.

Did she sense his magick in this adventure? Did she understand he would bring her into another realm? Magick dictates destiny. Was she ready?

"Turn off the light," she said.

Marc flipped the lamp switch off. With his left hand, he held her head and with his right hand withdrew the pillow to reposition it under her hips. He kissed her, drawing her breath into his to seal their vow. Cupping his palms at the sides of her head, he declared his first command in a soft but steadfast voice: "Turn over."

He commanded the darkness to soak through. He weaved a sheath for their cave. Her heart beat furiously; it penetrated clean into his chest. He understood this voyage for a woman to manifest her highest feminine powers—and he loved every second.

He knew to work her body until it swelled with excitement. He knew to penetrate her gently at first. He knew to keep it shallow. He knew to keep a rhythm on her front. He stroked, coming nearer to the quick of her. Pulse-beats of her sexual high merged with the pulse-beat of her racing heart. She shrank at first, fear shaking her legs.

"I'm right here. Draw me in." Inside the depths of his mind, he said the enchantments, streaming her name with the lyrics as she surged and burned.

He summoned the breaking soft fires of the stars. He called on the moon's streaming blanket to cool her. He evoked the afterglow of the burning sun and the white frost melting off the snow. From the towering oaks, he directed them to shed their strength on her. He beckoned the waves of The Lake, a final enchantment, blue and green mists rippling into her heart.

Charlotte released herself to him. Deep inside, he lifted the tender thrusts until she cried out, the stinging white fire waving through her. At the crest, a full-body shock of pleasure left her drowned in his arms.

Afterward, when her face lay on his chest, her body still hot pink, he held her, listening to each new breath, the rise and fall, now a daughter of the Water Goddess, moored to Vivienne and the rifted rocks of ancient Avalon.

When she parted her eyelids, he kissed the back of her neck.

Chapter Twenty-Nine

Owl Magick

Night vanished. Charlotte woke, her naked thighs white-hot beneath the sheets. Marc lay next to her, his body stretched across the bed, head buried beneath the pillow. At the window, morning broke into a slate gray. Stiff, groggy, and thirsty, she slipped out of the sheets, entered the bath, and ran a cold shower, drinking gulps from the water pulse. The lather-up with his lemon soap calmed her heat. She rinsed off and slipped into Marc's navy terry robe.

Downstairs, the rooms smelled fragrant from the leftover paella, dishes still on the table. Once she got the coffee going, she opened the back kitchen door. The wall clock displayed 8:30 AM. Getting back to Draakensky by ten would prove smart with four more sketches due this week, so she could keep ahead of Jaa's authority and ensure Jung May's support.

Two white Adirondack chairs on his patio invited her outside, even though the sky pressed with heavy fog. Lacey cages of mists rolled over the green pines and cedar boughs.

Robed in blue, coffee mug in hand, she walked barefoot on the cold earth, its heartbeats drumming against her soles, toes curling the soil. Wintergreen, bearded moss, and peat perfumes filled her. Dew rested on the grass. If she were a butterfly, she would spread her wings and float from tree to tree.

She stepped nearer to the trees bordering the lawn. Charlotte recognized hawthorn, rowan, broom, birch, oak, ash, apple, blackthorn—not a leaf among them—pine and evergreens, their branches holding hands. The tree trunks shone in the foggy light, bark flaking with age, knots, and creases. Several trunks wore vertical lines with crossing slashes. Tally marks?

Beyond the tree grove, a gray pond rippled wide circles. Calming air flowed up like a potion. An urge surfaced in Charlotte's mind to be that singular ripple on the water as it traveled the pond. More ripples followed. Watercolors bloomed in translucent blues, greens, and yellows.

In the mists over the meadow, a woman walked. She wore a blue nightgown, the image of polished glass, revealing small white feet as she stepped lightly. The woman's face reminded Charlotte of cellophane. Her long dark hair was tied back in a swaying knot. How fine it must be to rise at dawn every day, open your door and walk barefoot outside in your nightgown among trees, water, and sky.

On impulse, Charlotte walked in time with the woman, aligning her slow footfalls in a curve around the pond's edges—the edges in her own body melting into the haze. She saw through the fog, traced each tree limb and bough freed into the cloud banks. Charlotte was sure she could smell apple blossoms, an impossibility in late winter.

Walking back to the patio, she decided to sketch Marc's tree grove. The scene would be cracked for an ancient style. How would she draw the hush in the shadows, though? That *hushhh* kept repeating inside her head, Lady of the Wind in her ear.

She sat with her coffee and let her imagination work the scene. Feeling a presence behind her, she turned. "Good morning."

Marc sat down in the other chair. "Charlotte," he said her name deeply, arousing her the same way he had when he whispered it to her in bed. "Kind of cold this morning, isn't it?" He zipped up his hoodie sweatshirt.

"Not for me. I'm burning up here. Too much fervor last night?"

"Just right, m'lady." He grabbed a sip from her coffee mug.

"Your pond is splendid. I saw your neighbor walking the meadow."

"My neighbor?"

"The woman with the dark hair? Wait." She thought again. "Is she your neighbor?"

Marc shot his vision to the pond. "She lives nearby." He lifted her hand and kissed it. "You were magnificent last night. Your ascent into wildness. I loved it."

"Not nearly as magnificent as you were. I think I've fallen for you. I probably shouldn't have told you that."

"I will remain humble, promise."

"Where did you learn such handicraft?"

He shrugged. "Here and there."

"Get out," she kidded. "A man doesn't acquire such proficiency from here and there. My gosh, who are you?" She couldn't keep the elation out of her tone.

He leaned in. "Did you know the Celts have worshipped water deities for, oh I don't know, centuries? The deities have various names and personifications. But there is only one goddess. We call her Vivienne."

"Vivienne."

"All women can touch the goddess. She offers many secret paths to her power. The bridge I thread is only one of them. You know what's thrilling about secrets? There's always another one hiding it."

"The walls reach high on your secrets, don't they, Marc?"

He pushed back into the chair. "So. What do you think of that beautiful mist out there this morning?" he said in that sexy saxophone voice. "The mists of Avalon. My little fairy women are awake. Can you see them in the trees, Charlotte?"

She did see them floating about. The woman in the blue dress stood beneath the willow tree. The lady could have been a statue except that she tilted her head in a welcome. Then slowly, she faded into the pond's surface.

Who was this man she had fallen for? This man who made mysterious secrets his law, who wore a silver wolf head around his neck, who possessed magick in his body that he gave to her? *Magick, a higher self-awareness that fuels power.* Would she ever truly understand his magick? Dare she breach any of it?

"I love your tree grove. What are those cuts on the trunks?"

"The slashes are the Ogham alphabet symbols I carved on the bark. I duplicated my grandmother's Ogham grove when I rebuilt the barn. Most trees were here already, but I planted more. The Celts have twenty trees of wisdom."

"I'm dying to sketch it. You have all twenty trees?"

"Of course. The yew, that evergreen at the center, symbolizes the Otherworld, the threshold between life and death. The apple trees represent Avalon." He hooked his pinky with hers. "If you look closely, you can see the pools of light changing inside the mist. Watch the fog. Vivienne is a master fog-weaver. She leaves shining loopholes. I see a fairy in that oak on the right. And another. See them? Maybe a rain dragon hiding in the yew? Oh yeah, there he is."

"That silvery scaled figure with the curling tail? There are two of them. One has his mouth puckered. What do rain dragons do?"

"They kiss the raindrops."

"You're teasing me. Why would they do that?"

"So they can feed the raindrops into the tree blood."

"And you know this because?"

"Because Lady Vivienne commanded them to. Tell me what you see inside the mists, Charlotte."

"Hmmm. I think I see . . . wings . . . floating. Haunches too. Black and brown. Bruised. Moving haunches. No, not moving—flying! Marc?" She jumped up, coffee cup smashing onto the patio.

Marc sprang from his chair.

The evergreens filled with a mass of owls, spotted owls lurching overhead, brown owls tumbling the air, white owls plunging.

Stiff-winged gray owls torpedoed toward them. One striped owl with throaty hoots, feathers erect, flapping wildly, rocketed straight for Charlotte.

Angry crossed eyes zoomed at her. She stumbled back, a scream choking in her throat. The owl barreled into her belly like a wicked cannonball. Arching her back, she hit the pavement as Marc snatched its wing and flung it away. They both scrambled inside, through the kitchen door.

Charlotte struggled to catch her breath; her abdomen stiffened into a spasm.

"Your air is knocked out. Stay calm. Exhale through your mouth."

She coughed, tasting mud on her tongue. The owl's musty odor nearly made her vomit. Marc kept rubbing her stomach. "Breathe slowly."

Owls swarmed the house, clinging to the windows like hungry beasts. Three owls flew upside down in frantic circles in the backyard. More owls flipped over the barbecue grill. Some gathered at the dining room windows, hovering with wings bent into obscure angles, flattening their faces against the glass, mouths open, twisting their heads, blinking erratically.

Charlotte struggled to sit up against the cabinets, watching an owl crash on the patio, spurting blood into the air. "Get out! Get away!"

Marc ran to the front windows. "Sky Wolf's on the front step. She's pawing the door." The wolf howled a shrill so fierce Charlotte covered her ears.

Every owl screeched, spinning and zig-zagging in loops. Sky Wolf howled again and again. Each call reverberated, a megaphone in her head. Even the trees trembled, their trunks vibrating like jackhammers.

One by one, the owls dove, their wings in chaotic spirals, dropping dead into the muddy ground.

Within the hour, a Wildlife Control van pulled into Marc's driveway, Chief Jimmy Cruz behind them, red lights flashing. The lawn resembled a combat zone—birds belly-up, broken wings, heads smashed, trails of blood, feathers swimming the air. Charlotte watched from the half-opened front door. She didn't want to hear their assessments, but their words reached her.

"Rare—maybe an avian virus—bacterial infection—became disoriented. Seizures—geomagnetic disturbance—weather patterns."

Jimmy Cruz waved a thumbs-up to her from the rock wall. She gestured back an okay sign.

Some time later, Marc came rushing back into the house. "The control unit checked your car. No damage. They're removing all the dead birds for me. And they'll clean up the blood splatter on the lawn with a peroxide spray. Otherwise, the blood will attract bats."

"I better get dressed." She suddenly felt naked beneath Marc's robe.

"Wait. Jimmy's got an officer to check the rooms."

Curled up on the sofa, Charlotte waited for everything to settle down. She brought up happy places in her mind: Aunt Loretta's kitchen, playing tic-tac-toe on the wolf pup board, and climbing the elm tree in the backyard. She stayed with these thoughts, rubbing her bare feet together, tightening Marc's robe around herself.

Upstairs, the officer's footsteps hammered back and forth. Jimmy and Marc mumbled in the kitchen. She caught a few stray words: "Detective—Harrogate—footprints—Heida's ramblings."

Jimmy strolled into the room with the Wildlife Control staff. Marc followed behind them. He gave magnanimous thank-you handshakes to all three men. "All those dead birds. Makes me sick. How many were there?" Marc asked.

"We counted thirty-nine birds on the property," one man said. "I've not seen an owl parliament that big. Five or six is the normal roost for owls. We're finished spraying. You should be okay."

The police departed. Wildlife Control drove away. Marc waited until the cars were gone before coming back inside. He sat with her on the sofa. A sigh escaped, nearly a moan. "Thirty-nine owls. Dead. What a catastrophe. I lost them all."

"Owls are largely air," Charlotte told him.

"What?"

"That's what Jaa told me. What do you think she meant?"

"Owls are air? Jaa would know." He rubbed her thigh, soothing her, but maybe soothing himself, too. "You know, I adore the owls in my woods. I love their songs. When they stop hooting, there's this stillness in the air. Practically sacred. But this? This wickedness?"

"How could this happen, Marc?"

He fisted his hands. "Makes me sick. I don't know. You should have seen their bodies dumped in the van. Bulging and distended. Most were coated in a wind-burned dark orange. Hideous. Owls are such beauties."

"The owl that hit me, did it fly away? Or was it one of the dead thirty-nine?"

"That bird shot toward the roof. I've seen owls perched up there. I think the original barn here had been their nesting home. When I rebuilt the barn, they darted around the property for months. Hunting for a new roost. At dusk, they performed the most amazing aerial stunts. Kings of the night."

"Did Jaa cause this with her wind magick?" She had to ask.

"This wasn't Jaa," he said firmly.

On the coffee table, his cell phone buzzed. He snatched it up before she could see the I.D. "I need to take this call." He hurried to his study.

"I'm going upstairs to get dressed." With each step on the

staircase, she felt Marc watching her. When she reached the second floor, she heard him close the door to his study.

She walked into the bedroom, turned, and padded silently to the steps to listen. His words muffled, she could still hear: "Detective Horne, I'm happy to give you my full cooperation for the investigation. I hardly knew Harrogate." She made two steps down. "Today is not a good time. I've had a domestic mess here with birds—Oh, did you?—Well, the police were here, blocking access for safety reasons. Might we do this tomorrow? My attorney will join me if that's agreeable. I'll confirm the time later."

She snuck up the steps and got dressed. When she returned to the foyer with her bag, her stomach churning, she found Marc in his study, head down, scribbling notes in a desk planner.

Entering quietly, she stood by the bookshelf, waiting for him to respond, eyeing the photo on the middle shelf. Marc and another man with a young red-haired woman between them, heads touching, hands locked together like a link chain, faces bright as polished silver. She lifted the frame. "Family ties?"

He jerked his head up. "What? Oh. Yeah. My brother and Sheila, the baby.

"You call her the baby? With those snappy black eyes? I'll bet she's a regular spitfire."

"Sheila's an arborist in Concord, Massachusetts. She's got Mamó's eyes."

"You chat with Sheila every Sunday, too, like you do with William?"

"Sheila is Monday nights. She supervised the construction of my tree grove. What do you say we get out of here? Bar is closed today. Weather is going to clear up. We could spend the afternoon in Nyack. Take a sailboat ride on the Hudson. Kick back and talk, just you and me. Would you like that?"

She returned the frame to the shelf. "Today's been grueling. I've got these deadlines, Marc. Maybe another time?"

His mouth clamped shut. A flush crept up his face. His blood pressure rising? Sometimes his silence banged louder than a gunshot. She sat down in the chair. This man wore his secrets like armor. "Is there something on your mind?"

He looked like he might burst. "I need to tell you—a situation has come up."

She perched the chair's edge. "Must be pretty bad from the expression on your face."

"It sounds bad. Don't let appearances sway you."

"What is it?"

"It appears I am a person of interest in the Harrogate murder investigation." He paused. "The suspicions are groundless. I had nothing to do with his death. There's absolutely no evidence to support a single accusation."

She ran her hands through her hair. "What accusation?"

He avoided her gaze. "The detective has concocted a story. She claims I blamed Harrogate for Heida's death. Because . . . she suspects, I was involved with Heida romantically." Pausing again, his face hardened. "The accusation is that I killed Harrogate in the same manner that he killed Heida on Yew Crag, on the anniversary of her death."

"What? You mean a lover's revenge?"

"How cunning is that, huh? Ridiculous."

Still rattled from the morning's trauma and with her abdomen sore now from the hit, she struggled to remain calm. "Wait, what evidence does she have that you were romantically involved with Heida?"

He licked his lips. "Harrogate's ramblings in his memoir. A pack of misconceptions. False perspectives fed to him by Heida's fantasies."

Exhaustion suddenly hit her like a brick. She slouched back. "How does any of that square with the night of Thomas's murder? You were with me at the cottage."

"Time of death is estimated between 5:30 and 6:30. I was home, taking a power nap before bringing you dinner at Draakensky. Not exactly a solid alibi since there were no witnesses."

He held himself in such stiff reserve that it unnerved her. She thought back to that night, his phone call, his high spirits when he arrived. Certainly not the state of a person who had just killed a man. "So, Thomas's memoir is the only evidence the detective has about you and Heida?"

He glanced away for a second. "One other thing. The night of the bar fight in September. That night, I threatened Harrogate—with a gun."

"You didn't." She straightened, both hands gripping the seat.

"Harrogate attacked Heida. He had his paws around her throat. When I pulled the gun on him, he backed off. Now, that threat has become . . . what could be characterized as malice aforethought."

"Oh my God, Marc."

"I know it sounds bad. But they cannot prove I had an affair with Heida because I didn't. All they have is Harrogate's memoir, a man with a history of mental instability and depression. And they cannot place me at the crime scene either. They have nothing concrete. It's all conjecture."

Charlotte didn't know what to think. Malice aforethought sounded dire.

"It's doubtful this will go any further. At least that's what Robert says. My lawyer. No murder weapon. No fingerprints. No fibers. All they have are vague muddy bootprints with no specific impressions they can identify."

"Not your bootprints."

"No. Except, I happen to be the same shoe size as the prints. Robert says that's not nearly enough to indict or charge me. Jimmy doesn't think it's even enough for a search warrant."

"And the only reference to this affair is Thomas's memoir? Only his word?"

His pause, his intense eyes focusing on nothing, made her uneasy again. Charlotte's mind swam. Heida's love letter. The kiss in the office. The sleigh bed invitation. After reading that letter, she had thought for sure they had had an affair. And she didn't want to believe it was true. What would a detective think? If the detective had Heida's letter, would that substantiate Thomas's word? Would the letter incriminate Marc?

He kept his eyes on the bookcase behind her as if he could see through it.

"I don't know what to say," she managed in a calm voice.

"Charlotte, you know I did not have an affair with Heida. I had no cause to go after Harrogate. I'm not capable of murder."

She rose, trying to quell her insides from quivering.

"Don't leave." He jumped from his chair. "Please. I know this sounds alarming."

Heida's letter! Was he going to ask her about it? Did he expect her to hand it over to him or ask her to destroy it? Was it evidence? That letter sat in Heida's iris-painted box that very minute. What should she do with it now? What if the police came to the cottage looking for it? What if they questioned her about Marc and Heida?

A ripple of nausea set her balance off. She moved to the doorway, hand on the frame, and turned to face him. "I think I should leave. I don't know what all this means for you, Marc. I'm sorry. Right now I'd just like to be a rabbit and hide in a hole. Go ahead, laugh. But that's where I'm going. I've got important sketches to finish for Jung May."

"I would never laugh at you. I'm more likely to join you down that rabbit hole."

"Please. Don't."

Chapter Thirty

Kingdom of Mysteries

Charlotte found her sanctuary in a tunnel of white heat at the drawing easel. Despite the pervading tension, she plowed through Rilke's more difficult poems and worked straight through the day, half the night, and into Tuesday. She emailed the electronic versions to Jung May, crashed into bed late Tuesday afternoon, and slept dead to the world until Wednesday at noon.

She woke to light snow drifting outside the windows as pretty as lace. March snow. Phone messages and texts from Marc, Alice, Chief Jimmy Cruz, and her favorite Sister James. One text from Jung May reported she'd approved the three sketches and sent them on to Frederik.

Charlotte drank a pot of coffee and ate scrambled eggs before calling back Sister James. Her meditative voice, always a tonic, soothed Charlotte.

Sister James had been awarded a new position as Prayer Mother, securing secret prayer requests at the altar in St. Paul's Cathedral. A prestigious honor. "I'm so happy for you. When I get back to Chicago, I'm coming straight to St. Paul's to see you." They chatted for an hour, mostly about Marc.

"Are you in love with this man?" Sister James came straight out with it.

"I am finding many moments when I'm sure I am."

"Does he know?"

"Not in so many words. But he knows."

"And do you believe in him?"

"Believe in him?"

"Can you look him straight in the eye and say, I believe in you? Believe in his honor? His qualities? In his ability to love you? Because any love without genuine belief will struggle to survive. You must have learned that from all your troubles with Don."

Sister James, pragmatic as ever. "I don't know. Marc is hiding something, or protecting something important."

"Is he protecting himself or protecting you?" The pause hung between them. "Maybe, Charlotte, you'll know when you come back to Chicago."

After Charlotte hung up, she gave their conversation serious thought. She even went so far as to repeat the words, "When I come back to Chicago." *When.* Is that what she wanted? Or was it a big fat IF she returns to Chicago?

In the shower she lathered up, running her soapy hands over her body the same way Marc had run his palms gliding over her thighs and abdomen. Thinking of his touch aroused her. A muscle beneath her ribs ached and after rinsing off, a purple bruise appeared. She pressed the flesh and winced.

In the bedroom, she dried off and texted Marc.

Sorry I've been missing in action. I needed time alone. Time to work. I'm done with the rabbit hole. I might stop by the bar later. C.

Just as she prepared to call Alice Eve, the phone showed her ID calling. "Alice?"

"Well, it's about time," Alice said goodheartedly.

"Sorry. I'm terrible at returning calls sometimes. I've been working on the sketches. What's up?"

"I have a message for you from Jaa." Charlotte noticed a different tone in Alice's voice. "Jaa prefers you don't contact her this week. She said it's best not to see her any time soon."

"Why? I planned to bring her my sketches this afternoon."

"Don't do that."

"Is she ill?"

"Not that I can tell. I'm just the messenger."

"What's happened?"

"Jaa's seriously upset. Even declined her normal flower delivery for this week."

A sick feeling waved her stomach. "She's still angry with me about the 'Child in Red' sketch."

"Did you have a disagreement?"

"Conflicting opinions on the interpretation. The publisher approved the sketch and that's got her in a snit."

"This is more than a snit. She called your work fraudulent and derivative. You'd best give her cooling off time. Whatever you do, don't knock on her door. She's spitting fire and apt to slam the door in your face. One more thing. You know that owl feather you asked me to keep for you? Well, I mentioned it to Jaa, and she insisted I burn it. So I tossed it in the fireplace."

"I don't understand."

"Jaa senses a bad omen. She told me about the owl attack at Marc's house on Monday morning."

"How does she know?"

"Says she got it from Heida. Make of that what you will. I've got a customer. Gotta go, sister." *Click.*

Fine. If Jaa wanted to cut her loose, so be it. "I'm moving on to the next set of poems tomorrow. There's no falling back for me now."

The snow flurries gave way to a clear sky. Still rather cold, Charlotte dressed in her plum-colored velvet jumpsuit, side-swept her hair with a pearl comb, made a stop at the post office to drop an envelope and drove to The Grackle.

At five o'clock, she figured Marc would still be there. Jackson scurried the length of the bar, attending customers before he saw her at the corner stool.

"Marc's in a meeting," Jackson told her.

"Can you let him know I'm here?"

"He's has the Do Not Disturb sign on the office door. We can't text or call him unless it's an emergency. Can I get you a chardonnay?"

In Marc's office, Attorney Robert Sharpe made notes. "Marc," he said, "I thought you did quite well with the detective's questions yesterday, but I am concerned. This love letter by Heida Mead is troubling because it might be incriminating, especially if it corroborates Harrogate's claims you had an affair with Heida. Who else knows about the letter besides Charlotte?"

"Possibly Jaa Morland." Marc admired Robert, a lawyer with

an intimidating demeanor, wielding his big, Black boldness. The high self-confidence, the Afro-Caribbean accent, and especially the degree from Harvard all pointed to success.

Robert ran his hand over his bald head as he calculated the situation. "We don't want this letter turning up. Is there any possibility Charlotte would mail the letter to the police? Even anonymously?"

That thought nearly stabbed Marc in the heart. "Robert, I can't imagine Charlotte would betray me."

"And the sister, Jaa Morland. Would she have access to the letter?"

"Maybe. I know Jaa would stop at nothing to protect her sister's reputation."

"Exactly what is her sister's reputation in Bedford?"

Marc needed to be careful here. "We all knew Heida as a praise-worthy academic. She did the university lecture circuit. A benefactor in the communities here. Strong philanthropist, but on her own terms. She initiated the Homestead in Somers for children at risk. She found a little girl, Marguerite, abandoned in the streets in White Plains and got Patricia and Daniel Whitestone to take her in. That's when I got involved, donating food every month. Heida Mead is one of Bedford's local celebrities. Revered by most. For others, feared."

"Tell me about Heida's dark side. You didn't elaborate when I asked you earlier."

Marc stifled a moan. "Heida admitted one time she had a proclivity for Machiavellian-type men. She loved to manipulate men. I told you about her V list."

"You did. And how is it you know about her male companions?"

"Between the art of bar conversation and dirty gossip, there are some unsavory truths."

Robert nodded. "It may be necessary to get deeper into all that. For now, I'll leave it alone. If Detective Horne shows up at your door with a search warrant for those boots, be cooperative, be polite. Call me immediately. You cannot, under any circumstances, be suspected of hiding, manipulating, or destroying any evidence in the investigation, nor in a conspiracy. Should the letter come to light, we maintain the content reflects Heida's melodrama, her talents for fantasy, and that no romance occurred."

At the bar, Charlotte sipped her wine, spotting Sir Duncan at the far end. He gave her a head tilt, moved to a stool next to her, and they chatted about his Victorian art collection. His voice flowed in melodious inflections, crafting each word beautifully. She realized she hadn't captured the terrain of his face in her previous quick sketch, failing to accentuate the square chin and breadth of the eyes. Another study would be needed. "Would you be willing to sit for me again? In a more formal setting where I can do a portrait?" she asked.

"I'd be delighted. This isn't flirting, is it? Because I have a daughter your age," he tugged at his earlobe as if to suggest caution.

"Strictly professional. I promise. Marc will vouch for me. Could we do it in April or May?"

"Sure, call me." He gave her his card.

Jackson served him a Sexton and soda, placing it down on the bar top with a tap. Sir Duncan whistled at the drink. "Marc must be rolling in it. He's got Godinger Dublin cut glasses now? Fancy that bloke."

Charlotte admired the refraction of light in the prismatic design. Very noir, she thought, when the short tumbler suddenly tilted on its edge, spun and flipped upside down into Charlotte's lap.

"Whoa!" She jumped up. The glass crashed to the floor. "Did you see that?"

Sir Duncan handed her cocktail napkins. "Weirdest thing I ever saw."

Jackson ran over, waved for a busser to sweep up the glass. "So sorry. Did I do that? My apologies."

"You didn't, Jackson. You had already stepped away." Sir Duncan mopped up the seat.

Charlotte stopped drying herself off, her attention drawn to the rumbling above. Wineglasses hanging from the ceiling's steel rack above the liquor bottle display shimmied so hard she feared the ceiling might crack. All heads raised.

"What the hell—?" someone yelled. Random glasses popped off the rack and crashed on the bar top.

Sir Duncan pulled Charlotte away from the bar just as two glasses exploded into her seat.

"Get back!" Jackson shouted as he ducked to avoid pilsner glasses spinning down.

Everyone scrambled away. Glasses smashed, spewing shards. Tumblers hit the walls.

Charlotte, her feet rooted to the floor, stared at the metal rack swinging on its hinges. The steel bars buckled, ready to plunge.

In the glazed mirror behind the liquor bottles, an image formed. A bald woman in a red dress. Square forehead, white as porcelain. Distorted chin jutting out, ready to bite. The woman peered out with black oval orbs behind a feathered owl mask, bejeweled in green and blue stones.

Heida Mead. Charlotte resisted a scream.

Two hours later, Marc tossed the broom into the backroom closet, the shrieks of his bar customers repeating in his head. Images of their panicked faces made his stomach somersault.

"Goodnight, Marc." Jackson shut the back door behind him. Marc locked up and walked into the bar. The room emitted a taut silence. Never had he had seen such a foreboding haze inside his bar. He paused before the ceiling rack hanging precariously to one side. Matteo had secured it with a brace until repairmen could bolt it in the morning.

Marc squinted at the horrible crack in the glazed bar mirror—a straight vertical fracture with five horizontal cracks across the fracture. Exactly where Charlotte had told him she saw Heida appear wearing the owl mask. From the bar sink, he filled a pitcher with ice water and sat down next to Charlotte at a table near the front window. He drank down two full glasses.

"Are you okay?" she asked, genuinely concerned.

"Not at all." His chest tight, his neck throbbing, he stretched his shoulders. "The broken glass flying everywhere was bad enough, but what if that steel rack crashed on a person's head? I shudder to think. Might have killed someone."

"At least there were only minor cuts. Just four customers. A blessing no one had to be taken to the hospital."

He curled his fingers around the water glass. "Every single

person who walks through that door is in my care." His voice broke. "I've always made that my priority."

"You are an impeccable restauranteur. You're right that it could have been far worse. What about the mirror?"

"What about it?"

"Those odd cracks. Nothing fell on the mirror. Not a single bottle on that side was broken. The crack is too specific to be random shatters from the vibration."

He tried not to look at her, but he had to. His skin went hot then cold. He drank more water to flood out the sour taste. "This is Heida's work."

"How do you mean?"

"That vertical line with five horizontal short lines is the symbol of the yew tree. The Idho in the Ogham alphabet. Represents a portal between this world and the Otherworld. She's sending me a message."

"Which is what, exactly?"

It would kill him to say it because he knew language itself, each word, carried energy that could influence a course of events. He mouthed the words: *She has the power*.

Charlotte's eyebrows narrowed.

He hoped she wouldn't ask anything further.

"Marc, what are you not telling me about your relationship with Heida? The owls attacking your house, the murder accusations, and now this attack in the bar?"

In the darkened dining room with only the bar lights for illumination, the Idho letter on the mirror glared like a hanging ghost.

She kept her gaze on him. "Marc, did you give Heida your magick?"

His silence became an ocean between them.

"Neither confirm nor deny," she stated. "What am I to think?"

He felt suspended in midair with no landing in sight. Minutes passed. He listened to her light breathing, watched her fingers fiddle with the cocktail napkin. Charlotte had performed masterfully during their night together. A true warrior woman, greater than any other woman he had had in his bed. When she reached her breaking point, she soared, a firebird, wild with lust. How could he reassure her?

"Charlotte, I gave *you* my magick. That night, you were triumphant. You were the starlight. Orion would be proud."

A tear got loose. She whisked it away with her fingertips.

"I'm going to tell you again. I did not have an affair with Heida Mead. There was no love triangle between me and Heida and Thomas. I had no cause to kill Thomas Harrogate."

"I know you didn't kill Thomas," she said.

He breathed easier hearing those words. In the low light, she unzipped her velvet jumpsuit and exposed her abdomen.

"What is that?" He looked closer at the bruise.

"Blunt force. From the owl. Thomas died from blunt force."

"Yeah."

"The same blunt force that owl propelled into me. It punched my stomach so violently that I lost my breath. But the force didn't kill me. Maybe Thomas didn't see it coming. And no one was there to intercept the killer owl as you did for me."

In utter relief, his shoulders let go of days of tension. *Killer owl. Heida's owls.* He had thwarted the attack. Heida failed. And tonight she tried again.

"But, Marc, who covered Thomas's body with the yew tree branches? And what caused Heida's death on Yew Crag? Who caged her in the river?"

He wanted to look away and change the subject. "Sometimes, Charlotte, in the realm of the unknown, it's wiser to live with the mystery than the truth."

"What about reality?"

"Reality can be a prison. My father believed mysteries attract mysteries. He lived the unknown realms." With his thumb, he gently touched her bruise. The flesh was swollen and abnormally warm. "This is a wicked contusion. A doctor needs to see you. How bad does it hurt?"

"Hurts to bend."

"I don't want to be alone tonight," he blurted out. "Do you?"

Uncertainty flooded her face. "Marc, I can't—I'm—I want to believe in you, I do—but I don't know who you are."

There it hung, possibly his only opportunity. Should he take the risk? "Charlotte, I'm the man who loves you. I'm the man who cannot live without you. Today, tomorrow, forever. Will you . . . stay the course with me?"

Charlotte looked like she might cry any second. Relief tears? Happy tears? Surrender tears? Tears she would wipe away and fall into his arms? She worked hard to keep them from spilling out. Fight tears.

"Charlotte? Will you?"

She rose slowly, made silent steps toward the front door. A glance back. "Maybe."

The latch clanged, a bell tolling in his head.

He would have to live with the promise of *maybe.*

Book III
Be the Magick

"Magick revealed is magick unsealed. Beware."
—Merlin

Chapter Thirty-One

Spell-Craft

Over the next two days, Charlotte slept badly, waking with a dark curtain in the middle of everything: Marc, Jaa, Heida. Marc. Marc. Marc.

She selected the next poem in the series, "The Dark Hours of My Being," gave "Orpheus" a quick read, and dove into "Woman in Love," which was a woman's view of love. An evocative choice to do at the moment, she thought.

Whatever images came, her pencil dragged on the page. Her chalk strokes became chaotic, making a mess of her gradations. She kicked a pile of crumpled sheets across the room and rubbed her temples to soothe the pressure.

This section of the book explored Rilke's feminine principle. If she couldn't get these poems, how would she ever tackle Rilke's section on historical and mythical lovers?

She tried again, restless leg swinging, eyes blurring up, hands streaked in black and white chalk. Wedged inside the creases of her right palm, chalky flakes had gathered. Would Marc turn to dust in her hands too? Another relationship fallen into her past?

The ache in her chest drove her to pace the room. At the window, she swayed this way and that, darkened, muted, little white stars. Orion's stars. No way was she going to float away or disappear into the gloom. Admitting defeat, she burned the crumpled sheets in the fireplace, the clock ticking against her.

She texted Marc. I'M STRUGGLING HERE, DEADLINES ARE A DEATH WISH. I CAME DOWN WITH A CASE OF METROPHOBIA. YOU DOING OKAY? C.

He answered immediately. STEEL RACK IS REPAIRED. REPLACING THE MIRROR PANEL TODAY. WHAT'S METROPHOBIA? M.

FEAR OF POETRY. I'M A BLANK SLATE HERE. DISASTROUS. SCRIBBLING LIKE A TODDLER. C.

WANT TO ESCAPE WITH ME TOMORROW? TAKE A SAIL ON THE HUDSON AT SUNSET? M.

AH! JUST THE INSPIRATION I NEED. C.

PERFECT. M.

Charlotte's cell phone rang. JUNG MAY.

"The news is not good," Jung said without a greeting. "I'm so sorry to tell you, but Sterling Publishing has canceled Rilke's book."

Charlotte nearly dropped the phone. "What? Why?"

"We are within our legal bounds to reject a manuscript for any reason. As you might guess, we have artistic differences with Jaa. Frederik is beside himself. Jaa has rescinded the copyright to reprint Heida's essays and lectures unless we give Jaa full editorial license and meet her demands."

"Oh no! What are her demands?"

"I'm not at liberty to say. Again, my apologies. Frederik will send you a notification email. Stop all work, Charlotte."

Charlotte simmered down. "Can you publish the book without Heida's essays and lectures?"

"We're an academic press. Our readers are professors, scholars, students. The marketing values for this book *were* Heida's essays and lectures. Without them, I'm afraid we only have a book of Rilke's poems and illustrations."

"Jung, this is devastating."

"I know. We feel the same way."

"What if I speak with Jaa? Maybe I can get her to change her mind."

"Give it your best shot. Keep me posted."

Charlotte hung up, ready to punch the wall. Immediately she called Alice. If anybody could clue her in, it would be Alice. After blurting out the bad news, Alice admitted to knowing about it.

"What a standoff it must have been," Alice said. "I'm sorry. If it's any consolation, Jaa was in tears her sister's book is dead in the water. She didn't expect Frederik to kill the entire project."

Charlotte paced. She might have been Rilke's panther behind the black barred cage. "I could kill that stupid woman. She's blown the whole deal because of one illustration. I've lost everything here."

Charlotte moved her sight to the sketches on the wall. "Child in Red" dead center. Not until that very second did she see the slashes across the image. Someone had taken a knife to it, slicing an X top to bottom. "I have to go," she said.

Within seconds she banged at Jaa's door. "It's Charlotte. Jaa?" When no answer came, she used her key. She half expected Jaa to be sitting in her chair, too stubborn to answer. No Jaa in the kitchen, bedroom, or bath. On the second floor, the library held an unsettling aura.

"Jaa?" She's hiding in her secret attic; of course she was. Charlotte couldn't recall which bookshelf opened the attic steps. She ran her hand across the books and shelf edges to find the gap. "I'm coming up." She found the lever near *Alice's Adventures in Wonderland* and pulled the bookcase open. The staircase lightbulb burned harshly. Each wooden step whined as she ascended.

At the top, the attic space opened up to a small area with three windows, two overlooking the paths and boardwalk. Jaa might be on her walk or at the gazebo, but when Charlotte looked, she saw no one.

Half a dozen candles burned in various nooks. A small drop-lid desk and chair sat beneath the window. Nearby was a trundle bed covered in a faded patchwork quilt. An empty birdcage huddled a corner with a wooden ladder. Stacks of books, baskets of clothes, two steamer trunks, a box of old boots. *Old boots.*

From the array of dishes scattered about and a half-eaten box of Dutch chocolates next to a red rocking chair, Jaa had been occupying herself in the attic. By another window, a three-story Victorian, blue-and-white dollhouse—roof nearly reaching the low ceiling—fit snugly against the wall.

With a battered exterior caked with dust and paint peeled off, the dollhouse sported an odd charm. Most of the interior walls were broken, like someone had taken a hammer to it. Holes in the roof too, but the damages didn't diminish its whimsical appeal. In the dining room, two antique Victorian dolls wore puffy satin dresses, their porcelain faces still showing rosy cheeks. Long hair full of knots, heads crooked, their eyes open and blank.

The Victorian dolls sat at a tiny table draped in white linen with broken teacups—like two crazy sisters with their lips painted shut in chipped ruby red, gabbing about spells, magickal might, and wind beings.

Sitting on the stool before the dollhouse, Charlotte browsed the bedrooms showing mama and papa dolls sleeping in their beds, backs to each other. The kitchen sported two maids in kerchiefs. Near the chimney, the exterior wall wore an odd thickness. At a closer look, the structure wasn't a wall at all. A wide book held up the house. Charlotte carefully slid the volume out, expecting the roof to collapse, but it didn't.

Inside the worn leather covers, shabby pages poked out, although not terribly aged. Each page had handwritten notes. Lunar spells, moon phases in a list, and scribbled across the top: We Are the Magick of the Moon.

As she turned through the pages, she found a spell encircled in black crescent moons and clotted ashes.

BY POWER OF THE CRESCENT MOON, DRAW HIM HOME TO ME,
THIS MAN I LOVE.
I BURN FOR HIM, HE BURNS FOR ME,
LADY MOON, I SPEAK THIS SPELL, COME HITHER.
WHEN HE GAZES UPON ME, DRAW HIM HOME TO THEE,
COME HITHER, SO MOTE IT BE,
A KISS,
THESE MAGICK RITES WILL COMPLETE MY WISH,
COME HITHER,
THIS MAN I LOVE, DRAW HIM HOME TO ME,
MY SLEIGH BED, LADY MOON, SO MOTE IT BE.

More spells on each page: revenge spells, money spells, seduction spells, sex spells written in red ink, image spells with photos dusted in gray ashes.

A creak on the steps startled her—a cane tapping.

"Good afternoon, Charlotte," Jaa said sharply, taking the last step into the attic. She targeted the book in Charlotte's hand. "Snooping?"

"Caught me, yes, you did. This is a book of spells?"

Jaa heaved a sigh. "Spells, charms, conjures, and curses. It's known as a Book of Shadows."

"In Heida's handwriting. This is her Book of Shadows."

Jaa blinked slowly, then shrugged. "Heida's spell-craft. Nothing comes to her that she hasn't conjured."

"Spell-craft? What a kind way of saying witchcraft."

"I despise that word. My sister is not a witch." Jaa lifted her chin. "I hear you and Marc survived the owl attack. You have my greatest admiration. My sister's magick is difficult to thwart. But stop her, you did. Bravo." She gripped her cane with both hands. "Don't you want to know how Heida created such an event? All those wild owls attacking? Aren't you dying to know how she devised such a wicked airstream into so many birds all at one time?"

Charlotte shook her head. "Maybe I'd rather not know." Her vision kept shooting to the boots in the corner—men's boots with worn-out soles and ragged laces.

"My dear Charlotte," she said exasperated. "If you are going to battle through this, you'd better know how to swing your sword."

"Battle through what?"

Reaching into her dress pocket, Jaa withdrew a folded paper. "You need to see this. Heida chanted this spell to me thirty-nine times. I heard it in the wind. I think she attempted to ensure her success by snatching my energies to align with hers. Read it silently. Do not speak the words aloud."

Jaa sat down in the rocking chair, her face sagging, hands clutched on her lap. She rocked restlessly like a bad child told to sit still.

COME HITHER MY MYSTERY OWLS,
KILL AS I DO WILL, SO MOTE IT BE.
GLIDING THROUGH AIRY DAY AND NIGHT,
COME HITHER, HEAR MY WILD HOWLS,
WIELDING YOUR POWER WITHIN MY SIGHT,
MY CAMAROON OF FEATHERS AND AIR
HIT HARD THE BODY, CENTERED THERE,
IN TRIUMPH, WHACK, BREAK, AND KILL,
KILL AS I DO WILL, SO MOTE IT BE.
OH CAMAROON, THE MIGHTIEST OF FOWLS,
COME HITHER, MY WARRIOR THIRTY-NINE OWLS.
KILL AS I DO WILL, SO MOTE IT BE.

Charlotte raised her eyes. "Camaroon?"

"You've met Camaroon. On your car windshield at The Grackle. He will find you again. And when the time is right, he will strike."

"You mean the same way Camaroon's blunt force killed Thomas?"

Jaa popped a chocolate into her mouth.

Charlotte threw the paper into Jaa's lap. "And what if I kill Camaroon first?"

She popped another chocolate and chewed slowly. "There is no death for Camaroon. You don't understand how magick works, do you? It's soul work. Willful intention. This energy changes the material world. Or, defies it. As long as Heida has the power, so will Camaroon."

"Heida's thirty-nine owls are dead, hauled away by Wildlife Services. Marc is sick over this."

"Another thirty-nine will strike if Heida deems it necessary. She'll find a way."

"Where is Heida?" Charlotte asked, not even sure Jaa could answer the question.

"Where you would expect her to be. Where all spell-casters reside when they die in shame. In dishonor! They dwell in the shadows." Another chocolate into her mouth. She lifted the box. "Would you like one?

"No. You mean ghost-witches, don't you? Ghost-witches reside in the shadows. In tree shadows. Isn't that what your sister is now?"

Jaa stabbed a finger at her. "Don't you call her that name!"

"Thomas knew about her witchcraft, didn't he? And he wrote about Heida's sorcery in his memoir."

"I'm not sure what he knew. He told me he suspected Heida experimented in necromancy. Raising dead spirits. I didn't give it any credence. She dabbled in the Craft, certainly."

"Raising what dead spirits? Who would that be?"

"I shudder to think who she might have conjured. Heida overreached all the time. Now she seems more powerful than ever. I don't mind admitting, it frightens me. I've been stupid, so blinded by my own grief and guilt. I should have exposed Heida when we were girls."

"Heida resides on Yew Crag," Charlotte said, watching for a confirmation in Jaa's face.

"If you cross the bridge, you are trespassing into Heida's realm. Know your battlefield, Charlotte."

"What exactly does Heida want?"

"Heida wants you dead."

The words hit her like lead hands dropping abruptly on her shoulders. She slid into the desk chair and gripped the wooden arms.

"Charlotte, you've stolen her glory. You're walking with Rilke in his sunlight, illustrating his brilliance, and Heida is in the darkness. *You* will receive the applause."

"You put an end to that. Jung May called me. No book."

"Frederik and I failed to agree. The canceled book has sent Heida into a fury. My sister blames you and your ridiculous 'Child in Red' for ruining the entire project. I can feel Heida's rage right here in my stomach." She rubbed her abdomen.

Wind rattled the hatched windows. A purplish whip spread across the sky.

"That's Camaroon out there. He's diving among the trees. Here is your task, Charlotte. Go back to Chicago. Pack up and leave at once. My sister's magick has its limitations. Physical distance is one of them. I can tell you Nature cannot restore this imbalance. I've tried. Believe me, I have tried. You can be sure Heida's spells are not so rigorous as to reach you in Chicago. Do you understand?"

"You're telling me to run away."

"Didn't you run from your foster care? From jobs? From men? Didn't you run from Chicago to start over here? Well, do it again. What other recourse do you have but to run to safety? You are no match for Heida's fury or her sorcery. Nor am I. Charlotte, go home!" Her voice wavered with a sob.

Home? To what? Her sublet studio in Chicago? Home was Long Grove with Aunt Loretta. There was no going home. Charlotte knew running back to Chicago would be one more in her series of flees to nowhere and no one. "Jaa, I have spent so much of my life running away. I think I missed out on living it. I ran *to* Bedford. Everything I've ever wanted for my art and for my life is here now."

"I'm not your mother, nor have I been a mother, but my instincts are sharp when dangers are high. If you were my daughter, I'd be telling you to flee immediately. If you stay here, you will die on Yew Crag." She exploded into tears, her eyes raw blue with pain. "Charlotte, my dear girl, I couldn't bear to have that happen to you."

In a blink, Charlotte returned to the sheltering arms in the backyard trees. Only this time, it wasn't Aunt Loretta's voice calling her in from the approaching storm. "Jaa, I appreciate your affection. But, I—"

"Stop right there." Jaa raised her cane, frustration twisting her mouth. "Don't you understand? If you stay, not only do you risk a gruesome death caged on the river rock like Thomas, but you will continue to be the obstacle on Heida's path to her prize. She is determined to win. And win she will."

"Win what?"

"Oh my dear, it's not what she wants to win. It's whom."

Chapter Thirty-Two

Magick Has Its Laws

Jaa tapped her cane down the hallway to Marc's office at The Grackle. His voice carried a friendly but authoritative quality as he spoke on the phone. The second he saw her in the doorway, he waved her in.

She appraised her first visit to his office. Bodacious décor in bronze and copper colors, masculine and inviting. Even Marc's gray-tweed sports jacket, open blue-collared shirt, and neat jeans complemented the room's style. Would she expect anything less from *the* Marc Sexton of Bedford?

"I have to go," he said into the phone, "I have a meeting with an important lady who just walked into my office. So, two cases each: Irish Whiskey Tea, Irish Cream Tea, and Lady Grey? Your support, Howard, means the world. Can't thank you enough." He hung up.

"Good afternoon, Marc. I see you are making your preparations for the Sunday Afternoon Teas?"

"I am. Red Tea House came through with donating six cases. What brings you here?"

She whispered. "I've hit a wall. I need your help."

He rose quickly, grabbed a Do Not Disturb Sign, slapped it on the door, and closed it. "What wall is that?" He sat down. "You can speak freely. No one will overhear."

Jaa fingered the birch cane. Marc's grandmother's cane had brought her much comfort. "I need to know. Did Heida come to you for advice? You know what I'm asking?"

"Advice about—?"

"Your Ogham tree grove."

He placed his pencil down. "Oh. That. She did."

"And you told her about your yew tree magic?" She regretted the accusation in her tone.

"I have no yew tree magick."

His absolute tone gave her pause. "Isn't it true that the Celts believe in tree magick? The yew is the portal between the living and the dead, is what Heida told me. *Spell of knowledge*?"

He hesitated, his expression more than grave. "The Celts believe trees are spiritual energy. Sacred powers. Healing. Wisdom. The entire landscape is alive intellectually and spiritually for us."

"And your tree grove? It has magickal powers."

"My grove is a tribute to my grandmother. Mamó was a Lore Keeper in Ireland. I built the grove myself to honor her memory. The ancestral spirits did not create my Ogham grove. I carved the symbols into the trunks."

"But you practice tree magick, do you not?"

"I do not *practice* tree magick."

"What kind of magick do you practice?" She said, trying not to sound too impatient. "Heida insisted you know the ancient Craft."

His expression revealed nothing.

"If not tree magick, do you draw your magick from living things? Plants or animals?" she pressed.

Again, he offered her a blank expression. "Earth magick? Bird magick? Storm magick? Do you practice image magick from photographs?"

No answer. "What, then? Magick from supernatural beings? From the dead? Is that why Heida sought your advice?" What a poker face. "Or, Marc, am I to guess you practice all these elements like some shaman?" She looked deeply at him, hoping to see a hint of truth. Then it struck her. Right there in plain sight, dangling below his throat, on a silver-braided chain. "You practice wolf magick. The wolf realm."

"I practice no wolf magick."

"So why wear the wolf head? Where did you get it?"

"Australia. After my father died, I had a rough patch. The wolf symbolizes strength and helped me through the storm. Jaa, what's happened? Why are you asking me this now?"

"For Charlotte's sake and her well-being. What kind of magick do you practice?"

He swallowed hard. "I witness magick, the same way you

witness Frau Holle. We are not that different except you are far more gifted than me."

"You're a seer?"

"My grandmother taught me ways to understand the Otherworld and their thresholds. She had a Celtic eye. Mamó knew the ancestors' secret lore. You have your secrets. I have mine."

"Ah! You practice folklore magick?"

"Magick is controlling the uncontrollable world, often for personal gain, at the cost of someone else. I do not practice that principle."

"Hmmmm, I think a fish with his mouth closed never gets caught, does he?"

"I expect that's probably true."

Jaa paused. *Magick is magick. Knowledge concealed raises its powers and its value. Sources must always remain hidden.* She knew magick loses power when the core was revealed, or worse, the revealed magick could rebound horrifically. Marc knew the loopholes in the veil between this world and the next and had to protect that knowledge, or lose it.

She fondled Mamó's cane in her hand. He knew about yew tree magick, even if he didn't practice it as a craft. Respecting his confidentiality had to be a bargain of trust.

Squeezing the cane tighter, she said, "Answer me this, young man," pausing to summon her former librarian's stern voice. "Can a person conjure a spirit of the dead by yew tree magick?"

Again, he gave her his stone face. "That would not be wise," he said almost in a whisper.

"Unwise, but possibly effective. Because, Marc, I think that's what Heida attempted to do on Yew Crag on October 26th. I think she tried to steal the yew's magick in order to obtain power over the dead."

Marc tilted back in his chair. "That requires the highest powers of sorcery, and would illicit exceptional dangers. Magick can backlash with disastrous effects. You know that, Jaa."

"I do. I also know that Heida's spells, words I dare not repeat, had become powerful for her. I'm terrified she's been successful . . . in conjuring the dead. Dabbling in that dark realm."

"How long has Heida been practicing witchcraft?"

"Spell-craft. Too many years, I'm ashamed to say. My sister was born on the night of Samhain."

"Was she? Me, too. October 31st." Marc offered.

Panic stirring, she squeezed her hands together for strength. "You probably don't draw down the star constellations. Or, reverse the flow of the Mianus River, do you?" she teased with a twinkle for comfort. Then added, "What if Heida did steal or abuse the yew tree energies for her own spell-craft?"

He drew his eyebrows together and rocked his chair. "That would be a monumental offense. If tree spirits are threatened, they would have the wisdom, and the power to corrupt her magick. Maybe even strike her down."

"Could such a strike—kill her? A shock to the heart?"

He stopped rocking.

"Would it be akin to dying of fright?"

"Jaa, my understanding is that if a person abuses yew tree power, or if too much power is drawn, the result would be serious physical injury, insanity, or possibly death to the sorcerer."

"Is that a textbook definition?"

"That's Mamó's wisdom."

She nearly cried out but held herself together. "Marc, could yew tree magick . . . create a cage around Heida's body with its tree limbs on the river rock?"

Marc's face went white.

"Could yew tree magick trap her on the crag?" Jaa covered her mouth with her hand so he would not see her lips trembling. "Could yew tree magick make her a prisoner inside her own ill-gotten magick?"

"Magick has its laws," he said in an apology.

Jaa felt her cheeks flush. Sweat burst at her temples. "Shall I write a petition to the devil's forest? Send it up in flames?"

He flinched at the thought. "There exists no evil in magick itself. Evil exists inside the person's intention. Evil begets evil."

"And what of my sister?" She waited for him to answer. "I am afraid to say what's happened here. Heida's death is—what then?"

"You tell me what you think her death is."

"Is it . . . Heida's magick gone unspeakably wrong?"

Marc didn't nod. He revealed no answer but everything in his expression told her yes. Still, she had to know for sure. "What would your Mamó call it? And don't give me one of your one-hundred-yard stares with no answer!"

"Jaa, you don't know what you're asking."

"Tell me. What would your Mamó say caused Heida's death?"
He leaned forward, jaw clenched, holding the words back.
"Do not be silent on this!"

"Mamó would say," he spoke through tight lips, "Heida suffered Death By Magick."

The words stabbed her. She struggled to find her voice. "How would your Mamó know that?"

"Her sources are unknowable."

In the dead silence, they sat there, Jaa wiping away her tears, Marc stiff in his chair. Muffled chinks from the kitchen, waiters' voices, and bar chatter filtered into the office. Marc soothed her with kind words, gave her water and a shot of whiskey, which she knocked back without a blink.

Death By Magick. Jaa wanted to howl and weep. The image of her sister huddled inside the yew's hollow would not fade. Holding her stomach with both hands, she stood up, soldier-tall, and leaned on Mamó's cane.

"Thank you, Marc," she said with vaulting dignity. "I should tell you that Rilke's book has been canceled by the publisher. All contracts are now void. Don't ask why. I've sent Charlotte back to Chicago. She's leaving today."

He leaped from his chair. "What? She's *not* going back to Chicago. What have you done, Jaa?" He snatched up his phone.

With her cane, she struck the phone out of his hand. Meeting his red face and blazing blue eyes, she said, "Do not call Charlotte. She is on her way to safety, far beyond Heida's range. Don't you dare try to stop that girl!"

"You don't know what you're doing!"

"I know what my sister is doing. She is still spell-casting. Heida may very well have conjured the dead. She is determined to kill Charlotte. Beware of Camaroon. He is bewitched, a devious, fearless owl, and completely under Heida's commands. Don't think for a minute you've seen the last of that bird."

Rigid as a sword, he failed to blink.

"I know Heida killed Thomas with her owl magick and her spell that caged him on the river rock. She will do it again with Camaroon as her agent. I say this with a heavy heart. My sister is a murderer, twice in her life. A thief from age nine. Stolen magick from a baby owl. Do you want Jimmy Cruz to find Charlotte lying dead, trapped in a yew cage, mud in her mouth on the river rock?"

His chest rose with rapid breaths. "I can protect Charlotte. Heida's magick will deteriorate. She will weaken."

"You foolish young man! Don't underestimate Heida's power to conjure the dead. What if Heida is commanding death magick now?"

Marc shuddered. "Don't even say those words, Jaa."

"What if!" Jaa placed Mamó's birch cane at his chest, and with a mighty thrust, she sent him off his feet, a puppet, into his chair, arms and legs splayed.

Chapter Thirty-Three

Grackles

Temps dropped. Drafts blew through the cottage door gaps. Something scratched in the kitchen as Charlotte gathered her pencils and chalks into her bag. Outside birds hopped on the flagstone—sleek bodies, long legs with extended tails, iridescent blue-and-green heads. Grackles. Ravishing beauties, shimmering with their slick shoulders. Marc's grackles.

Two flew off; she followed their flight to the treetops. Were they running away from her? She had run from people and places. But not today. She refused to become paralyzed between options to run or stay.

She opened the kitchen door.

Draakensky spread out before her, an expanse of evergreens with a wild wind. A familiar *hushhh* circled her head. Lady of the Wind. How could she leave this? Leave Marc? Why should she flee? She wasn't a thief in the night.

In the iris box on the floor, Heida's owl mask lay askew.

"Sometimes an owl is just an owl. Isn't it?" She lifted the mask, slipped it over her face, and looked in the oval mirror on the wall. The masked woman who looked back made her step back. But then she moved in closer.

Ghosts must live inside you to see them. Where? If you are in there, show yourself. Right now.

The grackles called out whistles, catcalls, and clucks—ready-for-battle calls—as they zoomed past the windows.

"If you are really in there, show yourself, ghost. Let's see you, brave one."

Her reflection swelled in the glass. A hot energy surged up, flushing her neck and face, coiling her spine unlike she had ever felt before. The mirror slid down the wall. The crash echoed in a high-pitched wail, a voice clogging her throat. She coughed it out in sharp barks.

From the floor, she lifted the shards one by one and arranged them on the countertop into the original oval shape beneath the window—a beautifully patterned net formed with broken light.

She tore off the mask.

Charlotte greeted her image inside the broken reflection, a face liquid clear, and so sparkling, she drank it in. "Heida Mead, you do not live inside me. No ghost-witches do. Not now, not ever. Some people are haunted, but not me. Not today." She slipped into her red-hooded coat, grabbed her bag, and walked out the door to be with Marc's grackles.

They perched themselves in the evergreen branches. One by one, each soared up, following their leader, a blue-black grackle with an elongated furry tail. She followed the birds. Behind, her shoe prints made a pattern in the soil. Leaving her prints on Draakensky pleased her. The windmill spun furiously on the hill. *Who is that gale?*

Charlotte turned onto the river path, her thoughts flying with the grackles swinging across the curved sky. At the bridge, river waves pitched in silvery fishhooks. Sketching the yew tree and all its shadows would prove reality—prove Heida—if there existed a reality.

Surrounded by the soaring grackles, Charlotte crossed the bridge.

The yew stood, a trophy against the sky. Coiling pillars, the beastly trunks humpbacked each other. The tree's green roof spread out. Hidden thickets with rhubarb-red stripes drooped down. So many sad roots broken and shaved to the core on the ground. Could she capture the bereavement this tree held in its branches? Even the peak wore stunted lines pointing up in a dunce cap. The tales this tree could tell.

If I were a tree.

A milky ghost glided among the limbs. In a dark hollow, a woman covered in yew branches crouched over a mound of ashes. Her knuckled head, hard cheekbones, and square forehead shone in the daylight. Charlotte halted.

Heida Mead rose, throwing shadows around her. "There you

are, Charlotte Knight, our little trespasser. I am conjuring your death magick."

Charlotte shivered, tightening her fists, rooting herself into the mud, and gathering her strongest voice. "I am no trespasser."

"Trespassers are turned to stone. I have other plans. Your death will come as the river turns to thunder. The last sound you hear will be the water gushing into your ears. INTO THE RAPIDS YOU GO. *KILL AS I DO WILL, SO MOTE IT BE.* LITTLE MINERVA'S GIRL."

A sudden darkness hooked Charlotte by the neck. Alien smells of bloody feathers and rotted roots intoxicated her, limbs going numb, head drowsy. Caught in a tangled web, a gust swooped her up. Dangling. Swinging. Flashing faster and faster, her world blurred into a tunnel of the old dead crone. *Klatchhh . . . Klatchhh.*

Chapter Thirty-Four

What If?

After texting **Charlotte** and leaving a phone message—"Do not leave! I'm on my way." Marc rushed into the bar. "Jackson, call Vickie to cover my shift and have her close up tonight."

Above the liquor bottles, in the new mirror, a light blinked. He squinted at the glare. In his reflection, an owl's wing spread across in red and brown streaks. Camaroon! "Don't you dare, Heida," he muttered.

He dashed into his jeep and sped out of the parking lot, his foot on the gas all the way to Draakensky. He knew the death magick realm to be embedded with secret layers of malefic wheels spinning into the buried Forgotten Realms. The malignant dead. Ancient beasts. How could Heida possess powers to access even the first layer? Jaa had to be mistaken. *What if?*

The death magick wheels admitted no remedy by any human performance.

He gunned the gas, swerving the turns at breakneck speed. When he pulled into the carport, next to Charlotte's yellow Fiat, he fisted victory with a shout. Once inside the cottage, his elation dashed: no Charlotte anywhere.

In the kitchen, the broken mirror shards alarmed him. On the counter, the pieces spread out in a spider-webbed design. He placed his hand above it. A sting on his palm revealed the frequency. Mirror magick. Reflection tools to break spells. What had Charlotte done here?

Wind punched the kitchen door open, making him veer back. Through the doorway, leaves blew over Charlotte's footprints on the river path. "You didn't go there. Charlotte!"

Daylight would soon fade. He ran the trail to the river so fast that his heart beat into the roof of his mouth. Marc reached the cross bridge and paused to catch his breath. On the opposite side of the river, Sky Wolf faced him, fierce with determination.

"Easy, girl," he shouted.

The wolf made a dart, ready to charge, teeth bared, mouth drooling.

"Sky Wolf. I'm crossing over. Stay."

She jumped up on her hind legs, swiping the air with extended claws.

"Sky Wolf! Do not obstruct my path." Marc placed his foot on the bridge's first step. "Get back, girl."

The wolf leaped and yowled a brash call. Her bellow carried the volume and intensity of a sky full of wolves threatening to quake the earth. Marc jolted back in the vibration and hit the ground hard. Dirt scraped his face. A crack broke with ear-splitting crashes.

The wooden bridge split down the center. Bolts and brackets flew off. Planks, posts, and rails twisted in a frantic collapse, slamming into the river. The waves flooded up and sent the pieces downriver, the bridge swallowed up in seconds.

Unbelieving, he watched waves swell higher than the bank, bucket up from the rocks, and surge wildly into the beguiled air. "Sky Wolf! What have you done?"

With no other access to Yew Crag, he'd have to swim across. How could he manage the rocky falls, currents, and eddies? No helmet, no life vest. Getting across alive would be a death-defying feat. Sky Wolf dashed across the crag in a manic run, nose pointing north. Back and forth she ran, urging him—*north, north, north.*

Above, the edge of night hovered.

Chapter Thirty-Five
Make Me the Wind

Jaa reflected as she rocked back and forth in her attic rocking chair. In the force of a storm, trees shake themselves into new formations. In a hurricane, they huddle down and break. Wind can suck the world and yet the sky will remain strong. *Frau Holle, where are you?* Windmill sails spun from a hard north wind. Birds hurled through the sky. Grackles. A plague of them soared over Draakensky, window shoppers around the windmill, their bright heads inspecting the hatched glass portals.

Down the attic steps she went, cane in hand, out the door, wearing Heida's blue-fox fur coat and a bright yellow scarf tied on her neck. The wind frightened her now. Jaa smelled her sister's scent. That fleshy odor—ash-rich. "We've lost our way, haven't we, Heida? I cannot be with you in this darkness."

Breathing with Frau Holle, she flipped on the electric lanterns and cautiously walked Heida's boardwalk, each step a journey, her mind fuzzy, legs tired already. By the time she reached the gazebo, she ran out of energy, causing her chest to ache. Floodlights illuminated the river's lower rapids while Yew Crag sat in shadows. On the distant river rocks, phantom shapes shifted.

Chimes clanged. Grackles zoomed. "What magick is left here for me now? Heida, how do I make your death closer to me than your life? I still love you. Even if Dad made you feel forsaken, I am here for you."

Across the river, she spied the white wolf pacing the woods in anxious strides. Wind blasted down in white puffs. That wolf was in the wind; she knew it. Jaa recalled a fantasy game Heida used to play—seeing through a wolf's eyes—naming herself Wolfgang and leading the imaginary wolf pack up fantastical mountains to the queen's castle.

What did this white wolf see on Yew Crag? What did it know? The wolf leaped and ran downriver, a fierce gallop as if life depended on it. Whose journey was this wolf mapping?

"Frau Holle, give me this. Please! Make me the wind."

Chapter Thirty-Six

Prisoner of the Yew

With dusk approaching, Marc fled the river paths back to Draakensky, Sky Wolf running on the opposite bank, leading parallel the entire way. The Dutch windmill spun its blades, gusts charging out circles of light like a bright pinwheel.

Dashing to the backyard, Marc leaped up the boardwalk steps and tore across the walkway, lanterns guiding his safe footing. He reached the gazebo, no breath in his lungs, stumbling to the rail

Jaa seized his arm.

"The bridge is out," he said with little air. Each word stung his throat. "I have to get to Charlotte. She's gone to the crag."

"Heida has her now. You must cross the river." Jaa pointed to the gate. "Take the kayak." Her skin chalk white, she winced. "Paddle the top of the plateau to the bank. Hurry."

The ladder down the gazebo held him steady to the lower dock. In minutes he released, flipped, and lowered the kayak into the river. Once in the cockpit, paddle in hand, he pushed off under the lights, wind battering his head, blurring his eyes.

Jaa's gray head poised over the gazebo's rail, her long hair strewn out, yellow scarf flying. "Keep to the upper plateau. Direction straight northeast. I'll hold you! I'll keep you right here in my palms." With both arms extended over the river, she smoothed the winds, her face reflecting in the lantern lights, bright as an owl's.

The rapids broke open a fair distance below Marc's position. He paddled fast to keep the kayak straight. Waves thrust him forward. Kicked him backward. Rocked him sideways and pitched him up. He paddled left and right, fighting the currents ready to capsize him downriver into the falls.

"Steady the bow," Jaa called again. Marc glanced back. Her hands pressed the air, holding up a wall against the darkening sky.

A timber whacked the stern, tipping the kayak on its side. His head nearly hit the water. Tree debris banged the bow. Jaa streamed words into the gales, words he could not grasp. Instantly, the kayak found leverage. Steady on its course, the bow swerved left, then straight. A wicked gust broke through like some gigantic hand. It whirled him up in circles. Jaa screamed, releasing red smoke from her arms. The vapors swept him across and over the waves. He landed on a rocky apron at the river bank.

When Marc climbed out and planted both his boots on Yew Crag, he turned back to give Jaa a wave that he had made it.

Wrapped in the wind, bright as a yellow beacon, Jaa lifted her palm and blew him a kiss. "I am the wind!" she sang to him.

Then she vanished into the shining surrounding the gazebo.

With the boardwalk floodlights giving enough light, he beat a trail to the yew tree, his mind reeling with images of the river rock covered in a cage of yew tree branches. *What if?* As he approached the yew, he had to punch his way through the looping branches. Clouds parted as a full moon began its rise, shedding white light across the crag. *Klatchhh . . . Klatchhh* echoed like a metronome. Marc lashed the branches away, emerging onto the riverbank. *Klatchhh.*

Above, on an extended yew branch hanging over the river, a pendulum made with twisted vines and a timber log swung vertically, back and forth in the direction of the current, downriver, directly over the steepest falls. Charlotte clung to the swinging log, head dangling to one side, hands loose on the vines. Her red coat flapped in the wind.

His heart nearly halted. Not a breath in his lungs to shout her name. With every *klatchhh,* he recoiled. If she fell, she'd be gone in seconds. Panicked, he ran toward her, stopping short of falling in.

"Shall I stop it?" Heida's voice broke.

Inside the yew's cavernous hollow, Heida huddled, blackened

cheekbones below a bony forehead, eyes striped in orange. Ashy smoke brooded around her in a flowing cape. Heida directed the pendulum's rhythms with a wand. "Where is your applause for my spectacular pendulum magick?"

Klatchhh.

He practically choked on his anger. Holding onto a branch at the river's edge, he leaned as far over as he could and cried out, "Charlotte! Charlotte!"

"She cannot hear you. My spell deadens the ears. All she knows is the pendulum's daze. Until I halt the beat. Then she catapults off. Crashes into the rocky falls. Your little ragdoll." Heida twisted her hands to her lap and let the wand keep the pendulum beat, whisking the air on its own power.

"Heida! Reverse your spell," he commanded, averting her ghastly face.

"Calm yourself, my dear Marc. My pendulum magick is rather short lived, I'm sorry to say. We must act quickly. You and me. I knew you'd come to save her."

"Reverse the spell. Do it!"

She rose, a crooked hag, her body stiff as hard gel, hobbling over to him. "My poor Marc. Am I offending you?" Gyrating her hands, whispering an incantation, she brought up dark smoke and feathers and disappeared within the snaking vapors. As the smoke cleared, her chest and shoulders swelled with youthful vigor. Her wrinkles fell away.

Before him, the elegant Heida Mead of Bedford appeared: tailored white blouse, collar turned up, the grayish-brown hair coifed to perfection with flirtatious wisps framing her face. Her marvelous green eyes shined. And those alluring cheekbones that never failed to capture.

Poised before him, one hand in her trouser pocket, the other resting at her throat, shedding jasmine scent, stood the stunning woman Marc remembered from years ago.

Klatchhh. Charlotte's red coat hung lower. Her grip on the vines slid down. *Stay with Charlotte* was all Marc could think. *Charlotte. I'm with you. Defy the spell. Defy her magick.*

The free wand continued to click its rhythm.

"Here I am, Marc. Ever yours. I won't be able to hold this image spell for long. My powers have grown slippery."

He retreated from the riverbank, letting go of the branch once he found steady footing. "Reverse the pendulum spell. Abort the track. Bring her down safely. Do it!"

"Create a backward spell? You help me, and I will help her. You know the ancient Craft, Marc. You know how to get me out of this—release me from this—this—"

"Destiny?" He threw the word at her. "What I know is that yew poison drips from your layers. Each sunrise burns off another tier. You'll be left a powerless phantom, trapped inside your corrupted sorcery."

Her head jerked forward, her hands pleading. "Marc, if you care anything for me, do not abandon me now. Not in this exile. Even my sister and her worthless wind magick cannot assist me. You have the magick to create a path out for me. Did our friendship mean nothing?"

"I have no magick for you."

Charlotte lobbed her head up. He caught a glimpse without shifting his vision.

"You have wolf power," Heida said, coming closer.

Sky Wolf rested on the river rock. Paws apart, muzzle up, ready for a leap. "Look at that white beauty, Marc. You have her wolf magick. All I ask is that you share your power with me."

Marc kept a peripheral eye on Charlotte. "You are mistaken. I practice no wolf magick."

"Liar! You wear the wolf shield over your heart. White wolf magicians possess strength, speed, wisdom. You are Wolf Warrior. Wolf Warriors know the Otherworld. They know the Wolf Realm." She came close enough to touch him. He stepped back. "Do not fail me. Or would you rather watch your sweet Charlotte drown at the same time the rapids crush her bones, split open her skull, and smash her little face?"

"I cannot help you," he shouted in sheer desperation.

Heida's lips flattened; her face flooded orange. "I can have you killed right here on the spot. I still have enough might in my power to extract your magick from your dead belly. That's where it resides, yes?" She shoved her hand at his crotch. "Or, does it reside here?"

He stumbled back. Owls flew above, Camaroon diving among them. A fury shook Marc, urging his hands to reach for her throat. He could easily strangle her, but there was no strangling a ghost-witch entity. What would destroy her? Would she burn? Maybe even fire would not annihilate her.

Klatchhhhhhhh . . . Klatchhhhhhh.

Marc dug his heels into the earth. Whatever wisdom he might absorb from earth magick, from soil, sand, rock, tree and root, he drew it with deep breaths. Whatever speed he might gain from river magic, from the rapids racing unbridled before him, he pulled it with his eyes. Whatever strength he might capture from sky magick, from Orion's fiery sword, from the stars over Australia, he captured it with every bone in his body.

The words came quickly to him. "All Wolf Realms in the Otherworld are governed by the Water Goddess. I have no powers in the Wolf Realm. Only her powers can bestow wolf magick. Only Vivienne can redirect your destiny now."

Heida curled her lips in her famous saucy way. "Is that so? Then connect me to her. Request my release into the Wolf Realm." She gazed again at Sky Wolf.

Klatchhhhhhhh . . . Klatchhhhhhh.

"Reverse your spell. Right now. Bring Charlotte down safely and I'll see to your request."

Heida tilted her head with interest. "Perhaps I will. Or perhaps, I'll increase the pendulum's speed." With her forefinger, she lifted the wolf pendant from his neck and rubbed it with her thumb. "Give me your promise, Marc, as a man whom I love, and who still loves me. Promise me the glory of your Wolf Realm."

"My promises have no authority. As a male, I am not qualified to carry your request to the Water Goddess. Not me nor any man. Only a daughter of the Water Goddess knows the portal to Vivienne."

"I am a woman. I will request it. Take me to the goddess."

"You are *not* a daughter."

Heida jabbed him with her finger. "Then who is? Bring her here."

"She is here."

Rage flushed Heida's face. "That ridiculous child who thinks she can sketch the talented Rilke? Rilke is my poet. That girl's absurd 'Child in Red' renderings? Never."

"Charlotte alone has the means to bring your petition to the Water Goddess."

"I don't believe you. I'd sooner see her float up a mangled pulp downriver at the Mianus Old Mill. That is her destiny."

Klatch . . . Klatch. Charlotte now swung on a cross tilt. She had maneuvered herself off the timber seat—her legs dangling over the waves, red coat flaring, hands gripping the vines. She altered the pendulum's direction, rocking side to side, across the river.

Klaaaaatch . . . Klaaaaaaaatch. A smooth, slow buzz from Charlotte's new swinging motion from river bank to river bank spread over him. His chest swelled with relief.

Heida hissed. She spun herself around, snarling out her incantation, "Come hither—my fowls—of the night and—and—fright—*Kill. Will as I do will, so—so mote—mote—it be.*—My Camaroon—of feathers and Air . . . Kill. Camaroon!"

The owls spun in wild zigs and zags, losing their direction in the dark. A buzz from Charlotte's vibration filled the sky. One owl dove up only to tangle itself in the yew. Another zoomed fast as a bullet, crashing into the falls.

Charlotte sawed the air back and forth. The pendulum swung from riverbank to riverbank. Marc watched Charlotte pump beyond the bank and fly smack into the yew. What magick was she using? Wind magick? River magick?

There she jumped with the skill of a lioness, landing at the middle of the tree. Tangled up in the evergreen, Charlotte swung her limbs, arm over arm, hands gripping tight, leg over leg, from branch to branch, descending each level down. The yew's strength held her like a giant father bringing his child home. Reaching bottom, she let out a grateful swoon, falling gently onto the soft earth. The yew shook its branches, a thousand arms with hands extended up to the sky in silent applause.

Marc ran to Charlotte, lifted her up. He might have spun her in a victory toss, but he couldn't bear to release her, holding her tight, safe in his arms. She smelled of green and moss and mist from the river. "I was terrified I would lose you. How did you manage?"

"The river held me. With every exhale I turned the pendulum. Air is a transport, isn't it? It's not empty space at all."

Marc sometimes felt entirely stupid; he had no knowledge of air magick. Mamó had made no mention. But air magick had to be a sister of Mother Earth. How perfectly wise She was.

Charlotte turned her head. "Heida's standing there, waiting. I hear her petition."

"Are you willing? Do you know—?"

"I know the task ahead. I will carry Heida's petition to Vivienne. Will Vivienne agree to the passage?"

"Vivienne will bestow her gifts, if or as she pleases."

"Heida?" he called. "Charlotte will issue your petition to the Water Goddess. You best hold your tongue," he warned her. "Take a stand at the river's edge."

The darkness surrounding Heida grew deeper, her powers diminishing by the second now: shoulders drooping, hair falling to the ground, head shrinking. Marc looked away and moved under the yew, behind Heida.

Without hesitation, Charlotte threw off her coat and shoes. "I see her swans," she said and entered the river plateau. She waded out. The bursting muscles on each wave aligned with her. When she reached waist level, a swan floated near.

Gentle waves ebbed in circles. The words she enchanted, he could not hear, nor did he choose to know them. Her whispers calling upon the Water Goddess, appealing to her ladyship of the lake, would create its own magick.

Upper falls and lower falls slowed their tumbles. Water drums carried a crescendo beat. Another swan appeared. Then two more. Swimming in circles, they created a misty vortex at the plateau's center.

Heida steadied herself at the river's edge. She unlocked her hands to rest at her sides and stretched her head up, eager as if she were meeting her king. Had she abused the yew tree energies for her own purposes? Had she used her witchcraft to raise a dead spirit? Who did she raise? He knew Heida's spells likely walked the brink of her death.

He wondered if Vivienne would even hear the petition under such conditions. What right did he have to even initiate this to Vivienne? Words spoken made shadows, sometimes induced darkness. The Wolf Realm. His chest broke into a sweat. All he could hear was a clanking in his head if he had overstepped his position with the goddess.

The very earth trembled, or was it his body quaking? Every yew on the crag shook as if they heard his thoughts. He turned, not wanting to see but a part of him dying to see. Yew tree roots rose in tremors, wrenching the soil. Strips of bark bled sap. Wind in their branches whacked the sky and gnashed like teeth.

Charlotte moved deeper into the river. Mists whirled from the night sky—tender puffs, white as sleepy babes wrapped in linen. At the vortex, swans kept to their circles. Charlotte's enchantments weaved a quiet hymn. Three times she raised her hands to the sky. He heard only one line: "Lady of the Lake, dear Vivienne, give heed to a daughter. Hear my call."

Repeating the enchantment, Charlotte swam with the white swans inside the sparkling mist—a familiar scene he remembered from another time in another realm—watching an enchantress swim with her wild white swans beneath blue starlight, songs of nightingales, and flowering meadows.

Above, the moon dulled with a dense fog woven so thick Marc no longer saw Charlotte. Within the fog, a light sliced open. A shape emerged. Long rippling hair, dark as midnight, flowing over a blue gown. A silver-linked braid crowned her head. Her ancient features wore a shimmering haze. All eternity hid there. Her right hand held a white alabaster shield.

Charlotte's enchantments continued. Would the Goddess comply? What if she rejected the petition?

The yew tree suddenly snapped its branches.

One by one, the yew dropped thin timbers and green limbs around Heida, constructing a pyre. More branches blew in from the surrounding crag, dropping over Heida in concentric circles, building higher until they reached her shoulders. Only her bony skull remained visible.

"Marc?" Heida called in a terrified voice. "Are you here? Help me, please? You protected me so many times. You did love me, didn't you? Look what we did for little Marguerite. Please, Marc?" Her pleas twisted inside his belly. He had loved Heida, but not as a lover.

Please Vivienne, do this, were the only words in his head.

The air stilled. Raising both arms to the sky, the Water Goddess hurled a thunderbolt from her shield toward Heida. Earth-shaking. Hot. Inside the bolt, Marc saw a pack of speeding wolves. At the lead, a horrific black wolf dove through the mist. A beastly rags-and-bone wolf lord, hairy limbs spread, claws hooked, tongue sharply extended. The monstrous black jaws devoured Heida in a tremendous howling.

The force sent Marc cowering to the ground.

Black wolf magick! Vicious warriors at death's gate. Vivienne unsealed the gates to Black Wolf Realm? Dear God.

Black wolf vibrations penetrated the crag in echoes that could not stop growling. On the spot where Heida had been standing, rocks, soil, and timbers degraded into a swirling cavity, swallowing everything like a tornado's eye. The surface reformed into a solid rocky platform, every yew standing strong enough to scrape the sky.

Marc couldn't move. In the silence his head pounded, urging him to cry out. Wind pressed down, emitting a bitter odor as the fog lifted. No matter how hard he tried to block the black wolf's image out, the darkness of it lodged behind his eyelids. *Magick dictates destiny.* Words that his father had scored in his mind so many years ago.

Mists circled Yew Crag like smoke rings. Marc recognized wood nymphs flashing their tiny heads, flitting tree to tree. Overhead, grackles croaked, finding clean new rhythms.

Charlotte broke from the mist. She climbed the bank, soaked and shivering. She didn't speak. He knew why. They warmed each other, drying off, listening as the river returned to its thrashing. Sky Wolf bolted back and forth, sniffing the ground, pawing the dirt, barking short howls until she finally galloped to the path beyond the yews. They followed her to the cross bridge.

At the entrance, seeing the bridge spanning the river, Marc stopped. Sky Wolf leaped onto the planks and placed her bottom center stage, a queen on her throne. He couldn't dismiss the image of the bridge collapsing beneath Sky Wolf's howls earlier. Had her magick restored it? Or had her magick played illusory tricks on him?

He placed his hand on the rail and shook it. Solid. With Charlotte at his side, they crossed the bridge.

Moonlight lit the trails back to Draakensky. If a hundred voices spoke from the trees, Marc would not have heard them. His focus remained on Sky Wolf at the lead, her white fur acting as torchlight.

Charlotte rested her head on his shoulder as they walked. Her hand in his, he kept his stride with hers, feet in sync, heeding her slower pace. She led him to the oak tree near Draakensky and maneuvered him against the trunk. Instinctively, he embraced her. She pressed her body against his, her breath sweet with pine. She kissed him so deeply he thought she might slide inside him.

Holding his face in her hands, she said, "What is Black Wolf Realm?"

The words were not on his tongue. Even if they were, he lacked the courage to speak them aloud.

"What kind of magick rules there? Tell me."

A sharp pain in his forehead made him blink. "If I reveal that to you, or anyone, we would draw its power down upon us."

"Is it a—?"

He pressed a finger to her lips. "Speak no words. Magick revealed is magick unsealed. Do not look into darkness. It stares back at you."

Sky Wolf trotted across Draakensky's lawn. Beyond them, the windmill spun counterclockwise in a furious wind that might have split every sail in half. They watched it spin faster and faster, becoming a screech. Or was it a call?

Suddenly it stuttered and jammed to a halt. The wind dropped dead.

"Marc. Where is Jaa?"

Chapter Thirty-Seven

What We See, Sees Us

At the Village Green Cemetery, the light rain stopped. Sun emerged. Six pallbearers—Marc at the lead—carried Jaa Morland's white coffin into the family mausoleum. Charlotte slipped her hand into Marc's arm when he came to stand with her. She held on as they proceeded outside to the cemetery lawn with the guests. Over a hundred residents had come out for Jaa's funeral. The minister said his final prayers. He spoke about the mystery, light, and the path to peace. "Let us all watch our sister Jaa melt into the sun."

Chief Jimmy Cruz, in his usual dress blues, extended a pat on Marc's back. The tender exchange between the men caught Charlotte's attention. Jimmy's struggle to keep it together, wiping away a loose tear, secret words between brothers. She admired that part of Marc's life—how friends became family.

Alice Eve gave Charlotte a see-you-later wave, wiping at her leftover tears. She put her arms around Marc. "I brought this for you," Alice said, raising Jaa's birchwood cane. "Jaa loved having your grandmother's cane. I know she would want me to return Mamó's cane to you. You were like the son she never had. You know that, right?"

Marc went limp.

Sitting on the bench with Charlotte, he held her hand, absently rubbing his thumb on hers.

"Alice gave a lovely breakfast for the funeral guests, didn't she?"

"Five-star," he said flatly.

"She performed a stunning eulogy. A daughter couldn't have done it any better. Jaa would be proud."

"Beautiful that she called Jaa a great lady. I wanted to applaud." Marc said.

"Alice told me I could stay at the cottage for as long as I need."

"Jaa left the cottage to Alice?"

"Jaa left Draakensky estate to her. They read the Will yesterday."

"Quite a legacy for Alice. I'm happy for her." He scanned the headstones.

"Alice also inherited the copyrights for Heida's work. She suggested I call Jung May. We're going to meet next week about the book. Sounds promising."

"That's good news."

"You've been so quiet these last few days, Marc. Barely a word to me at all."

His vision appeared to be fixed on a yellow daffodil at a nearby headstone. The yellow reminded her of Jaa's scarf when they had found her dead on the gazebo floor. She squeezed his hand. "Jaa died from a heart attack, Marc. No one is to blame. The connection between the sisters played a role here, don't you think?"

"I suppose."

"Do you want to talk about this?"

A full minute passed before he answered. "Charlotte, Jaa gave me the last moments of her life. If she hadn't worked her wind magick to protect me, coaching me across the river, the kayak would have capsized and sent me down the falls." He brushed a stray hair off her cheek. "I've closed the bar today. Come back to the house. Will you stay with me tonight?"

"I hoped you would ask."

"I need a run this afternoon. I'm about to explode if I don't pound this tension out."

"Of course. I thought I'd go to Yew Crag and sketch for a while. That okay? I'll see you after your run."

Charlotte watched him make his way down the path to the exit gate, each step slow and unsure. He held Mamó's birch cane in his left hand. At one point he leaned on it, plodding along the path with the lacy tree shadows following him.

On Yew Crag, Charlotte settled down on a flat rock with her sketch pad. The thunderbolt had left the yew tree split open down the center, jagged as a broken heart. Sunlight poured through the trunk, green needles vibrant with moisture. Rendering the tree had its challenges: light glared; dampness chilled her; wind created too much movement. Funny how tree branches obeyed the wind's commands. Bend around. Shake down. Stretch out straight.

She worked on several images but was unhappy with the results. The river rolled and kicked loudly. That plateau where she had met the Water Goddess held a slight mist on the surface. Would she see Vivienne again? Or the lovely swans? She could still smell their acid breath.

Behind her a twig snapped. She spun around to the yew grove.

A man stood on the grassy path. Dark hair, buttoned suit, navy tie, woolen vest, light-colored shoes, and hands behind his back. The man watching her all these weeks.

He walked forward in timid steps, his shoes sinking into the moist earth. She nearly spoke but feared he might evaporate if she did. Maybe she had created this stranger. Seeing him at the cemetery. At the bookstore. The cottage window. The bar. A man haunting her. Her whole life she carried vague haunts of her mother, her lost father, Aunt Loretta.

"Hello. I'm Charlotte Knight."

He gave a gentlemanly bow.

"Do I know you?" she said.

The warm glow on his face held a reminiscence of a rose blooming out.

"I do know you, Sir. From where?"

"From the in-between. The dark hours." He handed her a folded page.

Her sketch of "Child in Red" jumped before her eyes. The red swing, tree, red shoes on the grass below a crescent moon—one of the renderings she had tossed away.

He tilted his head gently. "You know the shadows in my words. *Magnifique!*" His dark eyes gleamed like orbs looking through window glass. "Who shows a child his true world? I learn so much from my artist friends. I remain grateful to you and your work. I love the dark hours."

"Yes, I know you do," she said.

He lifted his shoulders and recited, " '*I love the dark hours of my being. My mind deepens into them. There I can find, as in old letters, the days of my life, already lived, and held like a legend and understood.'* "

Charlotte rose slowly. "That's your poem. 'The Dark Hours of My Being.' "

He bowed again. " *'Then the knowing comes: I can open to another life that's wide and timeless. So I am sometimes like a tree rustling over a gravesite and making real the dream of the one its living roots embrace: a dream once lost among sorrows and songs.'* "

" *'Then the knowing comes'* is my favorite line," she said. "Knowing the knower within, yes? Traveling inside it?" The man held his attention on her, an admiring spotlight that circled out across the crag. "May I call you René? Would you—?"

He dusted off his hands. "My path is now clear. I shall return to the evening."

"René, please don't go."

"The trees here are *magnifique*. Yet, the moving space between them even more dazzling. My dark hours made conscious. *Merci beaucoup*, Mademoiselle Charlotte Knight."

The poet stepped lightly on the grassy path. He crossed over to the yew tree. Sunlight burst through the split trunk. He stepped through, into the streaming gap, and departed Yew Crag, leaving narrow shoe prints tracked on the moist soil across the riverbank.

Chapter Thirty-Eight
Magick Dictates Destiny

Marc ran the backroads through his neighborhood, running his usual track up favorite hills, down sudden turns, through the bright meadows, jogging the soggy grass, pounding the gravel waysides and the wooded patches until his chest heaved out sharp breaths, the whole time three words running inside his head: *Jaa is gone.*

At a split-rail fence, the willow trees towering above, he let himself stumble to the ground. Sitting on the good earth, head against the post, he closed his eyes. *Jaa is gone.* He reminded himself she was only dead from this world, from his world, but alive in the Otherworld.

His pulse slowed; his body charged down; a breeze brushed his face. He caught the fresh scent. Salty. Clean. Ocean air. He practically heard waves hissing on a shoreline. A whispering ghost?

In his mind, Australia's gleaming Whitehaven Beach in Queensland surfaced—crystal white silica sands, turquoise-colored waves, and the ocean's whipping gusts against his cheeks. He envisioned that night in June from years ago, on the deserted beachhead, under the moonless sky. The brilliant-cut star constellation Lupus had hung overhead. At only twenty years old, he had found the courage to call down the stars on that summer night.

On the beach in Australia, the Lupus constellation contained the imaginary mythical wolf in its star formation, named The Wolf by the astronomer Ptolemy. Marc knew the imaginary to be reflections from realities behind the veil. Alone with Lupus glittering above, feet dug into the cooling sand, Marc's star lust fueled his highest magickal powers.

He sank his aim on the brightest star, Alpha Lupi, and let it burn into his thoughts. With his drumming enchantments, secret power words, the breathe-in, the breathe-out, he knew to manipulate the energies. Activating his highest vibration, he called down the star wolf.

Through the darkness, he found his white *Canis lupus*, Sky Wolf.

He had not witnessed Sky Wolf fall from the sky that night. But he felt it. The shock shot him up and slammed him into a dune, knocking him out. When he came to, the silver wolf head pendant, mounted on a shield, hung from his neck on a thick chain—the intense heat nearly burned his skin in its enchanted promise to ensure his safety and protect his powers against black magick.

Sky Wolf ran the beach. A silver phantom, streaking blue dust. As the sun peeked over the horizon, he found the wolf's paw prints along the shoreline. He followed the tracks until they suddenly vanished as if she had leaped into the sky from where she came.

Marc hadn't completely understood such magick. Mamó had instructed him how to draw down the stars, insisting star magick had a place in the Sexton ancestry. And he might have taken her advice and chosen it for his practice, but doubts redirected him. Later, he met Lady Vivienne at The Lake. The Water Goddess invited him in. Serving her and the daughters of Avalon became his magick.

Marc opened his eyes, head resting on the split-rail fence. Sunshine streamed down at his feet. Inside the beams, Sky Wolf sat on her haunches, white as a pearl, head held high, ears primed, and the posture leaning in, saying, *I'm here.*

Sky Wolf's eyes held a hypnotic spell. He couldn't even blink. Her gaze filled with peace and strength—those golden orbs saw it all.

"Hey there, girl."

She had a snout straight as a pistol, but he had yet to see her fire it. A wolf's powerful jaws could crush a femur in one bite. Bang. "Sky Wolf, are you ever going to let me touch you?"

He cupped his palm up slowly, mindful of her wild nature. She snuggled in and licked it, tongue thick and sandy. He carefully stroked her head. She had clean, soft fur. He didn't expect that. Would she let him rub her belly? Yes, she rolled over for him, and he stroked her with both hands. Her belly fur flattened out as if he were running his palm on white silk. He might have hugged her, had he the tenacity. Instead, he blew a kiss into the air. She licked his hand once more.

"Why are you here, Sky Wolf?" he said, holding her head in his hands. Her breath smelled tangy. Her rhythmic breathing beat like a chant.

Sky Wolf pawed the dirt anxiously, panting what might have been words. Her ears flattened. A shadowy fear broke into her eyes. She squinted up with a whine.

Words formed in Marc's thoughts. *Sharpen your sword.*

Chapter Thirty-Nine

The Realms

The front door swung open easily for Charlotte. All quiet. Marc must still be on his run and had left the door unlocked. She stashed her bags on the staircase. In the dining alcove, a huge arrangement of perfectly bloomed sunflowers demanded her attention. She estimated three dozen, all standing in a white whiskey barrel vase, not a closed bud among them. The card read:

Marc,
Keep the flame of these wild beauties. Follow the sunny wind.
All my love,
Alice

Charlotte sat down, tears bursting. Jaa's voice surfaced, *I can't bear to live without fresh flowers. They die so beautifully.*

The house was a quiet envelope. Through the windows, tall trees bent down to look inside. She sat alone, absorbing the shady lawn under a sky making room for the ghost in the wind.

The wind—*a wind walk*, as Jaa would say. Fresh air would be the nourishment she needed. Charlotte snatched up her pad, pencils, and chalks. Snug inside her red coat, hood up against the descending wind, she headed outside to the patio.

The temps grew slightly warmer. Sitting on the double-seat lounge, the late afternoon sun lowering, she chalked an outline of the Ogham tree grove. Structures, cylinders, trunks, crowns. Quickly, she completed the tree grove scene: yew, aspen, blackthorn, elder, hazel, rowan, ash, oak, apple, hawthorn. A good rendering. But a palpable emptiness emerged. The spaces between the trees hung too wide, yawning dead air. *Owls are largely air—Jaa.* Charlotte decided to fill the void.

The wind cooperated, slowed down to a breeze. As she drew, her vision intensified. The landscape grew into a tint in the approaching twilight. Fluttering. Expanding. Uprising. She drew each flutter inside the trees, fulfilling each stroke.

This was home.

Oval lean bodies. Wings extended. Sharp V-shapes. Then they hardened on the page, leaving a diffuse glow.

Everything you can imagine is real. Picasso. *Where your thoughts flow, so does energy flow,* she remembered from her art classes. *Draw from desire.*

She turned to a new page, starting again. Stroking in a tall figure on the lawn, she shaded the images without thinking, without stopping, using colored pencils now—reds, burgundies, brown and claret shades. Her right hand buzzed on the page. The vibration traveled into her chest and down to her belly with heat so strong she tossed off her hood. Drawing furiously, when the kitchen door banged, she jumped. "Oh! Marc, you're here. I thought you were still on your run. The house was so quiet."

He stepped out and she closed her pad.

"I needed a power nap. Longer than usual." He carried a bottle of wine and two stemmed glasses against his burgundy cable-knit sweater. Same image as the day they met at the bar. That relaxed gentleman with the swaggering voice and that *pow* smile that had melted her heart. "May I tempt you with a glass of cabernet?"

"You may. Feeling better?"

He sat with her on the lounge. "Do you ever cry in the shower?"

She rested her head on his shoulder. "Me? I do my sloshing into a bed pillow."

"I'll have to try that. All's well on Yew Crag?"

"All is well. You know what? You know the love letter Heida wrote you? Well, yours was not the only love letter in her spell-box."

"Dare I ask how many others were in there?"

"One other. To Rainer Maria Rilke. You weren't her only obsession. I think she may have wanted René more than she wanted you."

He sipped the wine. "Mmmm. I think you'll enjoy this cab. Bright. A bit jammy."

"Do you want to read the letter? She writes about meeting Rilke in the darkness beneath the starry trees. 'Come hither to me—awaken at my command.'"

"I do not. Let's not speak about her. I don't even want to say her name."

Half tempted to tell him about Rilke walking on the Crag, she saved it for later. "Are you still worried about the detective? The shoe prints on Yew Crag?"

"Forensics declared the prints inconclusive. Jimmy says the tread is not in any databases, domestic or international. Whose prints they are, we may never know."

"Some things are best left unknown—letters left unread, letters lost, letters forgotten."

He straightened up. "Letters lost?"

She kissed her forefinger and sealed the kiss on his lips. "Not every lost item needs to be found." She sipped the wine. "Mmmm, jammy. Delicious."

He gave her a knowing raise of his brows. "What are you sketching today? May I?" He peeked over her lap and flipped the drawing pad cover open to her rendering of his tree grove. After a rather long look, he shot his eyes to the trees.

She followed his gaze. Owls roosted in small gatherings in every tree, wings tittering, heads turning. A few *whoo-whoooos* strung the air. They flew, their sharp V-winged shapes ripping the sky.

The grove became a living duplicate of her illustration, right down to a white baby owl perched on a low branch. The setting left Charlotte numb in her seat, unbelieving her eyes.

Marc jabbed the air with his forefinger. "Thirty-seven, thirty-eight, thirty-nine owls. They're all back! You are incredible."

"But I didn't—no, I couldn't have—Marc, this was your magick at work here."

"I wish. I did not do this." He walked to the patio edge. From high in the sky, a massive whitish, black-and-brown owl flew in, wings spread as majestic as a king. The bird perched on the willow's top branch.

"Is that Camaroon?" she said, getting up. "Is it? Marc!"

"We're safe. All her spells are terminated."

He strode across the lawn. Camaroon soared up with an elegant swing. His ash-colored head shining, he sailed a circle around the grove. Slow. Gentle. Fluid. Marc gave a whistle and extended his arm. Camaroon landed on his forearm. Both remained there, locked together. Man and owl, the trees and rippling pond as background, the sky acting as the crowning light. And nothing but a triumphant expression on Marc's face.

Quickly she turned the page on the pad to her second drawing: Camaroon and Marc, owl in hand, standing on the lawn before the grove. An identical scene, Marc in his burgundy cable sweater and blue jeans. The owl sat on his left arm, precisely as she had drawn it, elbow slightly bent, his right palm up for balance.

How had she known Camaroon would fly into the grove? Or that Marc would lift the bird up on his left arm?

Camaroon flew off. He tipped his wings in a wave over the treetops and landed on the roof. There he perched.

Marc sat down, his face rapt on the thirty-nine owls still fluttering in the trees. "That was an amazing greeting by Camaroon. He's a jewel. What beauties these owls are. Just look at them, back inside my grove!"

Charlotte shook her head. How could she have caused thirty-nine dead owls to return to his tree grove?

He grabbed her hand. "You know, when I first moved into the house, I had moments when I wanted to grow wings and fly. Be an owl. Shift myself into a bird so I could sit with them inside the trees under the stars. Just for five minutes."

"And why didn't you?" she said, nearly afraid to ask.

"I have no powers to command such magick. That's not in my Realm. But you, Charlotte Knight," he tapped her drawing, "your sketch has manifested my thirty-nine dead owls back into our world. I love you so much for bringing them home."

She held her body tight, fearful she might come apart at the seams. "I wasn't aware you desired them back."

"I think you did know. Magick is direct knowledge. What else did you draw today?" He lifted her pad and viewed the page with Camaroon perched on his arm before the grove. "Oh, I love this! Extraordinary. Look how you captured his peace."

"Marc, I didn't draw Camaroon or the thirty-nine owls from the real world. This is not what I saw."

"Of course not. Because reality is a wall." He kissed her, letting his lips linger. "Sometimes knowing and seeing are reflected inside the same Realm."

She steadied herself. Was this artistic imaginative realism? Drawing the unreal, the unseen? Drawing images of the impossible? No. This transcended art. Dare she say it aloud? She struggled to settle her thoughts, searching for the right words. There were no right words. "Marc, what have I done?"

"You've entered the Realm." He held her in a steady gaze. "Magickal wisdom is so clever."

"You scare me sometimes. I'm shaking."

"You're safe with me. I would tear apart the world to keep you protected."

She did feel safe with Marc. Safe in his wisdom. In his strength. Especially in his love. Except . . . "I still don't know who you are," the words tumbled out. "Marc, are you the wizard in the attic?"

A full minute passed, his hand swirling the wine. She could read nothing on his face.

"Marc? What secrets are you not telling me?"

His gaze shot intensely blue; it could be a stab of starlight.

"Charlotte, it doesn't matter who I am. Or what you think I am. Or what I've done. Magick guards itself. And we guard its mystery."

"Please tell me. What magick do you practice?"

"I don't practice magick. I live magick. Because the world is magick. And I am compelled to live in that world." Marc opened his palm to her. "Take my hand. You tell me, Charlotte Knight, who are you?"

As twilight spread, the Ogham tree grove began to fade from sight. Charlotte watched the light sweep across the pond. The Lady of the Lake in her blue gown strolled the grass on the far side. Her white shield flashed. Vivienne hummed an ancient tune. She sent an airy stream across the lawn, settling on Charlotte. Their eyes met inside the mists of Avalon.

Charlotte felt ready to say the words, words she would never take back. "I am the woman who loves you, Marc. I am the woman who embraces and desires you today, tomorrow, forever."

"Will you live the magick with me?"

Like clear water suddenly let loose from an ice block, she buried her face in his chest. Her eyelids grew hot, tears ready to slide out.

"Marry me, Charlotte. *Be* the magick."

She held him, belonging to him entirely. "I'll always love you."

He placed a kiss on the back of her neck. "Is that a yes?"

For Marc, their magick shined complete as he sat beneath the evening shadows, Charlotte in his arms, Orion barely visible above. He called down The Hunter to glow brighter on him and Charlotte—the muscular starred warrior facing off at Taurus the Bull—what bravery.

Charlotte snuggled in, clinging, her hand on his chest, her fingers resting on the wolf head pendant. Someday, after she became his wife, if the time ripened, he would tell her about his Australian adventure on the beachhead with Sky Wolf. But then, he would have to lock his tongue. He knew in the fathoms of his heart he could not reveal the Sexton scorched ancestry from old Ireland; never reveal their shifting past inside the Otherworld; never reveal his father Matthew as the Realm Walker in the wolf kingdom. Secrets he vowed to keep for the safety of himself and those he loved.

For now, he would hold Charlotte in the enigmatic quiet with the sheen from the Water Goddess still lingering on the pond in a steady peace.

On the lawn, a figure emerged from the trees in a shaft of moonlight. High pointed ears. Eyes sparking red fire in bony sockets. A warped white skull with sharp bones. Paws big as sledgehammers.

The Ripper. Alpha male of Black Wolf Realm.

Hot winds slashed his fur into inky spikes as a chorus of frenzied howls broke the night wide open. Striking like a clock, his father's last words on the day he died thrummed into Marc's thoughts: *These wolves from Black Wolf Realm owe their souls to darkness.*

Warrior drumbeats pounded through Marc's body into ragged breaths.

Sharpen your sword.

Acknowledgments

Acknowledging magick as a spiritual power in Nature opened my journey to writing *Draakensky*. Yet, the deepest motivation came from the poet Rainer Maria Rilke. His untitled poem "I Love the Dark Hours of My Being" spoke to me, in fact, haunted me until I sat down and explored the story Rilke was telling me. My wholehearted gratitude goes to Rainer for his poetic musings about the human soul, Nature, and especially for his understanding of the power of solitude.

For Permissions, my thanks go to the following:

Translator David Need, *Roses, The Late French Poetry of Rainer Maria Rilke*, published by Horse & Buggy Press, 2014, for use of the poem "XIV." [*Les Roses*]

Translators Anita Barrows and Joanna Macy, *Rilke's Book of Hours, Love Poems to God,* published by Riverhead Books (Penguin Group, USA), 1997, for use of untitled ["I Love the Dark Hours of My Being."]

Graywolf Press. Rainer Maria Rilke, excerpts from "Child in Red" from *The Complete French Poems of Rainer Maria Rilke,* translated by A. Poulin. Translation copyright © 1979, 1982, 1984, 1986 by A. Poulin, Jr. Reprinted with the permission of The Permissions Company, LLC on behalf of Graywolf Press, Minneapolis, Minnesota, graywolfpress.org.

Special thanks to The Sexton Single Malt Irish Whiskey, Proximo Spirits, Jersey City, NJ. Please note that the historical references to the character Marc Sexton and his ancestors as the creators of Sexton Irish Whiskey are fictional. The true Master Blender for Sexton Irish Whiskey was created by Ms. Alex Thomas, made with 100% Irish malted barley, triple-distilled in copper pot stills, aged in oloroso sherry casks, and distilled by Bushmills in County Antrim, Northern Ireland, released in 2018. The signature cocktail, The Grackle, is my own recipe.

For my stellar editors, Bram Stoker Award 2023 Finalist

Richard Thomas at Storyville; Stephen Black of Black Thoughts Editorial Services in Northern Ireland; and John Robin at Story Perfect Editing Services in Canada. A heartfelt thank-you for a superb job in offering their keen insights into the characters, plotline, and the magickal storytelling world. Editors are the world's highest readers and every writer is blessed to have a good one. I've had three masters to guide me.

My research into Celtic traditions, folklore and myths, the Otherworld, Avalon, and the spirituality of Nature would require pages to name the 100+ books I have read and studied to understand our world, the magickal realms and their elements, the spiritual world beyond, poetry, and art. Thank you to authors Renee Baribeau, Steve Blamires, Joseph Campbell, Tom Cowan, Peter Berresford Ellis, Danu Forest, Sandra Ingerman and Llyn Roberts, Frank MacEowen, Sharon Paice MacLeod, Caitlin and John Matthews, John O'Donohue, Graham Philips and Martin Keatman, Gabiyell Sarom, Jhenah Telyndru, Rainer Maria Rilke, and Fred Alan Wolf, and more whose books were and still are treasures on this writing journey.

My experience with the remarkable wolves at the Wolf Conservation Center in Lewisboro, New York, thrilled me with a profound understanding that wolves and their beauty can walk among us in mind, body, and spirit.

I must mention my research and visits to the Mianus River Gorge Preserve in Bedford, part of a 42-square mile watershed, spanning five towns in two states, which inspired the river scenes in *Draakensky*.

Where would I be without my local libraries? Many thanks to the librarians at Bedford Village Library, Lewisboro Library, and especially Pound Ridge Library for assisting me with all my needs.

Deep gratitude and affection for my husband Ron who has remarkable patience and foresight these past years enduring all the magick and mayhem in our household; his steadfast encouragement has been monumental. I don't think I would be a writer without him.

My daughter Gina Casey and my son Jon-Paul Cappa provide the highest enthusiasm, appreciation, generosity, and dearest support for all my creative writing. They are a blessing in my life every day and an inspiration for every story I write. Thank you to Emily Zhang and Todd M. Casey for sharing their affection, strength, and goodness for our family and enriching all of us. Special thanks to still-life artist and author Todd M. Casey, *The Art of Still Life,* for his professional advice and insights about art, sketching, color, painting, and for assisting me in discovering the artist's soul for the character Charlotte Knight.

And, for the many writing muses who continue to wake me at three in the morning, floating around me with their ancient and mysterious inspirations. In Rilke's words, *magnifique*!

The End?

Not if you want to dive into more of Crystal Lake Publishing's Tales from the Darkest Depths!

Check out our amazing website and online store
or download our latest catalog here.
https://geni.us/CLPCatalog

We always have great new projects and content on the website to dive into, as well as a newsletter, behind the scenes options, social media platforms, our own dark fiction shared-world series and our very own webstore. Our webstore even has categories specifically for KU books, non-fiction, anthologies, and of course more novels and novellas.

About the Author

Paula Cappa is a multiple award-winning author of *Greylock, The Dazzling Darkness,* and *Night Sea Journey, A Supernatural Tale*—print editions published by Crispin Books, Milwaukee WI. She is known for her "quiet horror stories" and as an Amazon best-selling author. Cappa's short fiction has appeared in *The Lorelei Signal, Scribes, ParABnormal Magazine, Coffin Bell Literary Journal, Unfading Daydream, Dark Gothic Resurrected Magazine, Whistling Shade Literary Journal, SmokeLong Quarterly, Sirens Call Ezine, Every Day Fiction, Fiction365, Twilight Times Ezine,* and in anthologies *Journals of Horror: Found Fiction, Mystery Time,* and *Human Writes Literary Journal.* Readers can find many of her short stories as singles in ebook format on Amazon and Smashwords.

Cappa is a freelance copy editor and writes a short story blog, Reading Fiction Blog, at her website at paulacappa.wordpress.com. When she is not writing or reading stacks of books, she is Co-Chair of the Pound Ridge Authors Society in Pound Ridge, NY. You can contact her at her blog site or her author email: authorpaulacappa@gmail.com.

BookFest Book Awards, 2025, *Draakensky*
Readers' Choice Book Awards, 2024, *Draakensky*
Gold Medal, Global Book Awards, 2023, *The Dazzling Darkness*
Gold Medal, Global Book Awards, 2022, *Greylock*
Silver Medal, Global Book Awards, 2021, *Night Sea Journey*
Best Book Awards Finalist, American Book Fest, 2017, *Greylock*
Eric Hoffer Book Award Winner, 2015, *Night Sea Journey*
Chanticleer Book Award Winner, 2015, *Greylock*
Bronze Medal, Readers' Favorite Book Awards, 2014, *The Dazzling Darkness*
Gothic Readers Book Club Choice Award Winner, 2013, *The Dazzling Darkness*

Books by Paula Cappa

The Dazzling Darkness
Night Sea Journey, A Tale of the Supernatural
Greylock
Sky Wolf, a Novelette

Readers . . .

Thank you for reading *Draakensky*. We hope you enjoyed this novel.

If you have a moment, please review *Draakensky* at the store where you bought it.

Help other readers by telling them why you enjoyed this book. No need to write an in-depth discussion. Even a single sentence will be greatly appreciated. Reviews go a long way to helping a book sell, and is great for an author's career. It'll also help us to continue publishing quality books.

Thank you again for taking the time to journey with Crystal Lake Publishing.

Visit our Linktree page for a list of our social media platforms. https://linktr.ee/CrystalLakePublishing

Follow us on Amazon:

Our Mission Statement:

Since its founding in August 2012, Crystal Lake Publishing has quickly become one of the world's leading publishers of Dark Fiction and Horror books. In 2023, Crystal Lake Publishing formed a part of Crystal Lake Entertainment, joining several other divisions, including Torrid Waters, Crystal Lake Comics, Crystal Lake Kids, and many more.

While we strive to present only the highest quality fiction and entertainment, we also endeavour to support authors along their writing journey. We offer our time and experience in non-fiction projects, as well as author mentoring and services, at competitive prices.

With several Bram Stoker Award wins and many other wins and nominations (including the HWA's Specialty Press Award), Crystal Lake Publishing puts integrity, honor, and respect at the forefront of our publishing operations.

We strive for each book and outreach program we spearhead to not only entertain and touch or comment on issues that affect our readers, but also to strengthen and support the Dark Fiction field and its authors.

Not only do we find and publish authors we believe are destined for greatness, but we strive to work with men and women who endeavour to be decent human beings who care more for others than themselves, while still being hard working, driven, and passionate artists and storytellers.

Crystal Lake Publishing is and will always be a beacon of what passion and dedication, combined with overwhelming teamwork and respect, can accomplish. We endeavour to know each and every one of our readers, while building personal relationships with our authors, reviewers, bloggers, podcasters, bookstores, and libraries.

We will be as trustworthy, forthright, and transparent as any business can be, while also keeping most of the headaches away from our authors, since it's our job to solve the problems so they can stay in a creative mind. Which of course also means paying our authors.

We do not just publish books, we present to you worlds within your world, doors within your mind, from talented authors who sacrifice so much for a moment of your time.

There are some amazing small presses out there, and through collaboration and open forums we will continue to support other presses in the goal of helping authors and showing the world what quality small presses are capable of accomplishing. No one wins when a small press goes down, so we will always be there to support hardworking, legitimate presses and their authors. We don't see Crystal Lake as the best press out there, but we will always strive to be the best, strive to be the most interactive and grateful, and even blessed press around. No matter what happens over time, we will also take our mission very seriously while appreciating where we are and enjoying the journey.

What do we offer our authors that they can't do for themselves through self-publishing?

We are big supporters of self-publishing (especially hybrid publishing), if done with care, patience, and planning. However, not every author has the time or inclination to do market research, advertise, and set up book launch strategies. Although a lot of authors are successful in doing it all, strong small presses will always be there for the authors who just want to do what they do best: write.

What we offer is experience, industry knowledge, contacts and trust built up over years. And due to our strong brand and trusting fanbase, every Crystal Lake Publishing book comes with weight of respect. In time our fans begin to trust our judgment and will try a new author purely based on our support of said author.

With each launch we strive to fine-tune our approach, learn from our mistakes, and increase our reach. We continue to assure our authors that we're here for them and that we'll carry the weight of the launch and dealing with third parties while they focus on their strengths—be it writing, interviews, blogs, signings, etc.

We also offer several mentoring packages to authors that include knowledge and skills they can use in both traditional and self-publishing endeavours.

We look forward to launching many new careers.

This is what we believe in. What we stand for. This will be our legacy.

**Welcome to Crystal Lake Publishing—
Tales from the Darkest Depths.**